TAKEN BY THE FAE KING

JESSICA GRAYSON

Purple Fall
Publishing

Published in the United States by Purple Fall Publishing. Purple Fall Publishing and the Purple Fall Publishing Logos are trademarks and/or registered trademarks of Purple Fall Publishing LLC.

Identifiers:

e book: 978-1-64253-199-2.

paperback: 978-1-64253-398-9.

Cover Design by Kim Cunningham of Atlantis Book Design.

PRINTED IN THE UNITED STATES OF AMERICA.

CHAPTER 1

GRAYCE

I always hoped my marriage would be to someone I love, not to a stranger, and certainly not to my enemy —King Kyven of the Fae.

Standing on the castle balcony, I gaze at the courtyard below, my heart pounding as I watch the Fae King and his warriors approach.

My breath catches as I take in his imposing figure and the regal grace with which he carries himself. His face is set in a stern expression, his violet eyes scanning the courtyard and the castle guards at their posts. He is wearing a gold circlet crown. The sharp points of his Fae ears peek up through short, silver-white hair.

He is tall with broad shoulders, and dressed in black and gold armor that does little to hide the lean muscular form of the warrior he is beneath. A sliver of sunlight spears through the dark clouds, highlighting the clear, lavender panes of his wings, scattering brilliant colors across the ground.

Kyven is the key to my people's survival; tomorrow, I will become his queen.

It would have happened a few days ago, but our wedding was postponed due to the unexpected arrival of my cousin, Freyja, and her new husband—the fierce Dragon King Aurdyn.

Kyven is known as a fierce and powerful ruler, as adept in the field of battle as he is in politics. He insisted upon my hand to seal the alliance between our two kingdoms, claiming our marriage would ensure a permanent peace.

I hope he is right. We lost our father in a battle with the Fae, and I'd rather not lose anyone else I love.

A cool breeze blows through my long brown hair, and I draw my cloak firmly around my shoulders. Drizzling mist begins to fall from the dark gray clouds blanketing the sky, the weather seeming to match my mood.

Just beyond the castle's outer wall lie ruined and bloodied fields, reminding me why this marriage must take occur. It has only been a handful of days since the army of Kolstrad invaded our kingdom of Florin. We managed to defeat them, but just barely.

King Kyven of Anlora and a dozen of his Fae warriors arrived unexpectedly during the heat of the battle. They were under no obligation to assist us, but they did.

My brother, King Edmynd, is a proud man, but even *he* doubts we would have prevailed without their aid. Their powerful magic was able to counter that of the Mages and Wraith that marched alongside Kolstrad's army.

The Fae King and his warriors come to a stop below. Kyven looks up at me. A shiver runs down my spine as his intense gaze meets mine.

Fate is a hunter. I learned this long ago. The gift of foresight, passed down from my mother, has always felt more like a curse than a blessing. We met only a few days ago, but I knew him immediately. I have seen those violet eyes in my dreams for the past three years.

In my visions, Kyven offers me a purple rose. But like most of my dreams, I know not what it means. It could be a sign, or even a warning. I only know that the gods do not direct our paths without purpose, and for some reason, they chose to cross his with mine.

"Grayce," my brother's voice calls from behind, and I turn away. The look on Edmynd's face is nothing short of grave. He runs a hand roughly through his short, blond hair, his green eyes studying me in concern. "Are you certain you wish to go through with this?"

It comforts me that if I changed my mind, he would honor my decision. Our kingdom needs this alliance with the Fae. Without them, we could fall to the Order of the Mages and their Wraith. I do not make this choice lightly. "Yes."

My other brother—Raiden—stands beside him, his expression bordering on thunderous. "I don't trust him." He clenches his jaw, and his brown eyes sweep to Edmynd. "You're truly willing to offer our sister to the Fae King?"

"I am not offering up any—"

"Stop it," I snap. "Edmynd isn't forcing me into this. This is my decision, Raiden."

"We do not need this alliance," he counters. "We already have one with the Dark Elves, and now the Dragons. We don't need the Fae. Maybe it was a sign from the gods that your wedding was interrupted a few days ago," he points out. "Perhaps it is their will that this marriage should not be."

"This alliance could put an end to all the bloodshed along our borders," I tell him. "Think of how many lives could be saved if we joined forces with the Fae instead of constantly fighting them."

Raiden clenches his jaw. He knows I'm right. "I still don't like it." He rakes a hand through his short brown hair and then darts a glance at Edmynd before addressing me. "Just remember that if you change your mind, you will have our support."

Edmynd nods in agreement.

Emotions lodge in my throat. My brothers love me, and I am going to miss them so much. I embrace Raiden and pull Edmynd into the hug with us.

When we pull back, Raiden rests his hands on my shoulders, meeting my gaze evenly. "I want you to do me a favor."

"What is it?"

"When we meet with the Fae King today, do not look him directly in the eyes."

"Why?" I blink up at him.

"He's Fae," Raiden practically snarls. "There are tales of their kind enchanting human women and luring them into the woods to steal them away as their brides. I want to be sure he hasn't ensorcelled you into accepting him as your husband."

A startled laugh escapes me. Of all the things I thought he'd say, this was not one of them.

Edmynd rolls his eyes. "Those are stories, Raiden. Nothing more."

Raiden purses his lips. "Most tales contain a kernel of truth, do they not? And it's not just the Fae, it's the Dark Elves too," he insists. "I'm not entirely sure that Varys didn't cast a spell on Inara to make her agree to marry him," he says, referring to our youngest sister's recent marriage to the Dark Elf King.

"Here we go," Edmynd says, exasperated.

"Varys did nothing of the sort, and you know it." I playfully slap at his shoulder. "Inara is blissfully happy with her marriage. You've seen it yourself. Besides, I thought you said you liked Varys now."

Raiden crosses his arms over his chest. "I liked him better

before I found out he was friends with the Fae King. Thick as thieves, those two," he murmurs under his breath.

"You're being ridiculous." Edmynd blows out a frustrated sigh. He turns to me and offers his arm. "Are you ready?"

I nod and loop my arm through his. As we walk through the corridors to meet with the Fae, Raiden follows reluctantly behind us, obviously still stewing. Glancing over my shoulder, I shoot him a warning look, and whisper. "Be nice."

Sighing heavily, he nods. "Fine."

I'm nervous, but that is to be expected, and I'm sure it's probably true of most women with an arranged marriage. I know almost nothing of Kyven beyond his ice-cold exterior. But I do know that he asked me directly for my hand, instead of asking my brother, and I appreciated that. It shows a level of respect that many suitors before him were severely lacking.

Most of them sought only to negotiate with Edmynd, and that guaranteed them an automatic refusal.

The Fae are known to be cold, and I doubt there will be any love between Kyven and me. I seek little more from our marriage than mutual respect, and perhaps even friendship. I do not want to risk getting hurt again.

My heart was hurt once before by a man I thought I cared for, and who I believed cared for me in return. Nothing ever happened between us, and I did not know Joren well enough to say if it was love, but I do know that when he left without a word, the pain of his rejection is not one I ever wish to repeat.

As I walk with my brother, the stones beneath our feet echo our every step, their dull thuds a haunting reminder of the path I am about to embark upon. The walls of the castle are adorned with portraits of our ancestors, their eyes seeming to follow us as we move through the dimly lit hallway. The glow from the torches, flickering like the flame of my resolve, casts a warm light on the tapestries depicting scenes of valor and victory. The scent of beeswax mingles with the ancient mustiness, a combination as familiar as it is comforting.

Nervousness coils within me, tightening like a serpent with each step we take. The air in the hallway seems to grow heavier, pressing down upon my chest.

We approach the double doors to the small council chamber, the intricate carvings a testament to our family's history and legacy. Stags locked in battle, dragons soaring overhead - a world of magic and power, now intertwined with my fate.

Edmynd pauses, his hand resting on the worn brass handle. "Grayce," he murmurs, his voice steady and reassuring. "Remember, whatever you decide, we will support you."

I nod, grateful for his words, and he pushes open the doors. The council chamber is an intimate space, circular and draped with richly colored fabrics. A round table, hewn from a single piece of oak, dominates the room, the intricate carving of our family crest at its center. The chairs surrounding it are heavy and ornately carved. Built several generations ago by our ancestor, Ryckard the Great. He was the first to push back the Fae and regain the lands of his ancestors.

At the far end of the room, stands King Kyven, the Fae ruler who is to become my husband. His eyes, a piercing shade of violet, find mine immediately, a shiver running down my spine as they lock onto me. Power radiates from his form, a force as ancient and wild as the lands he governs. He inclines his head, a silent greeting, and I return the gesture.

Sunlight spills in through the large windows, casting his moonlight-pale skin in an ethereal glow, gilding the tips of his wings. Their lavender panes are edged with black, and they flutter behind him before settling as we approach.

Dressed in the dark armor of his people, he cuts a handsome figure with broad shoulders and a lean, muscular form.

As we stand before him, his violet eyes meet mine, their vertically slit pupils expanding slightly as he studies me with a gaze that seems to pierce my very soul.

Already, I have broken my promise to Raiden as I stand transfixed before the Fae King, completely mesmerized. He is more attractive than anyone I have ever seen.

My gaze travels over the pointed tips of his ears and his wind-blown, short silver-white hair. His face has sharp angles and masculine features, perfectly handsome in a way that only Otherworldly beings can be.

"King Edmynd," he says, dipping his chin in a subtle but respectable nod to my brother.

"Princess Grayce." The rich, deep timbre of his voice makes my heart flutter as he takes my hand. His palm is warm but callused, suggesting he is no stranger to work or weapons. Heat rises in my cheeks as he presses a gentle kiss to the back of my knuckles.

"King Kyven," I somehow manage to breathe out the words.

Releasing my hand, he straightens. The air shifts with his movement and the smell of fresh rain and forest fills the space around us. The top of my head is not quite level with his chin. As he stares down at me, I am caught in his sharp gaze, unable to move.

I've seen him so many times in my dreams, his face is as familiar to me as my own, and now I believe I know why.

For better or worse, this man is my fate.

CHAPTER 2

KYVEN

My heart clenches as her hazel eyes study me warily. As if I were no more than a stranger before her, instead of the man she once loved. And yet... I am not that man. Not to her, anyway. She does not know it was me who came to her almost every night, glamoured to appear as a human named Joren, trying to win her heart.

She is my Fated One. I knew the moment I saw her that she was my *A'lyra*. I should have told her then who I was, but our people have been enemies for so long, I worried she would reject me.

I had planned to reveal the truth of who I am, but then word came that my father and older brother were dying. I would have returned to her sooner, but the mantle of rule has been much harder than I imagined, especially under the weight of my grief.

I wish more than anything that I could tell her who I was, but I cannot. Not without risking the wrath of the gods.

These past few months that I've been away from her have been torture. My heart aches just looking at her face. She is even more lovely than I remembered. I am completely mesmerized as her gaze holds mine and a pink blush blooms across her cheeks and nose, spreading to her delicately rounded human ears.

My fingers ache to run through her long, silken chestnut hair. The delicate scent of rose oil with a hint of lavender floods my nostrils, her familiar scent stirring the primal instincts buried deep inside me—the longing to mark and claim her as mine.

Long, dark lashes frame her eyes—their golden-brown coloring flecked through with chips of green. I study the pattern of tiny spots that dot her cheeks and her dainty nose as her rose pink lips part slightly beneath my gaze.

She is dressed in a long, purple, silken gown—her favorite color. Try as I might, I cannot tear my eyes from her. I have seen many things in my life, but none of them more beautiful than Grayce.

She would have been mine two days ago, but our wedding was interrupted by the untimely arrival of the Dragon King —Aurdyn—and his human mate, Freyja—Grayce's cousin.

Our human ceremony is supposed to be tomorrow, but the revelation that Freyja is now mated to King Aurdyn has changed things. The Dragons of the Ice Mountains have agreed to an alliance with Florin.

Dragons are powerful beings. With Aurdyn and his warriors now on their side, King Edmynd may believe he has no need of a treaty with my people for protection against the Mages and the Wraith.

He asked for this meeting a few hours ago, and I have been on edge ever since, worried that he will confirm this, and that Grayce will inform me that she wishes to dissolve our betrothal and cancel our wedding tomorrow.

Despite the worry in my heart, I force my expression to remain impassive as I wait to hear what they have to say. Hopefully, Edmynd simply wishes to renegotiate some of the terms of our proposed treaty now that Florin is in a relative position of power with their new alliance with the Dragons.

If I am right, I will grant him whatever he asks. I have never wanted anything as much as I desire Grayce, and I will do whatever it takes to make her mine.

I bite back a growl when King Edmynd's advisor, Lord Marden, steps forward. I've never met anyone as disagreeable as this man. With his abnormally long, pointed nose and beady eyes, he reminds me of a weasel. He's the reason I brought Lord Torien with us.

Torien was my father's advisor, and now serves as my own. He and Lord Marden are the ones who worked out the tenuous truce between us and Florin after Grayce's father died in battle against our warriors. Her father declared war upon Anlora shortly after the assassination of his wife—the queen—Grayce's mother. He was convinced our people had something to do with her death, despite my father's vehement denial.

Lord Torien regards the humans warily, his brown wings fluttering slightly in agitation as his green eyes study Lord Marden. He combs a hand through his shoulder-length white hair and straightens his spine, staring across at them imperiously.

Lord Marden holds up the treaty, unrolling it on the table before us. He points to a line on the parchment. "You'll note here that we have updated the information regarding the current alliances of Florin to now include the Dragons of the Ice Mountains." His gaze shifts to Lord Torien. "We understand your people have a somewhat contentious relationship with the Dragons. Knowing they are now allies of Florin, are you still interested in signing the treaty between our two kingdoms?"

"Yes," I reply, relief flooding my veins. I will gladly put up with the arrogance of King Aurdyn and his Dragons if it means that I can have Grayce.

I desire peace as much as King Edmynd does, but my people have powerful magic; we do not need Florin. The treaty has never been my primary goal. I only proposed it so that I could take his sister's hand.

It seems the humans do not understand the advantage they now have, and I do not want to give them time to realize it, nor for Grayce to change her mind about marrying me. "We will sign the treaty tomorrow, immediately after the wedding."

Edmynd steps forward, his gaze meeting mine evenly. "I have a proposal for you to consider before we do that."

Worry creeps down my spine as he studies me with a calculating look. It seems I was wrong. King Edmynd does know that he has an advantage now, and I wait with bated breath to find out how he intends to wield it.

"What is it?" I ask, clenching my jaw. Edmynd has never negotiated nor bargained with a Fae as determined as I am now. The call of the bond stirs something dark and primal within, demanding that I claim my mate, and I will do whatever it takes to secure Grayce's hand.

"You have a younger sister. Are you willing to offer her up in this bargain?" Edmynd challenges. "Because we have yet to explore that option, King Kyven."

Grayce and Raiden's eyes widen slightly. It seems they are as stunned by this suggestion as I am.

"My sister is only twenty-two years old." I narrow my eyes. "She is not yet of age to join with another. I will not marry her off to—"

"Who said it has to be now?" Edmynd cuts me off, a faint

smirk on his lips because he knows he has me. "I am in no hurry to marry. We can arrange a betrothal and then I will simply wait until she is of age."

It seems I have underestimated this human king. He is as well-versed in bargains as one of my people.

One of my favorite pastimes is a board game of strategy. *Kal'var* is difficult to master because each player must think at least three steps ahead before making a move. Studying King Edmynd, I consider the options and their potential outcomes. The likelihood of winning this negotiation is heavily weighted in my favor. He may not need our alliance as desperately as he did before, but he does want it. Of that, I am certain.

We sit across from each other as equals, but in truth, it is Anlora that is the stronger of our two kingdoms. It is time to remind the humans of that. If I do not, Edmynd and I will circle each other endlessly.

"It seems you are not as interested in peace as we are," I state impassively, and Edmynd's mouth falls open. "A pity because I believe we could have achieved something great this day."

Without waiting for him to reply, I stride toward the door. We're almost there when Grayce calls out. "Wait!"

I halt abruptly and turn to face her.

Her gaze holds mine as she walks forward. If not for the slight trembling of her hands and the sour scent of her fear, I would never think her afraid as she stands unflinchingly before me. She looks back at her brothers. "I wish to speak with King Kyven alone."

I motion for Lord Torien and my guards to leave.

My personal guard—Aren—moves to my side. His blue wings flutter agitatedly as he leans in and whispers in *Faeri-nesh*. "This could be a trap. At least one of us should remain to guard you."

"I assure you, it is not a trap," Grayce says in heavily accented Faerinesh. "You are guests of Florin."

My jaw drops but I quickly snap it shut. I thought I knew everything about her, but I had no idea she spoke our language.

Aren gapes at her in shock before I turn to him. "Wait outside the door. I will be fine."

Aren is not just my personal guard, he is close to me like a brother. We served on the Great Wall together for five years before I became king. His blue eyes meet mine and it is easy to see the worry that flashes behind them before he bows low, his short black hair falling over his brow before he smooths it back as he straightens. "As you command, my king."

He levels a warning glare at Grayce's brother, Prince Raiden, as he moves up behind his sister.

Raiden wraps his hand around the hilt of his sword as he gestures to his older brother and the rest of their guards. "Go. I will stay here to ensure Grayce is protected."

"You too, Raiden," Grayce cuts him off. "I will speak with Kyven alone."

It seems Aren is not alone in his suspicions, but that is to be expected, I believe. After all, our people have been enemies for hundreds of years.

Instead of arguing as I'd expect, Raiden levels an ice-cold glare at me that promises death if I hurt his sister. Little does he know that I would sooner end my own life than ever harm her.

I dip my chin in subtle acknowledgment of his threat, and he walks out into the hallway, closing the doors behind him and leaving us alone.

When I return my attention to Grayce, she stares up at me proud and unafraid, despite the acrid scent of her fear. "If

13

my hand is the price for peace with your people, I will pay it. But only on two conditions."

She is as strong as she is brave and selfless. I remember Varys telling me how she offered herself up to him to spare her sister, Inara, from wedding the Dark Elf King. Fortunately for me, he refused. Inara is his Fated One, just as Grayce is mine.

I know Grayce. I spent weeks following her, studying her, learning everything I could, including how she thinks. She is as strong as she is selfless, and will agree to a betrothal to protect her family and her kingdom. This is not how I imagined our marriage would be, but I vow to make up for it by doing everything I can to make sure she never regrets this decision.

"What would those be?" I ask.

"You will treat me as your equal in all ways."

"Done," I reply without hesitation. I would have it no other way. "What else?"

"Swear to me that you will protect me and any children we may have. That you will be loyal to us above all else and will father no offspring outside of our union that may threaten their right to the throne once you pass."

All of this I would have given her freely. My people mate for life, but it seems she does not know this. So, now I will make sure she does not doubt my commitment.

In one smooth motion, I pull the dagger from my belt and draw the blade across my palm, coating the sharp edge with my blood. Her eyes widen as I drop to one knee and present it to her and speak the vow of protection. "I swear myself to you. My blood upon this blade is the promise that I will protect and defend you, from now until the moment I draw my last breath."

She gasps as swirling silver light winds around the knife. "Magic," she whispers.

"An unbreakable vow of loyalty and devotion," I reply solemnly. "If you accept me as your mate."

Her gaze drops to the blade and Grayce swallows hard. "I accept," she whispers as she reaches a trembling hand out to grip the handle. She inhales sharply as silver light swirls from the blade, winding around both of our hands and our wrists before disappearing.

Her luminous hazel eyes search mine, and I fight the urge to pull her into my arms. My fangs lengthen as the dark and primal part of me unfurls from deep within, longing to sink them into her tender flesh to give her my claiming mark.

I clench my jaw as need burns through my veins. Knowing that she will be mine, tomorrow cannot come soon enough. Since we are to be bound, I wish to drop the formal form of address. "Please, call me Kyven."

"Kyven," she repeats. A faint smile crests her lips. "You may call me Grayce."

My heart is full as I gaze at the female who will be my mate, my queen, and the mother of my children. I take her hand and place a tender kiss to the back of her knuckles. "I will meet you at the temple tomorrow, Grayce."

"Tomorrow," she agrees.

CHAPTER 3

GRAYCE

After I inform Edmynd that the wedding is still moving forward, he instructs one of the servants to lead the Fae back to their guest chambers. My eyes track Kyven until he rounds the corner, disappearing from view.

I can hardly believe I'll be married tomorrow.

As soon as the Fae are gone, Raiden spins to face me. He puts the back of his hand to my forehead, as if checking for a fever. Then, he cups my face with both hands, staring deep into my eyes with a strange look.

I frown. "What are you doing?"

"Checking for any signs of enchantment," he murmurs. "Some sort of love spell or—"

Rolling my eyes, I gently push him away. "He did not cast a spell on me, Raiden."

"I doubt you'd know it if he did," he murmurs under his breath.

I love my brother, but sometimes his protective nature can be a bit overbearing. "All is well," I reassure him. "Truly."

I turn to Edmynd and cross my arms over my chest. "When were you going to tell me about your plan to offer yourself for the alliance instead?"

"Is it not the same thing you tried to do for Inara?" he asks, reminding me of how I offered myself to the Dark Elf King in her stead when I found out he had asked for her hand. "You're strong, Grayce, and you always put everyone else's needs before your own. I just want you to be happy."

"We both do," Raiden adds.

I love my family and I want them to be safe. Powerful allies, like the Fae, mean greater protection for them and all of Florin against the Mages and their Wraith. Marrying the Fae King is a small price to pay for this. "I appreciate your concern, but there is no reason to believe that I could not find happiness with Kyven."

"Have you had any more visions of him?" Edmynd asks.

I told my family about the dreams I'd been having for the past three years. It was the same for my sister, Inara. She dreamed of Varys before they met. "Only the same one I've had in the past, where he offers me a purple rose."

"What do you think it means?" Raiden asks. "Do you think it's a warning?"

It's difficult to interpret a vision. It is not enough to dream of something, the emotions behind the dreams are important as well.

"It feels like a sign." Chewing my bottom lip, I struggle to find the right words to describe it. "Like a symbol to watch for to know that I am on the correct path."

"I hope you are right," he replies. "But know this: If he ever upsets you, I will—"

"She *knows*." Edmynd says, crossing his arms over his

chest. "*Everyone* knows. I'm sure even the Fae King knows you will end him if he upsets her in any way."

I laugh as Raiden narrows his eyes in mock irritation. "Is it wrong to care for my sister's happiness?"

"No," I reply. "And I appreciate you. Both of you," I add. "But I have a big day tomorrow and I'd like to get some sleep." I look at Edmynd. "Is everything still in place for the wedding and the reception?"

"Yes."

"Good." I hug them both. "Then I will see you in the morning."

With that, I head down the hallway to the family wing. I'd love to talk to Inara, but it's late and she and Varys are probably already asleep.

As I make my way to my room, I think about Kyven. For all his brooding intensity, I cannot deny that I'm attracted to him. But it worries me also. He was very insistent that our alliance could only be sealed through marriage. And while I understand his reasoning behind it, I cannot help but think there is something he is holding back.

I cannot explain why I feel this way; I only know that I do. And I learned long ago to trust my instincts.

I felt something similar with Joren. As if there were some part of him that he was hiding from me. But I was a fool. And I ignored the warnings in my mind, allowing my heart to rule my decisions.

He promised me his undying devotion, and then left soon after, as if I'd meant nothing to him.

It is well-known the Fae cannot lie. Kyven gave me his word when I presented my two conditions, but his people are rumored to be masters of turning words and bending phrases to serve their own advantage. I worry that I may have missed something in his vow. A way for him to avoid keeping the promises he made to me.

Perhaps I would not be so wary if I'd never had my heart hurt before, but I cannot change the past. I can only push forward and look to the future. Besides, I am not the first woman to have suffered rejection and I will not be the last.

I refuse to allow my experience with Joren to ruin my life. He did not deserve my affection and I will not allow him to take up any more space in my mind or my heart. I am strong and I will not let the past cripple me.

CHAPTER 4

KYVEN

L ord Torien unrolls the treaty parchment on the table before me, pointing to the last line. "Everything on here is to *their* advantage, *not* ours," he says. "What do we gain from this alliance that we truly need?"

"Peace between Anlora and Florin," I reply. "And a queen."

"A human queen," Torien mumbles. "I fear the people will not accept her, my King."

"She will be my mate. They will have to."

"You are a direct descendent of Queen Ilyra," he points out. "You should reconsider the option to take a Fae consort —one of the nobility—as your true mate. One that the people would bless."

"Let me guess." I arch a brow. "You mean someone like your daughter—the Lady Amalthea?"

This isn't the first time Torien has tried to push his daughter on me. His is one of the oldest noble families in

Anlora and he has always had ambitions to see one of his blood upon the throne.

I exchange a knowing glance with Aren. He has never liked Lord Torien and warned me the male would try to dissuade me from taking Princess Grayce as my mate. As always, his instincts were right, which is part of the reason he makes such an excellent personal guard.

"I only offer the suggestion, my King." Torien bows low. "It would be a shame to muddy the royal line with human blood."

"Enough!" I snap, and all the color drains from his face. "Watch how you speak of my betrothed, Lord Torien. I will not tolerate anyone disparaging my future queen."

Trembling, he bows even lower. "Of—of course, my King. I—I meant no disrespect."

"See that it does not happen again." I seethe.

"Forgive me, my King, but you are still new to this role." He reminds me again that I was never meant for the throne. It should be my older brother—Lyrian—ruling our people, not me. His sharp green eyes dart briefly to mine before lowering again. "I have dedicated my life to the royal family. As your advisor, and your father's before you, I am only here to offer counsel to the crown."

"Leave me." I command. "I've had enough of your *counsel* this night."

I curl my hands into fists at my sides, as he slinks out the door like the sniveling worm that he is. Breathing in through my nose and out through my mouth, I try to calm the anger swirling within me. "You were right," I tell Aren. "Even now, he would still try to put his daughter on the throne."

"He is nothing if not persistent," Aren says, crossing his arms over his chest as he leans against the door. "But he is right about one thing."

"What is that?" I ask.

"Our people have been enemies for a long time, and I believe there will be many who will have a hard time accepting a human as their queen." His eyes meet mine evenly. "She will be the only human living in Anlora, and her people do not possess any magic, which will make her an easy target to any who would mean her harm. I suggest the formation of a queen's guard as soon as possible."

I hate that he is right. It worries me to think of Grayce in any danger, especially at the hands of my own people.

"We have always been honest with each other," he says a bit hesitantly. "I would ask permission to speak freely right now."

"What is it?" I frown. "Tell me."

"As your true mate, she will be closer to you than anyone else." His blue eyes search mine. "Do you trust her?"

I understand his worry, but his fears are unfounded. "She is a princess, not an assassin."

"Anyone can kill," he says darkly. "Her father thought one of our people was responsible for her mother's death. What if this is some sort of elaborate trap for revenge?"

"I trust her," I tell him, trying to put his concerns to rest. "She will not harm me."

"How do you know?"

"Because I know her," I reply, inwardly cursing myself for giving too much away. Aren doesn't know my secret. Varys knows, but he has been bound by magic to reveal nothing, and I'll not risk telling anyone else. Even my best friend and personal guard.

His brow furrows deeply. "But you only recently met."

"If she had any ill intent toward me, I would have sensed it when I touched her hand," I explain.

His eyes widen slightly before he nods, seemingly satisfied by my answer.

Only a few of my kind possess the ability to read

someone through touch. I am one of them. I have been feared by many because of it. Even my own parents were afraid when they learned what I could do.

This ability is one that gave birth to some of the rumors humans used to have about my people. They believed we could read their minds and ensorcell them simply by staring into their eyes, which is just as ridiculous as the myth that Fae could not tell any lies.

It is a crime among my people to read another Fae without their permission, which is why I was trained to create a mental shield between myself and others at all times. Since Grayce is human, this law technically does not apply to her, but I would never search her mind without her consent. But I tell Aren this now so that he will not question my trust in my future queen.

"It is late," I murmur. "I will see you in the morning."

"I'll be next door if you need anything," he says, bowing before he leaves the room.

Night has fallen, but I am too anxious to sleep. I pull the handkerchief from my tunic pocket and lift it to my nose, inhaling the subtle scent of my mate deep into my lungs.

It was a gift she gave me while I was disguised as Joren. A pang of longing stabs my chest as I study the silken material. She embroidered it with scrolling vines, covered with tiny purple flowers along the edge. I have kept it with me ever since. It was my only connection to her while we were apart.

I think back to the first time I saw her. My father had suggested marrying me to her younger sister, Inara, to secure a peace with Florin. I was a second born son, and he assumed her brother—King Edmynd—would be more likely to marry her off for an alliance rather than Grayce, who is next in line for the throne.

Using a glamour to appear human, I came to Florin only

to glimpse Inara—wondering about the woman my father would try to barter me away to, but instead I saw Grayce.

Instantly, I knew she was my A'lyra. I've heard others describe the pull of the fated bond, but I never realized how all-consuming it would be.

I shadowed her every move, and learned everything I could about her. Her favorite color is purple, and roses are her favorite flowers. She chews her bottom lip when she is deep in contemplation. She has an inquisitive mind, and spends long hours in the palace library researching various languages and cultures. She loves reading romance novels, but she hides them beneath her mattress to avoid being teased by her brother, Raiden.

He often jokes that she is a hopeless romantic, but I know something that she does not. He is too. Raiden reads as many of those novels as she does, but no one would know it, the way he makes fun of such things.

When Grayce cannot sleep, which is most nights, she climbs down the vine trellis of her balcony to the palace gardens below. Her favorite spot is the rosebush-lined wall along the southeast corner.

I am not ashamed to admit that I shadowed her for days to learn her patterns. Once I did, I made sure to place myself in her path, making it appear as no more than mere happenstance. Presenting myself as a simple palace gardener, tending to her favorite plants. I made sure to accidentally drop a copy of a romance novel I knew she liked.

In truth, I did enjoy *The Queen's Knight*. It has led me to seek out other such novels in my own library back home. Of course, each one that I read I now imagine myself and her as the main characters in the story.

Many nights I snuck into her balcony window to watch her sleep. I convinced myself that all of this was harmless because I never touched her, but in truth, I allowed it to go much too far and now... everything inside me wants to gather her in my arms, tell her who I am, and kiss her as I have longed to do ever since we met, but I cannot. To do so, I would risk losing everything.

It has only been a few hours since we spoke, but I long to see her again. If she has not broken from her normal, nightly routine, she is probably in her room now. Every evening she drinks a cup of lavender tea with two chocolate biscuits, sometimes three if she has had a particularly long day.

With a heavy sigh, I walk onto the balcony and look out over the palace gardens. With neatly trimmed bushes, and perfectly aligned rows of flowers, it's all so orderly and... somewhat strange. As if they've been forced to grow in a certain way, rather than allowed to flourish naturally. So unlike the wild, untamed beauty of my own home in the Fae realm.

I spent much time with Grayce in this space, and I know how much she enjoys it. Especially the rose-bush lined wall near the back gate. It is the place where I used to meet her often.

Where Joren met her, I remind myself bitterly.

She mentioned once that she often wondered if the gardens of the palace of the High Elves were as beautiful as she'd heard.

I have seen them, and while they are impressive, they pale in comparison to those of my kingdom. It is my hope that she will love the gardens of my palace as much as she loves these.

I search for the balcony that belongs to Grayce. It is dark, but my people have sharp night vision. The light of a half-moon provides enough illumination that I am able to see very clearly. My heart stutters and stops as she steps outside.

The cool breeze tussles her long, chestnut hair as she gazes down at the gardens. Dressed only in her sleep gown, I watch as she wraps a heavy cloak around her shoulders. A smile crests my lips as I observe her climb down the vines that hang from her balcony. Her movements are graceful, and I am fascinated by her daring and stealth.

I know I should not, but I cannot resist the urge to follow her. Carefully, I drop over the side of my own balcony, extending my wings to drift quietly to the earth below. Quietly I make my way through the shadows, trailing after her through the palace gardens, her steps light and sure.

A half-moon casts silver light across her features as she slips among the hedges toward the wall along the back. I am completely and utterly entranced by her beauty and her spirit, and intense longing fills me as I recall all the nights we met here in secret when she thought I was someone else.

I know I should not be here, and that I should not alert her to my presence, but I cannot resist the pull of her allure.

When she agreed to marry me, concern was easily read in her eyes, despite her attempt to appear stoic. To her, I am a relative stranger, and I want nothing more than to put her mind at ease. To show her that I am a good male—worthy to be hers.

I want only to speak with her and reassure her that she has nothing to fear from me. I will always place her needs above those of my own. Drawing in a deep breath, I steady my nerves as I follow after her, my heart hammering in anticipation as I try to decide how best to approach.

CHAPTER 5

GRAYCE

It is late, but I cannot sleep. Mist swirls around my ankles and feet as I make my way along one of the many worn garden paths toward the back wall. Winter's approach has rendered the roses dormant, but their branches are still green and covered with leaves.

This has always been my favorite place to escape. It is far enough away to be hidden from view and so peaceful since it is not along any of the main paths that lead back to the castle.

Tomorrow, I will marry King Kyven, sealing an alliance between our two kingdoms. While I know it is the right decision, I cannot help but wish I knew more of my future husband.

His cold and calculating manner during the negotiations was somewhat intimidating. And yet, his expression softened when he addressed me directly. I love that he not only listened to what I had to say, but he cared about my thoughts. So, perhaps those are signs that he will, at least, be a partner that listens when I speak.

As I ponder this, I lie down in the grass and gaze up at the stars. The ground is soft and spongy beneath me from the almost constant rains of the past few weeks.

From a logical standpoint, I understand that marrying Kyven is the right thing to do, not only for our kingdom, but also for my family. An alliance with the Fae would mean no more bloodshed between our two peoples, but also more protection against any other attempts of invasion by the Order of Mages.

Even knowing this, I cannot help but wish for some sort of confirmation that I am on the right path. Sending a silent prayer to the gods, I ask for a sign. Something, anything to confirm that the decision to marry Kyven is the right one. Sighing heavily, I close my eyes.

"Grayce?" a man's voice speaks softly, and my eyes snap open. I inhale sharply as my gaze lands on Kyven standing over me, worry etched in his features. "Are you all right?"

I jerk up to sitting. "I—I'm fine. What are you doing here?"

"I… could not sleep," he says.

I'm surprised by his answer. "I couldn't either." I start to stand but settle back on my hands as he takes a seat beside me.

"It's quite lovely out here," he muses, looking up. "Clear skies, a half-full moon, and a blanket of stars."

"It is," I agree.

I study him a moment. His head is tipped up to the sky, his wings relaxed at his back, and his expression thoughtful and contemplative. As if his only concern were to count the stars and survey the moon overhead. As if an important decision that will affect both of our lives and that of our kingdoms was not looming over our heads.

"Do you normally have trouble sleeping?" he asks, his gaze still fixed on the sky.

"Only when I am anxious about something," I reluctantly admit.

"Me too." He sighs and then turns to me, arching a brow. "Do you want to talk about it?"

I frown. What sort of game is he playing? Surely he knows what I am concerned about.

When I hesitate, he asks, "How about I go first?"

I study him a moment before nodding.

"I asked a princess to marry me, and she agreed. But I cannot sleep for worry that she may change her answer in the morning." A mischievous smile tugs at his lips as he adds, "And I heard rumor that you had a proposal from a king."

Despite my initial trepidation, I cannot help the faint grin that curves my mouth at his sly humor. "Not just any king," I tease lightly. "A Fae one."

"Ah." His violet eyes sparkle with barely contained amusement. "I've heard Fae males are very handsome." He smirks. "*Especially* their king. Very intelligent and brave, that one… sharp wit as well."

A soft laugh escapes me, and he puts his hand to his chest, feigning shock. "You disagree?"

I arch a teasing brow. "You forgot to mention he is very vain and proud."

He laughs—a rich, rolling sound that makes my heart flutter. He flashes a devastatingly handsome smile. "Well, this Fae King of yours sounds like a keeper."

Narrowing my eyes, I pretend to study him with a piercing gaze even as a smile threatens to break through. "Perhaps."

A gorgeous grin stretches his lips.

Despite the lightness of our teasing, I feel compelled to be direct with him. I've always been one to face things head on, never enjoying the subtle games that people often play with each other, where one must guess what the other wants

29

through thinly veiled conversation. If we are to be together, we must have honesty between us. I steel myself as I give him the truth. "It worries me that we are to marry, and I barely know you, Kyven."

His expression sobers. "What do you wish to know? Ask me whatever you want, and I will answer."

It is well-known that the Fae cannot lie. They may be able to speak around a truth, but having grown up in a royal court, I can easily detect such things. He has offered to answer any questions I have, and I've decided to take him up on it. After all, this is a huge decision, and the more information I have, the better. "Can I truly ask you anything?"

A smile quirks his lips. "Yes."

"Why me?"

He frowns. "Why not you?"

I do not want to play games. "Answer me plainly, please."

"Of course." His keen gaze holds mine. "Our marriage would cement the alliance between our kingdoms better than any signed parchment ever could. It would mean one less potential enemy for my people, as well as an ally in our fight against the Mages and the Wraith."

I shake my head. "I understand the politics behind it but that is not what I am asking."

"Then… what?" he asks, studying me curiously.

"If you were going to marry outside of your species, why not a Dark Elf or a High Elf? They have magic, like your kind do. Surely, they would make for better allies than humans."

He leans in, arching a brow. "Is this you gently telling me to find someone else?"

"No," I deny. "It's just that… aside from humans having no magic, I've always heard your people find mine plain." I look down at my hands. "In truth, your kind are very handsome and beautiful and I—"

"You find me handsome?" He flashes a gorgeous grin.

"I—no." His face falls. "I mean… yes." He smiles again as I stumble over my words, completely flustered.

"Thank you." He dips his chin. "As for the rest of your kind, I cannot speak. But you, Princess Grayce, are quite the opposite of plain."

Embarrassment heats my cheeks, but I clear my throat, pushing it back down as I draw upon my courage to ask the questions I need answered. "Will our marriage be in appearance only, for the sake of an alliance? Or will you take me as your true wife?"

"You would be my true mate in all ways, Grayce," he replies solemnly. "My mate, my queen, and the mother of my fledglings."

I'm surprised that he answers this without hesitation. But there is something else I must ask to be sure. "And if we cannot have any… fledglings?" I ask, using the same term he did. He is Fae and I am human, after all, so it may not even be possible for us to have children.

"I would like a family, but if no children resulted from our union, I do have a younger sister to pass the crown to," he replies. "Her offspring would then continue the royal line."

I'm surprised at this. Most high lords, especially kings, desire heirs above all else. But as I consider this, an ugly truth rears its head. There is something else that Lords will kill and go to war for. Power. I wonder if Kyven knows of my abilities. The gift of foresight—the curse I inherited from my mother.

Kyven is friends with Varys—the Dark Elf King. My sister, Inara, has this ability as well, and I know not if she has told her new husband that I do too. And if she has, did Varys then tell Kyven?

In the wrong hands, my curse could become a weapon. Is that why he truly wants me?

Fae are unable to speak a falsehood, so I will ask him for the truth.

"Do you know of my sister's curse?"

"Curse?" He regards me a moment before answering. "If you are speaking of her visions, Varys has told me of them. Though some would consider this ability a rare gift."

Perhaps some might think so, but not me. It has only ever been a burden. "Did he tell you that I have them too?"

"No, he did not."

"Now that you know, would you use my... ability against your enemies?"

His brow furrows deeply. "If you were my queen, they would be *our* enemies," he says pointedly. "But no, I would never force you to use your gift if you did not wish to."

"It is hardly a gift." Lowering my gaze, I fold my hands in my lap. "Truth be told, it is not something I can call upon at will anyway. It simply happens sometimes when I dream. Magic has only recently become accepted in Florin, now that the Mages are no longer in control. And my visions are still something that many people fear because of it."

"Were you in danger because of this?" he asks.

My eyes snap up to his. Before they were our enemies, the Order of Mages were the protectors of not only Florin, but several other human kingdoms. They used their dark powers to keep the Fae, Elves, and Otherworldly beings from using their magic in our lands. But according to their laws, any humans found to possess any hint of magic, were put to death.

"Yes. High Mage Ylari knew our secret. He helped us hide it from his own people. I would have been put to death, along with my sister, if the Order of Mages had ever found out." I swallow hard. "And I will be if they ever manage to defeat Florin and bring us back under their laws."

"That will not happen," he states firmly.

"How do you know?"

"The Order is strong, but not strong enough to stand against both my people and the Dark Elves. And our alliance would mean we would come to Florin's aid if they were to invade again."

His reasons are sound, but I still have more questions. And because he is incapable of speaking an outright lie, I will ask them bluntly so that I may have the naked truth. "You vowed to treat me as your equal, but is a wife considered the property of her husband according to Fae law?"

"Property?" His head jerks back. "Is that how human males regard their mates?"

"It is how some treat their wives," I answer honestly. "Especially those acquired as part of a treaty."

His violet eyes meet mine evenly. "You have my most solemn vow that I would never do that to you, Grayce."

"Is there anything else I should know about you?" I ask.

"Yes." He gives me a hesitant look. "I understand what it is to be feared by others. I am one of the few among my kind with the ability to read someone's mind through the act of touch."

My mouth drifts open.

"Forgive me. I should have mentioned it sooner." Guilt shines in his eyes. "I am so used to hiding my... ability. I have not used it in years," he adds. "It is against Fae law to delve into the mind of another without their permission. I was taught to create a barrier—a shield of sorts to prevent the transfer of thoughts or emotions through touch. And I am always so careful to keep my shields up. I did not think it would ever be a problem."

"Are you able to maintain your shields while you sleep?"

He hesitates a moment before replying, "I believe so, but I am uncertain."

I bite my lower lip, considering. "I suppose we could place some pillows between us at night while we're asleep."

His head jerks back. "You would sleep in my chambers?"

"We are to be husband and wife, Kyven." I give him an incredulous look. "Where else would I sleep?"

He blinks several times. "Most Fae couples have separate rooms. They only share a bed for the act of mating, but otherwise—"

Kyven stops talking as I stare at him in confusion. He cocks his head to one side. "Is that not how it is done among humans?"

"Most married couples share a bed," I tell him. "My parents did. At least... until my father's infidelity. After that, my mother kept her own chambers."

"So, it was his punishment then," he murmurs. "Your mother sleeping away from him."

"Yes, but it was also more than that. It was broken trust." My mother still loved my father, but it was a distant sort of love. A tempered love meant to protect her heart from any further pain.

"If you have changed your mind about bonding with me, I understand," he says, his voice hesitant. "My ability is... a curse that I cannot find a cure for, no matter how hard I have tried."

A Curse. His words resonate deep within. Is that not what I have always thought of my visions? Perhaps we have more in common than I thought.

All the fear and uncertainty that has trailed me all my life because of my own curse comes crashing to the forefront of my mind. Swallowing hard, I meet his gaze evenly. "I understand what it is to live with such a secret, Kyven," I whisper. "I know what it is to be considered an outsider, even among your own people."

"I should have told you before now." His violet eyes

search mine. "And for that, I am truly sorry, Grayce. Can you forgive me?"

He is asking forgiveness for withholding things from me. And yet, have I not done the same to him as well? If Kyven were to ever link with my mind accidentally, he could discover my past. I would rather tell him about it first. Sighing heavily, I clench my jaw. I had not wanted to ever speak of Joren to anyone, ever again. But now, it seems that I must.

"There is something I need to tell you, Kyven. Something that I—" I pause, unsure how to begin, wondering if it is wise to bring up another man to the one I am to marry.

Worry flickers across his expression. "What is it?"

I thought I was in love with Joren, and although nothing ever happened between us, I am not sure how Kyven will take this. But I want no secrets between us. Not now. Not ever. I draw in a steeling breath. "I was involved with someone before you."

His eyes widen slightly, whether in shock or anger I do not know.

CHAPTER 6

KYVEN

Worry twists deep within. I am certain she is speaking of Joren. I want so much to tell her the truth, but I also know the dangers of ignoring the guidance of the gods.

"His name was Joren." Her voice quavers. "Nothing ever happened between us. In fact, we never touched. We simply talked. But I—" her voice catches. "I had strong feelings for him. Part of me even thinks I may have loved him, but I have nothing to compare it to, so I do not know for sure."

Guilt and sadness unfurl deep within. Knowing that I am the cause of her pain is almost more than I can bear.

Sadness mars her expression. "All I know for sure is that he did not return these feelings."

My heart stops. Nothing could be further than the truth. "Why do you believe this?"

Surely, she knew that she was everything to me. To *him*, I think bitterly.

"Because he left me." She clenches her jaw. "He did not give a reason or any warning before he disappeared."

I hurt her. Deeply. I hate that she believes she was simply cast aside as if she were nothing to me. "Perhaps he had no choice," I offer. "Maybe something happened."

Her brow furrows deeply. "You would defend another man to the woman you are to marry?"

I reach forward and gently cup her cheek, the sadness in her eyes threatening to tear my soul in two. "I would not see you so... hurt by the past."

Grayce studies me a moment before speaking. "You are not upset?"

"Only that you were hurt," I reply. "That is my only concern."

A faint smile curves her mouth, but it falls away as she lowers her gaze. "I must admit something else to you, but I'm afraid."

I brace myself, wondering what it might be; worried she may have changed her mind about our marriage. "What is it?"

"I am not one to trust so quickly, Kyven. And yet, I find myself already trusting you." A smile crests my lips. She continues. "It worries me how easily you disarm me with a smile or a few gentle words." She swallows hard. "I trusted Joren, and he—"

"He hurt you." The words are like bitter acid on my tongue. I take her hand, wishing to offer some sort of comfort. "I am sorry," I whisper. "Truly, Grayce."

Her eyes snap to mine as if she cannot believe what I am saying. If only she knew the guilt I carry in my heart. I hate that I hurt her like this, and if I could, I would take it all back. But I cannot.

"My mother always said that people who come into your life are either a blessing or a lesson." She draws in a deep breath, tipping up her chin. "I have accepted it as a painful lesson, and I have moved on."

I want to promise that I will never hurt her, but I cannot ignore my lies. So, instead I will offer what I can. Cupping her cheek, I stare deep into her luminous eyes. "I vow that if you marry me, I will never forsake you, Grayce."

"Are you offering me a Fae bargain?" she asks tentatively.

I wasn't, but if this is what she wants, I will promise it. I am completely and utterly hers, but she does not know this yet. And as such, I have no issue devoting myself to her entirely. "Will you accept it if I am?"

She extends her hand out to me, and my gaze drops to the plush bow of her lips. "Fae bargains are not made with a handshake, they are sealed with a kiss."

A crimson flush blooms across her cheeks and the bridge of her nose, highlighting the small dusting of pigmented spots across her skin. I swallow hard as she moves closer to me. How many times have I dreamed of the taste of her lips?

CHAPTER 7

GRAYCE

My heart pounds as Kyven curls one arm around my waist and pulls me to him. I rest my palms against his chest, acutely aware of the solid layer of muscle beneath his tunic. He cups my cheek with his other hand. "Are you certain you want this?"

I'm surprised by how much I do as his violet eyes stare deep into mine, and I nod.

His masculine scent of fresh rain and forest fills the air around us. His hand slides to the back of my head, and his fingers thread through my hair as he leans in, brushing his lips against mine.

A soft sigh escapes me, and I melt against him. I've never been kissed before. His mouth is soft and warm and as his tongue strokes lightly against mine, a spark of desire ignites deep within, ready to consume me if I let it.

My heart pounds, and I fist my hands into his tunic, holding onto him.

When he finally pulls away, I'm breathless and slightly

dizzy. Gently, he drops his forehead to my own, his violet eyes piercing mine. I'm surprised by not only my response to his kiss, but by how easily I could lose myself in his gaze. I must be cautious. I cannot allow myself to fall so easily. Not after what happened before. I do not think my heart could take it if—

I force myself to cut off this line of thought, attempting to fortify the walls around my heart. "I do not know what came over me," I tell him. "I should not have—"

"You do not have to apologize for kissing your betrothed," he says, a faint smile playing on those soft, perfect lips that were only a moment ago claiming mine in a tender kiss.

Muffled voices draw our attention. We both stand, but I can see nothing. Kyven scans the area. "Two guards," he murmurs. "They are coming this way."

Alarm spikes through me. "We need to hide."

"Why?"

I don't have time to explain the fact that the Fae were our enemies only a handful of days ago and the Florin guards still carry some hostility toward Kyven and his people. "There will be too many questions," I whisper urgently.

Thankfully, instead of questioning me further, he nods. "What if I hide us both?"

"You can do that?"

He nods, and then steps closer, lifting his open arms out to me. "May I?"

I step into the circle of his arms, and Kyven tugs me to his chest. The wind shifts around us in a rush of air before settling. I blink as my gaze travels over the strange shimmering barrier that surrounds us. It reminds me of a soap bubble, and as the guards approach, I hold my breath, worried they will discover us.

"It is all right," His voice is warm in my ear. "They cannot see us in here."

My palms are pressed against Kyven's chest, and I'm acutely aware of the hard planes of muscle under my fingers and the strong and steady beating of his heart beneath my left ear. He tightens one arm around my waist, while the other cups the back of my head, holding me close, my body molded to his.

He smells like fresh rain and forest, a captivating scent that makes my pulse race. The Fae are rumored to have exceptional hearing. My heart is pounding so loudly surely Kyven can hear it.

We remain silent and still while the guards walk past us, completely oblivious to the fact that we are here. When they finally leave the gardens, Kyven removes the concealment barrier, and his gaze drops to mine. "Is there anything else you wish to ask me?"

The castle's clock tower strikes on the quarter hour and worry fills me when I realize what time it is. "There isn't time. It's almost midnight. We need to get back to the castle."

He frowns. "What happens at midnight?"

"It's bad luck for the groom to see the bride after midnight on the night before the wedding."

He frowns. "Bad luck?"

"Yes." I turn my gaze back to the clock tower. "Go, before it's too late. I'll make my way back to my room."

"I can fly you back to your balcony, if you wish," he offers, and I nod.

He places one arm on my back and another behind my knees and hoists me to his chest as if I weigh nothing. Warmth fills me as he flashes a gorgeous grin. "Hold on to me."

I wrap my arms around his neck and his wings begin to flutter furiously behind him. Slowly, we lift into the air. I gasp and tighten my grip as the ground falls away beneath us.

"I will not let you fall." His warm breath whispers across

my skin, carrying the soft scent of mint. "You are safe with me, Grayce."

When we reach my balcony, he touches down so gently I'm not even sure he has landed until he carefully lowers me to my feet. He keeps his hands wrapped around my waist for a moment to make sure I am steady, and I cannot shake the feeling that something has shifted between us.

He takes my hand. The gentle touch warms my skin as he slips his palm into my own and entwines our fingers. "I vow that I will prove myself worthy of you, Grayce. If you will give me the chance, I will do whatever it takes to do this."

"Then, I must ask one thing."

"What is it?"

"Please, be patient with my heart," I speak softly.

I hold my breath, waiting for his answer, knowing that what he says next will tell me if I am right to choose him or not. After what feels like an eternity, he brushes his thumb along the inside of my wrist. "Always, Grayce."

The tightness I had not realized was in my chest, eases at his words. The last bit of my hesitation falls away. "Thank you, Kyven." Gently, I squeeze his hand. "I will see you at the altar in the morning."

"I'll be the one with the purple wings, standing next to the brooding Dark Elf," he teases lightly, and I laugh.

Heat floods my cheeks as he kisses the back of my knuckles. It seems the rumors are true about the Fae being as charming as they are handsome. "I will see you tomorrow."

"Tomorrow," he repeats. A faint smile curves his gorgeous lips. "Until then, be assured that I'll not sleep a wink."

A soft laugh escapes me, but I quickly cover my mouth, not wanting to risk awakening my siblings.

He steps back and then flaps his wings, rising into the air. "Good night, Grayce."

"Good night, Kyven," I whisper in reply as he turns and flies back to his balcony.

When I step into my room, I make my way to the bed. I remove my cloak and fall back onto the mattress with a heavy sigh. Closing my eyes, I think of our kiss, and the feel of his body against mine while we hid from the guards, and I swallow thickly. How is it that he already affects me so? We only met a few days ago, and yet, it feels as though I've known him much longer.

Our conversation was comfortable instead of awkward. Kyven is handsome and charming, and has an easy way about him. Even as I think this, warning bells ring in my head for I already know that my heart is in danger. I could easily fall for this man—my soon-to-be husband.

I walk to my desk and pull open the top drawer. Lifting away the false bottom, I stare down at the letters Joren would leave for me under a rock in the garden. I unfold the top one and my gaze drifts to the last line. *Yours always*, he had signed with his signature in curling and elegant script.

Shaking my head, I tuck it back beneath the ribbon binding them all together. I held onto them after he left, searching for any hint or a sign that I may have missed, but I found none. I do not know why he left me, and I have accepted that I will never have an answer.

I walk over to the fireplace and then toss the stack into the burning hearth, watching as the flames consume the pages. I will not allow Joren's memory to cast any shadows over my life with Kyven. It would not be fair to him or to our future.

I reach up and touch my lips once more, remembering our kiss. Gods help me, I am already at risk of losing my heart to Kyven and we are not even married yet.

CHAPTER 8

GRAYCE

I smooth a hand over the silken skirt of my wedding gown as I study myself in the mirror.

Inara stands behind me, adjusting the gold circlet crown atop my head, making sure it is straight. "It's perfect now." She grins and rests her hands on my shoulders. "You look absolutely beautiful, Grayce."

Her golden hair spills down her back in thick waves as her hazel eyes sparkle with happiness. I've always heard that pregnant women have a glow about them. Looking at her now, I believe it to be true. She just recently announced she and Varys are expecting.

Her expression falls. "Are you all right?"

She's my sister. And while I don't want her worrying about me, I know she will understand what I'm feeling now. After all, it was not long ago that she married the Dark Elf King to forge an alliance. He was a stranger to her as well. "I'm just a bit nervous," I admit. "I still cannot believe that I'll be leaving here tomorrow. It will be hard leaving home."

"I promise it will get easier," she says, wrapping her arms around me and resting her head against mine. "At first, I missed home so much. And I still do miss being here, and seeing you, and Edmynd, and Raiden, and Lukas. But I love Ithylian. It feels just as much like home as Florin to me now."

"I hope I feel the same about Anlora." I glance at her stomach. "Do you think you could come visit before the baby is born?"

"Of course." She smiles. "And you will have to visit me as well. Varys and Kyven are as close as brothers. I'm sure they would love to spend time together too."

A knock at the door draws my attention, and I move to answer it. A smile crests my lips when I find my brothers standing outside. I'm not surprised to find Lukas standing behind them as well. His golden eyes lock onto me, and he rushes forward and gathers me into his arms, lifting me into the air and spinning me once before setting me back down.

"I'm glad you came." I smile. "I've missed your bear hugs."

"Wolf hugs," he corrects, and I laugh.

Lukas is the Wolf Shifter prince of Valren—our closest neighbor—but he practically grew up with us, and I've always thought of him as a brother. "Wolf hug," I repeat, and he flashes his signature wolfish grin.

He combs a hand through his short brown hair, smoothing it back into place as he straightens. "I wouldn't have missed it for the world." He exchanges a glance with Raiden. "But are you sure about this? Marrying the Fae King?"

"I am."

Lukas doesn't trust the Fae. The Wolf-Shifters of Valren have a long and bloody history with the kingdom of Anlora. I hope that my marriage to Kyven and my friendship with Lukas will help create peace between them as well.

He hugs me again and whispers in my ear. "I love you as if

you were my own sister. If you get to Anlora, and you are unhappy, I will come for you." He pulls back and meets my gaze evenly. "My kind are immune to magic. The Fae could not keep me away from you if they tried."

Although I doubt I will need to be rescued from my new husband, Lukas's words are comforting all the same. Wolf-Shifters are not just immune to the effects of magic, they are fierce in battle, and heal faster than the other races. It's why the Fae, the Elves, and even the Orcs are hesitant to cross them.

"Thank you. But I do not think you need to worry. Kyven has been nothing but kind to me so far."

"Even so, you must be wary," he warns. "It is not just him that worries me. You will be in Anlora, amongst Fae who have viewed humans as their enemies for centuries. Any one of them could try to harm you." He presses the hilt of a dagger into my hand. "I gave one to Inara when she wed Varys and I want you to have one as well. Keep it with you at all times."

Ice-cold dread twists deep inside me at his ominous words as I glance down at the blade. The memories of my mother's death flood my mind. She was murdered by an assassin; she died protecting me and Inara.

I reach up and feel the thick scar just below my left collarbone. The masked attacker tried to kill me after he was finished with my mother. He stabbed my chest, but I pulled the dagger from my body and slashed a line over his eye and down the left side of his face.

The black blood on the knife was the reason my father suspected the Fae in mother's death. In truth, it could have been any Otherworldly being. The color of their blood is all the same; none of them bleed red like humans.

I tuck the dagger into my dress pocket and lift my gaze back to Lukas. I know he does this because he cares for me.

He has no idea of the trauma I still carry from that day. No one does. I hide it well. "Thank you."

It's nearly time for the wedding. Lukas and Raiden leave for the temple, while Edmynd waits off to the side.

Inara gives me a quick hug. "You look beautiful." She smiles brightly. "I'm going to get Varys and we'll meet you at the altar."

Varys is standing in as Kyven's best man, while Inara will be my maid of honor.

When she leaves, I turn back to the mirror and study my reflection once more. Edmynd rests a hand on my shoulder. "Whenever you're ready."

Drawing in a deep breath, I loop my arm through Edmynd's and we start down the hallway. Our footsteps echo along the stone floor, each one bringing me closer to the destiny that awaits. Today is the day I will wed my former enemy.

WHITE FLOWERS and ribbons adorn the towering columns of the castle temple, on either side of the large wooden doors. I would think the decorations were lovely, if not for the worry in my heart. Smoothing my hands down the silk skirt of my wedding gown, I take a deep and steadying breath.

"You look lovely," Edmynd offers, but it is easy to read the sorrow in his expression. One would think he was leading me to the gallows instead of preparing to walk me down the aisle to my future husband.

My wedding dress is a masterpiece of delicate lace and silk, the bodice tight and fitted, the skirt decorated in an intricate pattern of small crystals and pearls.

It was my mother's, and I wish more than anything that she was here with us today.

My long, chestnut hair is styled in an elegant twist of braids atop my head, adorned with a gold, circlet crown of diamonds, and my hazel eyes are lined with kohl. Despite my nerves, I give him a faint smile. "Thank you."

Edmynd offers me his arm, and I loop mine through his. I'm a tangle of nerves as the guards open the doors to the temple, and everyone stands and turns to stare at us. Some of them gazing at me with looks of approval and others with pity.

The aisle is decorated with lovely flowers and ribbons. Scattered pink and white rose petals line the carpet, and the air is thick with the sweet scent of incense.

My eyes immediately find King Kyven, standing beside the altar. Sunlight spills in through the large windows, casting mosaic patterns on the stone floor and gilding the tips of his lavender wings.

Dressed in his gold and black armor, which does little to conceal his lean, powerful form beneath, he is strikingly handsome to behold.

When we reach the altar, Kyven's violet eyes meet mine, their vertically slit pupils expanding as he studies me intensely. The pointed tips of his ears stick up from his short silver-white hair. He has an aristocratic nose and brows, and a masculine square jaw that could cut glass.

He is so tall the top of my head does not quite reach his chin. I've always heard the Fae were the very definition of handsomeness and beauty. Gazing up at him now, I know that these rumors were not wrong. He is the most handsome man I have ever seen.

My heart hammers as we stand across from each other, and my cheeks flare with heat. If he is nervous at all, he is excellent at hiding it. His face is an impassive mask.

I swallow hard, trying to appear stoic to hide my uncertainty. In truth, I am pledging my life to a man I barely know, a man who is king of a people that mine have been fighting against for over a hundred years.

The weight of this moment is nearly overwhelming, but I hold my head high, determined to be brave.

My younger sister, Inara, stands beside me as my matron of honor, dressed in elegant Elvish robes, similar to her husband—King Varys—who stands next to Kyven. His own silver robes are a stark contrast to his gray-blue skin, short, black hair, and glowing blue eyes.

Their union gives me hope that my marriage to Kyven could be successful.

Out of the corner of my vision, I see Raiden staring daggers at my soon-to-be husband, his brown eyes narrowed as he looks him up and down.

Lukas stands on the other side. His golden eyes meet mine briefly before sweeping to Kyven with a threatening glare.

I stop short of rolling my eyes. They make a wonderful pair—each of them ready to murder my new husband at a moment's notice.

My cousin Freyja, and her husband, King Aurdyn—the Dragon King—sit beside them. A smile lights her face as Aurdyn curls his left wing around her shoulder, tugging her close to his side. I pray that my marriage will be as blessedly happy as theirs seems to be.

Edmynd kisses my forehead, and then relinquishes my arm to take a seat in the front row beside the rest of my family.

Kyven takes my hands, his grip firm and steady. His callused palms are warm in mine.

I force my voice to remain steady as I speak my vows. When I promise to love, honor, and cherish him, something flickers behind his eyes—an emotion I cannot quite place.

Despite my nerves, the rich, deep timbre of his voice

makes heat rise in my cheeks as he promises the same in return.

When he is finished, the priest looks at us both. "It is time for the exchanging of the rings."

One of his guards hands him the ring, and Kyven steps closer. The air shifts with his movement, and the smell of fresh rain and forest fills the space around us.

As he holds out my ring, my eyes travel over the delicate silver band etched with tiny leaves. I inhale sharply when I notice the purple moonstone setting in the shape of a rose.

My heart hammers. This is my sign. It is the purple rose I saw in my vision.

I lift my eyes to Kyven, and I'm caught in his intense violet gaze, unable to move. I have always trusted my instincts, and in my heart I understand now that the gods are directing my path.

Our fates are entwined.

CHAPTER 9

KYVEN

Lifting her delicate hand, I carefully slip the ring onto her fourth finger. Surprise flits across her expression as she studies it before she lifts her gaze back to me.

My heart clenches as her hazel eyes search mine. She is stunningly gorgeous, dressed in her long, white gown with tiny crystals embedded in the bodice and trailing down the elegant fabric like starlight.

The sunlight catches on her chestnut hair, twisted in a series of small braids and appearing like a crown atop her head. A few spiraling tendrils frame her lovely heart-shaped face accentuating the delicate features of her brows, nose, and chin and the plush bow of her soft, pink lips.

The delicate scent of rose oil with a hint of lavender floods my nostrils, her familiar scent stirring the primal instincts buried deep inside me. I long more than anything to seal her to me, so that none will doubt that she is mine.

Long, dark lashes frame her eyes—their golden-brown

coloring flecked through with chips of green. A lovely and unique combination that never fails to fascinate me. I study the pattern of tiny spots that dot her cheeks and her dainty nose as her rose pink lips part slightly beneath my gaze.

When she places my ring on my finger, I am surprised by the detail of the band. Intertwining vines of silver with tiny thorns and flowers carved into the metal. A smile crests my lips when I realize they are roses. Our rings are a match even though we did not confer upon this before our wedding, and I am in awe of the workings of fate.

I lift my gaze back to my human bride. A lovely pink flush spreads across her cheeks when the priest instructs us to kiss at the end of the ceremony.

Grayce stretches up on her toes, and I lean forward just enough until her face is nearly even with mine. The soft mint of her breath fans across my skin. My heart pounds as I close the small gap between us and brush my lips against hers in a tender kiss.

When we pull away, her eyes meet mine, a flicker of uncertainty in their depths. She is nervous, and understandably so. She has just sworn her life to a veritable stranger. And while I wish more than anything that I could tell her the truth... that I was Joren, I cannot. Not without risking the wrath of the gods.

* * *

THE CELEBRATION HALL is large enough to hold at least two hundred people. Thankfully, there are probably no more than one hundred here right now, making it easy to navigate our way to the table near the front and center of the room for the wedding feast.

Great platters of meat, bread, cheeses, and fruit are laid out before us. Large goblets of wine are poured to overflowing and I notice Aurdyn, Grayce's brothers, and Lukas partaking heavily of the drink, whereas Grayce merely sips at her wine, and I do the same.

It is a human tradition to consummate the marriage on the wedding night, and if she wishes to keep this tradition, I want to be clear-headed and focused. I want only to please my mate, especially upon our first joining.

When it is time for dancing, I stand and take her hand. Music played upon stringed instruments fills the air. I rest one hand on her lower back and pull her close as she rests a hand on my waist, and I take her free one in my own. Together, we begin to dance and whirl across the floor. Her steps match mine in perfect synchronous movements as we spin and weave through the crowd.

She is so lovely I cannot take my eyes off her. Desire thrums through my veins as I hold her close. My gaze drifts down to the elegant curve of her neck and my fangs extend with want to mark her as mine.

I do not know how Varys went for so long before finally sealing his bond with Inara. The instinct to fully claim my mate is a fire in my veins.

The next song is a group dance. Thankfully, Varys and Inara are beside us and I only have to switch off with him instead of someone else, when I reluctantly am forced to relinquish my hold on Grayce as we spin and weave among the other dancers.

As I make another turn around Inara, my head whips toward Grayce to find Lukas has cut in. A low growl vibrates my chest as the song changes and he pulls her away, spinning and twirling with her through the throng of dancers.

Bright sparkling laughter leaves her lips and jealousy flares brightly within. *How dare he take her from me.*

I start toward them, and his gaze snaps to mine, a smirk

playing on his lips. That vile dog knows exactly what he is doing.

A hand on my shoulder stops me abruptly, and I spin to find Varys. "He did the same to me with Inara when we were wed," he murmurs in my ear. "Do not let him goad you. She considers him like a brother."

"You are certain he does not desire her as his?"

"I am."

Even so, murderous thoughts fill my mind as I watch Prince Lukas dancing with Grayce. Magic sparks between my fingers, threading through them like small bits of lightning before I close my hands into a fist to snuff it out.

As I speak with Varys, my eyes never leave my new bride. We are married, according to the human tradition, but our bond is not yet complete.

My kind are intensely possessive of our mates, and until I fully claim her, and give her my mark to seal our bond, the urge to fight off every unbonded male that comes near her will be nearly unbearable for me.

"Have you told her yet?" Varys asks.

In this moment, I regret having told my friend my terrible secret. The truth of how I courted Grayce in the guise of a human. I admitted this to him in a moment of doubt and weakness. Thankfully, I bound his tongue with the unbreakable promise spell before I told him what I'd done, rendering him incapable of speaking of it to anyone but me.

"I would if I could, Varys," I say defeatedly. "But I cannot."

I would tell her if not for the warning given to me by the spirit of the heart tree—a being who speaks for the very gods themselves. The gods can be giving, but their cruelty knows no bounds if you ignore them. My father learned this the hard way, and I will not repeat his mistakes.

"If you do not tell her, and she finds out later, I fear it will be worse for you," he warns. "A secret like that can destroy any bond you form with your mate."

"What would you have me do?" I ask defeatedly. "Risk angering the gods? Chance altering my fate?" I shake my head. "I *cannot*. I *will* not. Not after I saw the price my father paid for ignoring their will."

Varys sighs heavily. "I understand your concern, but I worry for you, my friend."

I swallow hard. "I do too."

We remain silent a moment before he changes the subject. "You should expect to be threatened by the males in her family this evening."

"Threatened?"

He nods. "It is a human tradition for male family members of the bride to threaten the life of the groom at the reception."

My mouth falls open, but I quickly snap it shut as Raiden makes his way toward me.

His face is red and his breath reeks of wine as he glares at me, backing me into a corner. "If you ever hurt her, I'll kill you," he grinds out. "Do you understand?"

His words would be considered an act of war if I did not realize they were spoken out of brotherly concern for his sister, and that it was a tradition. "I would never harm her, Prince Raiden. I vow this to you."

"Good."

I turn back to Varys, but instead find myself face to face with King Aurdyn. His silver-white wings flare out behind him as his green eyes lock onto mine in a stern look. He points a clawed finger threateningly at me. "Know that if you ever upset your mate in any way, I will burn you to ash and raze your kingdom to the ground."

What in the seven hells? Anger flares brightly within. "How dare you threaten to—"

"Aurdyn!" Freyja—his mate, and Grayce's cousin—snaps at him. "What do you think you're doing?"

I observe in shock as the fierce Dragon King is chastised by his human mate.

She places her hands on her hips. "Why are you threatening Grayce's husband?"

"We are mated now, and I am part of your family." He gestures to Raiden, standing off to the side. "He told me it was tradition for male family members of the bride to threaten the groom at the wedding reception." He puffs out his chest with pride. "I have successfully fulfilled my familial obligations, my beautiful Freyja. But if it pleases you, I will threaten him again."

Freyja stops short of rolling her eyes and looks up at me. "You'll have to excuse my mate." She loops her arm through his, and narrows her eyes in Raiden's direction. "Come on. We're going to go have a friendly chat with Raiden."

Before Aurdyn can say anything else, she leads him away.

I glance back at the dance floor and see Grayce dancing with Edmynd. She is truly stunning to behold.

Prince Lukas walks up beside me. From the look on his face, I'm almost certain a threat similar to the one Raiden and Aurdyn gave me is about to be spoken. Crossing my arms over my chest, I turn to face him. "Have you come to threaten me as well?"

"No," he replies, surprising me with his answer. "I do not have to." He lifts his right hand and studies his nails, extending them into sharp black claws. His golden eyes snap to mine, narrowing. "You already know what will happen if you hurt her."

Out of the corner of my eye, I notice Varys speaking with Raiden. Raiden claps his shoulder and laughs with him at some shared joke. Not long ago they considered him their enemy. I can only hope to be on such good terms with them as my friend seems to be now.

I can profess all I want that I would never hurt Grayce, but I understand that actions are more powerful than words. So, I will do everything in my power not only to prove myself to her, but to her family as well.

* * *

THE SUN IS low on the horizon by the time most of our guests have already left the reception. Grayce hugs her family, and I bite back a growl as she embraces Lukas as well. She loops her arm through mine, and we follow one of the temple priestesses to the room where we will consummate our marriage.

Fierce possessiveness floods my veins. The pull of the bond is strong, calling forth the instinct to claim my mate. Now that we are wed according to the customs of her people, I am eager to seal her to me.

Until we fully seal our bond, I worry that I will be constantly on edge, especially if she is around unbonded males. It is a primitive urge that all Fae males struggle with in the early days of a bonding. And it will not be sated until she is carrying my mark.

CHAPTER 10

GRAYCE

We follow the temple priestess down the candlelit hallway, my heart pounding with equal parts anticipation and anxiety. She gestures for Kyven to go into one room and directs me into another, two doors down.

This part of the castle is normally reserved for guests, but it seems a few of the rooms have been repurposed to serve as a wedding suite for me and my new husband.

Husband. The word sounds strange, even in my head. I can still hardly believe I am married now.

When I enter the richly appointed chamber, one of the servants helps me to remove my wedding dress. I step behind a dressing screen to discard the rest of my clothes and change into a silken gown of joining.

I gaze at myself in the mirror. The sheer fabric is cool against my skin, and shimmers like moonlight, leaving nothing to the imagination. I can't help but feel exposed, vulnerable beneath its silver, gossamer folds.

With nimble fingers, my lady's maid loosens my hair from its braids and carefully combs it out so that it spills down my back and shoulders in soft waves. She moves in silence, her quiet efficiency a stark contrast to the chaos of emotions swirling inside me.

Once she has finished, she leads me to a door off to one side. I step into the bedroom, a sanctum of candlelight and shadows. The four-poster bed stands as the room's centerpiece, its ivory linens and silk drapes glowing in the dim light. I stand at its edge, fingers brushing against the smooth fabric, my heart threatening to beat out of my chest.

I can't help but wonder what Kyven is thinking as he prepares for our union. I wonder if he has done this before. I've heard the first joining can be painful, and I pray he will be gentle with me, understanding of my inexperience and nervousness.

The door across the way creaks open, and I hold my breath as Kyven steps through the threshold. He wears a similar sheer robe, but it is so dark I cannot make out his features beneath the fabric.

His gaze locks onto mine, and for a moment, time seems to stand still, suspended in the space between us.

With a grace that belies his size, he crosses the room, his movements fluid and confident. When he comes to a stop before me, my gaze travels over his broad shoulders and the chiseled planes of his chest and abdomen.

I have seen images of male anatomy in books of medicine, but they did not look quite like him. He is larger than I expected. His shaft is lined with ridges along the top and rows of smaller bumps along the side. A large bulb of extra tissue rings the base. His manhood is hard and erect, straining against the sheer fabric of his joining gown.

Careful to retract his claws, he cups my chin, tipping my

face up to his. His violet eyes search mine. "Are you sure you wish to do this?"

My heart hammers in my chest. I'm nervous, but it is tradition to consummate the marriage on the wedding night. It is how the union is sealed. "Yes."

"You are more beautiful than anything I have ever seen," he whispers as he studies my face. His pupils expand so that only a thin rim of color is visible around the edges. He leans down and gently brushes his lips to mine with a tenderness that takes my breath away.

His masculine scent surrounds me—a delicious and heady mix.

One kiss bleeds into another until I'm no longer sure where one ends and the next begins. I open my mouth and his tongue finds mine, curling around it.

He slides his hand around my waist and pulls me closer. A soft moan escapes me as he molds my body against his and threads his fingers through my hair, tipping my head up to angle my mouth to his own.

I'm completely lost in sensation as his tongue strokes against mine in a sensuous dance of give and take.

Without breaking our kiss, he lifts me into his arms and walks to the bed. I'm breathless and panting as he lays me gently beneath the blanket. He crawls over me. Bracing his weight on his elbows on either side of my arms, he captures my mouth in a searing kiss as he settles between my thighs.

I inhale sharply at the hard press of his length against me. We're still dressed in our joining robes, but the material is so thin, the weeping tip of his manhood leaves a trail of warm liquid along the tender flesh of my inner thigh.

He cups my left breast in his palm, and I moan as his thumb brushes over the sensitive peak before he trails his hand down my body and grasps the hem of my dress, pushing it up to my hips.

He kisses a heated trail along my jaw. He moves down my neck and I gasp as something sharp scrapes lightly across my skin.

He pulls back and fear spikes through me. His eyes are obsidian black, and his fangs are fully extended.

CHAPTER 11

KYVEN

Her eyes are wide. The acrid scent of her fear is thick in the air around us, overpowering and replacing the sweet scent of her arousal.

Quickly, I lift away from her and stand from the bed. "You are afraid of me."

It is not a question, but I pray that she denies it.

Her entire body trembles slightly as she pulls the blankets to cover herself. "I felt your fangs on my skin," she murmurs. "Why?"

Inwardly, I curse myself as I retract my fangs. She is human, not Fae. I should never have assumed that our ways would be the same as theirs. "It is instinct to mark one's mate during the first joining," I explain. "Forgive me. I should have realized…"

"Your eyes." She swallows hard. "They were different… completely black."

"I am sorry I frightened you, but I promise that you have nothing to fear from me, Grayce. I would never harm you."

She relaxes slightly at my words, and the scent of her fear begins to dissipate. Even so, I want only to reassure her. I would sooner take my own life than ever harm her.

I pull a fur blanket from the bed. "I will not come to your bed again until you wish it."

"You do not care if we consummate our marriage?"

I meet her gaze evenly so she can see the truth of my words. "I vow that I will never take anything you do not willingly give."

I spread my blanket on the ground. "I will sleep on the floor." She opens her mouth to speak, but I quickly add, "Rest now, Grayce. We have a long journey ahead of us tomorrow."

Without waiting for her to reply, I lie down. Her shadow moves in the darkness as she shifts onto her side, curling beneath the blankets.

I hate that she fears me when I want only to care for and protect her. She is my fated one—a blessing from the gods that every Fae hopes to find, but few ever do.

Clenching my jaw, I stare up at the ceiling. I vow that I will do whatever it takes to prove myself to her.

CHAPTER 12

GRAYCE

When I wake, Kyven is already gone. I make my way to the cleansing room and dress. A soft knock at the door is one of the servants with a tray of tea and breakfast.

"Your new husband asked us to send this up to you, my lady," she says as she walks it inside and carefully sets it on the table. "He said to tell you he is waiting downstairs whenever you are ready."

I nod and she leaves quickly.

A knot of worry forms in my stomach. I'd hoped we could perhaps talk about last night before we leave, but it seems there will not be a chance. I hate the way I reacted to him. Especially since he has been nothing but kind and respectful of me since we met.

Sighing heavily, I eat a few bites of egg and some toast before drinking my tea. When I'm finished, I go to my chambers and find five trunks packed full of my belongings.

When I open them, I realize that most are clothing with

only a few personal items. I'm not sure I want to take this much with me. Especially since it is such a long journey. It would be a strain on both the horses and the carriage.

I quickly search through the trunks, pulling out only enough clothing to fill one trunk, tossing in a few personal items, including my copy of "The Queen's Knight."

I feel a bit guilty taking it from the palace library, but it's my favorite novel, and I'm not sure that I'll find any romance books in Anlora. At least, not ones that I can easily read.

I've studied a bit of *Faerinesh*, but not enough to speak or read it fluently yet. That will have to be remedied rather quickly, I believe.

I place Lukas's dagger inside as well. Kyven gave me one the night before our wedding, and it's small enough to conceal in my hidden pocket while traveling.

Instructing the servants to only bring down the one trunk, I make my way downstairs to find Kyven barking orders at his men, readying for our departure.

The moment I step out into the courtyard, his head snaps to me and he walks over.

"Did you sleep well?" he asks, his eyes full of concern.

I hate that things are so awkward between us. I'm still nervous to be leaving behind everything I've ever known, but I'm not afraid. Not anymore.

Kyven is a good man, who actually cares what I think and what I feel. If he did not, he would have insisted that we consummate our marriage last night, and he wouldn't have been so upset about my fears.

"Yes," I lie.

In truth, I only slept a few hours. My mind would not rest. While I cannot deny that it was somewhat startling to see him with his fangs extended and his eyes pitch-black, I have to remember that Kyven is not human. And I cannot expect him to look and act human either. He is my husband, and I must accept him as he is, just as he has accepted me.

"Good." A faint smile crests his lips. "We are ready to leave when you are."

Tears sting my eyes as I prepare to say goodbye to my family.

I wrap my arms around Inara. I hate that I'm leaving her so soon when it feels as though she has only just returned recently from Ithylian. "You'll come visit me soon, right?"

"I promise, Grayce."

"Gods, I'm so nervous, Inara," I whisper, allowing my worry to escape unfiltered. "I have no idea what I'm doing."

When I pull back, she takes my hand and glances down at my ring. "You have a sign you are on the right path. Just take things slowly and everything will work itself out."

"How do you know?"

"It worked for me and Varys." She hugs me again. "Use the time you are traveling to ask questions and share stories. Get to know him better."

"I will." I hope she is right.

"You are both welcome in our kingdom anytime you wish to visit," Varys says as he bids me goodbye.

Freyja hugs me tight and Aurdyn dips his chin in parting.

Edmynd, Raiden, and Lukas take turns giving me great bear hugs. When they finally pull away, Edmynd turns to Kyven, his expression full of concern. "You are sure you do not wish for any carriages?"

He shakes his head. "It's faster and safer to fly, I believe."

Fly? My head whips to him, my eyes wide. I had just assumed we'd be traveling back to Anlora by carriage.

"My sister cannot make the journey like that," Raiden snaps. "She is—"

"It's all right, Raiden," I cut him off.

I'm sure he was about to reveal that I'm terrified of

heights. I give him a warning look. I do not want to appear weak in front of my new husband and his warriors.

"A carriage is more vulnerable to attack by the Wraiths," Kyven explains. "With all the recent sightings along our borders, flying is the safest choice."

Raiden still has a stern expression on his face, but he remains silent, probably weighing the options in his mind, like me. If given the choice between fear of heights or fear of Wraiths, I would rather risk the heights.

I comfort myself with the thought that perhaps it will not be so bad. After all, Kyven did fly me up to my balcony the other night and it was fine. Drawing in a deep breath, I steady my nerves and push down my fear, forcing myself to focus on something else.

I'm glad I packed light, but now even the one trunk with my belongings seems like a burden.

Reading the concern in my expression, Kyven tells me. "I will be the one to carry you, my queen."

My queen. It is strange to hear my new title. I knew this is what I would be once we were married, but to hear it aloud is a stark reminder of all the changes ahead. My life will never be the same and I'm still not sure if that is a good thing or not.

As I glance once more at my sister and Varys, I can only hope that Kyven and I can have a marriage like theirs someday.

Two of Kyven's guards take my trunk, and Edmynd frowns. "Is that all you are taking?"

"I didn't want to burden the carriages or the horses." I glance at Kyven and his guards. "But perhaps this works out better anyway. I wouldn't want to ask anyone to carry anything else. Besides, I do not need so many clothes. I'm sure the fashions in Anlora are different from Florin."

He gives me a pitying expression. "If you wish for

anything else, send word and I will have it brought with me when we come visit."

Sadness tears at my heart and I step forward and wrap my arms around his neck, hugging him close. He loops his arms around me in return.

"I'll miss you," he whispers.

"And I will miss you."

Swallowing against the lump in my throat, I finally manage to pull myself away and return to Kyven's side.

A Fae with vibrant blue wings and bright blue eyes approaches. He bows low. "We are ready to depart whenever you are, your Majesties."

Kyven turns to me. "Grayce, this is Aren—my personal guard and my good friend."

I'm surprised by the familiar way he addresses his guard, but then I realize he is telling me this to let me know how much he trusts him.

"My Queen," Aren says as he thumps his fist to his chest and bows again. "It is an honor."

"It is lovely to meet you as well." I offer him a warm smile. "How long have the two of you been friends?"

"Five years," Aren replies.

"He saved my life on the Great Wall in a fight against the Wraiths," Kyven adds. "We have been friends ever since."

My eyes widen slightly. I've never been to the Great Wall, but I understand it is a dangerous place. To know that my new husband has been there, defending the kingdom from the Wraiths, tells me he is not only brave but as dedicated to the safety of his realm as my own brother is of Florin.

From what I have witnessed of many of the nobility, it is rare for them to do anything that places them in harm's way. Only the bravest among them actually take up arms.

"The King is too kind," Aren says. "He has saved my life more than once as well."

"And mine," another guard chimes in.

Kyven jerks his chin toward his men. "We all trained together when we were younger."

I'm surprised by the familiarity he has with his guards, but it speaks volumes about his character. It is easy to see he has the complete loyalty of his warriors. An indication that he is a fair and just King.

When we're ready to leave, Kyven carefully places one arm behind my back and the other up under my knees and lifts me to his chest.

"You're sure you can carry me the entire way?" I ask, concerned that I'll be too heavy, and he might lose his grip.

"My people are stronger than yours, Grayce," he reassures me with a handsome smile. "You are very light in my arms. Are you ready?"

Swallowing back my fear, I nod. With a final wave goodbye to my family and friends, we lift into the air.

His wings flutter behind him and the ground falls away beneath us as we ascend toward the clouds. The last time he carried me like this, we were only a few feet off the earth. As I look below me, my stomach begins to churn with nerves.

"Are you all right?" he asks.

Swallowing against the bile rising in my throat, I wrap my arms tighter around him, burying my head against the curve of his neck and shoulder. His masculine scent fills my nostrils, and it's oddly reassuring. "Just a bit... nervous," I somehow manage. "I've never been so high up before."

He tightens his grip on me, curling me into his chest. "I will not let you fall, Grayce. My vow."

His words calm my racing heart as I focus on my breathing. "How long is it until we reach Anlora?"

"We will stop for the night to rest, but we should be there before midday tomorrow."

A low groan escapes me.

"Do you want me to turn back?" he asks. "I can take your brother up on his offer of a carriage."

I'm about to say yes, please, but stop short. "You said this was the safer route, right?"

"Yes. Wraiths have been spotted along our borders and Orcs have been seen wandering in the Forest recently."

"Do you know which Clan they belong to?" I ask. I've studied Orc culture in great detail. I had to when Edmynd negotiated a truce with Clan Ulvad a few years back. But I know that not all Clans are the same. Some are violent, and some are not. It depends upon their leader.

He hesitates a moment before replying. "No."

"It's probably safer to fly," I tell him.

"My guards and I will protect you if you wish to travel by carriage."

"I'm not going to put anyone in danger just because I'm a bit uncomfortable, Kyven." I do my best to keep my voice even despite my churning stomach. "Besides, this is how you normally travel, is it not?"

"Yes."

I lift my face to his. "Then I will learn to get used to it."

His expression softens. "You are certain?"

I nod and then duck my head back to the crook of his neck. I breathe in through my nose and out through my mouth as I focus on calming my heart rate and breathing. I love his scent of forest and fresh rain. "You smell good." Heat rushes to my cheeks, and I inwardly curse my nerves as the words leave my lips unfiltered.

A warm puff of air blows across the top of my head. "So do you." He gently nuzzles my hair. "Like roses and lavender."

Cautiously, I lift my head. I'm acutely aware of Kyven's warriors watching me. I cannot deny that it's unnerving being the only human amongst so many Fae, and the last thing I want is to appear weak and afraid.

His guards appear to have a great deal of respect for their king, but our people have been enemies for so long, I wonder how many of them harbor animosity toward humans and dislike the idea of their king marrying one.

"We should reach the Wyldwood soon," he says, interrupting my thoughts. "But if you wish to stop along the way, let me know."

"The Wyldwood?"

"I believe your people call it the Dark Forest," he replies.

The Dark Forest covers a vast area between Anlora and Florin. Wild and untamed, neither kingdom claims it as their own. It is said that the trees are as tall as castles and their branches so thick and heavy with leaves that they blot out the sun. I've also heard that monsters make their home in the forest. Lord Brandar even swore that he saw a herd of unicorns near the edge of the woods once, and I wonder if it is true.

"I've heard there are unicorns in the Dark Forest," I tell him. "Have you ever seen one?"

"Yes. Many of them make their home in the Wyldwood. They are beautiful creatures," he says. "But extremely territorial. If we happen upon one, you must be very cautious."

My ears perk up despite his warning. "I've always wanted to see one."

"You have?"

"Yes."

"Then I will make it a point to find one for you, my beautiful mate."

Heat sears my cheeks at his term of endearment, and my heart flutters as he flashes a devastatingly handsome smile. Gods help me, my new husband is already breaking down the carefully built walls around my heart.

CHAPTER 13

KYVEN

I am completely enchanted as her cheeks flush a lovely shade of pink. Grayce is the most beautiful female I have ever seen, and I can hardly believe that she is mine. I want only to please her; to make her happy. And if she wishes to see a unicorn, then I will do everything I can to make sure she does.

"I was so fascinated with them when I was younger," she says. "I read every book I could find in the palace library about unicorns. And then I went through a phase where I was obsessed with maps. And that led to an interest in learning about languages."

"I used to dread my language lessons," I admit. "But my father insisted upon them."

She laughs softly. "And those were the lessons I looked forward to the most." A wistful smile crests her lips. "I always felt like that was the key to really learning about other cultures. When you learn someone's language, you don't just learn how to speak and read in their tongue, you learn a little bit about how they view the world."

Her answer intrigues me. "What do you mean?"

"In my native tongue we describe the elements as earth, air, fire, and water. But in Elvish and Faerinesh, there are dozens of words to describe these, suggesting you have a much closer relationship with nature than my people possess."

"We draw our powers from the elements," I explain. "But we also strive to live in balance with nature. We infuse our magic into the land, to ensure we give back at least as much as we take so we do not deplete the life force of the world around us."

"How do you do that?" she asks.

"All magic is an act of balancing a scale. Each spell, no matter how small, has a consequence."

Her eyes light up. "That is why the Faerinesh word for *magic* is also the same as the word for *balance*, isn't it?"

I smile. "Yes."

"What about the word: *mate*?" she asks. "It is the same word as *forever*."

"Because when my people take a mate, it is for life."

Her mouth drifts open. "There are so many stories about Fae males luring human women into the woods. But they must all be complete fiction then."

I arch a brow. "Perhaps it did not happen with humans, since I know of no interspecies bonding between our kind before now, but there is a kernel of truth to those tales. In ancient times, this was a courting ritual among my people.

"Males would often woo a female by enticing her to follow him into the woods. If she accepted his advances, they would seal their bond in the forest beneath the moonlight. This is why our bonding ceremonies take place beneath the light of a full moon."

"That is why the word for bonding ceremony is so similar to the word for moon in your language," she murmurs, more to herself than to me.

"Yes."

As we continue our conversation, I am fascinated by the inner workings of Grayce's brilliant mind. Although I have spent my entire life suppressing my ability to read someone through touch, I long more than anything to feel the brush of her mind against my own.

I am completely and utterly obsessed with my mate.

When we reach the Wyldwood, Grayce stares at the forest in wonder. "I've never seen trees this big." She gapes. "How old are these woods?"

The ancient trees with trunks as large as castle towers seem to stretch toward the heavens. Their bark is as dark as midnight and their thick branches are heavily laden with dark green needle-like leaves that blot out the last light of the sun as it retreats from the sky.

"No one knows how old this forest is." It is said that these colossal guardians have stood sentinel since the dawn of time, their roots burrowing deep into the earth, tapping into the very essence of magic that pulses through the land. "It predates our written history."

We reach a small clearing, and she gasps when she looks down, as if only now realizing just how high above the ground we are.

She quickly buries her face in the crook of my neck, and fierce possessiveness uncoils deep within. My fangs extend. The primitive desire to mark my mate is all-consuming as her warm breath puffs against my skin.

If she were Fae, she would mark me, just as I long to do to her in return. But she is not, and her fear of me last night gives me pause. I do not know enough of human mating rituals to know if marking is something her kind does as well. I did not notice any claiming marks on the citizens of Florin, but perhaps humans leave them in places on the body that are concealed by their clothing.

"My king," Aren says as he comes up beside us. "It is getting late. Do you want me to send a few scouts ahead to secure a campsite?"

"Yes," I reply, thankful that he is such a competent warrior. He is always thinking ahead, and I trust his judgment in regards to our safety. "See that it is done."

He dips his chin and leaves to relay the order to the others.

Scanning the woods below, I search for any sign of movement. All the reports I've had of Wraiths and Orcs have been farther north than this, so we should be relatively safe for the night.

I'm sure Grayce must be tired. Despite my reassurances that I will not let her fall, her body is still slightly tense. She has relaxed a bit as we've talked, however, but I imagine she will probably be exhausted once we stop for the night.

"We are almost there," I murmur into her hair.

"Thank the gods," she breathes out the words like a sigh. "I cannot wait to set foot upon solid ground again."

Worry snakes through me at her statement. We are not going to make camp like humans. We are Fae. We set up our shelters in trees, where it is safer. "We are not going to be on the ground."

She lifts her head. "What do you mean?"

"We sleep in the tree branches."

She gulps but says nothing.

I open my mouth to reassure her, but Aren interrupts, gesturing up ahead. "The shelters have been prepared."

All the color drains from her face as we approach the tarps and bedding strung between the tree branches.

Aren directs us to the closest one. I notice my men have strung extra material on three sides for some privacy.

The sour scent of Grayce's fear permeates the air as we alight on a branch, and she clings even tighter to me.

Aren flies over to us, his nose wrinkling slightly at the strong smell. His gaze darts briefly to mine, full of concern, before he bows low to her. "All is well, my Queen. The others and I will take turns keeping watch throughout the night."

He is a good male, and I appreciate his attempt to allay her concerns.

"Thank you, Aren." She offers him a faint smile. "I trust you know what you are doing."

His face lights up at her faith in him. "I will be on first watch," he says before he flies off, leaving us alone.

CHAPTER 14

GRAYCE

I study the pitiful tarp strung between two thick branches that is somehow supposed to serve as my bed for the night. *Our* bed, I correct myself as I glance at my new husband. A blanket and two small pillows are arranged on top, and closed in on three sides for a small measure of privacy. Another tarp hangs overhead to protect us from rain.

My heart hammers as my gaze drops to the forest floor far below us.

Carefully, Kyven lowers my feet to the branch. As soon as my slippers touch the bark, panic seizes my chest, and I grip him even tighter.

"Grayce," he murmurs as I cling to him as if my life depends upon it, worried I will fall. He smooths a hand across my shoulders and cups my chin, tipping my face up to his. "You are safe," he murmurs. "I promise I will not let you fall."

Despite his words, I cannot force myself to relinquish my death grip on his arms.

"You must relax your hold a bit so I can guide us to the bedding."

"I'm trying." An unbidden tear slips down my cheek. "I just need a moment."

He slips his arms around me, rubbing a hand soothingly up and down my back. "You're safe, my beautiful mate. I have you."

I hate this. This is not who I am. Drawing in a shaking breath, I struggle to push down my fears. "I once tumbled out of our tree house when I was a child. Fortunately, I only sprained my wrist, but I still remember how terrifying it was."

"Humans have homes in trees?" He cocks his head to the side. "I did not know this."

A soft puff of air escapes me in a nervous laugh at his confusion. "No. They're built for children to play in." My entire body trembles as I carefully peel myself away from his body, putting a small bit of space between us so we can move. "But they can be a bit dangerous."

It's only a few steps to the tarp, but even that does not appear very stable to me as I swallow against the knot of worry in my throat. Breathing in through my nose and out through my mouth, I shore up my courage as I hold Kyven's hand as he guides me to the tarp.

Carefully, I sit on the blanket, crossing my legs in front of me.

I watch curiously as he kneels beside the branch and rests his palm on the rough bark. He bows his head, and a faint glowing light winds around his hand before disappearing. When he is finished, he lifts his gaze to me again.

"What were you doing?"

"I was thanking the trees for allowing us to shelter in

their branches, and promising that I will not use any of my magic to manipulate their growth in any way."

"What do you mean?"

"If we were in Anlora, I would have used my powers to weave a tight shelter of thick vines instead of using the tarps. But this forest is ancient; older than any found in our kingdom. And the trees here remember a time when others tried to use their magic to bend them to their will."

I stare at him in astonishment. "I had no idea you were able to speak with the trees."

"It is not exactly a conversation, per se, it is more of a feeling... an understanding. When we use our magic to encourage growth, we are communicating with the plants. I will show you what I mean when we visit the palace gardens."

I've heard stories of the famed gardens of Anlora's castle, but I've never talked to anyone who has actually seen them. "I've always wanted to see the gardens in Ryvenar."

He grins. "I believe you will enjoy them." He moves to stand. "I will fetch some food and drink."

His wings flutter behind him, readying to lift off, but I grip his forearm, stopping him abruptly. "Please, do not leave." I wince inwardly at how weak and pitiful I sound. This is not who I am. I am strong, and I am not a coward.

He sits next to me. "I will stay with you."

Everything inside me wants to tell him it's all right to go. I hate being afraid. But when I open my mouth, the words die in my throat as I glance down at the ground once more.

One of his guards brings us a platter of food. Sliced meat, bread, and cheese with a few pieces of fruit and some water. As delicious as it looks, I eat only enough to sate my hunger, worried that eating more will irritate the knot in my stomach.

When we're finished eating, a slight twinge in my lower

abdomen makes me grimace. I turn to Kyven. "Could you please help me get down?" My cheeks warm as I force the words past my lips. "I need to relieve myself."

He scoops me up into his arms and flies a short distance away from our encampment. Far enough that we can have privacy, but still close enough to call out if we run into trouble. His eyes sweep over the forest around us, searching for any signs of danger before he sets me down.

Kyven pulls a dagger from his belt and hands it to me. I still have the one he gave me before our wedding, but this one is larger. Bracing myself against my terrible memories, I take it from him. My pulse pounds in my ears as I grit my teeth and hold my arm tight to my side to stop it from trembling.

I am strong and I am brave. I repeat the words like a mantra in my head. *I will not be afraid.*

Kyven gestures to a nearby tree. "That is a good spot."

As I start toward it, so does he. I whip my head to him and frown. "I'd like some privacy."

"It is dangerous," he points out. "There could be Orcs out here."

As much as I fear the Orcs, I also know that there is no way my bladder will cooperate with him standing over me. "Then, just wait on the other side of the tree," I state in a tone that leaves no room for argument.

Reluctantly, he stalks away. Quickly, I relieve myself. The Fae truly must have excellent hearing because as soon as I'm done, he reappears around the corner.

"Let us go."

He takes my hand, and a warm tingling sensation spreads over my palm, up through my arm, and across my body. The fresh scent of rose and lavender fills my nose, and I glance down to see my clothing appears pristine. "Was that a cleansing spell?"

He grins. "Rather convenient, is it not?"

"Yes." How considerate of him. "Thank you."

He gathers me to his chest, and we fly back up to our shelter. When he sets me down on the tarp, he flashes a gorgeous smile. Just one look seems to loosen something inside me. I'm still nervous, but not quite as scared as I was before because I know he would never put me in danger.

I glance at the guards around us, settling onto their tarp beds and I'm suddenly very self-conscious about the thought of sleeping beside my new husband with an audience nearby.

Even though three sides are relatively shielded with extra material, it is not much.

As if sensing my concern, Kyven waves his hand and a soft glowing barrier forms around us. Aside from the very faint glow, it has the appearance of a soap bubble. I can see out at the others. "Is this for protection?"

"For extra privacy," he explains. "We can see out, but no one can see in." He turns his gaze back to the forest. "As for protection… Aren has erected an invisible barrier around our entire group. It will repel most things, and alert us of any trespassers."

I try not to focus on how he said "*most* things," not "*all* things." My mind begins conjuring all sorts of terrifying images of what sort of dangers he may be speaking of. Closing my eyes briefly, I force myself to push down these dark thoughts as I settle onto my side.

He lies down next to me and carefully pulls the blanket up over my shoulders. "Thank you," I somehow manage to speak despite my nerves. I'm not sure if I'm nervous to be sleeping beside him or worried about how far up we are. Sighing, I realize it's probably a bit of both.

A cool wind blows through the trees, causing the branches to sway slightly, and I freeze in place as an entirely new fear snakes through me. If I fall asleep, I could easily roll off this tarp. And if Kyven is sleeping when it happens, I could fall to my death before he even awakens. At the very least I'd definitely break something.

I glance around for anything I can use to tie myself off to the branch. So if I roll off the tarp, I won't fall. Or at least, not too badly. I'm sure I'd still have some sort of injury from the initial tug on the rope and then I'd probably slam against the trunk, and—

"I can scent your fear, Grayce." Kyven raises his arm. "Come here. I will not let you fall."

I move close to him, and he loops his arm around my waist, tugging me the rest of the way until I'm flush against him. With my palms pressed against his chest, I can feel the hard planes of muscle under his tunic and the strong and steady beat of his heart beneath my fingers.

"You are safe with me, Grayce," he murmurs.

I lift my head to find his violet eyes studying me with a piercing gaze.

"You will not fall. I have you." Gently he tucks a stray tendril of hair behind my ear. "My vow."

I shiver slightly and he tucks the blanket up around my shoulders and then cautiously wraps his wings around my form like a second comforter. Gently, he nuzzles my temple. "Are you warm enough?"

"Now I am."

I'm surprised by how flexible his wings are. At first glance their colorful panes appear delicate and almost brittle, but they are not. They have the consistency of leather and as they tighten around me, I'm surprised by their strength.

The nocturnal sounds of the forest drift along the breeze. As I settle into his embrace, I realize just how much I trust him. We haven't known each other long, but it feels like forever in a way. Wrapped up in his arms and wings, I feel safe. Like he would never allow anything to hurt me.

And while I'd think this a good thing since he is my husband, there is still so much I do not know about him. With his strong arms looped around me, I breathe in the heady smell of his masculine scent.

I cannot deny that I am attracted to him, but I do not yet know if my heart would be safe in his care. I trusted it to someone before and they cast it aside as if it were nothing. And I vowed that I'd never endure such pain again. I'm not sure my heart could take it.

Kyven has asked nothing of me beyond giving him a chance to prove himself, but in truth, I know he is asking for everything. He does not just want my hand, he wants my heart. And I'm not sure if that is something I can fully give him yet. I only pray he will be patient with me as he has promised.

If I'm honest with myself, I'm already falling for Kyven.

"Sleep, Grayce," he murmurs. "I will keep you safe."

And just those words reassure me, and I close my eyes and relax in his arms. After what feels like forever, I finally begin to drift away into sleep.

CHAPTER 15

KYVEN

Grayce shivers slightly in her sleep, and I curl my arms and wings tighter around her, holding her close. She releases a soft sigh of contentment and nestles into my chest. She fits so perfectly in my arms. As if we were made for each other.

She is lovely, my new bride. Completely and utterly captivating. But then, I knew this from the moment we met. Yet, I never had a chance to study her like this before. As she sleeps, I gaze at her beautiful heart-shaped face.

As I gaze at her, I wonder if she senses the connection between us. If she does, she has said nothing.

Gently, I reach out and run my fingers through her long silken hair as my gaze travels over her delicately curved, human ear. Long lashes cast shadows against her high cheekbones, the faintest hint of a smile playing upon her lips. I wonder what she is dreaming.

Imagining the feel of her skin beneath the tips of my finger, I long to read her thoughts and explore her mind. All the time I spent watching her when I was disguised as a human, I thought I knew everything there was to know of Grayce. But it seems I was wrong.

I am obsessed with my mate. Each time she speaks it is like seeing the world through a new lens, and I hang on her every word. I want to know everything about her.

Her lips part slightly and I can smell the soft mint of her breath. My eyes drop to the plush bow of her soft, pink lips. The memory of our first kiss fills my mind. I long to press my lips to hers and feel her open for me, allowing me to taste the delicate flavor of her kiss.

The humans have many stories about my people. One of them involves a Fae male who became obsessed with a human maiden. He found her asleep in the woods and stole a kiss from her as she slept.

I am not sure how much truth there are to these tales, but I do know that despite their recent claims otherwise, my kind have always been fascinated by hers.

I had not anticipated that she'd so readily share a bed with me so soon in our bonding, and I am pleased by how much faith she has in me already.

Even as this thought crosses my mind, guilt twists deep within. She does not know who I am. Who I was. If she were to discover this, she would probably hate me. At the very least, she'd be hurt and all the trust we are building right now would be forgotten.

Several times I have wanted to tell her. And I would have if not for the warning given to me by the spirit of the heart tree—one who speaks for the very gods themselves. The gods can be cruel when their will is ignored, and I'll not repeat the mistakes of my father.

They warned him not to go to Drathal. But when he discovered the Trolls were amassing there, readying to invade our lands, he felt he had no choice. How could he send his warriors to fight when he would not?

While he was defending the border, a regiment of Trolls snuck past his lines, surrounding my father and his warriors. He and my older brother were mortally wounded in the fray. I learned then how great the cost could be of ignoring a warning from the gods.

A flash of blue wings catches my eye, and I turn to find Aren approaching. He cannot see inside the magic barrier I've erected, and I am loath to lower it because of how intimate this moment feels with my mate, but I know that I must.

Carefully, I lower the shield. "What is it?" I keep my voice low so as not to wake my bride.

His gaze sweeps down to Grayce, his eyes widening slightly, probably surprised to find her already in my arms and wings, before he returns his attention to me. "One of our scouts detected a band of Orcs nearby. At least a dozen of them, maybe more. They are heading this way."

"Seven hells," I curse under my breath. Orcs may not have wings, but they do have magic, and they are formidable warriors.

But if we leave now, we risk being attacked by Harpies or any other manner of nocturnal flying predators that make their home in these infernal woods. Last time we were here, we stumbled upon Harpies. They were easily defeated, but I do not want to risk fighting mid-air with Grayce. If we travel by foot, we chance running into Orcs or other dangers.

I gaze at the sky. Dark clouds roil overhead, covering the light of the stars and the moon. My people are possessed of excellent night vision. At least, in the darkness we'd stand a better chance of going unnoticed by others if we flew.

As if reading my mind, Aren says, "It is pitch black. We have a better advantage in the air than we do on the ground."

"Gather our warriors. We must leave at once." I dart a glance at my A'lyra, still sleeping soundly in my arms. "And bring me a tunic and pants."

His brow furrows, but he gives an affirmative nod before flying away.

As soon as he is gone, I whisper. "Grayce. Wake up." Her eyelids flutter open. "We have to leave. There are Orcs coming this way."

With a sharp inhale, she jerks up to sitting. Tentatively, she reaches for me. "Kyven?" Her voice is barely a whisper as she touches my arm. Tracing her hand down to mine, she grips it firmly. "I can barely see anything. You'll have to guide me."

My heart clenches as her scent sours with fear. I'd forgotten how poor human night vision is compared to ours. With the moon and the stars covered by the clouds, I wonder if she can see anything. I would cast a globe of Fae light, but we'd risk being discovered by our enemies. "We're going to fly from here, quick and fast. We—"

I stop talking as Aren returns. His fluttering wings stir the air around us, scattering the smell of her fear into the forest. The Orcs will scent her for sure if they get any closer.

He hands me the clothing and I press it into Grayce's hands.

"What is this?"

"You need to change into a tunic and pants," I explain. "While we're in the air, I may need my arms free if we're attacked. So you will have to hold onto me if that happens, and you cannot do that very well in a dress. Do you understand?"

She nods.

"We must hurry."

Swallowing hard, she bites her lower lip and draws in a shaking breath. She reaches behind her to undo the lacing on her fine dress, and I grit my teeth in frustration. I'll never understand why human fashions are so complex. At this rate, it's going to take forever for her to undress.

"They're nearly here," Aren whispers urgently.

Panic spikes through me, and I extend my claws. "Forgive me, Grayce," I whisper as I slash through the laces, careful not to hurt her.

She inhales sharply as the bodice sags forward and the dress falls from her body, pooling around her feet and leaving her only in a light shift. Each of my warriors turns away, knowing better than to stare at my mate in such a state of partial undress.

I rest her hands on my shoulders and drop to my knees as I hold out the pants. "Left foot," I instruct, and she lifts her leg so I can slide the left side onto her. "Now, the right." I do the same and then quickly pull them up her body.

She is smaller than one of our females, and the pants are long and loose on her form. Quickly I slice away the material to shorten them, and then swiftly remove my own belt and speedily tie it around her waist in a knot to keep them up.

I tuck her dagger into her belt and place her palm on the handle. "Do not hesitate to use this if we are attacked."

She nods quickly. To her credit, she remains still, allowing me to work fast, and I slip the tunic over her head. It is so large it fits her like a dress and hangs off one shoulder. I slice away more material to free her hands and then pull her close to me.

Without hesitation, I lift her into my arms, and she wraps her legs around my waist and her arms around my neck while I support her with one hand on her backside and another looped around her back. "Ready?"

"Yes," she replies, and we lift into the air.

CHAPTER 16

GRAYCE

My stomach drops as Kyven takes off. His wings beat furiously as he weaves through the trees. It's so dark, I can only make out the vague outline of his wings and body and I can see nothing of the ground below us. I only know we're not above the canopy when Aren hisses. "Keep low and move quietly. We'll use the trees for cover as long as we can."

Panic twists deep inside me, but I force it back down as I hang onto Kyven.

His warm hand finds my face. *"Are you all right?"* he asks, and it takes me a moment to realize he is speaking in my mind.

"Yes," I think the words back to him, wondering if it worked. *"Is this the mind link? Can you hear me?"*

"Yes."

"How far is it to Anlora?"

"Still at least half a day from here," he replies grimly. *"There*

JESSICA GRAYSON

is a shorter route, but Wraith have been spotted along that way, so we took this one to go around. And now, it seems this path is not any safer."

"If it makes you feel any better: Between Wraith and Orcs, I'd prefer Orcs any day," I reply.

"Truly?"

"There are some Clans that are relatively peaceful," I tell him. "Edmynd negotiated a treaty with one of them."

"All the Orcs I've ever dealt with would sooner slit our throats if given the chance. Or take us prisoner to sell at one of their auctions."

A small shiver runs through me. He's right that there are some that are bloodthirsty and cruel. I've seen several people who were liberated from Orc slavers. I cannot bear the thought of being taken.

He tightens his grip around me. *"I would die before I let anyone hurt you, Grayce."*

Through the link, I feel the conviction of his words. He means this. He would truly give his life for me. Knowing how much he cares gives me comfort. Whatever happens, he will not abandon me.

We fly for what feels like forever. The clouds thin overhead, allowing soft moonlight to filter through. When I look up, I can make out Kyven's entire face instead of just a vague shape like before.

"I'm going to set us down on that branch," he says, pointing to a large tree up ahead. "We should be safe to stay here for the night."

The rest of his warriors gather around, each of them taking a different spot on the same massive tree.

The branch is at least the width of three people. Even so, when my feet touch the bark, a flash of panic arcs through me, afraid I might slip and fall. I grip Kyven's arm, clinging to him as he guides me toward the trunk. "I suppose now is a good time to tell you that I've never been particularly fond of heights," I tease lightly, trying to mask my nerves. "It's actually one of my biggest fears."

His head snaps to mine. "Why did you not say anything? We could have taken a carriage, Grayce."

I shrug. "I've always considered myself to be a very practical person—the kind who prefers to face things head on. This is my new life, so I may as well start getting used to it now."

His brow furrows. "I do not want you to be uncomfortable, Grayce. I—"

"Is it safer up here?" I ask, cutting him off. "Or down on the ground?"

"Up here."

"Then, that decides it," I state firmly. "Safety is much more important than comfort. I will be fine."

"Forgive me, Grayce. I am a terrible mate to you. We've only just been wed, and this"—he gestures to the branch and the tree—"is where I've taken you."

I'm stunned by not only the sadness in his eyes but the true regret in his words. "You've kept your promise." I cup his cheek. "You protected me from danger. You still are. That means you are not as terrible a husband as you think, Kyven."

"Truly?"

"Truly." I grin.

A handsome smile curves his mouth. "I shall make all of this up to you on our *m'eala*. My vow."

"What is that?"

He frowns. "Do human bonded pairs not go away with each other after the ceremony for a few days?"

"I've heard that some do," I reply as my cheeks heat thinking of all the stories I've heard from the palace staff about such things. "But not all."

A flash of light catches my eye, and I turn to find a small

glowing, golden orb floating toward us. As I study it, I realize it's a tiny woman with golden skin and hair, and wings. "Is that a pixie?"

"Yes," Kyven replies in a low voice.

I've heard of them, but never seen one up close. She gives me a close-lipped smile and extends her small hand out to me, flying closer. "You're so beautiful," I murmur as I reach for her. "You—"

Lightning fast, Kyven grips my wrist, pulling it away from her.

"What are you—" I start, but my jaw goes slack as her lips curl back, revealing two rows of tiny razor-sharp fangs.

"She is a night pixie," he growls and waves his hand at her, shooing her away. "They have a nasty bite."

She snaps her dagger-like teeth as if to emphasize his point and I lean further into him. "Thank you," I reply a bit shaken, unable to tear my eyes away from her as she flies away. "I had no idea." I gulp. "Is there anything else I need to know?"

He opens his mouth to speak but another pixie approaches. This one with golden skin and silver streaked through her gilded hair. She bows low and holds out a tiny purse. He places his hand just below it, and she drops it into his palm. "Apology accepted," he says, a hard edge to his voice. "Alert us if anything approaches this tree and I will consider us even."

She dips her chin and then turns to fly away, joining at least twenty others in the distance.

I look down at the tiny pouch. "What is that?"

"Pixie dust." He places it in my palm. "It is yours. You never know when you might need a pinch."

"What does it do?"

"It is a surprise spell. A boon of sorts," he explains. "It

depends upon what type of magic the pixie used to make it. It can be anything from a teleportation spell to a cloak of invisibility, but you will not know until you use it."

Studying the pouch, I frown. "How would one know when to do that?"

"The magic will call to its owner when the time is right."

This sounds like a boon indeed. I hold it out to Kyven. "Are you sure you do not want to keep it?"

"I want you to have it, Grayce." He takes my hand gently between his, curling my fingers over the pouch in my palm. "Keep it with you at all times. Your safety is important to me."

His words warm my heart. Lost in his luminous gaze, I realize how easy it would be to fall completely if I'd let myself.

Aren flies up beside us. "The perimeter is secure. Cyral will be on watch until dawn."

Kyven nods, and Aren leaves.

I tuck the pouch into the pocket of my tunic. "Well, it is not calling to me now. So… perhaps that means we are safe for the moment." At least, I hope that's what it means as I wait for his reply.

"Indeed." He turns his gaze back to me. "You should rest, Grayce."

I know he's right, but after all the commotion this evening, I doubt I'll get much sleep. Especially up high in the trees like this. I glance over the side, peering into the darkness below, wondering just how far up we are right now. I'd been afraid of resting on the tarp, but now, with just a branch, I'm even more worried.

One claw tipped finger hooks under my chin, pulling my gaze away from the drop. His violet eyes stare deep into mine. "I will keep you safe, Grayce. My vow."

"What if we both fall asleep and... I tumble over the side before you wake?" I voice my concern aloud, wincing at how pitiful I sound. This is not who I am. I am the strong one in my family, not the one who needs protecting. Until now.

"Come." He pulls me into his hold. With his back braced against the tree trunk, he settles me between his thighs so that my back is to his front. He wraps his strong arms solidly around my waist and tugs me into his chest.

He shifts slightly and folds his wings around my form, cocooning me in his masculine scent and the warmth of his body. A slight vibration begins at my back, and I twist my head to glance over my shoulder. "What is that?" The low rumbling grows even louder, and I blink several times. "Are you... purring?"

"My kind do not purr." He lifts his chin. "We *tr'llyn.*"

It certainly sounds and feels like a purr, but much stronger.

"Does it bother you?" He tips his head to one side. "If it does, I can stop."

"No. If anything it feels... soothing," I answer honestly. "Do all Fae—" I start to say 'purr,' but instead use the term he provided, "tr'llyn?"

His vertically slit pupils widen. "Only Fae males do this. They tr'llyn for their mates to calm them."

"Why?"

"Our healers claim it is a primitive instinct passed down from our ancestors. It has a calming effect and is believed to encourage closeness and intimacy."

"Is it meant to hypnotize me?" I tease gently.

"No." A faint smile quirks his lips. "It cannot do that."

Despite my earlier fears, the tension begins to ease from my body as the vibrations from his tr'llyn move through me. I lean back against him. With my head resting on his collarbone and my face turned toward the crook of his neck, every breath fills my lungs with his intoxicatingly rich and masculine scent.

My eyes blink open and closed as I struggle to remain awake. "You're right about the calming effect," I murmur sleepily. "I can barely keep my eyes open."

He gently nuzzles my hair, and his breath is warm against my ear as he whispers. "Then, sleep. I will make sure you are safe, my beautiful mate."

Warmth floods my veins. As I drift between that place of sleep and wakefulness, my thoughts catch on the memory of my wedding ring and my vision. "I dreamed of you before we met."

He stills behind me.

"And I wanted to tell you, but I was waiting for my sign."

"What sign?"

"In my vision, you gave me a purple rose." I lift my hand, studying my purple moonstone wedding ring. "Just as Inara dreamed of Varys and the green ribbon he gave to her with his betrothal. I knew when I saw this that our paths were meant to align."

His arms and wings tighten around me and his tr'llyn grows stronger. "I believe you are right."

"How did you know?" I mumble.

"Know what?" he whispers.

"Purple is my favorite color and roses are my favorite flower."

His tr'llyn falters a moment before he answers. "It... felt right."

Something about his hesitation snags at my subconscious, but I'm too tired to pursue this line of thought as exhaustion begins to pull me under.

"You are mine to care for and protect, Grayce," he whispers into my hair. "And I vow to do so until I draw my last breath."

His soothing words and his tr'llyn dissolve the last of my tension, and I lose the battle to remain conscious and fall away into the beckoning void.

CHAPTER 17

KYVEN

The forest is alive with the various sounds of nocturnal creatures making their way back to their homes. A thin line of pink and orange spreads out across the horizon as the dawning sun begins to rise.

I glance down at Grayce, still asleep with my arms and wings folded around her. Sometime during the night, she repositioned herself, curling her legs up to her chest and twisting to the side so that she could snuggle against me, with her dainty hand resting against my chest, directly over my beating heart.

Aren flies over to us, alighting on the branch before me. He arches a brow as his gaze travels over Grayce, before he turns his attention to me. "One of our scouts reports another band of Orcs further north. There are more of them in these woods than we thought," he says grimly, making sure to keep his voice low. "I suggest we avoid that route and fly directly for Corduin instead."

"Corduin is less than a stone's throw away from the Great

Wall," I hiss. "You cannot truly be suggesting I take my new queen to such a dangerous place."

"It is *our* fortress. Full of *our* warriors," he points out. "She will be safe for one night."

I can hardly believe what Aren is suggesting. But I realize he is right. Flying to Corduin is the safer choice.

More importantly, I trust the warriors that guard the Wall. I served with them. They were like brothers to me. The Fortress of Corduin was my home for five years, training as a warrior and a healer. As a second born son, I would have lived out my life there if my brother had survived to become king.

"And if she sees what we do along the Great Wall, she can report it to her brother, King Edmynd," Aren says, pulling me back from my thoughts. "Maybe then he will agree to your proposal of expanding a joint presence there to increase our defenses."

I glance down at Grayce and clench my jaw. Aren is right. Grayce should see it. If for nothing else, then because she is now queen of Anlora, and should be apprised of everything that affects the safety of our kingdom.

"Fine," I agree. "Inform the rest of our warriors. We will stay at the Fortress of Corduin tonight, and then continue to Ryvenar."

He bows low and then flies away to relay my orders.

Sighing heavily, I glance down at my mate. Unable to stop myself, I press a tender kiss to the top of her head. "Grayce, you must wake up." She stirs gently and nestles into me further. "Grayce." I try again, and this time her eyelids flutter open.

"Where are—" She stills, her entire body going tense a moment before relaxing again as she lifts her gaze to me.

"It is morning. We must ready to leave. We will travel to

Corduin today. We'll spend the night in the fortress and then continue on to Ryvenar tomorrow."

"Corduin? Isn't that close to the Great Wall?"

"Yes." Guilt rushes through me. I am a terrible mate to my new bride. We have not even been married a handful of days and she has already been in danger several times. "I had not planned on going there, but our scouts have reported another band of Orcs nearby and this is the best route to avoid them."

When she opens her mouth, I think she means to protest. Instead, she says, "I've never been to the Great Wall."

"The fortress is heavily guarded. It has never been breached," I add. "If you are worried about your safety, I—"

"I'm not," she denies.

I'm stunned. "You're… not?"

"No." Her hazel eyes meet mine and a faint smile crests her lips. "I know you would never put me in danger, Kyven."

Trust. That is the look she is giving me right now and it is humbling beyond measure. I return her smile with one of my own. "You are right."

I stand and pull her up with me.

When she looks down, I detect the panicked beat of her heart as her fear scent perfumes the air. Grayce holds onto my forearm with a white knuckled grip, her face pale as she lifts her chin, trying to appear unafraid. "It's much higher than I thought." A nervous grin crests her lips. "I suppose it's fortunate I could not see how far up we were last night, or I'd probably have been unable to sleep at all. I probably would have kept you up talking all night."

"I would have liked that." The words escape unfiltered, and she frowns. So I move quickly to correct myself. "What I mean is that I enjoy talking to you."

"You do?"

"Very much so."

"Good." Pink blooms across her cheeks. "Because I'd like to practice speaking *Faerinesh* with you."

As I listen to her speak, pride fills me when she finishes the last half of her sentence in the common Fae tongue. I'm sure it will not be long until she has completely mastered our language. Her Florinesh accent is still audible, but not so much that it takes away from anything she says.

"Very well." I smile as I reply in kind and hoist her to my chest. "Let us practice then."

CHAPTER 18

GRAYCE

The sun is high in the sky when we stop to eat and rest. We sit on our tarp and I force my gaze to remain on Kyven instead of allowing myself to look down at the ground, far below. He hands me a platter with fruit, cheese, and bread. I eat enough to satisfy my growling stomach and then pass the plate back to him.

"Are you sure you do not want more?" he asks.

"I'm fine," I reassure him.

A cool breeze whips through the trees and I shiver slightly. He quickly removes his cloak and drapes it around my shoulders.

A smile crests my lips. He is so attentive and attuned to my needs. "Thank you."

He calls Aren over to sit with me while he goes to relieve himself.

Aren offers me a cup of tea. "It will help settle your stomach if you are nervous about the flight."

"Is it that obvious that I have a fear of heights?" I tease lightly before I take a small sip.

"Just a bit." He grins. "There is no shame in this, though. Every Fae has experienced this fear at some point in their lives."

"They have?"

"All of us go through it. Learning to fly can be a terrifying experience for any fledgling. I imagine it must be difficult since your kind do not have wings, but you seem to be handling the journey well."

Aren strikes me as a kind person and I know Kyven trusts him completely. If he did not, he would never have left me in his care. I decide to take a risk and voice my concerns aloud. "Is there anything I should know before we reach Corduin?"

"If you are concerned about the Wraiths, the fortress has never been breached," he reassures me. "And the King is well-liked and respected among the warriors at Corduin Fortress. They will feel honored that he has brought you to meet them."

"Even though I am human."

"Yes," he replies without hesitation. "It is the royal court at Ryvenar that may be a challenge, I believe. Many of the nobles hoped the King would choose from among them for a mate. Some will not be pleased that he has chosen a human as their queen."

I already suspected this, but I do not voice it aloud.

His blue eyes study mine with a piercing gaze. "If I may speak plainly."

"You may."

He leans in a bit. I notice he darts a glance in the direction of Lord Torien before he lowers his voice so as not to be overheard. "You are very direct in speaking your mind. You stood your ground on several points that Lord Torien tried to have removed from the treaty negotiations. I believe this will serve you well, and I have no doubt you will be able to navigate the royal court."

He's telling me not to show any weakness, and while I already knew this from having grown up in the royal court of Florin, I appreciate the warning.

* * *

As we make our way to Corduin, Kyven and I continue speaking in Faerinesh. The conversation is helpful to keep my mind occupied so I don't dwell on how high up we are.

"We are nearly to the border," Kyven says, gesturing up ahead. "You can see the *Veil* wall from here."

In the distance, the glowing, blue barrier of the Veil cuts through the trees. A magic wall that marks the official edge of the kingdom of Anlora.

I note a small section that does not glow as brightly as the rest. "Why does that look different?"

"This part of our border is difficult to maintain." He purses his lips. "The Wyldwood is full of many creatures that possess magic: Orcs, Unicorns, Harpies, Griffins, and such. They are constantly challenging the power of the Veil. Our patrols must replenish it regularly."

Worry ripples down my spine as I wonder what sort of magical creatures are trying to push through the Veil.

"You must hold my hand as we cross," Kyven says. He shifts his hold and slips his palm into mine, entwining our fingers.

"Will I always have to do this when we go through?"

He shakes his head. "Once we fully seal our bond, the magic of the Veil will recognize you as Fae. The same is true for other protective wards and spells. But until then, we must approach each barrier with caution. There are some that are so strong, it would not matter if we were touching when we approached them. They would not recognize you as Fae without my claiming mark."

My face heats at the mention of sealing our bond. I'm not quite sure I'm ready to fully consummate our marriage yet. And the thought of a claiming mark worries me. I've never liked pain and I wonder if it will hurt.

Shaking my head softly, I push these troubling thoughts away as we draw closer to the border.

A tingling sensation skitters across my skin as we pass through the Veil. It's not painful, but it is unpleasant, and I'm glad we are through it.

"We are almost to Corduin," Kyven says. "You can already see the Great Wall from here."

I peer into the distance and notice a glowing ribbon of blue light stretching as far as the eye can see to the east and the west. It reminds me of the Veil, but much larger. The magic of this wall is the only thing keeping these lands from being overrun by Wraith. I've never traveled to the Great Wall, but my brothers have.

Raiden is the one that father sent regularly to check on the Florinesh portion of the Wall. Bitterness fills me. As the second born son and also illegitimate child of his mistress, I remember one of father's advisors hinting that Raiden was expendable and that's why it made sense for him to represent our family at the dangerous outpost.

As we draw closer, the town of Corduin comes into view. I've heard of the wonders of Elvish and Fae architecture, but to see them in person is another thing entirely.

The entire town is a forest of trees, nearly as large as the ones in the Wyldwood, connected by beautifully designed wooden bridges and homes that seem to have been carved into the massive trunks of the trees and yet also somehow expanded out from them as well. As if the homes were an extension of the wooden base instead of something attached afterward.

"We use our magic to shape and mold the wood to create our homes, buildings, and bridges," Kyven answers my unspoken question.

A thin line of orange spreads across the sky as the sun begins to set in the distance. Soft golden light spills out from the windows, casting the entire city in an ethereal glow. And while it appears lovely, it also looks delicate and fragile in a way. An entire city built in the trees seems vulnerable to me. "What about fires?" I ask.

"We use our powers to solidify the wood, making it hard as stone and impervious to such things," Kyven explains. "And our magic feeds the trees, helping them remain strong."

On the opposite side of the town is a larger structure that connects several massive trees lined along the Great Wall. Their bridges and walls are almost completely solid, with only the barest hint of light spilling out through small, slit-like windows. That has to be the fortress that guards the city and the borders of Anlora from the Wraiths that roam on the other side of the Great Wall.

"We will be staying in the Fortress this night," he says, and a small frisson of fear ripples down my spine.

I'm terrified of the Wraiths, and I never thought I'd be this close to the Wall. But I also know that the Fae have powerful magic, and if anyone can counter the dark powers of the Wraiths, it is them. Without Kyven and his warriors, Florin would have surely fallen.

Several Fae fly back and forth throughout the city, while some of them walk along the intricate network of bridges made of branches and vines. As we approach, they watch silently, their gazes fixed intently upon their king and his strange human queen.

The guards bring their closed fists to their chest in salute while the rest of the people bow low in respect. My heart hammers under the weight of their stares. As if sensing my nerves, Kyven tightens his arms around me and leans close, whispering in my ear. "They are merely curious. It has been many years since our kingdom had a queen."

"I'm not a queen yet," I tell him. "We have not had our Fae ceremony."

"It matters not." His eyes meet mine. "We are bound according to the ways of your people. The Fae ceremony is merely a formality for the nobility and the court."

Although he has already addressed me as such, I had no idea the rest of his people already considered me their queen. I glance down at my borrowed outfit, wincing inwardly. Mother always ingrained in us the importance of our appearance. She would never have appeared before her people dressed like this. "Oh, Kyven," I murmur. "I should have changed before we arrived."

"Why?"

"I'm wearing your clothes. What will they think of me?"

"Because you are dressed in my clothing, you carry my scent. And scent-marking is very important between mates. This is more important than what you are wearing, because it means that you are mine." His violet eyes stare deep into my own, full of possession. "None will question that you are my mate and my queen."

Warmth pools deep within at his heated gaze, and I force myself to look away, lest my body betray my inner desire. Kyven is the most handsome man I've ever seen, and it would be so easy to lose my heart to him completely, if I would only allow myself.

I turn my gaze to the massive fortress that stands guard

along the wall. It is a daunting sight, with high, thick walls that stretch up toward the heavens. Several guards are perched atop the towers, ready to defend the kingdom from any threat.

Kyven lands just outside the massive doors. Carefully, he sets me down on my feet, keeping his hands on my waist until he is sure I am steady.

The doors are made of wood so dark it is almost black, and when I touch it, it is as cold as stone and just as hard.

Unlike the city before it, the fortress is neither beautiful nor inviting, but I suppose that is to be expected. This place is the first line of defense against the Wraith that live on the other side of the Great Wall. A sense of fear and dread moves through me, as I ponder the dangers that lurk just beyond the safety of the kingdom.

Looping my arm through Kyven's, I straighten my shoulders and lift my chin, hiding my fear behind an impassive mask. I want his warriors to see that I am brave, and proud to stand beside their king.

Two Fae guards open the doors, and Kyven leads me inside. Warriors are lined up on either side of us. They thump their closed fists to their chests and bow low as we enter. Their curious eyes track me as we pass, some with open fascination and others with looks that I cannot quite discern.

Our footsteps echo as we walk through the entryway and into a wide, cavernous space. A narrow set of stairs along the right wall leads up to another three levels consisting of surrounding balconies that look down upon the first floor.

Everyone here can fly, and I wonder why there are even any stairs at all, but when a Fae warrior approaches, dressed in full armor, and bows low, I notice the bandage on his left wing joint, where it attaches to his back.

His hair and wings are gold, and his eyes are gray, like

clouds gathering before a storm. Only the fine lines in the outer corners of his eyes betray that he is any older than my new husband. I wonder how old he is, since the Fae age much slower than humans.

"My king," he says. "It is good to have you among us again."

"It is good to see you as well, Commander Caldyr." Kyven gestures to me. "This is my mate. The Princess Grayce of Florin, now Queen of Anlora."

The commander's eyes widen a moment before he bows even lower. "It is an honor to meet you, my queen."

The soft fluttering of wings draws my attention, and I lift my gaze to find at least double the number of warriors now staring down at us from the upper balconies, all of their eyes on me with expressions ranging from awe and wonder to shocked disbelief.

"Tell me, Commander," Kyven says, and Caldyr's eyes snap to him. "Is there anything new to report? Your last message said that it had been rather quiet along the Wall."

"Word has reached us about feral Wraiths that have been found further south of here," he says. "But if there are any breaches along this section of the Wall, we've yet to find them."

Kyven darts a glance at me. "Now that we have a perma-nent alliance with Florin, I'd like you to send a messenger to their Outpost along the Wall to discuss the possibility of shared patrols."

"I'll send someone immediately." He dips his chin. "We have last meal already prepared in the main hall. And after dinner, we could give the queen a tour of the fortress. Unless you would prefer to eat in your rooms."

Kyven looks at me. "What would you like to do?"

I love that he asks me before giving an answer.

"Dinner in the main hall." I smile. "Then, a tour before we retire for the evening."

The commander's eyes light up, obviously pleased by my response, and a smile tugs at Kyven's lips as he offers me his arm again. "Shall we?"

I nod.

Commander Caldyr leads us up the stairs to the second level. As we walk through the quiet halls of the Fae fortress, our footsteps are silent on the polished wooden floors. The walls seem to breathe, their gentle whispers a testament to the living trees that form the very heart of this place. The air is heavy with the scent of ancient wood and earth, a testament to the magic that thrums through every fiber of the fortress.

The hallway is wide and long, stretching ahead of us. Each space is carved into the massive trees, masterfully created to blend seamlessly with the natural world. The walls of the corridor are adorned with only the most necessary embellishments: a few Fae lights, their flickering flames casting dancing shadows across the floor, and carefully made carvings that tell the stories of the Fae. The designs are both wild and graceful, a testament to the dichotomy of the Fae themselves.

Though sparse and utilitarian, the Fae fortress maintains an air of elegance that is difficult to define. The very essence of this place is woven with an otherworldly beauty. The quiet of the fortress is both soothing and unnerving, a reminder of the dangers that lie beyond the Great Wall.

We turn down a long hallway to the right until we reach a set of double doors. Caldyr pushes them open and inside is a large dining hall with long rows of dark wooden tables, each of them full of warriors already seated for the evening meal. There are four massive, decorative bowls in each corner of the room, stacked with *l'sair* crystals to give off light and heat.

Several orbs float overhead, their Fae light casting soft golden color throughout the space. I know this is a fortress, but it is as fine and elegant as any dining hall I've ever seen in any royal court.

All the warriors stand as soon as we enter and bow low as we take a seat at a table in the center of the room. This must be where the commander normally eats because it is the only empty table.

Large platters of meats, cheese, breads, and fruits, along with goblets of wine are placed before us in a veritable feast. I take a tentative sip of the wine and my cheeks immediately flush with heat. I set it down and ask for water, worried that if I drink anymore Fae wine Kyven may have to carry me to our rooms.

I've heard rumors of Fae and Elvish wines. I thought the Dark Elf wine at Inara's wedding was strong, but it was nothing compared to this.

The commander stands and offers a toast. "A warm welcome to our king and queen." He turns to Kyven and raises his glass. "Welcome back, our warrior brother on the Wall."

The warriors all stand and raise their glasses as they repeat. "To our warrior brother on the Wall."

The commander claps a familiar hand on Kyven's back, and the room erupts in cheers. A warrior with short black hair and amber eyes and wings walks over to us and grips Kyven's shoulders in greeting. "It is good to see you again."

Kyven grips his shoulders in return. "And you as well, Talyn." Kyven turns to me. "Talyn and I trained together when we were first stationed here five years ago. He is an excellent warrior and a skilled healer."

"It is wonderful to meet you," I reply, doing my best to

hide my surprise. I knew he had been here before, but I had no idea Kyven was assigned to the Wall.

More of the warriors come forth, welcoming him as they would a brother, and I watch as he greets them warmly in return. It seems there is much I do not know of my new husband, but I find that I am eager to know more.

CHAPTER 19

KYVEN

I t is good to be back here. I have missed my fellow
warriors. And while I am glad to introduce them to my
A'lyra, I wish it had been done after our bond was
already sealed. Having Grayce here, surrounded by so many
unmated males is difficult.

My people are extremely possessive of our mates. Especially in the early days of a newly formed bond. And until it
is sealed with the first mating and the claiming mark, it can
be difficult to control our aggression toward others.

Fortunately, Grayce is wearing my clothes and covered in
my scent, appeasing the primal part of me that claws just
beneath the surface, desperate to fully claim her and give her
my mark so that every male will know she is my mate, and I
am hers.

Commander Caldyr leads us on a tour of the fortress. We
climb up to one of the watchtowers and Grayce stares in
silent contemplation at the land beyond the Great Wall.

I remember the first time I saw this cursed landscape. I'd been stunned into silence as well.

Much of the terrain is a barren wasteland of ice and snow. A handful of rather pitiful trees are visible, along with a few scraggly bushes. It is so different from the lush green lands on this side of the Wall that are only covered by a light dusting of powdery snow.

The last light of day casts lines of orange and pink across the land as I lead Grayce to the royal chambers. It is the second time I will have used them. The first was when my father brought me to the wall when I was barely thirteen. I realize now that he was preparing me for my future. The one he thought I would have, at least.

When I returned again, years later, it was with the understanding that although I was a prince of Anlora, I was a second son. My life would be that of any other warrior, with the choice to live as I pleased. And it pleased me to live simply. But that life is no more.

When we reach the fortress library, Grayce is immediately drawn to the clear display case in the center of the room. She gazes at the necklace that belonged to my great ancestor—Queen Ilyra.

"What is this?" she asks.

"It is the necklace of Queen Ilyra," Caldyr says proudly. "She died defending the Wall from the Wraiths."

I study the teardrop-shaped crystal pendant on the silver chain. It appears much like any other gemstone, but the magic that radiates from it speaks to its power.

"It's beautiful," Grayce remarks.

She is right. It is lovely, but it is also dangerous. That is why it remains here, under heavy guard at the fortress.

"It is one of the most sacred objects of our people," Caldyr adds. "A reminder of the sacrifice of a Queen for her kingdom."

When we are finished with the tour, Caldyr directs us to our chambers.

Grayce's gaze travels over her rooms as we enter, her expression unreadable. The double bed along the far wall is covered with thick blankets and furs to ward against the chill. A large bowl of l'sair crystals sits in the corner of the room, providing light and heat to the space.

A plain white sofa and chair are positioned next to it, and across the way is a door that leads into the cleansing room. There is no bath here, however. It has only a shower, a sink, and toilet in a smaller room attached.

Grayce remains silent as I show her where everything is, and I worry that she is disappointed, so I move to reassure her that this is not the level of comfort she should expect in Anlora. "These lodgings are sparse compared to those at the castle."

"Sparse?" Her brows lift. "It is beautiful here. I'd not expected this level of luxury in a fortress." My mouth drifts open as she continues. "Not that I've been to many, but... the ones I have were rather bare. Besides, this is by far more preferable than sleeping on a tarp exposed to the elements."

I open my mouth to apologize but laugh instead when I notice the teasing smile that plays on her lips.

"I was simply trying to manage expectations early," I joke in response. "This way, when we reach the castle, you'll be so thoroughly impressed by its opulence, you will wonder why you did not think to wed me sooner."

She laughs, and it is a lovely sound of pure delight. I had not thought it possible to be any more in love with her, but my feelings are growing even stronger the more time we spend together.

"Why ever did I not think of such a thing before now, I wonder?" She flashes a teasing grin and then we're both laughing together.

When I bid her goodnight and turn toward the door, her voice stops me abruptly. "Where are you going?"

I spin back to her. "To my rooms. They are next to yours."

"Oh." Something akin to disappointment flashes across her face, but it's gone too quickly for me to be sure. "I thought—" She gives me a faint smile, but it does not reach her eyes. "Never mind. Goodnight, Kyven."

Indecision roots me in place. It is Fae tradition for a bonded pair to sleep apart, but I know she said humans do not. She has also indicated that she is not ready to fully seal our bond, and I do not want her to feel pressured to do anything she does not want, including sharing a bed.

There was no choice in the forest, but here... I want her to feel secure in the knowledge that *she* will be the one to decide how and when our relationship progresses.

Indecision wars within me. I want to stay with her, but I also want her to know that I respect her, and I will wait to share her bed until she indicates otherwise. After a moment, I bid her goodnight and leave the room.

When I enter my own, I want more than anything to return to hers, but I force myself to remain in place. This room is a mirror image of hers. Memories flood my mind as my gaze travels over the space. I remember sitting on the sofa with my brother, playing cards while my father paced back and forth as he listened to the commander's report.

Caldyr grew up with my father. They were as close as brothers. Perhaps that is why I feel so close to him. He is a reminder of what I once had.

A subtle knock at the door is Aren. "I came to see if you needed anything. I already checked on the queen."

I'm glad he thought to check in on her first. It tells me he understands how important she is to me. "Thank you, but I am fine. I would, however, like for you to send someone to purchase clothing from the town for her."

"Already done." He grins, obviously pleased with himself. "She has been given a sleeping gown and a fresh set of clothes for travel tomorrow: a tunic dress, pants, and travel boots in a size more… suited for her."

And this is one of the reasons I value his presence. He is always thinking ahead. "Thank you."

"There is another item we should discuss."

"What is it?"

"Talyn," he says. "We spoke about forming a Queen's guard, and I believe he would be a good fit."

"Do you think he would wish for this post?" Talyn is one of our fiercest warriors, and most capable healers. He takes great pride in guarding the Wall. He descends from a long line of warriors that have devoted their life to defending the kingdom from Wraiths.

"I do." He gestures to the door. "He is outside. I took the liberty of telling him you wish to see him."

I purse my lips. "What if I had said no?"

"Then, it would have been just for a friendly visit." Aren arches a teasing brow. "You would have wished to speak with him anyway, would you not?"

He knows me too well. "Yes."

Aren opens the door, and Talyn walks in, his amber eyes crinkled as a smile lights his face. He looks between me and Aren. "I am glad to see you both well. It has been too long."

"It has," I agree. I motion for him to take a seat on the sofa while I sit in the chair across the way. "I have an offer for you."

He tips his head forward in attention. "What is it?"

"You are a good male, and I trust you with my life." I meet his gaze evenly. "I'd like to assign you as personal guard to my queen."

He blinks at me in astonishment. "I—of course." He stands and thumps his fist to his chest. "I would be honored."

"Good." I clap my hand on his shoulder. "It is settled then. You will come with us to Ryvenar."

"There is something you should know, in regards to the safety of you and the queen," he offers. "We have just received word that two of our scouts have located an Orc encampment not far from here, just on the opposite side of our border."

Aren looks at me. "It could be the same group that our warriors discovered last night, in the Wyldwood."

"If so, it would seem as though they are tracking us. But why?" I clench my jaw. "And why would they make camp so close to Corduin and the Wall?"

"I do not know," Aren replies. "But I suggest we send a dozen of our best warriors to confront them, and—"

"Start a war?" I ask. "No." I shake my head. "They are not inside Anlora's borders, and we have no idea of their numbers. Send two of our best warriors to track them discreetly. Let us find out why they are so close, and how many of them there are."

He dips his chin, and then he and Talyn leave to investigate.

Sighing heavily, I make my way to the cleansing room and shower before changing into my soft knit pants for sleep. If not for those bloody Orcs we'd already be in Ryvenar. Grayce would be secure in the castle and in my quarters.

I lie back on the bed, already missing the feel of her in my arms. I wonder if she feels the same or if she is glad to have her own space.

It matters not. I will do whatever it takes to win her heart. I won it before, and I will win it again. And once I do, I will claim her and seal her to me.

CHAPTER 20

GRAYCE

The warm water of the shower is soothing, but my entire body is still tense. I know the Fortress is well-protected, but I'm on edge knowing how close we are to the Wastelands and to the Wraith. The Great Wall is heavily fortified, but it is not perfect. If it were, no one would have to guard it.

When Florin was attacked by Kolstrad's army, the Order of Mages fought for their side. They controlled the Wraiths with their powers, using them in the battle against our people and the Dark Elves.

If Kyven and his warriors had not arrived when they did, and helped us, I fear we would have lost. Having seen up close the devastating magic of the Wraiths, I cannot silence the worry in my heart at the knowledge that there are who knows how many of them just on the other side of the Great Wall.

It is a good sign, I believe, that Kyven does not seem worried about an attack. He was stationed here, and he knows these warriors and what they are capable of. That he has such faith in them to guard his kingdom gives me a measure of peace.

In the dining hall earlier, it was nice to see the way he interacted with the warriors—his brothers on the Wall. It was as if seeing a glimpse of who he was before he had to take up the mantle of rule.

Like Edmynd, Kyven is a young king. Unlike my brother, however, he was a second son. He was not raised with the expectations of inheriting the crown. I wonder if he misses the life he would have had if his older brother had lived.

Finished with my shower, I wrap a towel around my body and grab another to dry my hair as I walk back into the bedroom. The wind howls outside the fortress and as I gaze out the small window of my room. I'm not surprised to see snow falling on the city, blanketing it in white.

It's chilly in here, so I move closer to the large bowl with the l'sair crystals, trying to stay warm while I rub the towel over my hair to dry it. As I lean to one side, wringing my hair with the towel, movement catches the corner of my eye.

Paralyzing fear snakes down my spine as I squint into the darkness, searching the shadows for any sign that something is there.

After what feels like an eternity, I detect no movement. Blowing out a frustrated breath, I inwardly chastise myself. I'm nervous. That's all. Being so close to the Great Wall is putting me on edge. I need to—

Something scrapes across the stone floor, and my veins fill with ice as a shadow moves in the dark corner. Indecision locks me in place. If I cry out, I risk being attacked before anyone can reach me. And if I try to run, I may not be fast enough, and—

Glowing red eyes blink at me from the darkness and a terrified scream rips from my throat. "Kyven!"

CHAPTER 21

KYVEN

A scream pierces the darkness, and I jerk up in bed, instantly alert. "Kyven!"

Raw panic claws at my throat as I race to Grayce's room. Half running, half flying, I cannot reach her fast enough.

The sound of something crashing to the floor is quickly followed by another panicked cry.

I throw open her door and find the large I'sair bowl knocked over, crystals spread across the floor like broken glass. Wearing only a towel Grayce stands before it, her feet spread in a defensive stance and dagger firmly in hand.

"Grayce!" I rush to her side. "What happened?"

"There's something in here." She breathes shakily, gesturing to the dark corner. "I saw red eyes."

I scan the darkness and relief fills me when I see a mountain squirrel hiding behind the chair, its tail flicking back and forth in agitation. They are four times the size of a regular squirrel, and far more destructive. They always seem to find their way into the fortress despite our best efforts to keep them out.

"It's all right," I reassure her. "It's only a—"

The squirrel darts out from its hiding place, and rushes toward us. Grayce throws the knife, barely missing him before she scrambles up my body, clinging to me in terror.

"It's all right." I curl my arms solidly around her. "It is a mountain squirrel. They are harmless. Well… unless they get into the food stores, that is," I amend.

"A mountain squirrel?" She pulls back just enough to look down at it, cowering by the sofa, probably as terrified of her as she is of it.

The squirrel rushes toward the window, climbs up the wall, and scurries back outside.

The door crashes open behind me as Aren and two other guards rush in. Grayce ducks her head under my chin as if trying to shield herself, and it takes me a moment to realize it is because she is not fully dressed.

"My king," Aren's voice calls out behind me. "We heard—"

"It is fine," I tell him, trying but failing to suppress a low growl as fierce possessiveness floods my veins. "A mountain squirrel startled the queen. It just went out the window."

"Do you want us to check for others?" Aren's booted steps start toward me, but my fangs lengthen, and I glance over my shoulder.

"No. Leave us."

Aren halts abruptly. "Yes, my king." He motions for the other two guards to leave the room before his gaze finds mine again and he dips his chin. "I understand."

Clenching my jaw, I force myself to remain still as they leave the room, willing myself to calm. Aren knows what this is, and so do the others. It is a dark and primal instinct that affects every Fae male when he first takes a mate.

Intense possessiveness flares deep within, triggering by

the primitive instinct to protect my mate. I know that none of my warriors would ever try to take her from me, but until Grayce and I have fully sealed our bond with our first mating, it will be challenging to suppress my aggression toward other unbonded males.

Now that they have gone, I am acutely aware of how close we are. With her legs wrapped around my waist and her arms around my neck, her entire body is molded to mine, just as it was when we flew last night. At that time, I was distracted, searching for any sign of danger. Now... I can think of nothing but her as I support her backside with one hand while my other arm is looped around her waist, holding her firmly against me.

Carefully, I lower her feet to the ground, but keep my hands on her waist, unable to force myself to step back. The desire to seal her to me and mark her as mine is a fire in my veins.

She lifts her eyes to me, pausing briefly on my bare chest and torso. Her cheeks are redder than I've ever seen them. Nervously, she tucks her hair behind her curved ears. "Thank you. I'm sorry to have... awakened you for something so ridiculous."

"It was *not* ridiculous," I reassure her. "You are my mate. I will always come for you when you call."

"But I've made a fool of myself in front of your warriors."

"They are your warriors too," I point out. "They would not dare disparage their queen. They are honored to protect you, and I have found you a personal guard from among their ranks."

"Who?" she asks.

"Talyn. You met him earlier, in the dining hall. He is one of our best warriors, and I trust him. But it is ultimately your decision, and if you would rather choose someone else—"

"No. Talyn will be fine." Her hazel eyes search mine. "You trust him. That is enough for me."

Pride swells my chest. "Aren will make sure he is acclimated to the capital when we arrive."

"Thank you."

The breath puffs from her lips in the chilled air, and I rip one of the furs off the bed and drape it around her. "Here." I instruct her to sit on the sofa while I right the l'sair bowl and stack the crystals back inside it, adding a few extra for more light and warmth.

"I'll be right back," she says, disappearing into the cleansing room. When she returns, she is dressed in her sleeping gown and robe.

She looks up at me. "I suppose you probably wish to return to your bed."

"Actually, I'd prefer to spend more time with you, if you are not tired."

A smile crests her lips, and she motions for me to sit on the sofa. She takes a seat beside me, curling her leg beneath her as she turns her body to face mine. "You did not tell me you lived here before," she says, a questioning look in her eyes.

"I was a second son," I explain. "And, unlike my older brother, I disliked life at the royal court, so... when my father decided to send me here, I did not complain."

"Did you like it here?"

"I loved it," I answer honestly. "Aside from the constant threat of the Wraiths, it was very"—I stop short, searching for the right word before finally deciding upon—"freeing."

She rests her hand on mine. "You must miss it then."

Sighing heavily, I glance out the window. "Here, I was not the son of the king, I was just... Kyven. Another warrior, like everyone else, and they are like family to me. Commander

Caldyr was my mentor. He taught me how to be a warrior. I had also recently started studying to become a healer."

"I used to dream of becoming a warrior." A timid smile curls her mouth. "My grandmother was a shield-maiden of Ruhaen, and I always wanted to be like her. Fierce and brave."

"But Ruhaen is a human kingdom." I frown. "I've always heard that your people do not train your females to fight or wield weapons."

"I notice there are not many females here among your warriors either," she points out.

"That is because our males outnumber our females by at least three-to-one."

"I did not know this," she replies. "From what I have seen, the human kingdoms seem to have an even number of both men and women, but Ruhaen is a bit more forward thinking compared to most of the others." She pauses. "In Florin, it was considered improper for Inara or me to train." She lowers her gaze. "But that does not mean that we actually listened. Not that it did me any good, when we were attacked…" Her voice trails off.

"When?" I ask, concerned. "Are you referring to the battle with Kolstrad and the Mages? I thought the castle had remained untouched."

"Not then." Her gaze drifts to the opposite wall with a faraway look. "I meant when my mother was attacked."

"You were there?"

My heart clenches as she nods. I can only imagine how terrible that was to have seen her mother killed by an assassin.

"It all happened so fast," she murmurs. "There were three of them. One of them stabbed my mother, and he came next for me." She tugs at the collar of her sleep gown, revealing a scar below her left collarbone, dangerously close to her heart, and I inhale sharply. "I nearly died that day."

It is hard to look at her injury, knowing that this wound could have easily been fatal. She could have been taken from this world before I ever met her. The thought is nearly unbearable.

She continues. "I pulled the knife from my chest and turned it on him." Tears brighten her eyes. "But he was so quick, I only managed to slice a line from his left brow, down to his cheek before he escaped."

From what I know, they never caught the men who attacked and killed her mother. "Do you remember what he looked like?"

"No. But I would know the mark I gave him if I saw it. The blade was made of iron, so his scars would remain, just like mine have." She swallows hard. "Whoever he was, he was not human."

"How do you know?"

"His blood was black instead of red."

"That's why your father thought they were Fae," I murmur more to myself than to her.

"Yes." Her eyes search mine. "Edmynd said you swore that you know nothing of any Fae involvement in our mother's death."

"I do not," I repeat solemnly. "My vow."

"My father was not exactly a peaceful ruler. He had many enemies, so I suppose it could have been anyone." She draws in a deep breath. "But my brother is not like him. Edmynd is a better king, I believe."

"I agree. And it is easy to see that he cares greatly for his family."

"If you only knew how many times he asked me if I was sure about marrying you." She laughs softly. "He nearly went mad with worry after Inara married Varys as well. So, we must be sure to send him a raven straight away when we reach Ryvenar, and let him know it's going well."

"Is it?" I arch a teasing brow. "I mean… we've only been wed a few days and you've been forced to sleep sitting up in a tree, and now I've brought you to the Great Wall, which many could argue is the most dangerous place to take one's new bride and—"

She bursts out laughing, and it is such a lovely sound, I want only to hear more of it.

I continue. "Once they hear of all this, I wager it will be less than a fortnight before your brothers and Lukas show up at the castle, ready to make good on the threats they made to kill me if I did not take care of you."

She covers her face with her hands. "Oh, Kyven, I'm so sorry," she says, practically wheezing with laughter. "Truly, I was so embarrassed when I saw them corner you. Freyja said that Aurdyn threatened to roast you as well."

Crossing my arms over my chest, I narrow my eyes in mock irritation. "Your laughter suggests you were more amused than embarrassed." A smile tugs at my mouth. "It is rather troubling to know that my mate finds threats of violence against her new husband so hilarious."

Her bright laughter rings throughout the room. "Do not be so put out. They did the same thing to Varys when he married Inara, and now they practically adore him."

"Truly?" I am shocked to hear this. I thought her brothers, especially Raiden, were still a bit upset that Inara had married the Dark Elf King.

She nods.

"And… do you think they might come to regard me the same?" I ask hopefully.

She eyes me with a playful smile. "I suppose it depends upon the message I send with the raven."

"Then perhaps we will have to embellish a few details of

our journey thus far." I grin. "You can say I took you on a tour of a majestic forest, followed by a relaxing stay in a lovely and quaint town along the border of the kingdom."

Both of us dissolve into laughter, and my heart has never been so full. I thought I was in love with Grayce before, but now that I am getting to know her better, I realize that what I had felt was only the beginning of something so much deeper.

But the more of herself that she allows me to see, the more my guilt eats away at my soul. I hate having to keep such a huge lie from her, but I cannot risk her finding out the truth. And my heart aches when I think of how much she already trusts me.

I am so undeserving of her trust that it nearly breaks me every time I think about it for too long. She leans closer to me on the sofa, telling me stories of her childhood. She is everything to me, and I am so afraid to lose her.

When we reach Ryvenar, I will go back to the heart tree and ask the spirit for guidance. I have never questioned her before, but I will now. I must know why it is so important to keep this truth from Grayce. Because with each hour that passes, it weighs heavy on my soul, and I fear that I will be unable to keep this secret for much longer.

CHAPTER 22

GRAYCE

As the night wears on, Kyven and I trade stories of our childhood. And every time he flashes one of his devastatingly handsome smiles, my heart melts even more. Despite trying to be cautious and take things slow, I am already losing my heart my new husband.

A deep ache settles in my chest as I regard him. Deep down, I do not feel like Kyven would ever betray me, but my experience with Joren has made me so afraid of being hurt again.

It is late and my eyes blink open and closed as I struggle to stay awake. I enjoy Kyven's company, and he makes me feel so safe. And while I am not ready to consummate our vows, I *am* ready to embrace the intimacy that has already developed between us.

I know we only spent one two nights together before now, but I cannot deny that I was looking forward to this one, remembering how wonderful it felt to be folded in his arms and wings.

"Do you want me to leave so you may rest?" he whispers, and I realize that my eyes have closed.

"No. Stay with me," I murmur, halfway between sleep and wakefulness. I lean into him, my head resting on his shoulder. He curls his arm and wing around me, tugging me close as he settles onto his back on the sofa, gently pulling me so that we're both lying down.

His heart beats a steady rhythm against my palm, strong and reassuring. Wisps of memory float to the surface of my mind and my thoughts escape unfiltered. "Please, be careful with my heart," I murmur against his chest.

He stills a moment, and then presses a tender kiss to the top of my head and whispers, "Always," as I fall away into the void.

* * *

I'M STANDING before the Great Wall. A great crack rends the air, and I snap my head up as stone and mortar crumble to dust, the wall collapsing before my eyes.

Mages and Wraith rush toward the opening. They clash with the Fae warriors of Corduin, leaving a trail of broken bodies in their wake, staining the snow black with their blood.

A dark twisted form looms over me and bony fingers with black claws curl around my throat. Glowing, blood-red eyes burn with rage in a skeletal face as the Wraith snarls, revealing two rows of dagger-sharp fangs. "We are legion," he growls. "We are the darkness, and nothing can stop us."

MY EYES SNAP open as I wake with a start.

"Grayce?" Kyven's voice cut through the fog of my nightmare. "It's all right." He pulls me to his chest, and I unashamedly curl into him, instinctively seeking comfort.

"You are safe." He smooths a hand down my back. "I am here."

My heart hammer as I draw in a shaking breath.

"You were dreaming," he murmurs.

I wish he was right. "It was not a dream," I murmur, "It was a vision, Kyven."

He stills. "What did you see?"

I love that he does not question how I know; he simply trusts that what I say is the truth. "The Wraiths… somehow they tore down the Great Wall." Fear tightens my chest as the terrible image replays in my mind. "There were bodies… so many dead left in their wake."

Closing my eyes briefly, I draw in a deep and steadying breath. "I hate the nighttime," I admit. "I am always worried of what I will dream. I seldom ever get a vision of something good. It is usually something terrifying. That's why I have so much trouble sleeping."

"Is that why you walk through the gardens so often?"

I nod.

"My grandmother had the same ability that I do. She was able to link with the minds of others through touch," he explains. "Whenever me or my siblings had nightmares, she would often use it to help us sleep."

"How?"

"May I show you?" he asks, holding his hand out to me.

If he had asked me this when we first met, the answer would have been no. Even though we haven't known each other long, I trust him. Completely.

I slip my palm into his, and he entwines our fingers. The featherlight touch of his skin against my own pulses with a light tingling energy that seeps into my very soul. Closing my eyes, my head falls against his shoulder as warmth suffuses my entire body, as if wrapped up in layers of soothing comfort.

I open my eyes, and I'm standing in a garden. I tip up my chin, reveling in the warmth of the sun upon my face as my gaze travels over the beautiful landscape before me. Flowers grow in wild clusters, their colors blending together in rich hues of red, blue, and orange.

Streams weave among them, their crystal-clear waters cascading over small waterfalls. They follow along winding pathways, lined with trees with beautiful heart-shaped purple leaves. The ground is covered with green moss with tiny white flowers interspersed throughout.

Kyven stands beside me and takes my hand in his. "Is this a dream?"

"It is a recollection," he whispers, and I observe in wonder as day turns into night and the garden lights up with vibrant, glowing colors.

In awe of the rich and vivid detail, I turn to him as understanding dawns. "You are sharing your memory with me."

He nods. "I thought it might help soothe your fears."

The image changes and we're in the palace gardens of Florin. My mind drifts to our conversation the night before our ceremony, and then to the memory of our wedding night. Heat pools low in my belly.

Tentatively, I reach up and trace my fingers across his full, perfect lips that part slightly beneath my touch.

He studies me with a half-lidded gaze. "I wanted to kiss you from the first moment I saw you," he whispers. "I had never seen anyone more beautiful."

Warmth fills my heart.

"Close your eyes," he murmurs.

"Why?" I whisper, a smile tugging at my lips.

"Because it is already morning, my beautiful mate."

When I open them again, we are back in my room at Corduin Fortress. A light thrumming vibrates in his chest. It is Kyven's tr'llyn. I lift my head, and he gives me a sleepy smile. "Good morning."

"Good morning."

As my mind fully awakens, I realize that we are completely entwined with each other. My head is on his bicep. His left arm and wing are curled tightly around me. My hand is on his chest, with his free one resting atop it.

My heart pounds as I realize that my leg is draped over his hip, and his length is a hard bar against my inner thigh. My gaze drops to his mouth, and I bite my lower lip, remembering the taste of his kiss.

He cups my face, and his eyes search mine, tracing the pad of his thumb lightly across my cheek, leaving a trail of fire in its wake. Slowly, he leans in. His lips brush against mine in a featherlight touch, before he pulls back just enough to study me, gauging my reaction.

I reach out and trail my fingers lightly across his cheek, studying him in return. He is so handsome it almost hurts to look at him. "May I kiss you again," he whispers.

"Yes," I breathe out the word and then his lips are on mine, soft and tender.

A small sigh escapes me as his tongue begins to stroke gently against my own.

I grip his shoulder, urging him onto his side, and he groans into my mouth as our bodies align. His hard length presses insistently against my entrance, through our clothing, and desire coils tight in my core.

He dips his hand beneath the hem of my sleep gown. Anticipation races through my veins as he skims his fingers along my outer thigh before splaying his hand across the small of my back. Kyven rolls his hips against mine, and I moan into his mouth as delicious friction builds between us.

His sharp claws dig lightly into my already sensitive flesh as he grips my thigh and pulls me closer. And my heart stutters, not from fear, but from need so intense it is a maelstrom within me.

A soft knock at the door startles us both and we pull apart, each of us breathless and panting.

Kyven sits up and gently tucks the fur blanket around me before he stands from the couch, and then moves to the door.

I'm glad when he only opens it enough to see who it is, instead of inviting them inside.

"My king." I recognize Aren's voice. "Two of our warriors captured an Orc. He was found near the Wall."

"How did he manage to get so close undetected?"

"He was using a shade stone," Aren replies.

I sit up, drawing the blanket around my shoulders. "What is that?"

Aren looks around Kyven to me. "A stone with a glamour enchantment that can alter one's appearance. He used it to disguise himself as one of our people."

I had no idea such a thing even existed.

"What was he doing there?"

"We do not know," Aren says. "He is refusing to answer any questions."

"Bring him to the great hall," Kyven growls. "He *will* answer to me."

CHAPTER 23

KYVEN

Closing the door, I turn back to Grayce. Her hair is disheveled, and her cheeks are flushed a lovely pink hue. She stretches her lithe form, and the fur blanket bunches around her waist. She is still in her thin, night shift, and my fingers ache with want to touch her again. She is the most beautiful female I have ever seen, and I hate that we were interrupted, but it cannot be helped.

I must deal with this Orc. It is concerning that he was so close to the wall, and I wonder where the rest of his Clan are. Orcs rarely travel alone.

"I will deal with this and return to you as soon as possible, Grayce."

"I'm going with you." She stands from the sofa and starts for the cleansing room. "It will only take me a moment to ready myself, and then—"

"No," I state firmly, stopping her in her tracks. "I do not want you anywhere near the Orc. They are dangerous."

"I accompanied Edmynd when he worked out a treaty

with one of their Clans. I am well aware of the danger as well as what to expect when negotiating with them."

"We will not be negotiating anything. I will be interrogating him and—"

"I think that is a mistake."

"Why?" My head jerks back. "He is an Orc."

"Not all Orcs are bad," she says. "Once we find out which Clan he is from, we can—"

"*We* will not do anything." I meet her gaze evenly. "*You* will remain here, where it is safe."

"No, I will not." She clenches her jaw. "I am your queen. You promised to treat me as your equal. And as such, I will come with you to speak with this Orc."

Indignation burns in her eyes. I have made a grave error. She is angry with me. She doesn't understand. I do not do this because I think she's inferior. I'm asking her to stay here because I want her safe.

I cross the room in three steps and take both her hands in mine. "You *are* my equal, Grayce. The only reason I want you to remain here is because I cannot bear the thought of you in danger. Orcs are volatile and aggressive. I do not want you anywhere near him."

"This is a fortress full of warriors. All of them sworn to protect us," she points out. "If I am not safe here, I am not safe anywhere." She lifts her chin. "I have dealt with Orcs before. I sat in on the negotiations with Edmynd." My eyes widen as she continues. "I have studied their culture. I can be of help, Kyven."

She is determined and will not be dissuaded.

"Fine. But please, remain by my side at all times." I grab the dagger her dagger from the table. "Keep this on you." I place it in her hand. "And do not hesitate to use it if things go wrong."

She nods, but I note the slight tremor of her hand as she

takes the blade from me. "I'll be ready shortly," she says, walking toward the cleansing room.

I glance down at my sleep pants. "I must get dressed as well. I will meet you back here and then we will leave together."

When I walk back to my room, Aren is already there waiting for me. "Double the guards accompanying us to the Great Hall," I command. "And make sure the Orc is bound securely before he is brought before us."

"Us?" Aren frowns.

"The queen wishes to be present during the interrogation."

"You would bring her before an Orc?" His brows shoot up to his forehead. "They are dangerous. I—I do not think it wise to bring the queen before such a creature."

"She insists upon coming." I clench my jaw. "I do not like it either, but I cannot deny her the right to be there."

His gaze holds mine a moment, disbelief written across his features, before he finally dips his chin. "I will alert the guards."

After he leaves, I dress and then return to Grayce's room. She is dressed like one of my people. Wearing a green tunic dress and pants, along with a set of leather boots. Her silken hair is unbound and hangs down her back and shoulders in long chocolate waves.

It does something strange to me to see her dressed in the garb of my people. The rich fabric is a perfect complement to her lovely hazel eyes. Pride swells my chest. She truly looks like a queen of the Fae.

I offer her my arm, taking note that her dagger is tucked in her belt and within easy reach. She loops her arms through mine and we make our way to the Great Hall.

When we enter, there are at least two dozen warriors already waiting. Several of them gape at me as if I've lost my mind, bringing her here. And perhaps I have. Maybe I should have insisted she stay back in her room, where it is safe, but another part of me knows that if I had, she probably would not have forgiven me. Especially when I vowed to her that she would be my equal in all ways.

Guilt fills me. I have kept the secret of who I am from her —an unforgivable lie of omission. The least I can do is keep the promises I made when I asked her to marry me.

The lit torches along the wall cast dancing shadows across the floor. The Great Hall is normally reserved for meetings with the commander, but it has been repurposed as a throne room today. Grayce and I each take a seat in the heavy wooden chairs on the raised dais, at the far end, while we wait for the guards to bring in the Orc.

The doors open and everyone falls silent as the Orc walks in surrounded by four of my guards. He is bound in heavy chains that scrape along the floor with each step. Despite them, he holds his head tall and proud as he stalks toward us, glowering at each of my warriors as he passes.

A leather loincloth hangs around his waist, leaving his upper half bare. A beaded necklace hangs around his neck. At least a dozen scars mar the green skin of his heavily muscled form. Two leather bands etched with scrolling patterns circle his massive, tattooed biceps.

His chest heaves with each breath, his dark claws extended as if ready to fight his captors. A snarl curls his mouth, accentuating his sharp tusks jutting up from his bottom lip as he levels a dark glare at me.

His people are formidable warriors, and although he is bound, everything inside me wants to demand that Grayce leave. That she return to our rooms, far away from this great hulking savage.

He stops in front of our thrones, and his brow furrows deeply as his gaze darts to Grayce and then back to me.

"My warriors said you were found wandering near the Great Wall," I tell him. "Why were you there?"

His brown eyes are locked on mine as he clenches his jaw, refusing to speak.

Grayce leans forward in her chair. "From the markings on your arms, you are from Clan Arzul, is that correct?" she asks in the Orcish tongue.

His head snaps to hers as does mine and the rest of my warriors.

"I am," he says, his voice deep and low.

"I am Queen Grayce of Anlora, and Princess of Florin. This is my mate, King Kyven." She gestures to me, and his scowl deepens.

The Orc studies her with a piercing gaze but says nothing.

She stands from her chair, and as she starts to step off the dais, I shoot up from my seat. "Grayce!"

She stops abruptly, and Talyn and Aren rush forward, placing themselves directly between her and the Orc, preventing her from stepping off the platform.

Grayce looks at the Orc. "Give me your word, as a warrior, that you will not harm us if we release you." She continues to speak in his language.

"My word?" Shock flickers briefly over his features, and his nostrils flare. "I can scent your fear, and yet... you would take my word?"

"My brother, King Edmynd, negotiated a treaty with your brother Clan—Ulvad, to keep the peace between us, granting your two Clans the use of the forest along our border. I know that you are an honorable people. Now, give us your word, and we will release you."

To my great shock, he drops to one knee and bows his head low before her. "You have my most solemn vow that I will not harm any of you if you free me."

Grayce studies him a moment and then turns to the guards. "Unchain him."

Their heads whip from her to me, uncertain, while the Orc studies her warily.

I look at her, and she stares back at me with an unwavering expression. I turn to the men and give them a subtle nod.

Aren and Talyn move close to her side as the guards unchain the Orc.

She steps down from the dais, and I do the same. Magic arcs across my fingers like lightning, ready to end the Orc if he dares to threaten her in any way.

"What is your name?" she asks.

He straightens, tipping his chin up proudly. "I am Kurnag of Clan Arzul."

"Hon'latu, ushatar," Grayce speaks in Orcish, the words: *"I see you, warrior."*

Surprise flits briefly across his stern expression before he answers, "Hon'latu, hurum'ash." The Orcish words for *"I see you, brave one."*

My mouth falls open as does several of my guards and warriors. She steps closer, and my heart hammers in my chest. He is right. She is brave to stand within arm's reach of him, and it takes everything within me not to pull her behind me.

As if reading my mind, his gaze shifts to me over her shoulder and then drops to my hands, his eyes narrowing as magic crackles along my palm before he looks to her again.

"Why were you at the Great Wall?" she asks.

"Our Clan has encountered several rogue Wraiths and Shadow monsters in the Wyldwood," he says. "I was sent to scout the Wall; search for any signs of how they may be crossing... for any gaps in the barrier."

"Shadow monsters?" Grayce frowns. "What are those?"

Before the Orc can answer, I turn to her. "They are created by the Mages. Made with dark magic, they are a ruined and twisted form of life. You may know them as shadow assassins."

"I've heard stories, but never seen one."

"Pray you never do," the Orc says grimly.

Grayce turns her attention back to him. "What did you intend to do if you found any weakness in the Great Wall?" she asks the question I want an answer to as well.

He raises his hand and a flicker of glowing white light travels across his palm, a small demonstration of his power. "I was tasked to repair it."

Orcs have magic, like most Otherworldly beings, but theirs is able to tap into the ground, moving earth and stone much like the Dwarves are able to do.

"Is that all?" I challenge. "Your kind are known for raiding and pillaging, leaving behind destruction and ruin in your path. How do we know you were not a scout sent to spy on Corduin, searching for a way to invade?"

"You speak of other Clans," he grinds out. "Ours is peaceful. We only seek to protect our people, just as you wish to protect yours."

"I assume it was your Clan that pursued us in the Wyldwood." I level a dark glare at him. "Why?"

"We were curious," he explains. "We smelled a human female among you and wondered why that would be since it is well-known that your kind are enemies."

"Not anymore," Grayce interjects. "Our bonding has created an alliance between Florin and Anlora." She looks back at me and then addresses him again. "You claim that you want peace and safety for your people."

He nods.

"Deliver a message to your Clan leader," she says. "Tell

him that if he truly wants peace, to arrange a meeting to discuss it."

"A meeting?" His head jerks back. "How do we know this would not be an elaborate trap meant to capture the Orc who would be our king if our home had not been destroyed?"

He speaks of the Orc capital of Grunden in the Ashkar Mountain and of King Arokh. A rogue kingdom invaded their mountain and set fire to everything, killing hundreds of their people, scattering the Clans to the winds.

Anger tightens his jaw. "Since when have the Fae ever been interested in making peace with my people?"

Grayce moves to my side and takes my hand. "They made peace with mine, and we had been enemies with them far longer than yours have been."

His gaze drops to our joined hands, his brow furrowed deeply. "I will deliver your message to King Arokh." He thumps his fist to his chest and dips his chin to Grayce. "Or'-vat, hurum'ash." *Farewell, brave one.*

"Or'vat, ushatar." *Farewell, warrior.*

He narrows his eyes at me. *"Ilid'ren,"* he practically snarls the Orcish word for Fae. Apparently in his opinion, unlike my mate, I do not deserve any further address of honor.

He thumps his fist to his chest again, and she does the same before he turns and leaves.

My chest swells with pride as every warrior in the room turns to her with expressions of awe and admiration.

She has been Queen of Anlora for only a few days, and already she has earned the respect of our greatest warriors. I am certain word will travel far and fast of what happened this day.

CHAPTER 24

GRAYCE

After the Orc leaves, we make our way back to our rooms. Although we are walking arm in arm, Kyven is silent, and I wonder if I may have made a mistake. I invited the Orc King to meet us for a peace treaty.

Kyven said we would be equals, and *because* we are equals, I probably should have discussed it with him before I made the offer. I may be the Queen of Anlora now, but that doesn't mean that I understand everything about their history and any policies they have for negotiating with others: Orcs and such. And I do not know how deep the hatred and distrust runs between their two races.

When we step into our room, Kyven closes the door. I turn to him. "Did I overstep?"

He frowns. "What do you mean?"

"Telling Kurnag to deliver a message to his king about meeting with us."

"That was brilliant." A handsome smile curves his mouth. "And something that wouldn't have happened if not for you."

"What would you have done?" I ask, curious.

"I would have interrogated him, and probably thrown him in a cell," he says flatly. "But you found a path that may lead to actual peace between us and the Orcs. No wonder your brother was so hesitant about my marrying you." His lips twist into a slight grin. "I'm sure he was upset to lose his most capable politician."

Pride fills me, and I cannot help the smile that lights my face at his praise.

A subtle knock at the door is Aren. "We should probably leave soon," he says.

"Is Talyn with you?" Kyven asks.

"I'm here," Talyn replies and he steps into the room.

Kyven gestures to him. "Talyn has been assigned as your personal guard. He both a warrior and a trained healer."

Talyn's amber wings flutter behind him as he bows low. His short, dark hair falls over his brow, but he brushes it back when he stands again. His amber eyes meet mine as he places his closed fist to his chest. "It is an honor to serve you, my Queen."

"My mate speaks very highly of you." I smile. "I thank you for your service."

A bright grin lights his face. "It is I who am honored to protect the Sanishon Queen of the Fae."

Aren's eyes snap to Talyn, widening slightly and I notice Kyven's do as well. "Sanishon... it an ancient term in the original tongue, before Great Division. It means Outsider, does it not?"

"He means no offense, my queen." Aren turns to me.

"There is none taken," I reassure him, and then turn my attention to Kyven. "I've heard my sister's Dark Elf guards refer to her as the Sanishon Queen of the Dark Elves."

"She is the first human—Outsider—to bond with one of

143

their kind," Kyven explains. "Just as you are the first to bond with a Fae."

Something about the way he says this suggests there is more he is not saying. But I know we must leave, and I resolve to ask Kyven about it later, when we are alone.

When we walk out into the main entryway, dozens of warriors have gathered to see us off, each of them bowing low. Commander Caldyr bows as well, and Kyven rests a familiar hand on his shoulder. "It was good to see you again, Commander."

"And you, my king," he replies and then looks to me, his gaze shining with admiration. "It was an honor to meet you, my queen."

"And you as well."

Kyven hoists me to his chest. His purple wings flutter furiously behind him as we lift off and into the sky.

Against him like this, I'm acutely aware of his strong arms and the thick cords of muscle that line his chest. As he pulls me closer, I breathe deep of his heady masculine scent. My thoughts returns to our kiss, and I wonder if he is thinking about it as well.

Despite my fear of heights, as we fly out over the city and into the forest, I am not afraid because I know he would never allow me to fall. He leans in and the soft mint of his breath fills my nose. "I apologize again for bringing you to Corduin, so close to the wall. I know this is probably not what you had in mind for the early days of our marriage."

Although I do not want him to feel any guilt in bringing me here, I do like that he cares what I think. Father never particularly cared about our mother's opinions and it was my worry that I might someday find myself in a similar situation. I am pleased that it does not appear to be this way with Kyven. "I'm glad we came, Kyven. I've heard so many stories, and I've always wondered about the Great Wall."

He frowns. "You were not afraid?"

"At first, I was. But it was lovely meeting the people you spent so much time with."

A faint smile quirks his lips. "They are like brothers to me."

It is easy to see he has their admiration and respect. "Do you miss it?" I ask. "Living in Corduin? Guarding the wall?"

His brow furrows deeply. "It was not an easy life, but it was a simple one."

"Guarding the wall hardly seems like a simple task," I reply. "It's dangerous."

"That is true." He frowns. "But on the wall, you know exactly who your enemy is. In the royal court, it is often difficult to discern friend from foe."

This I understand. "It was the same in my brother's court," I offer. "So many claim to be loyal, but are not. Is there anyone in particular that I should be cautious of?"

"Unfortunately, I believe there may be many." He lowers his eyes. "I turned down several of the Fae nobility when they approached me about bonding, including Lord Torien's daughter," he explains, referring to his advisor. "And now I have chosen a human as my mate and my queen. There are those who still hold anger toward your kind for the battles and wars we've fought with each other over the past few hundred years."

This is nothing new. I already expected this, and I am not afraid. "It will take time for those wounds to heal, but I believe they will."

"I believe so too," he says. "But I must insist that you have Talyn with you at all times. I will not risk your safety. You are too important to me."

Panic spears through me, but I push it back down. This would be a healthy precaution for any new sovereign. Even so, it is still unsettling.

He must read the unease in my features because he quickly adds, "I will protect you, Grayce. I vow I will keep you safe."

"You cannot promise this, Kyven," I reply as dark memories creep in. Despite my mother's guards, she was still assassinated in her own kingdom, and now I go to a foreign one, where I am even more vulnerable to an attempt upon my life. "No one can."

He opens his mouth to protest, but I put a finger to his lips. "My father swore to keep my mother safe, but he could not. And I have seen what that broken promise did to his soul." I swallow against the lump in my throat. "It is the reason he went mad and declared war upon your kingdom without any proof the Fae were responsible." I cup his cheek. "I know we are new to each other, but I would not see you destroyed over a promise you could not keep."

"It was not madness that drove your father to seek revenge. It was love, Grayce."

He tightens his hold on me. Heat scalds my face at the intense look on his face, and I wonder, not for the first time, if his feelings for me run deeper than I thought.

I force my gaze from his as my entire body flushes with warmth. It worries me how strongly I already feel toward him after such a small amount of time. Despite my attempts to guard myself, I am already losing my heart to my husband.

But I want to be cautious. I have been hurt before, and I don't think my heart could take the pain of being hurt again.

CHAPTER 25

KYVEN

As we approach the village of Nyllthar, a soft glow radiates around it. Grayce notices it at the same time I do. She points to the barrier. "Is that magic?"

"Yes."

"Is that... normal?" she asks, her tone wary.

"No." Worry tightens my chest, but I force my expression to remain impassive, not wanting her to know I am alarmed.

Aren flies up beside me, and the rest of our guards gather in a protective formation around us, each of them scanning the forest for any signs of danger.

A barrier like this is strong, but also difficult to maintain. It is only used when the threat to a town or a village is high.

"Harpies?" Aren murmurs beside me.

"Or Griffins," Talyn says.

Grayce goes tense in my arms, the scent of her fear flooding my nostrils. I glare at Aren and Talyn—a silent warning for them to be quiet. My gaze travels over the woods, searching for any unusual movement, but the tree canopy is thick. Anything could be hiding in the branches, and we would not know it until we were nearly upon the village.

We pick up our pace. My wings beat furiously behind me as I race toward the barrier. Once we're inside, we should be safe.

"Kyven!" Grayce releases a pain-filled cry before she curls into my arms, shivering violently. "Something's wrong!"

My heart seizes in my chest. Even though she is touching me, the barrier is repelling her as it would whatever else it is meant to keep out, because she is not Fae. It is too strong for us to cross without harming her.

Without hesitation, I spin and fly away from the village, putting more distance between us and the magic shield.

I call over my shoulder to one of the guards. "Get inside the barrier and order them to lower it! Now!"

He zips past us, rushing toward the village.

"Kyven." Grayce's voice trembles as tears track down her cheeks. "What was that?"

"The barrier is strong. The magic of the shield repels anyone who is not Fae." I pull her close to my chest. "Forgive me. I should have realized this sooner."

"It's all right," she replies. "I'm fine now. I—"

"Griffins!" Talyn yells out, pointing to the left.

At least a dozen fly straight for us. Their massive wings slice through the air, their talons outstretched and ready to rip us apart. Their razor-sharp beaks and golden feather glint beneath the sunlight as they charge forward.

Bracing my hold on Grayce with one hand, I lift the other as I call upon my power. Raw energy crackles between my fingers, and I unleash a bolt of magic at the nearest Griffin, sending it hurtling to the ground.

My guards surround us in a protective formation as they use their magic to strike out at the remaining predators.

"There's too many!" Aren calls out. "We need to get inside the barrier! Now!"

"We must wait until it's down," I tell him. "I will not risk the queen."

"No!" Grayce lifts a determined gaze to me. "It's too dangerous to remain here. Fly to the barrier."

"It will hurt you," I protest.

"You sent one of the guards to take it down so we could enter," she counters. "Fly toward it, and we'll pray that they lower the shield before we reach it."

"No, I will not—"

"I'll not have you or any of the guards dying because of me," she states firmly. "Now, go!"

I'm vaguely aware of the guard's heads snapping toward her.

As much as I hate to admit it, she is right. There are too many Griffins. We have to try for the barrier or else risk losing everything. "Fly to the barrier!"

Two dozen more Griffins burst from the trees, joining the first group in their attack. We are severely outnumbered. If we cannot reach the village, there is no way we can fend off this many without casualties. They are as dangerous as they are lethal.

I grit my teeth as we draw closer, and the barrier is still intact. A pained cry rips from Grayce's throat as she writhes in pain.

Guilt floods my veins. If I had given her my mark and sealed her to me in a Fae ceremony, the barrier would recognize her as mine and allow her to pass as a Fae. But because I have not, she is an Outsider, and she is suffering as if she were an enemy of our people.

"Kyven!" Her scream tears a hole in my heart.

Three more Griffins erupt from the trees, forming a wall between me and my warriors. I spin toward them and send two bolts of powerful magic racing toward the group, scattering them as it explodes in their midst in a brilliant display of heat and light.

One swoops around the side, and before I can react, sharp talons rake across my upper arm and shoulder. Searing pain arcs through my arm as the venom burns in the wound. Furiously, I flap my wings, fighting to stay aloft as we spiral to the ground.

"Kyven," Grayce's voice fills my ears, but I can barely focus as I struggle to land.

"To the king!" Aren's voice rings out overhead, but it's quickly drowned out by the deafening shriek of the Griffins as they descend, ready to claim their prey.

I twist onto my back at the last second as we crash to the ground, protecting Grayce from the impact. Pain rips across my back and wings as we slam to the earth.

CHAPTER 26

GRAYCE

Kyven cries out in pain as we crash to the ground. Panic rises in my chest as three Griffins swoop down and start toward us like predators stalking wounded prey.

"To the king and queen!" Aren yells above us, but his voice is quickly drowned out by the ear-piercing shrieks of the Griffins as they battle the Fae.

Kyven pushes up to his feet, helping me to stand with him. He grips my forearm and tugs me behind him. His right wing is bent at an unnatural angle and black blood trails down his back, dripping onto the ground.

"Run, Grayce." His voice is low and deadly as he bares his fangs at the Griffins. "Go. Quickly."

Despite my fear, I stand my ground, pulling the dagger from my belt. "No. I'm not going to leave you."

"You need to run, Grayce," he grinds out. "Now."

Without warning, the Griffins charge forward.

Raising his hands, Kyven sends an arc of magic, striking

the closest one and throwing it back. But the two others close in quickly, undeterred by their fallen brethren, lashing out with their razor-sharp talons.

Kyven hits another with his power, but the third one swipes out. He twists to one side, but not fast enough. He cries out as its claws rake across his torso, slamming him sprawling.

The fear in my heart is swiftly replaced with rage as the Griffin closes in on my mate, readying to attack again. Time slows as I rush forward, dagger in hand. Panic grips me when I realize I will not reach Kyven in time to stop another attack.

Intense warmth fills my chest, flowing through my veins like fire. Heat gathers in my palms, and I glance down in shock as an orb of green fire hovers above my skin. Reacting on instinct, I raise my hands and fling it toward the predator.

An arc of green lightning rushes forward, hitting the ground at the Griffin's feet as it twists out of the way. Angry that I missed my mark, I somehow conjure another. But before I can throw it, thick green vines explode from the earth, their whip-like tendrils lashing out at the Griffin, catching its wings and limbs, wrapping tightly around it and slamming it to the dirt.

Rage blisters through me and the vines tighten, caging the Griffin to the earth. Another Griffin drops to the ground before me, and a surge of power bursts from my hands, sinking into the ground.

Vines erupt from the dark soil, twining around the Griffin's body and pinning it down. My arms tremble and sweat beads across my brow. Everything aches, and darkness gathers at the corners of my vision. But I grit my teeth and force myself to remain standing. I cannot give up. Not now. If I do, we are dead.

The Griffins twist and writhe in their binding, shredding at the vines with their talons.

Fear spikes my chest. I cannot allow them to break free. Mustering the last of my strength, I stumble forward. Gripping my dagger firmly in hand, I plunge it deep into the first one's chest. It sinks into the Griffin's flesh with a sickening squelch, and the light fades from its eyes.

Gritting my teeth, I start for the second one, but a bolt of power slams into it, incinerating the Griffin to ash. I glance back and see Kyven, his hands extended as he sends another arc of magic to a Griffin circling above us.

Aren and a few of the other warriors take care of the remaining few and then alight beside us.

Exhaustion steals through me, and I drop to my knees. Kyven rushes to me, hoisting me to his chest. "Grayce." His panicked gaze finds mine as he brushes the hair back from my face.

Unable to keep my eyes open any longer, my head falls back, and I surrender to the darkness.

CHAPTER 27

GRAYCE

As my mind slowly drifts back into awareness, the sound of humming fills my ears. I blink my eyes open and find a beautiful Fae woman standing over me. She has long, flowing silver-white hair, and her eyes are a lovely shade of violet that matches her flowing tunic dress and pants.

"How are you feeling?"

"I'm fine." I squint against the light, struggling to make sense of where I am and how I got here. My head is heavy as I lift it from the bed, and my thoughts are shrouded in a fog-like haze.

"I'm so glad you're finally awake." She smiles brightly. "We were ever so worried about you."

Myriad images flood my mind and alarm bursts through me as I recall Kyven injured and bleeding. "What happened?" I jerk up to sitting. "Where am I?"

"You collapsed." She rests her hand gently atop mine. "But all is well now. You are safe in the palace in Ryvenar."

My gaze sweeps over the room. The walls are carved out of a massive tree trunk, the tan wood gleaming in the soft light filtering through the window. The ceiling is high and arched, with intricate designs etched into the walls. The furnishings are simple yet elegant. The large bed is covered in silken sheets. There is a fireplace in the corner, stacked with l'sair crystals for light and heat. "Where is Kyven? Who are you?"

"I suspect he will be here any moment." A lovely smile curves her mouth. "He has hardly left your bedside since you arrived. I am his sister, Emryll. My brother flew through the night with an injured wing to get you here as quickly as possible. He will be so glad to know you are awake."

"Is he all right?" Concern spikes my pulse. "How is his wing?"

"My brother has been sick with worry. He will be better now that he knows you are well." A grin tugs at her lips. "Healer Draymon will be glad also. Kyven went to retrieve him. He has been badgering all the healers since you arrived, demanding to know why you had not yet awakened."

"How long have I been unconscious?"

Before she can reply, noise draws my attention to the door.

"I assure you that my wing is fine," Kyven's voice rings out, sharp and crisp with a hint of irritation lacing his tone. "Now, please, check on my mate, Healer Draymon."

"Kyven," Emryll calls out. "She is already awake."

His head snaps to me, and he rushes to my side, taking my hand. "How do you feel?" His eyes shine with worry as he brushes the hair back from my face. "Are you in any pain?"

"No," I reassure him. "I'm fine."

He sits on the edge of the bed and pulls me into his arms. A deep trilling hum builds in his chest, vibrating against my ear as he smooths a hand down my back. "Thank the gods you are awake. I was so worried."

"My king," a man's voice calls out behind him, and Kyven tenses. "I need to check your wing to ensure it is healing properly."

"Later," Kyven replies in a tone that brooks no argument. "I am tending to my mate."

"As you can see for yourself, she is well, my dear brother," Emryll says behind him. "It is you who must now be tended."

"Not now," he grumbles.

I push back just enough to lift my gaze to his. "Allow the healer to assess you, Kyven. I'm all right. Truly."

He cups the back of my head and drops his forehead to mine. The gesture is so intimate, my heart fills with warmth. "I was so afraid when you collapsed," he murmurs.

His whispered words melt my heart. If ever I doubted how much he regards me, it is plain to see in this moment. He cares for me. Deeply.

"How long was I unconscious?"

"Too long." A weary sigh escapes him. "A day and a half, but it felt like an eternity."

Myriad thoughts flit through my mind and I glance down at my hands, frowning at the memory of the power I was somehow able to conjure.

Before I can ask him about it, he glances over his shoulder. "I would like to speak with my mate, alone."

I wait until Emryll and the healer both leave, shutting the door behind them before I speak. "I used magic, Kyven. But how is that possible?"

He takes both my wrists, turning my palms up in his grasp. "Just as your sister, Inara, inherited some of Varys's magic through their bond, I believe you inherited some of mine in the same way."

"I—I don't understand."

Something akin to guilt flashes behind his eyes. "I should have told you sooner."

Worry slithers down my spine. "About what?" He promised there would only be truth between us, and already he admits to holding something back. "What is it that you have not told me?"

"You are my *A'lyra*. My Fated bondmate." His gaze holds mine as if gauging my reaction to this revelation. "I knew it the first moment I saw you."

"Why did you not say anything?"

"I wanted to, but you are human. Your people do not have fated bonds, and I didn't know how you would react. I did not want to scare or upset you. And I was also worried your brother would use this knowledge against me during the treaty negotiations." He cups my face. "It is not just that. I wanted to protect you."

"I don't understand."

"It would be easier if I showed you." He glances down at my hands. "May I?"

At first, I don't know what he means, but then I realize he is speaking of the mind link, and I nod.

Kyven slips his palms into mine, entwining our fingers. A light tingling sensation flows across my flesh at the contact.

He closes his eyes and whispers. *"A'lyra."* The word echoes in the space between us, resonating within—a recognition and an awakening deep in my soul. "Reveal the bond to me."

Glowing silver threads spread out from his chest and mine, floating in the space between us. Their ends swirl and dance around each other, but only a few of them touch. I stare transfixed as three of them tangle together, weaving into a thick braid.

When I reach for them, my fingers pass through as if nothing were there. "What is this?"

"The first threads of our bond linking together." His voice

is full of awe-filled reverence. "A tether from your soul to mine."

He whispers words in the Fae tongue that I do not understand. Slowly, the threads of the bond begin to fade and then disappear completely.

He lifts his gaze to mine, and in his eyes it is easy to read that he holds something back. I'm not sure how I can read him this well already, but I do not question it. "What else is there that you are not telling me?"

"There is a prophecy in the ancient tomes of the Lythyrian about the Great Uniters," he explains. "They are Outsiders—Sanishon—that will unite the various races and usher in an era of peace. And I believe you are one of the Sanishon that was foretold."

Wisps of memory float to the surface of my mind. "Inara spoke of this. She said Varys and the Dark Elves believe she is part of a prophecy as well," I tell him. "But the tomes were written thousands of years ago. Why do you believe they are true? And what makes you so certain that I have some part in it?"

"Because no Fae has ever had a fated bond with one outside of our race. The same is true for the Dark Elves and Dragons." His gaze pierces mine. "The fact that your sister has the fated bond with Varys and your cousin, Freyja, with the Dragon King... all of this points to the prophecy now unfolding. And there are those who would do anything to stop it."

"It is believed the prophecy speaks of the Mages and their Wraiths. The Sanishon are the Great Uniters who are foretold to bring about their end, ushering in an era of peace among the various races."

I lower my gaze. "I'll admit that when Inara spoke of this prophecy, I didn't want to believe it. Because believing it is true means that my sister is in danger. And now... you're telling me that I am too?"

Guilt mars his expression. "I'm sorry, Grayce. Most believe I married you only for the sake of an alliance. If they knew the truth of what you are to me, they could use it against us." He looks down at our joined hands. "I am a new king. The people loved my brother, but me... I was a warrior on the Great Wall. I am not the one who was supposed to wear the crown." He clenches his jaw. "I have enemies. Some I know and some I suspect. And until I know who is loyal, I will trust no one with the knowledge that you are my A'lyra."

"What about your warriors? And Lord Torien?" I ask. "What if someone saw me use magic when we were attacked?"

"Aren witnessed you using your powers, and I told Talyn as well." His gaze meets mine intently. "And I trust them both with my life, Grayce. They will speak of it to no one."

"And your sister?"

"She is aware," he replies solemnly. "My sister is one of the most powerful among us, and she will help keep you safe, but I will not risk confiding this knowledge to anyone else."

A maelstrom of emotions swirls deep within. I lower my gaze, unsure how to respond. I'm disappointed that he withheld this from me, but I also understand why he did.

As if sensing my inner turmoil, he says, "Forgive me, Grayce. I should have told you sooner."

"You're right. You should have," I reply sharply, and he blanches. "But you are also right that my brother would have used this against you. Any skilled negotiator would have," I point out. "I understand why you withheld this. But I also need you to understand something as well."

"What is it?"

"I may be human, but that does not mean I am weak," I state firmly. "I entered into this marriage fully expecting that

I may be in danger, simply *because* I am human. All monarchs have enemies both within and without their courts. That is not something unique to the Fae. I have lived my entire life under the scrutiny of others. I will not break under pressure, nor bow to threats. But when I agreed to marry you, you promised that we would be partners. True equals in all ways."

"You are right." Regret mars his features. "It is instinct to want to protect one's mate, and I find that the more time I spend with you, the more difficult it is to ignore this primal urge."

For some reason his answer bothers me. All of his care for me... his emotions... Is that what it is? An urge? An instinct? "Is that the reason you are so protective of me? Because of the fated bond?"

"No." He takes a step closer. My breath catches as his violet eyes meet mine, full of love and devotion. His intense gaze focused upon me with blazing intensity. As if I have lived my entire life in shadows and only now have seen the sun. Gently, he tucks a stray tendril of hair behind my ear. "I protect you because you are mine, Grayce. Because you are everything."

Although he does not say the actual words, his declaration makes my heart flutter and my cheeks flush with heat.

Something shifts deep within me... a strange pull deep inside. I think of the bond between us and the threads of fate that dance around each other, but do not yet meet. We are connected. Of that I have no doubt, but I do not fully understand what it means. I cannot deny that this makes me afraid. I have never been fond of the unknown. It is part of the reason why I spent so much time in the palace library.

For me, knowledge is not just power, it is mastery of the world around me.

My mother taught me this. She used to say that fear is just ignorance. Those words have stayed with me my whole life.

Any fear I've ever had, I chose to face head on. To learn what it is so that with that knowledge, I may no longer be afraid. But *this* is something that I can only learn from him.

I have always prided myself upon my independence. This is the first time I cannot rely upon myself to find the truth that will allay my fears. I need him. And that in and of itself makes me worry.

I glance down at my hands, remembering the power that flowed through them. "I do not know how I conjured magic, Kyven. What if it happens again? What if I cannot control it?"

He wraps his hands around my wrists in a gentle grip, studying my hands. "It is the same for all Fae when they come into their magic," he reassures me. "The first time my powers manifested, it was instinct—a reaction to perceived danger. Just as it was for you." He slips his palms into my own, squeezing gently. "I will teach you, Grayce. Just as I was taught. And I will show you how to wield and control it. But we must do so in secret. If anyone learns that you possess this, they will know that you are my A'lyra.

A soft knock at the door is Aren. Kyven's hands slip from mine as he turns to face him, and I find myself already missing the warmth of his palm in my own. "What is it?" he asks.

"There are a few matters that need your attention."

Kyven hesitates a moment before his sister steps into the doorway. "It's all right." Emryll smiles. "It will give me a chance to get to know my new sister better while you are gone."

I'm glad of the warm welcome Kyven's sister has given me, and I can't help but smile.

Kyven presses a tender kiss to the back of my knuckles. "I will return to you as soon as I can."

When he leaves, I look down at my hands and the wedding ring he gave me for our human wedding. I can hardly believe that was less than a handful of days ago. And now I will be bound to him in a Fae ceremony. And while I'm not quite sure what that entails, I find myself already worried.

Before I agreed to this marriage, I thought it would be one made out of the necessity of politics and built upon mutual respect and perhaps even friendship. After what happened with Joren, I erected a wall around my heart, vowing to protect it.

But in less than a week, my new husband has already begun to crack the walls I have built with his care of me. How could I not fall for a man who goes to such lengths to put my needs and my welfare above his own? And yet, his statement about instinct and news of the fated bond concerns me. Along with the fact that he withheld this information from me until now.

Does he do these things because he is falling for me as well? Or is it simply instinct—a pull of the bond that he cannot ignore? Until I know which it is, I must be careful. I cannot allow myself to completely fall until I know for sure that I will not be hurt.

CHAPTER 28

GRAYCE

Emryll flashes a bright smile. "How are you feeling?"

"Fine."

"Are you hungry? Thirsty?"

"No, but I would like a bath and"—I glance down at my dress—"a fresh change of clothes."

"Of course." She gestures to a door across the way. "The cleansing room is in there. I will have someone bring you some new clothing."

When I enter the cleansing room, I'm surprised to find a raised pool in the corner, jutting out from the wall. It is already full of water, a light mist of steam rising from the surface. Beside it is a shelf with two bottles. When I remove the stopper, the calming scent of lavender and jasmine hits my nostrils.

I remove my clothing and step into the pool. A sigh of contentment leaves me as I lower myself into the water. The warm liquid surrounds me like a soothing balm, easing all of the tension from my body.

A light knock on the door is one of the servants. I'm startled when she simply walks in as if I'm not in the middle of a bath. But then I remember I'm in Anlora, not Florin. The Fae, it seems, do not have any qualms about nudity.

"I hope these are to your liking, my queen," she says, setting the clothes on a low bench, beside the pool. "Is there anything else you require?"

I shake my head. "Thank you."

Her mouth curls up in a polite smile before she disappears through the door.

When I'm finished bathing, I quickly dry off and then change into my new clothes. My cheeks heat when I notice the undergarments are little more than scraps of silken lace. The tunic dress and pants are a lovely shade of purple, the fabric soft as silk against my skin. It's strange however, to feel the air on my back through the slit-like openings for the wings I do not possess.

The tunics I received at Corduin did not have these. It seems the seamstress there recognized that I would not need them.

I wonder about my trunk that I brought from Florin, but as I recall the fight with the griffins, I would not be surprised if my belongings were lost in the battle.

It's best, I suppose, to dress in the fashions of my new home. Perhaps it will help the Fae to accept me more readily.

When I step back out into the room, I find Lord Torien waiting for me. "Good." He pins me with an assessing stare. "I see they have found more Fae clothing for you. Your human clothes were left behind, but they should be arriving no later than tomorrow."

"I will not be needing them," I inform him. "I quite like the Fae style of dress. These are very comfortable." I gesture to my pants and tunic dress. "In fact, I believe I much prefer this fashion to those in Florin. The only issue is the openings for the wings."

"That can be easily remedied by a clothier. It's a pity your kind do not have wings," he says grimly. "It would certainly make things much easier for his Majesty."

His words draw my attention. "How so?"

"As I'm sure you are aware, the king is a direct descendant of Queen Ilyra."

I did not know this, but I nod as if I do. Something tells me not to show any lack of knowledge in front of this man. I'm surprised, however, that Caldyr and Kyven did not mention this when I asked about her necklace in the fortress library.

"And while it is not your fault." He spreads his hands wide. "Many will be displeased that her line could either end if it is found that humans and Fae cannot... reproduce, or if a child were to be born of your union with... unusable wings."

"As for the wings, I can do nothing about that," I reply, trying to appear unfazed by his statement. "But as for the issue of the ending of her line, Princess Emryll is directly descended from her as well, is she not?"

He purses his lips. "Yes, but she is not in direct line for the throne." He sighs. "There is an option that has yet to be discussed."

"An option?" I frown. "For what?"

"As you are aware, our people mate for life. If the King were to seal his bond to you, he may be left in a situation where he is unable to provide an heir. This could undermine the stability of his rule. Without someone to pass the crown to, that the people would fully support, it could create problems for his reign."

Anger floods my veins, but I force my expression to remain impassive, not wanting to betray anything just yet. I want to give him enough leeway to hang himself first. I clasp my hands in front of me and lift my chin. "As advisor to his Majesty, what would you suggest, Lord Torien?"

His beady eyes light up as if he truly believes he has me in his snare. "Have an official bonding ceremony with the King, but do not seal it. Be queen to his majesty in all ways but… physical ones. Allow him to take a Fae consort that can provide him with the stability that, through no fault of your own, your biology cannot."

He stands and clears his throat. "After all, this is not the first time such an arrangement has been made in the royal line. The King's famous ancestor—Queen Ilyra—was born of the King's consort as he too married a queen for an alliance while his heart had already been bound to another."

"Have you spoken of this to the King?" I ask, my voice tight. "Does he know of your concerns?"

"He does, but… he is a young King and inexperienced." He breathes out a long-suffering sigh. "And it is my duty to do all that I can to ensure the crown remains stable and—"

"He told you no, didn't he?"

His eyes snap to mine, worry beginning to crack his façade of feigned helpfulness. Now, I understand why Aren looked to him when he gave me his warning about the nobles of the royal court. Torien is one of the snakes he was referring to.

"You are late with your scheming, Lord Torien," I say bluntly because men like him understand nothing else. "And you forget that I have lived my entire life in a royal court. I assume you must have a daughter or someone close to you that you would see in my place, am I correct?"

He clenches his jaw, confirming my statement. He doesn't know that Kyven already told me that Torien tried to convince him to marry his daughter.

"That's what I thought." I clear my throat. "I've heard that humans cannot have children with the Fae, but they supposedly couldn't have them with Dark Elves or Dragons either, and yet, my sister and cousin both carry the children of their mates. Be mindful to whom you speak, Lord Torien, for one day my child may sit on the throne and there will be no room for such scheming and prejudice in their court."

Anger flashes in his eyes, and he opens his mouth as if to speak, but I take a step closer. "You may go," I dismiss him, reminding him I am queen.

As he slinks out the door, Emryll walks in, her brow furrowed slightly. "I meant to return earlier. I hope Lord Torien did not put you in a foul mood, as he so often does my brother," she says, narrowing her eyes at the door. "He is a difficult man, Kyven only kept him on as counsel to help in the transition of his reign. But hopefully soon, he will choose another advisor."

"All is well." I smile. "I grew up in a royal court. It is nothing that I have not dealt with before."

"Good." She flashes a grin. "Would you like a tour of the castle?"

"I would love that."

As I follow her, I do my best not to gape. The castle is nestled amongst towering trees. The entire structure is carved into the trunks and branches, just like the city and the fortress of Corduin. But where the fortress was somewhat sparse and utilitarian, the palace of Ryvenar is wondrously beautiful. Vines and flowers weave throughout the palace, a lovely contrast to the light gray wood of the trees.

Branches and leaves form intricate patterns on the ceiling above and the air is filled with the sweet scent of blooming flowers. The floors, walls and ceiling are so smooth and polished that I cannot help but admire the craftsmanship that must have gone into creating the palace.

I'm in awe as we make our way through the castle. Each room is more breathtaking than the last, with high vaulted ceilings and carved archways. The walls are adorned with tapestries depicting scenes of the forest and the Fae. The furniture is delicate and intricate, made from the same wood as the rest of the castle.

This castle is not just a home, it is a work of art—a living, breathing entity that is as much a part of the forest as the trees themselves.

When Emryll leads me outside, I'm struck by how high up we are. The city is an extension of the palace. The entire structure is built in the trees, connected by rope bridges and carved stairways.

"Your people have wings." I turn to her. "Why are there bridges and stairs?"

"Fae fledglings cannot fly until they are three years old," she explains. "And there are many who, for one reason or another, have either lost their wings or lost the use of them. Some even use *nylluan* to get from one place to another."

"Nylluan? What is that?"

"They are similar to griffins, but a bit smaller," she says. "They have the body of a spotted snow cat, an owl's head and wings."

A shudder runs through me at mention of griffins. "Nylluan are... friendly?"

"Yes, and they are easily tamed, highly intelligent, and fiercely loyal." She gestures to a tree next to the castle, with several large openings ringed around the trunk. "There are many in the palace rookery."

I step onto one of the rope bridges to get a better view. It looks out over the entire city. There are several areas carved out for gardens and green spaces. They are so large, it would be easy to forget one was high up in the trees instead of on the ground.

"It's beautiful," I murmur. "Like something out of a dream."

"If you think this is beautiful, wait until you see the palace gardens. I'm sure Kyven will want to be the one to give you a tour of them." She flashes a grin. "He spends much of his time out there in the evenings."

Emryll leads me to the dining hall. Intricate carvings line the otherwise smooth, wooden walls. Floor to ceiling windows across the room look out onto the elegant city below.

Ryvenar is so different from Florin. It is light and airy, whereas Florin feels so closed in and heavily fortified.

As we walk down another hallway, I notice a portrait of a Fae Queen. With vivid green eyes and wings, and long, flowing white hair, she stands tall and proud. A pendant with a teardrop-shaped crystal gem hangs around her neck. I immediately recognize it as the one from the fortress library. "Is that Queen Ilyra?" I point to the picture.

"Yes. She is one of our ancestors." Emryll places her hand to her chest in a solemn gesture. "She gave her life to save our people from the Wraith." She points to the necklace. "You see the gem she wears?"

I nod.

"Her mate gave it to her. He was a prince from the Great Divide. The stone came from that place."

"What is the Great Divide?"

"It is known as the World Between Worlds," she explains. "A place of magic so great that only the strongest of casters, or those immune to such power can navigate its path."

I frown. "Why have I never heard of this before?"

"Because the portal to enter is heavily guarded, and our people are forbidden from trying to access it. The last person to survive crossing the Great Divide was King Danryk—Queen Ilyra's mate."

"Why is it so dangerous?"

"It is said that the magic there is wild and untamed. But beyond that, I do not truly know."

Although I have more questions, I realize that I'll have to find the answers somewhere else. Fortunately, I've always enjoyed learning and I'm looking forward to unraveling the rest of this story.

The setting sun casts a golden glow over the city. The sky is a gorgeous display of oranges, pinks, and purples. Ryvenar is bustling with activity as people go about their business, their wings glistening in the waning light.

The streets are lined with lanterns, containing Fae lights, which flicker to life as the sun dips below the horizon. And the air is filled with the gentle hum of magic, and the distant sounds of music and laughter.

Soft light spills out from the various houses carved into the trees. Their purple leaves cast a lovely, muted glow. Gold and silver lights dance and zip among the branches.

"Are those night pixies?" I ask, shuddering inwardly as I recall their tiny razor-sharp teeth.

"Yes. They are mischievous creatures." She shrugs. "But they rarely bother anyone here in Ryvenar."

I'm not sure that statement is as reassuring as she thinks it is. I'd hate to be one of the *rare* people they might decide to take an interest in.

One of the servants approaches, folding at the waist a low bow. "The king has sent his regrets that he will be unable to join you for evening meal. He has pressing matters to attend to but will return as soon as he is able."

I hide my disappointment behind a polite nod of acknowledgment. I suppose this was to be expected. After all, Kyven has been away longer than he'd intended. I'm sure there is much he needs to see to, now that he is here.

Stuffing down my tangle of emotions, I turn my attention

to Emryll. She pins me with an assessing gaze and a slow smile spreads across her face. "You are disappointed."

Am I truly that easy to read? "I—"

"Forgive me," she says quickly. "I should have warned you."

"Of what?"

"My gift." She grins. "Kyven is able to read people through touch, but I am able to get a sense of their emotions simply by being near them."

"Oh," I reply, somewhat startled by her honesty. I'm so unused to people having any powers, much less freely admitting to them. After all, it was not long ago that the Order of Mages governed the laws as they related to magic in our lands. Anyone found harboring any sort of power was sentenced to death.

My sister and I lived in fear for most of our lives, terrified that someone would discover that we possessed the ability of foresight. Fortunately, High Mage Ylari taught us how to suppress and hide our powers by taking *nylweed*. Now that there is no need to conceal my abilities, I wonder how powerfully they will begin to manifest.

"I can assure you." She flashes a grin. "My brother is likely just as disappointed, if not more so, as you that he is unable to join you for dinner."

"Are there many Fae who possess these kinds of powers?" I ask, curious. "The ability to read someone's thoughts through touch or someone's emotions simply by being near them?"

"No." Her gaze turns thoughtful. "Our history suggests that many of our ancestors possessed these particular gifts. But now, only a handful do." She arches a teasing brow. "The rumors your people have that the Fae can sense lies... it is from people like Kyven and myself."

Although I should probably be concerned that they can

read people so easily, I find that it doesn't bother me in the least. I have nothing to hide, and I have always valued honesty and sought the truth above all else.

Emryll cocks her head to the side, frowning. "I worried this knowledge would unnerve you, but I sense only fascination and... approval? Is that correct?"

"Yes."

"Strange," she mutters more to herself than to me before her expression softens. "Perhaps that is why the goddess has matched you with my brother."

"What do you mean?"

Sadness flits briefly across her expression. "As I mentioned before, the ones with these gifts are few among my kind. The rare few that possess these abilities... they have difficulty finding a mate." She sighs. "I suppose the idea of someone being able to read your innermost thoughts or parse your emotions simply by proximity would be disturbing to most."

"Everyone harbors secrets... pieces of ourselves that we keep hidden from the rest of the world. But I have always valued honesty." I lower my gaze. "After witnessing the devastation that lies can have upon a marriage, as it did between my parents, I decided that when I wed, there would be no secrets between me and my partner."

Emryll rests her hand gently atop my own. "The goddess has chosen well for my brother, and I am glad." She gives me a watery smile. "I would be honored to call you my sister, if you will allow it."

Happiness blooms in my chest. I'd not expected to be received so warmly, especially by Kyven's sister. But I am happy to know I was wrong. "I would like that."

Joy seems to radiate from Emryll at my response. Grinning, she leans forward on her elbows. "Tell me all about your human ceremony. I wish I could have been there."

She sighs as I relay the details. "It sounds so lovely that your entire family and all your friends may gather for such an occasion."

I frown. "Is that not true for a Fae ceremony as well?"

"No," she says, a bit hesitantly. "Has anyone spoken to you about the Fae ceremony, and what it entails?"

"I have heard very little about what is expected." I reply honestly. "But I would appreciate it if you would tell me. I dislike the idea of being unprepared for anything, especially my own bonding ceremony."

"To receive the highest blessings from the goddess, it is best to bond during the full moon," she says, leaning back in her chair. "You are fortunate that it will not only be full tomorrow night, but also a silver moon."

"Why?"

"It is a good omen," she explains. "Almost every Fae ruler that has been wed beneath its light has had a long and prosperous bonding."

"What should I do to prepare for the ceremony?"

"As Kyven's closest family member, I would be honored to guide you through the process." Her small brow furrows. "Although, I'm unsure how your mating flight will work since you haven't any wings. But I suppose Kyven will figure something out. He—"

"Mating flight?"

"Yes." She releases a wistful sigh. "I've heard it's the most romantic part of the entire ceremony."

I listen in stunned silence as she begins to explain exactly what that entails.

CHAPTER 29

KYVEN

I hated having to leave Grayce after she had only just awakened, but I also know Aren would not have interrupted us without a very good reason. There are many things I have to attend to that have been put aside during my absence.

"We've received a raven from Corduin." Aren hands me a scroll. "They discovered a few… strange creatures in the forest, matching the descriptions given by the Orc. Shadow assassins as well as Wraiths."

Quickly, I scan the message, trying to appear calm when I am anything but. This is disturbing news. When I finish reading, I turn to Aren. "Double the guards around the perimeter of the city. We must strengthen the wards around the castle as well." I pause. "I need you to draw up a list of our best warriors—candidates for the queen's guard. I want my mate to be well-protected at all times."

He nods and then motions for one of the guards to come to him, and relays my message. When he turns back to me, dread floods my veins, because I already know what he is going to say.

"When did you know she was your A'lyra?"

Aren is not just my personal guard, he is close as a brother to me. Guilt twists deep within. If anyone, besides my sister, I should have told him. "I felt the bond the moment I saw her."

A deep frown mars his brow as he lowers his head and nods subtly.

"I regret not telling you," I admit. "If that means anything now."

"It is not my place to judge you, my king."

My king. He *is* upset. He never addresses me so formally when we are alone.

"Isn't it?" A half grin forms on my lips. "We trained together back in Corduin. We fought side by side and—"

"Different times," he says solemnly. "Back when we were nearly equal... or as equal as a spare prince sent to guard the wall and a common warrior can be, I suppose."

"You know I trust you, Aren. I simply—" the words escape me. How do I describe the feeling of terror that claws at my chest when I think of Grayce in danger? How do I tell him that the primitive, possessive instinct to hide her away from everyone, including him, is so overwhelming it threatens to swallow me whole?

"I cannot explain it," I finally admit. "I only know that the need to protect my mate is stronger than anything I've ever felt before. And the need to claim her is even greater."

"It is because you have not fully sealed your bond." His blue eyes meet mine evenly. "If you were wise, you would do so as soon as possible."

"I cannot push her into something she is not ready for. She is my mate. I will not take her until she asks."

"What if she never does?" He arches a brow. "What if she

never feels for you what you do for her? What then?" he challenges. "She could have died at the barrier to Nyllthar because you have not sealed her to you. Our magic will not recognize her as one of us until you seal your bond."

He is right. It is dangerous the longer we wait to complete our bonding, but I refuse to rush her into it.

"On the Great Wall, there can be no secrets between you and your fellow warriors," he reminds me. "You know this. They ingrain this in us during training. It is how we live, how we fight, how we survive." He studies me with a piercing gaze. "Each member of your personal guard was with you on the Great Wall. You chose us because the relationships we forged at Corduin were bonds forged in battle and blood."

Shame fills me. His words are spikes through my very soul. I chose him as my personal guard because I knew that he would not only protect me with his life, but he would also not hesitate to tell me the truth… even if it were something a guard might never tell his superior. Especially a king.

"You believe I should tell them she is my Fated One."

"Not just them," he says. "The entire kingdom should know what she is to you."

I'm shocked. Aren knows I have enemies at court. "Why? It would only put her in danger."

"She is already in danger, Kyven. She is a human living in the Fae kingdom of Anlora. Our people have been enemies for centuries. Even if she were Fae, she would still be a target for anyone who hates the crown or its king." He meets my gaze evenly. "But if you tell the people that she is your A'lyra, more of our people would accept her."

"Why?"

"Do you not understand what she is?" Disbelief mars his features. "What she means for our people?"

"Why do you think I have kept this secret from the moment I first saw her?" I ask incredulously. "She would be in even more danger if people thought she was one of the Sanishon spoken of in the prophecy."

"You already suspected, and you did not tell me," he says accusingly. "How am I supposed to protect you without the truth?"

"As you always have," I remind him. "Unfailingly."

"You are making a mistake keeping this secret, Kyven. She is the first Outsider to have a fated bond with one of our kind. She is one of the Sanishon foretold in the ancient tomes of the Lythyrian.

"The Sanishon will usher in an era of great peace. She is the blessing that every warrior hopes for when they are contemplating battle." He clenches his jaw. "We have fought against the humans, the Orcs, the Wraith, the Trolls, the Order of Mages..."

He holds up his palms. "My hands have been covered with so much blood, they will never be clean. All I have done, I have done in the hopes that the future generations will never know war." He shakes his head. "Warriors have died for that hope—the belief that one day our people could finally live in peace."

His eyes shine with tears. "Many have fought and died believing in this, Kyven. A dream that we fight for, even knowing that we may never live to see it come to pass. I never thought that world was for us." He gestures toward the castle. "But to know now that the herald of peace, foretold in the prophecies, is here—" He swallows hard. "Warriors would give their very lives to protect her, Kyven."

He is right about my king's guard, but as for the rest of our people, I am still uncertain.

As if reading my mind, he adds, "If you do not want to tell the people, at least tell your guards. They were with us on the Wall. They are good males, and they will keep your secret if you ask them to."

177

"All right," I reply. "Inform the guards. But we will keep this from the general public for now."

He dips his chin.

As I make my way through the hallways of the castle and back to my mate, I pray to the goddess that I have made the right decision.

CHAPTER 30

GRAYCE

When we're finished eating, one of the servants brings us two cups of tea. I lift it to my face, inhaling the lovely fragrance of peppermint before taking a sip, hoping it will calm my nerves over our upcoming ceremony.

"It bodes well for your bonding to be wed under the full moon." Emryll sighs wistfully. "The goddess will bless your union so that your years will be filled with happiness and love."

Love. I turn the word over in my mind. We have only known each other a handful of days, but it feels as if I've known him far longer than this.

Despite my attempts to shield myself, I realize that it is too late. Somehow, Kyven has already broken through the walls I've placed around my heart, and he did it so easily that I did not even realize it had happened until this very moment.

Even so, I cannot help but be nervous about our ceremony. I may be falling for my Fae husband, and I know the mating flight is part of their tradition, but I'm not sure I'm quite ready for that. Instead of voicing my doubts, I listen as she continues explaining the rest of their marriage rituals.

"Before the mating flight, the priestess will instruct you to disrobe," she says, and I spit out my tea.

"What?" I ask incredulously. "In front of everyone?"

"That part of the ceremony is private." She laughs softly. "Only the priestess will remain as witness while you paint the sacred runes on each other."

"Paint the sacred runes?" I swallow hard. "What does that mean?"

"Do not fret." She smiles reassuringly. "I will teach them to you. They are easy to learn. Trust me."

That's not the part I was worried about.

"Aren told me what happened in Corduin," she says, changing the subject. "Your encounter with the Orc is all the warriors have been talking about since they returned. By tomorrow, I suspect the entire capital will know of it. By the end of the week… the entire kingdom."

"Is that a good thing?"

She nods. "Many of our kind still hold prejudice against yours. The story will do much to instill confidence in your rule as our new queen."

Because she is Kyven's sister, I trust her enough to voice my concerns aloud. "Do you think most will accept me?"

She gives me a hesitant look. "It is my hope that our people can see beyond preconceived prejudices, but there will undoubtedly be some who cannot."

I appreciate her honesty.

"It may take time," she says. "But I believe the majority of the people will come to accept you, Grayce."

"It does not help that my father declared war against your

kingdom and blamed your people for my mother's death," I murmur more to myself than to her.

"Even before that, there are several instances of our people trying to invade your kingdom," she offers. "Unfortunately, there have been atrocities committed on both sides, but I believe your bonding will change all of that."

"I hope so."

When we're finished, Emryll leads me through the maze of hallways to my rooms. Several pairs of eyes observe as we pass, some with expressions of wariness and others with open fascination. I am the first human to come to Ryvenar in over one-hundred years. Some of them have never seen my kind, but there are many who have lost someone in the conflict with Florin.

I keep my back straight and my head held high. I will not allow any to see my worry. If I am to earn their respect as their queen, I must be strong and not show any fear.

At the end of a long hallway is a large set of double doors carved with a beautiful depiction of scrolling vines and leaves. Emryll pushes them open, and my breath catches.

The room is massive, with vaulted ceilings and lovely designs of nature scenes carved into the walls. In the center of the room, hanging from thick vines, is a large bed. The comforter is made of a lovely green iridescent fabric that shimmers in the soft light filtering in through the windows, from the balcony. The headboard is adorned with delicate, gold filigree and the pillows are plump and inviting.

A door across the way leads to a cleansing room. It has a similarly designed, carved out pool in the corner, like I bathed in earlier, but this one is much larger. It appears as though it could easily fit four people.

Just like the other one, it is filled with crystal-clear water, a light mist of steam rising from the surface.

"It is spelled to remain warm at all times," Emryll explains.

A small bench nearby has a couple of bottles of soap. They smell divine, like a bouquet of fresh spring flowers. I thought our castle in Florin was grand, but it is nothing compared to the beauty and wonder of this majestic palace built within the trees.

Emryll leads me back into the main bedroom and to the balcony. My breath catches at the view of the enchanting garden below. It is just as it appeared in Kyven's memory that he shared with me.

The flowers are of every color imaginable, and their sweet scent fills the air. There are several winding pathways lined with streams that turn into small waterfalls throughout. Gold and silver pixies flit among the large trees with purple, heart-shaped leaves. A few of them land on the ground, attracted to the tiny white flowers that dot the thick, green moss.

"Kyven loves the garden," she says. "He spends much time there."

"Have you had a chance to tour them yet?" his rich voice sounds behind us.

I turn and he flashes a gorgeous smile that arrests my heart.

Emryll looks between us both, and winks. "Since you have returned, my dear brother, I shall take my leave so you may enjoy the rest of the evening with your mate."

She leaves, shutting the door behind her.

My heart rate quickens as Kyven moves closer. The warmth of his body radiates to mine, and his clean, masculine scent fills my nose. When he turns his piercing violet eyes to mine, all thought leaves my mind, along with the ability to form words.

How is it that he already has this effect on me?

"Come." He holds his arms out to me. "I will give you a tour of the gardens."

I step into the circle of his embrace, and he slides one arm behind my back and the other up under my knees, lifting me easily. He gathers me to his chest and takes off from the balcony, fluttering his wings as he gently lowers us to the gardens below.

He flashes a handsome grin, and my heart skips a beat.

When I agreed to this marriage, I thought it would be built upon respect and mutual goals... perhaps even friendship if we were fortunate. I did not expect this. I'm falling for Kyven, and it worries me.

My new Fae husband is dangerous, and not just because he is powerful, but because in the span of only a handful of days, he has already managed to crack the barrier around my heart. He has slipped past all my carefully placed defenses, and I didn't even realize it until it was already done. When he offers his hand, I slip my palm into his without hesitation.

CHAPTER 31

KYVEN

Carefully, I lower Grayce's feet to the ground, and offer her my arm. My heart swells as she loops hers through mine, resting her hand on my forearm. Her gaze travels over the gardens, her face full of wonder.

Having seen Florin's gardens, I try to view these through her eyes. The vegetation glows with an otherworldly light. The purple, heart-shaped leaves of the trees shimmer like precious gems, and the flowers emit a soft, ethereal glow. Pixies flit back and forth through the trees and bushes, like starlight dancing on the wind.

A small stream winds along the path before disappearing into the dense vegetation. "It's like being in a forest," she whispers in awe.

When we reach the end of the path, her eyes widen as she gazes at the back wall. The tangle of vines and branches scale the entire length of the stone barrier, covered in dozens of white buds.

I reach up and touch the closest branch. Closing my eyes briefly, I concentrate my power and infuse the plants with a bit of my magic. Light travels across the branch, spreading out across the vines and leaves.

Slowly, the buds unfurl into glowing purple roses twice the size of the ones in Florin's palace gardens.

Grayce's mouth drifts open, and she traces her fingers reverently over the soft petals. "Beautiful," she whispers.

Her eyes travel over the garden, wide and full of wonder. "Is all of this magic?"

"It is an exchange of energy."

"What do you mean?"

"As I mentioned before, my people strive to live in balance with nature. We draw power from the world around us. It is the source of our magic. In return, we offer some of our energy as well. It is how we shape our homes and our cities in the trees. We do not seek to conquer the land, but to live in harmony with it."

I gesture to one of the buds. "Would you like to try using your magic?"

Uncertainty flashes behind her eyes, but she nods anyway. Tentatively, she reaches for the bud and cradles it in her hands as though it is made of glass.

Moving closer, I lean in and whisper against the round shell of her delicate ear. "Close your eyes and concentrate."

Her small brow furrows as she closes her eyes. "How?"

"Imagine the flower opening. Picture it in your mind."

A soft glow spreads across her palm, stretching toward the bud. Slowly, it twists open into a full bloom.

A lovely smile crests her lips. "It worked." She turns her gaze to mine, and my heart stutters and stops. She is truly enchanting, and I am completely enthralled.

A row of hanging vines trail down from a nearby balcony, swaying in the breeze like living curtains. She wraps her hand around one, closing her eyes and concentrating.

My mouth drifts open as it unfurls, growing longer. Tiny blue flowers spring up along the length. I'm surprised by how quickly she is learning to use her powers as she moves from one plant to another, wielding her magic and causing plants to grow and bloom.

Grayce moves to another, but her hands tremble slightly, and she pulls it away.

Concern fills me. "What is wrong?"

"I suppose I must be tired," she replies.

It is strange. Most feel invigorated after using their magic, not drained. Then again, she is human, and all of this is new to her. "Would you like to return to our rooms?"

"Not yet."

Grayce lifts her gaze to mine and through our bond I can sense a sort of hesitation, but I do not understand why. "Is something wrong?"

"I wanted to speak with you about our Fae bonding ceremony." Lowering her eyes, she wrings her hands, and suddenly I understand. She is nervous.

My chest tightens. I wonder if perhaps she has changed her mind, and decided she doesn't want to bond with me after all. Swallowing hard, I brace myself and force the words past my lips. "You have concerns."

It is not a question for I can feel the hesitance across our faint connection.

She nods, and my heart begins hammering in my chest. "Have you... changed your mind?"

"No." Her eyes snap up to me. "It's not that."

Relief fills me and I release the breath I had not realized I'd been holding. "What is it then?"

"The painting of the runes." She bites her lower lip as if searching for the right words before finally saying, "I'm nervous about being unclothed with you during the ceremony."

Does she truly believe I would try to take advantage of her? The very thought sickens me, and I want nothing more than to reassure her. I take her hand and meet her gaze evenly. "Grayce, I swear to you that I would never force myself upon you. I—"

"It's not that. I just… dislike the idea of being nude before a stranger." She draws in a deep breath. "In my culture, most humans only undress in the presence of their mate. Not in front of others, Kyven."

Understanding dawns. Humans have a general aversion to nudity, whereas mine do not have such compulsions. "You are speaking of the priestess."

She nods. "You are my husband. Only you should ever see me undressed. No one else."

For all I thought my kind were evolved, something dark and primal uncoils from deep within, reveling in the knowledge that *I* am the only one allowed to view her bare form.

My fangs extend with want to sink deep into her tender flesh, claiming her completely, but I force my instincts back down. "If you do not wish to be nude, we can forgo that part of the ceremony."

It is the most sacred part of the bonding, but I would never force her to do anything that makes her uncomfortable.

"But you followed human wedding traditions." Guilt flits briefly across her expression. "It would be wrong of me to not honor your customs in return."

My heart clenches at the sincerity in her eyes. I cup her cheek. "You are my mate, Grayce. I would never ask you to do anything you did not wish. Your happiness is more important to me than anything."

"What if we compromise?" she asks.

I cock my head to the side. "What do you suggest?"

"What if we wear our undergarments? So we are not completely nude, but we can still draw the runes."

It would work, and it is an excellent idea, but I want her to know for sure that she does not have to do this part of the ceremony at all if she does not wish. "It is a good plan," I offer. "But if you would rather forgo the runes, we can."

"Thank you, Kyven." She squeezes my hand. "It pleases me to know that you care so much about what I think."

"You are my mate." I stare deep into her eyes so she can see the truth in my heart. "Yours is the opinion that matters most."

Her lips curve into a stunning smile. "Then, we will wear our undergarments for the ceremony. I will not be so nervous that way."

"I'd rather you not be uncomfortable at all."

"I think it's normal to be a bit nervous on one's wedding day," she adds. "Don't you think?"

I'm not. I've wanted her from the first moment I saw her.

"A wedding is so important," she continues. "It's the day we start our lives together as one. A day that our children may ask about when they are older." Her cheeks flush, and she looks down at our joined hands. "If we are able to have any, that is," she corrects.

I love that she is already planning our future. That she is contemplating fledglings. I have always wanted to be a father someday, but we are the first human and fae pairing, and it may not be possible.

Knowing that her sister, Inara, is carrying Varys's child, and that her cousin, Freyja, is carrying the Dragon King's fledgling is encouraging. I only pray that we are blessed someday as they are. Even if we are not, I have no regrets taking Grayce as my mate. She is everything to me and I would never wish for another.

"Where is the temple where we will wed?" she asks, interrupting my thoughts. "Is it somewhere here in the castle?"

"No. It is on the mountain, behind the castle." I point in the general direction. Clouds obscure the towering peaks behind us, and because it is dark, I doubt she can make out the narrow bridge that spans the gap. "It is shielded with a barrier similar to the one I used in the gardens of Florin, to hide us from your guards."

"Why?"

"Because it is a sacred place," I explain. "One that must be protected from outsiders. The very first heart tree that was ever created, grows on the temple grounds."

"I've never seen a heart tree. But I've read about them in the Great Library in Florin." She regards me a moment. "It is said that each heart tree contains a spirit that is connected to the gods. That this spirit can grant visions to those who seek its truth. Is this true?"

"It is. And it is tradition that each sovereign connects with the heart tree to receive guidance from the spirit."

A frown creases her brow. "Including an Outsider?"

I take both her hands in mine. "You are my A'lyra. And once you receive my mark, the magic of this place will recognize you as its own, Grayce. So you will be an Outsider no more." A faint smile crests my lips. "Besides, you would not be the first non-Fae to seek knowledge from the tree. The High Elf King came here a few years ago for guidance."

"Did he receive a vision?"

"If he did, the spirit of the heart tree must have told him not to share it."

"Why?"

"It is believed that some visions of the future may be altered if they are spoken aloud."

She studies me a moment. "Have you received any visions?"

JESSICA GRAYSON

I wish so much that I could tell her the truth, but I cannot. The spirit of the heart tree said it would alter my fate.

Before I can conjure a lie, a slight smirk pulls at her mouth. "You did, but you cannot tell anyone. Am I right?"

I nod.

"I understand."

Guilt floods my system. If she only knew, I doubt she would be so understanding.

She yawns, covering her mouth.

"Perhaps we should return to our rooms," I offer.

I love that she does not hesitate to step into the circle of my arms so I may lift her to my chest and carry her, flying us back to the balcony.

I'm surprised when I land and notice her eyes are closed, her head resting against my chest. She is already asleep. She must have been more exhausted than she admitted. Quietly, I walk to the bed and gently lay her down. I carefully slip her shoes off her feet and then tuck her in beneath the blankets.

As much as I wish to join her, I cannot. She fell asleep in my arms at Corduin, but that was different. She asked me to stay with her. Now, she is not awake for me to ask what she prefers, and I will not simply assume that she wishes to share a bed with me just yet. Even if it is only to sleep.

Despite the blankets, Grayce shivers and I move to the hearth and add a few more l'sair crystals for heat. I settle into the chair across the way and lean back. It is not the most comfortable way to sleep, but I would rather remain near her than return to my rooms.

Closing my eyes, I try to relax, but my body remains tense. Something within me is unsettled, but I do not understand why. Sadness and fear wash over me like a giant wave, and I realize it is not coming from me. It is Grayce.

"No," she murmurs, writhing beneath the sheets, in the full throes of a nightmare. "No!"

I rush to her side. "Grayce, wake up," I call gently. "You're having a nightmare."

"No," she whimpers. "Please."

"Grayce." I touch her shoulder, and her eyes snap open full of fear.

She blinks several times as if coming back to herself. "Kyven?"

"You were having a nightmare. I could feel it through our bond." I wrap my arms around her. A low trilling hum vibrates in my chest as my body instinctively responds to her fear by offering comfort. "You are safe."

"I dreamed of my mother." She draws in a shaking breath. "The man who took her life… he was standing over me with a dagger. He—" her voice hitches. "I dreamed he found me, Kyven. That he'd come back to make sure I was dead."

My heart clenches. I can only imagine her fear at being attacked and the horror of watching an assassin take the life of someone I loved.

Anger tightens my chest as I think of the thick, pink scar just below her collarbone. She could have so easily died from this wound and been taken from this world before I ever even met her.

"I think my dream was a warning," she whispers. "Whoever killed my mother wants to take my life as well."

A long tendril of fear unfurls from deep within, and I curl my wings tighter around her.

My father swore he had nothing to do with the assassination of Grayce's mother, but that does not entirely absolve my kind from this heinous crime. There are many who harbor hatred toward humans and the kingdom of Florin. Any of them could have acted on their own.

"Promise me that you will go nowhere without one of the guards," I tell her.

She lifts her head. "You think my father was right."

"It is a possibility that cannot be ignored," I reply grimly.

Fierce protectiveness floods my veins. I slip one arm behind her back and another up under her knees and lift her to my chest.

I love how she automatically wraps her arms around my neck so trustingly before asking, "Where are you taking me?"

"To my chambers," I reply without halting my steps. "You will be safer there."

CHAPTER 32

GRAYCE

Using his magic, Kyven opens the doors. Talyn and another guard snap to attention. He turns to Talyn. "The queen will be staying in my chambers from now on," he informs him. "I want you and another guard to watch over her at all times."

"Yes, my king," Talyn replies.

At the end of the hallway, we enter a large set of double doors. When we step inside, I realize this room is a mirror image of mine.

Kyven walks me to the bed, and heat rises in my cheeks as he gently lays me down beneath the covers.

My heart hammers in my chest. We fell asleep on the sofa together in Corduin, and we are married according to the laws of my people, but I'm not quite sure I'm ready to share his bed.

As if reading my worry, his eyes meet mine. "Just as I swore to you on our wedding night, I vow that I will never expect anything of you that you are not ready to give, Grayce. I only wish to keep you safe."

I trust him. After everything we have been through the past few days, I know he is a man of his word.

"When I felt your fear through the bond, I have never been so afraid." He clenches his jaw. "The instinct to protect you and keep you close is not one I can easily ignore."

He pulls a fur blanket from the sofa and walks over to the chair in the corner. "You can have the bed and I'll sleep here."

While I'm not exactly sure I want to sleep as man and wife just yet, we are married and it's ridiculous to make him sleep in an uncomfortable chair when this bed is large enough for both of us.

I scoot toward the opposite side of the mattress and then pull back the covers. "You can sleep here."

His brows rise. "Are you certain?"

"I trust you."

From the moment we met, Kyven has proven over and over again how much he cares for and respects me. I know he would never cause me any harm or force me to do something I do not want.

A soft knock at the door interrupts us and Kyven goes to answer. It's one of the servants with a bundle of clothing. When he closes the door, he turns back to me. "Magra brought you a sleep gown."

It's only now that I realize I'm still dressed, except for my shoes. I take the gown from him and quickly change in the cleansing room as I ready for bed.

When I step back into the bedroom, my breath catches as Kyven removes his shirt, leaving his torso completely bare.

He is dressed in only a pair of soft-knit pants. With his attention fixed on the bed, I allow my gaze to travel over his muscular body, from his broad shoulders, to his strong arms, and sculpted chest and abdomen. He is perfect. His lavender wings rest at his back, their beautiful panes reflecting in the moonlight that spills through the window.

Nervous heat flushes my entire body as I pad over to the bed. I slip beneath the covers and move to one side to make room so he can lay down next to me.

A moment later, the mattress dips behind me. I turn to face him, but find him lying on his side, facing away. His beautiful lavender wings are draped at his back. I reach out and gently touch his wings. "Are they completely healed now?"

He stills, and I immediately pull away. "I'm sorry," I murmur. "Do they still hurt?"

"No, they do not. I was just... startled, that is all. You did not hurt me." He glances over his shoulder. "You may touch them if you like."

He's wrapped his wings around me before, but I never truly studied them before now. "They are beautiful," I whisper, tracing my fingers lightly along the beautiful panes, marveling at the soft, leathery texture. Their fragile, dragonfly wing appearance belies their true strength.

"I am glad you like them. I was worried you would find them strange."

"Only in that I cannot imagine what it must be like to have them." I sigh wistfully. "It must be wonderful to have such freedom... to be able to fly anywhere you please."

When my hand moves close to the main joint along his back, he inhales sharply. "Not there." He turns to face me. "My wings are very sensitive near the joint."

Worry fills me. "Did I hurt you?"

"No." A dark flush spreads across his face. "I meant... they are sensitive in a different way."

I frown, not quite understanding.

He continues. "The main joint where our wings connect to our back is considered a... pleasurable area. Just like the pointed tips of our ears."

"Oh," I reply, embarrassment flushing my cheeks.

"It must be hard for you," he says, changing the subject. "Living in a place like this when you have a fear of heights, and being unable to fly yourself."

"I'm getting used to it much faster than I anticipated," I reply. "Besides, the way the city is built, it is easy to imagine that we are still on the ground. It's lovely that there are bridges and stairs throughout, but I do dislike the idea of being a burden anytime we travel."

"It is no hardship to carry you." He frowns. "You are my mate. I will gladly carry you wherever we go."

"I know." I offer him a faint smile, because I know he means what he says. Still, I have always taken pride in my independence, and it bothers me to be so reliant on him for travel. "It's just that I'm used to being able to do things myself." I shrug. "But it's not as if I can simply grow a pair of wings. I did try to make myself a pair once, however, when I was a child."

He grins. "What did you use?"

"Branches and sheets." I grin. "Raiden and I were going to sail off the balcony, but my mother thankfully caught us before we did."

He stares in astonishment. "You could have been hurt."

"Edmynd had placed two mattresses on the ground in case it did not work." I smile. "We were well prepared."

"It certainly sounds like it." He laughs. "Your mother must have been a very patient person."

"Most of the time she was." I lower my gaze. "She was a good mother, but... not to Raiden."

"Why not?"

"He is not her son. He was born of father's mistress."

"But she agreed to raise him, did she not?" He frowns. "I thought she chose to do this."

"She felt as though she had no choice." Bitter memories rise to the surface. "Father's mistress died in childbirth. I love my brother, and I always hated that Mother treated him different." Tears sting my eyes. "It was something we argued over many times." I shake my head. "We argued before she died. Not about Raiden but something else. I was young. In truth, I do not even recall what it was now. But I just wish—" My voice catches. "She died trying to protect me, Kyven, and I hate that my last words to her, before she was attacked, were spoken in anger."

I've never told anyone this, and I'm not even sure why I'm telling him now. I only know that something inside me says that I can trust him, and right now, I do not feel like questioning it.

"My father was not an easy male to live with." His gaze drifts to the wall with a faraway look. "We seemed to always be arguing about one thing or another as well. When he first sent me to the Great Wall, I did not want to go."

"Why did he send you then?"

"I was a second son. It was expected. A tradition passed down through the royal line to ensure that the rightful heir would never be challenged by another." He sighs. "Even my sister would have eventually been sent away—probably bound to a High Lord unless she decided to dedicate herself to the goddess."

He continues. "I was angry at my mother for allowing Father to send me away. Accused her of not caring for her second born son—a throwaway spare." He swallows hard. "She cried when I said that, and it was the last thing I told her before I left for the Wall. When I received word that she was dying, I rushed home as fast as I could." Tears gather at the corners of his eyes. "I begged her forgiveness, but she was so ill, I was not sure she even heard me."

My heart clenches as he continues.

"With the last of her strength, she opened her eyes and took my hand. She told me: You are my son. And I love you more than anything you could ever do wrong." He pauses. "They were the last words she said to me."

I take his hand, squeezing it gently.

"Despite this, things with my father somehow grew more tense between us after her death. And when I received news that he and Lyrian were dying, I rushed home again."

"Did you get to speak with him?"

"When I arrived, Lord Torien and the guards bowed low, greeting me as their king." His voice hitches. "I knew then that I had arrived too late." He lowers his gaze. "Father's last words to Emryll were that he loved her, and he asked her to tell me that no matter our differences, I was his son, and he loved me more than anything."

A tear slips down my cheek, but he gently brushes it away with his thumb. "I tell you this not so that you may feel sorry for me, but so you would understand. Your mother died trying to protect you. That kind of love… it is unconditional, Grayce. There was nothing to forgive or to be forgiven because what you had with her was an unbreakable bond between a mother and her daughter." He threads his fingers through mine. "I'm sure she knew how much you loved her." His gaze drops to my collar. "You nearly died trying to save her, Grayce. I am certain she knew."

Tears clog my throat, and I cannot speak. He wraps his arms and wings around me, holding me close. "I am so sorry," he whispers. "I wish I could take away your pain, my A'lyra." He presses a tender kiss to the top of my head. "But know that I will defend you with my life. As long as I draw breath, I will protect you."

His words warm my heart, but I cannot help but ask. "Is it part of the bond? Is that why you feel as you do about me?"

"If you are asking if I would still want you without it, I would." Gently, he brushes my hair back behind my ear. "You are brave, intelligent, kind, determined... stubborn..." A hint of a teasing smile crests his lips, and I playfully bat at his shoulder.

"All the things I would have searched for in a mate," he replies.

"You do not care that I have no wings?" I ask.

Gently, he brushes the back of his fingers across my cheek. "It gives me an excuse to hold you in my arms, my beautiful Grayce."

His violet gaze holds mine, and I am completely lost in their depths. When we wed, I was determined not to surrender my heart. But now it is too late. I am already in love with my husband, and I find that I have no desire to pull away.

I lower my eyes to his mouth, remembering when we kissed. Cautiously, I lean in and gently brush my lips to his.

They are soft and warm against mine. He tightens his wings around me, pulling me close, and I mold my body to his.

He threads his fingers through my hair, cupping the back of my head as he deepens our kiss. His other hand moves down my body, tracing over the curve of my hip, setting my entire body ablaze with his touch.

Someone knocks at the door, interrupting us, and we both pull away.

"One moment," he calls out.

He stands from the bed, and I pull the blankets and furs over myself as he walks to the door. When he opens it, Aren strides past him, stepping into the room. "I informed the priestess that—" He stops abruptly as his eyes meet mine.

His jaw drops but he quickly snaps it shut and bows low. "Forgive me, my queen." His eyes dart briefly to Kyven. "I did not mean to intrude. I simply came to let you know that I personally inspected the wards around the temple and the caverns to ensure you will both be protected and undisturbed for your ceremony tomorrow."

"Thank you, Aren," Kyven replies. "I'd like you and Talyn both to be nearby tomorrow."

"Of course, my king." Aren dips his chin in acknowledgment before he leaves.

Kyven returns to the bed, lying down beside me. Although he is my husband, all of this is still new, and I cannot help the blush that warms my face when he turns and opens his arms in invitation. "May I hold you while we sleep?"

I scoot toward him, and a smile crests my lips as he loops his arm around my waist, pulling me the rest of the way. He folds his wings around me, surrounding me in a makeshift cocoon as I rest my head on his bicep.

"Sleep, Grayce," he whispers, gently tucking my hair behind my ear. "I will wake you if your nightmares return."

His words erode the last of the barriers around my heart. Somehow, this man has managed to find his way into my very soul, and I find that I no longer want to keep him at a distance. Kyven makes me feel safe. More importantly, he cares for me in a way that I never expected.

I'd always worried I would be relegated to a loveless marriage—a sacrifice for my kingdom's safety. But as I lie in Kyven's arms, I know that is not the path the gods have chosen for me. He accepts me—visions and all—without question. Already, I feel closer to him than I've ever been to anyone else.

Part of me is afraid that I am trusting him too easily. But another part insists that because it feels so right, it cannot be wrong. With a soft sigh of contentment, I close my eyes. Nestling further into him, I allow myself to drift away into sleep.

CHAPTER 33

GRAYCE

Standing in front of the ornate mirror, I study my reflection. The small scraps of silk that cover my breasts and pelvis are quite different from the modest attire I'm used to in Florin, but at least I have something to wear.

The Fae ceremony is meant to be done without any clothing, and even though only a priestess is supposed to be present, I cannot deny how uncomfortable I'd feel standing there nude.

Emryll hands me my robe, and I draw it around my shoulders, tying the sash securely around my waist. The material is green and softer than the finest silk and smooth against my skin.

"Do you want your hair up or do you wish to leave it unbound?" Emryll asks.

"How do most Fae wear their hair for their ceremonies?"

"Unbound."

This is my home now, and I wish to honor the ways of my new people. "Then, I will leave it down."

She rests her hands on my shoulders, a smile on her face as she studies my reflection. "You are lovely. My brother will probably lose the ability to speak when he sees you standing before him."

I like the idea of having this sort of effect upon him. I'm certainly speechless every time I see his bare chest.

"Do you remember the words and how to draw the runes?" she asks. "Or would you like to go over them again?"

"I remember," I tell her. And I should. We practiced all morning because I wanted to make sure that I would not forget anything during the ceremony.

"It is time then."

Drawing in a deep breath, I steel myself and follow her to the temple.

* * *

SILVER MOONLIGHT SPILLS in through the temple windows. The entire structure is a living, breathing testament to the ancient power of the Fae. Towering trees, their trunks twisted and gnarled with age, cradle the sacred space with an otherworldly grace. Vines adorned with glowing flowers, a vibrant dance of blues, pinks, and purples, weave their way through the branches above, casting a mesmerizing, ethereal light.

I wait before the altar, heart hammering in my chest, as I gaze up at Kyven. He stands tall and regal, with a crown of twisting silver adorning his white hair. His eyes meet mine, and my knees weaken beneath me.

My pulse quickens with a mix of anticipation and desire clouding my senses. His captivating violet eyes lock onto mine, the intensity of his gaze like a physical touch.

The priestess lifts a wreath of flowers from the altar and gently places it atop my head before putting a wreath of vines on Kyven. She then instructs us to follow her.

The full moon bathes the ground in silver light as she leads us outside the temple and to a circle of glowing l'sair crystals. Kyven takes my hand, leading me into the center before turning back to face me.

This is the moment I will become his true queen, bound to him by blood and magic, forever.

My heart hammers as I unfasten the sash of my robe. Drawing in a deep breath, I lower my gaze as I carefully allow it to slip from my shoulders. It slithers to the ground, pooling at my feet.

I understand the purpose of this ritual, but I am still nervous. The Fae bare themselves to each other as they speak their vows as a symbol of trust.

Kyven's robe drops to the ground. Swallowing against the knot of nerves in my throat, my gaze travels up his body. My heart swells when I note the loincloth tied around his waist.

A smile crests my lips. He did this for me... for my comfort.

My hand trembles as I reach for his, and he takes it gently in his own, his touch sending shivers through me. A faint pulse of magic travels across the tenuous connection, filling me with warmth.

The high priestess steps forward, her voice solemn as she begins the ceremony. I can barely concentrate on her words, my mind too caught up in the maelstrom of emotions churning through me.

She presents a small bowl to Kyven. He dips his finger in the silver paint and then gently touches my forehead.

The paint is cool against my skin as he draws the first rune, speaking words in the ancient Fae tongue of love and devotion eternal before moving down to my chest.

The paint glows on my skin, beneath the moonlight. I inhale sharply as the tip of his finger slides between the valley of my breasts as he draws the next rune. He studies me with reverent focus. My entire body hums in awareness, responding to his touch and the intensity of his gaze.

He kneels and then paints the next rune upon my abdomen. Goosebumps pebble my flesh as he draws the Fae symbols of fidelity and fertility intersecting one another.

When he is finished, his eyes lift to mine, his gaze both possessive and tender as he stands and then hands me the bowl.

A shaky breath escapes my lips as I struggle to calm my nerves. I know how sacred this moment is, and I'm so worried I'll do something wrong.

He lowers himself just enough to bring his forehead nearly level with mine so I can draw the first rune. As I speak the Fae words, magic thrums beneath the surface, responding to the call of the ancient vows.

Kyven straightens, and I draw the next rune on his chest. The silver moonlight accentuates the finely carved muscles of his body. He is masculine perfection and my heart skips as I paint the final rune on the V of his lower abdomen.

When I'm finished, the priestess takes the bowl. Kyven lifts his palms to me, and I do the same, pressing them together.

The priestess recites a prayer to the gods, and I inhale sharply as the glowing runes pulse with warmth that seeps into my skin and flows through my veins.

Kyven's eyes are twin pools of black—only a thin rim of violet around the edges—as they remain locked onto mine. Everything fades away, and we are alone in the world, bound together in this moment as the priestess begins the sacred winding.

With my left palm pressed to his right, she threads the

ribbon between our fingers and then around our wrists, binding us together.

From what I understand, the Elves follow this tradition as well. It is meant to remain in place until morning.

She holds out a chalice, filled with sacred Fae wine. Kyven and I each take a sip and intense warmth flows through me, mixing with the magic of the bond.

With a trembling voice, I repeat the vows that will bind us together, for better or for worse, until the end of time.

"Flesh of my flesh, heart of my heart, bone of my bone. Two souls together, now become one," we repeat solemnly.

"I give you my heart, my soul, and all that I am," Kyven says, his voice full of emotion. "I am yours, now and forever."

"I give you my heart, my soul, and all that I am," I repeat. "I am yours, now and forever."

The priestess bows low and then walks away, leaving us alone in the circle.

Kyven's gaze holds mine, full of fire and possession as he moves closer. It does strange things to me to be so close to him like this. My entire body is tense in anticipation of what comes next.

Gently, he drops his forehead to mine and closes his eyes. He loops his free arm around my back and pulls me close. "Hold on to me," he whispers, and I nod against his chest.

His wings flutter, and he lifts into the air. I wrap my legs around his waist, and he groans, his wings stuttering a moment, as his hardened length presses firmly against my inner thigh.

"Sorry," I whisper, biting my lower lip.

"You will be the death of me, my beautiful Grayce." He breathes into my hair, and I smile.

He flies us to the top of a waterfall, above the temple. Gently, he sets us down in the soft grass beneath the light of the full moon. A yawning cave mouth in the mountain beside us draws my attention.

The cool air embraces us as he leads me inside. Kyven curls his left wing around me, tugging me to his side and warming me with the heat of his body. As we walk further in, the shadows give way to the light and my breath catches in my throat.

The cave is full of bioluminescent plants. They create a lovely glow, bathing the cavern in beautiful shades of blues and greens. Delicate tendrils of ivy climb the walls, their tiny flowers winking like hundreds of tiny stars.

The sound of dripping water echoes through the stillness. Kyven leads me further in and onto a ledge overlooking a vast pool of still water below. It glows with a light blue color, reflecting the gorgeous plants all around us. I gaze over the edge at our reflections. A faint pulse of energy thrums through the air.

I lift my hand as if I could somehow touch it. "Is this magic that I feel?"

"Yes. The mountain is a source of natural power and energy. It is the reason my ancestors chose this place for our capital," he explains.

"Who created this?"

"We do not know," he replies. "And if our ancestors did, that knowledge has been lost to time."

"It's beautiful," I whisper.

"I hoped you would like it," he murmurs. "The mating flight is meant to seal the bond between a couple." Heat rises in my cheeks as he continues. "But I meant it when I said that I would never ask you for anything you do not willingly give. So, I brought you here instead so you could see what it is to fly on your own."

"How?" My brow furrows.

My hand is still bound to his as he steps backward off the

ledge, hovering in the air, while his wings remain still at his back. I stare at him in shock. "How are you doing that?"

"It is part of the magic of this place," he answers.

Gently, he pulls on my hand. Taking a deep breath, my heart hammers as I take the first step into thin air. A smile spreads across my lips as I remain suspended above the water. "This is amazing."

"Fae ceremonies are quite different from humans. But I enjoyed the dancing at our reception in Florin." He bows slightly and then grins. "Would you care to dance, my beautiful mate?"

Happiness blooms in my chest. "Yes."

He flashes a devastatingly handsome smile that melts my heart as he tugs me to him. With a flick of his wrist, he casts a spell and soft music echoes throughout the cavern. As if a string quartet were playing here, just for us.

Kyven curls his free arm around my waist and splays his hand across the small of my back, drawing me closer.

"Are you ready?"

"Yes." Excitement and anticipation thrum through my veins as he leads us in a waltz. Spinning and whirling through the air, my heart swells with the love and trust that anchors me to him. I glance at our reflection in the still water below as it mirrors the beauty of our dance among the glowing flora.

Kyven tightens his arm around me, and I lean into him, reveling in his solid warmth. My pulse races as we glide across the dreamscape of the cavern. He flares his wings out at his back. Their gorgeous panes reflecting and scattering the light in a brilliant display of beautiful color.

"Is this how Fae men used to lure my kind into the forests long ago?" I tease.

"Perhaps." He grins. "Is it working? Are you enthralled? Do you feel compelled to kiss me?"

Something about this moment makes me bold, and I nod.

Desire burns in his eyes as he cups my jaw, tipping my face up to his. "May I kiss you?"

Gently, I nod and lean in. Time slows as my lips brush against his.

"Open for me," he whispers.

I part my lips, and his tongue finds mine, our kiss igniting a fire within me burning brighter than the sun as our mouths mesh repeatedly. A low moan escapes me as he strokes his tongue against my own, gentle and exploring at first before it turns into something more.

Kyven pulls me flush to his body, and the world fades away. I'm consumed by love, lost in the embrace of this man who has claimed my heart and my soul. His free arm tightens around my back, crushing me to his chest as he kisses me like a man possessed, stealing the breath from my lungs.

Desire sparks within me as I kiss him back. Need coils tightly within as passion flares brightly between us.

He pushes me against the wall. The vines and foliage a soft blanket beneath my bare skin as he kisses a heated trail down my body to my breasts. He tugs at the lace of my bra, freeing my left breast. I gasp as he closes his mouth over the already stiff peak, laving his tongue over the sensitive bead.

Desire ripples down my spine, straight to my core. The pleasure is too much and not enough all at once. I thread my fingers through his hair, holding him to me as he turns his attention to my other breast.

His fangs graze over my sensitive flesh, the slight sting only heightening my pleasure. He cups the soft globe of my right breast and then lavishes attention to the peak, driving my desire even higher.

I've never felt anything like this before.

He moves down my body, pausing at the slight dip of my abdomen to trace his tongue over the rune he drew earlier.

Heat pools low in my belly, and I cup the back of his neck, trying to pull his lips back up to mine, but he resists.

He lifts his head to me, and his gaze holds mine as he whispers. "Open for me, my beautiful mate."

Anticipation thrums in my veins as I slowly part my thighs. Carefully, he pulls the silken scrap of fabric down my legs, discarding it. Now that I am completely bare, he traces his fingers up my inner left thigh to my center. "May I taste you?"

Trembling slightly with a combination of both nerves and desire, I nod and part my thighs even more to his gaze.

His eyes turn black with desire as he studies me. "You are perfect," he whispers.

He lowers his head, and I gasp as he slips his tongue through my already slick folds. A sharp cry of pleasure escapes me when he reaches the small bundle of nerves at the apex.

"Kyven." I breathe his name out like a prayer as he concentrates his tongue around the sensitive pearl of flesh. "Don't stop."

A deep growl rumbles in his chest, the vibration moving through me and sending ripples of pleasure straight to my core.

I've touched myself before, but it's never felt this intense.

Desire coils deep within and my entire body tenses in anticipation. As if poised on the edge of a cliff.

"Kyven." My voice quavers as I hover on the edge of everything I've ever known, afraid to lose myself in my pleasure. "I don't know what to do."

He grips my hand even tighter. The ribbon binding us together pulses with magic, glowing as his tongue teases my over sensitive flesh. His violet eyes meet mine as he continues to lap at my folds. "Let go," he whispers. "I have you, Grayce."

CHAPTER 34

KYVEN

Her entire body is flushed a lovely shade of pink. Her half-lidded gaze is locked on to mine, her mouth parted slightly as I continue to tease my tongue through her folds.

I stare deep into her eyes as I gently slip one finger just inside her entrance. She is so tight I worry she will be hurt during our joining unless I prepare her. She moans, and I slip another finger inside.

A low groan rises in my throat. I long more than anything to sink deep into her warm, wet heat. Her entire body trembles as I continue to give her pleasure. Her channel flexing and quivering around my fingers.

She is everything I have ever wanted, and I love the way she responds so beautifully to my touch. My stav is hard and painfully erect with want to join my body to hers. I desire more than anything to claim her and fill her with my essence. To give her my mark and make her mine completely.

Her gaze holds mine, and my heart clenches at the trust and the vulnerability in her eyes.

"Kiss me," she whispers, tugging at my shoulder.

I move back up her body and seal my mouth over hers. She moans as her channel begins to tighten around my fingers.

She reaches between us, and I growl as she unties the string of my loincloth, leaving me bare. She tries to wrap her hand around my length, but her fingers do not quite meet. I grit my teeth as she gently squeezes my stav. The tip begins to weep. I'm so close to erupting in her hand.

A tortured groan escapes me as she glides the tip of my stav through her slick folds. My nostrils flare at our combined scent.

Scent marking is important in my culture, and I grind my teeth as my stav pulses with the want to release. The thick, viscous fluid of my essence mixing with hers is driving me mad. I am desperate to be inside her.

Her entire body goes taut, and she arches into my hand, crying out my name as her channel clamps down around my fingers and she reaches her climax.

"Mine!" I roar as her orgasm triggers my own. My stav pulses strongly as I erupt, covering her abdomen and pelvis with the thick white ropes of my release.

Shaking with the aftermath of intense pleasure, I drop my forehead to hers.

Both of us are panting heavily, and I pull her to me, our joined hands pressed to our chests between us. I seal my mouth over hers in a claiming kiss.

My stav is still fully erect, pressing insistently against her lower abdomen, but the keen edge of my need has been dulled slightly. My fangs are fully extended and my gaze drifts to the elegant line of her neck. I lean in and gently nuzzle her soft skin, desiring more than anything to mark her.

She pulls back just enough to look up at me. "I—" She starts but stops, lowering her gaze as if unsure of something.

"What is it?" I brush the damp hair back from her face and stare deep into her lovely hazel eyes. "Tell me, Grayce."

"I know it is our bonding night, but I—" She swallows hard. "I am nervous about what comes next."

I'm unsure if she is referring to the act of mating or if she speaks of my mark. Either way, I want only to reassure her. "Nothing will happen that you do not wish, Grayce. I vow this to you."

Her eyes shine with such trust it nearly breaks me. "Then can we just touch and kiss for now?"

A smile curves my mouth. How many nights did I dream of touching her like this? I lean in and brush my lips to hers. "Anything you wish, my beautiful Grayce."

CHAPTER 35

GRAYCE

When I wake, we're lying on the ledge, just inside the cavern entrance. The faint light of early dawn filters in, casting brilliant rays of color across the walls. The cool morning air blows gently on the breeze. Completely wrapped up in Kyven's wings, I snuggle into his warmth.

With my head resting on his shoulder and our joined hands on his chest, I lift my head and find him already awake. His violet eyes study mine with a look of intense devotion.

I bite my lower lip. I'm not sure why I'm embarrassed, especially after what happened between us last night, but I cannot help it. And now that it is light, I worry about how we'll get back to the castle without our clothing.

He tightens his arms around me and squeezes my hand. "What is wrong?"

"How will we get back to the castle without someone seeing us?"

"We have the temple and the grounds to ourselves this morning. And there should be fresh robes waiting for us just outside. But first"—he gestures to the ribbon joining our hands—"I must remove this."

Carefully, he loosens the ribbon, freeing us from the binding. I notice that he takes great care to keep the knot intact on the end. He holds it up to me. "It is bad luck for a couple if the knot comes undone. It would mean that their bond is not strong."

I smile. "Then it is good that it remained."

"I agree." He grins.

He walks to the exit and returns with new robes. We slip them on and then he hoists me to his chest as if I were light as a feather. Before I can ask what he is doing, my heart slams in my throat as he spreads his wings wide and flies us back to the castle.

Embarrassment flushes through me as he walks us through the castle hallways and back to his rooms. I glance over his shoulder and see Aren and Talyn several paces behind us.

He takes me straight to the cleansing room and carefully lowers me into the heated water of the bathing pool.

It is pleasantly warm. When we are finished, he carries me out of the water and gently sets me on my feet. Before I can stop myself, my gaze travels over his body, following the rivulets of water as they trail down his skin.

Softly biting my lower lip, my eyes drift down to his stav. Rows of thick rings of ridged tissue line his shaft, and I note the strange bulge at the base.

"My knot," he explains, having followed my gaze.

"What is a knot?"

"Human males do not have these?" he frowns.

I shake my head. "At least… not from what I have heard."

"A male's knot expands during mating," he explains.

"Essentially locking him to his mate for a short period of time after release, enhancing the chances of conception."

I look down, hoping he doesn't notice the flush of my cheeks. "Will it hurt?"

"I have heard that many find it pleasurable. But it is possible to withdraw before it happens." He cups my chin. "If that is what you wish, I will do it… when the time comes," he adds. "And I will also make sure that you have tarin tea."

"Tarin tea?"

"It is an herb that prevents conception."

"We don't even know if it's possible for me to conceive," I tell him.

"Even so. I would give you the choice, Grayce."

His words warm my heart. He truly is considerate of my wants and my needs. Unlike Prince Darnel who once sought my hand. I had not even given him permission to court me, and he was already informing me that I would need to bear him two heirs before our third year together.

"I do want children, if it is possible between us," I tell him. "But… not just yet."

He dips his chin.

"Perhaps next year," I muse. "So that our child can hope-fully grow up with Inara and Varys's, and perhaps even Freyja and King Aurdyn's."

CHAPTER 36

KYVEN

I love that she is planning our future, but it is difficult for me to imagine any child of mine playing with King Aurdyn's. The Dragon King is known for his short temper and the last few times we talked, before I helped his mate in Florin, were rather heatedly charged at best.

We're not even completely dressed for the day when Aren knocks on the door.

I open it just enough to peer out, making sure to shield my mate from his eyes. She is only partially dressed, and my instincts are still on edge. If we had fully mated, I would not be so possessive, but because we did not, it is difficult to tamp down my aggression.

Despite that Aren is my personal guard and as close to me as a brother, he is an unbonded male. The dark and primal part of my nature demanding that I hide my mate from him. "What is it?" I ask, trying but failing to hide the irritation in my tone.

He arches a brow. "Why did you not seal your bond?"

"How did you know?" I narrow my eyes.

"Because you are acting as though you think I mean to storm inside and snatch your mate from you."

A growl rises in my throat, and he rolls his eyes. "See?"

Coming back to myself, I clear my throat. "Forgive me."

"Seal your bond," he gently chastises. "I have a job to do, and I cannot do it if you see *me* as a threat."

He's right, but I cannot do this yet. So, I will simply have to force myself to focus. "Why are you here?"

Inwardly, I curse myself as my words come out much sharper than intended.

He purses his lips. "If you are finding it difficult to control yourself around me, I wonder how you will handle this," he says dryly.

He holds out a small parchment. "What is this?"

"It is from the border," he explains. "But our scouts report they are already nearing the edge of the city."

My eyes widen as I scan the message. "Orcs?"

"You *did* invite them," Aren reminds me. "Or have you forgotten?"

"Of course I have not forgotten," I reply tersely.

I glance over my shoulder at Grayce and sigh heavily. Despite how skillfully she dealt with the Orc scout at Corduin, I do not want her near a dozen of them. But I doubt she will remain in our rooms while I speak with them alone.

"What of the queen?" Aren asks, guessing at my troubled thoughts.

"As much as I hate the idea of her in the same room as Orcs, I also know that I need her if I am to reach any sort of accord with them," I reply resignedly. "She understands them better than I do."

"Better than all of us," Aren points out.

* * *

When we reach the throne room, several members of the High Council have already arrived, waiting to see what will happen. It is not every day that Orcs come to Ryvenar. The last time was well over two-hundred years ago, if I remember my history correctly.

Grayce takes the throne beside mine. Everyone is watching her. No doubt word of what happened at Corduin has already reached their ears. She ignores their curious stares, her gaze impassive as she waits for the Orcs to enter the room.

The doors open and a collective gasp sounds from the crowd as they walk in. Dressed in simple leather loincloths and covered in the inked markings of their Clan, they walk toward us, their very appearance menacing as they approach.

But my mate appears unfazed. The closest one steps forward, and I recognize him immediately as the scout from Corduin. Behind him is another Orc. This one wearing a plain golden band across his forehead for a crown and a deep scowl as his raven-black eyes scan the crowd. He must be King Arokh.

They come to a halt at the base of the raised dais.

"Greetings, Brave One," the Orc scout addresses Grayce in Orcish. He dips his chin to me. "Fae King."

"Greetings, Warrior," Grayce replies in their language.

The Orc wearing the crown steps forward. He thumps his fist to his chest. "I am Arokh." He bows to her. "I have heard much of you, Brave Queen."

"It is an honor to meet you King Arokh," she says, and something akin to regret or sadness flits briefly across his otherwise stern face.

"I am king no more." He lifts his chin. "But leader of Clan Arzul."

She stands from her throne and Aren's hand goes to the hilt of his sword as she starts down the steps toward them. I quickly move beside her, ready to pull her behind me at a moment's notice if any of the Orcs show signs of aggression.

They are unpredictable and prone to violence.

Tension is thick in the air. My every instinct is on high alert as we stand before them. Energy crackles between my fingers as magic courses through my veins like fire. The need to protect my mate overriding all sense of diplomacy in this moment.

Lightning fast, Arokh pulls a hidden dagger from his belt, and I grip Grayce's forearm, pulling her behind me as I bare my fangs.

"Touch her and you die," I growl.

Arokh stills, narrowing his eyes as the others surround him protectively, scanning the crowd and growling deep in their chests.

Swords drawn and pointed at the Orcs, my guards completely encircle them.

"It's all right," Grayce says. She touches my back and then moves to my side.

"Grayce," I murmur, reaching for her. "Get behind me."

"Trust me, Kyven." She looks at the guards. "Lower your swords."

Arokh and the others watch with narrowed eyes as they reluctantly do as she commands.

He draws the blade across his palm and then raises his closed fist, allowing blood to drip to the floor.

"You honor us, Warrior, with the gift of your blood," Grayce says in his language.

Aren frowns in confusion, exchanging a wary glance with me.

Grayce pulls her dagger from her belt and my jaw drops as she does the same, allowing her red blood to drip onto the dark blood left by him.

Arokh's eyes light. "You honor me, Brave Queen, with the gift of your blood."

He waves his hand over the spot and a circle of magic forms around them.

Everyone in the High Council and the audience watch in rapt fascination and disbelief as my mate stands proud and unafraid before the Orcs.

I would be proud of her bravery, but I am too afraid for her life at the moment to think of anything other than that I would much prefer to end them all than to allow them to be so close to her.

But I also know enough that I understand I should trust her. Grayce has dealt with the Orcs before, and she understands their culture and their language in a way that my warriors, advisors, and I never have.

"The Wyldwood is full of monsters," Arokh explains. "Their numbers are growing by the day."

"What do you mean?" I ask. "What sort of monsters?"

His dark eyes sweep to mine. "The kind that should not exist."

"Tell us what you have seen," Grayce encourages.

"The Wraiths are evolving as are the Shadow Assassins. They have always been creatures of shadow and death, but now they can take the form of nightmares. Whatever you fear, they become."

I blink at him, stunned.

He turns to the Orc scout. "Tell them what you saw."

He steps forward, bowing slightly before he begins. "Humans killed my family. A group of males—hunters," he corrects. "I was a child, but the memory remains." He clenches his jaw. "The fear does as well."

Grayce's eyes brighten with tears. "I see your pain," she replies solemnly in Orcish. "May the goddess guide them to the lands beyond all suffering."

The Orc scout dips his chin in acknowledgment before he continues. "The monster I encountered. It took the shape of the man who slaughtered my mother. When I fought it, it turned back into a Wraith."

"How did you defeat it?" she asks.

"They are still susceptible to fire, magic, and blade." He growls. "But you must first free your mind from their illusions meant to disarm you. Any who are unable to resist are drained of their life force," he says grimly. "And some are even drained of their blood."

Arokh steps forward. "Somehow, they are crossing the Great Wall, and they are killing the forest, feeding upon the energy of living things to fuel their dark magic. They must be stopped before they devour everything like they have in the Wastelands beyond the Wall."

"The Wall is intact," I tell him. "If any portion of it had fallen or if the magic was not holding, my warriors at Corduin would know."

"Would they, Fae King?" He arches a brow. "Are you so certain of that?"

"What are you suggesting?" I ask sharply. I'm in no mood for subterfuge or games. "Speak plainly, Orc."

His gaze shifts back to Grayce. "Your people were once allies, but are now enemies of the Order of Mages. And from what we have heard, the Mages are controlling the Wraiths."

He clenches his jaw. "Mages are powerful beings. My people believe it was their dark magic that made the Wraiths, just as they created the Shadow Assassins. But that same power was used to strengthen the Great Wall to contain them. And now the Mages have decided to use the Wraiths as weapons. It would not be hard for them to create a weakness in the very Wall they helped to fortify."

"I believe he's right." Grayce turns to me. "The Wraith attacks along the borders of Anlora, Ithylian, and Florin…

they are not random. The Wraiths in the Wyldwood, near Corduin... what if they are meant to distract us? To divide us. To keep our attention while the Mages amass a bigger army."

Arokh's gaze darts to Grayce before he turns back to me. "When my scout told me you had taken a human as your queen, I knew the time of the Sanishon has come. That the prophecy of the Great Uniters is unfolding even now."

Several people in the crowd gasp at his statement.

"Did you come here for talks of peace or to speak of a prophecy that may be little more than myth?" I challenge.

"How can you not believe?" Arokh gestures to Grayce. "Your mate is the Sanishon queen of the Fae, her sister is Sanishon queen of the Dark Elves, and I've heard rumors the Great Dragon King Aurdyn of the Ice Mountains has taken a human mate as well." His brow furrows deeply. "The Great Uniters will stand against those who seek to control the darkness. Can you not see that the prophecy is speaking of the Mages who control the Wraith?"

Arokh meets my gaze evenly. "I would not be here, standing before you and asking to ally ourselves against a common enemy if not for your queen." He allows his gaze to sweep over the crowd. "Your people have the Ancient Tomes of the Lythyrian in your Great Library. If you doubt my words, why not investigate them yourselves?"

"Why is it so important?" Grayce asks.

"Because if the prophecy is coming to pass that means there will be war before we have peace." He glances over his shoulder at his men. "And I would do whatever it takes to minimize the losses of my people when that war comes. Including allying myself with a former enemy," he says pointedly.

"My people have the magic of earth and of stone. Your powers are of nature and living things. If we had access to inspect the Great Wall, we could find what it is that your people may have missed." His storm gray eyes meet mine. "What say you?"

While I am loath to admit any belief in the prophecy, an alliance is preferable to being enemies. Grayce's gaze drops to the dagger at my belt, and I understand what she is trying to tell me.

I pull the blade free and drag the sharp edge across my palm, just enough to make it bleed. I hold my closed fist over the blood the Orc and Grayce left on the floor between us and allow it to drip in the same spot.

I study him. "We will meet to draw up a treaty and—"

"Orcs do not make alliances with paper." Arokh's eyes drop to the blood on the floor, and his lips twitch slightly in the approximation of a smile. "We make them with blood, Fae King."

He glances back at his men. Each of them thumps their fists to their chests as their gazes fix upon me and Grayce. Arokh steps forward. "From this day forward, we are brothers of blood, and axe, sword, and shield," he says in Orcish.

Grayce and I exchange a glance, and we both nod. Together, we repeat the words in the language of his people.

CHAPTER 37

KYVEN

It is difficult to host the Orcs, even if it is only for a night. They are so loud and boisterous, I'm sure the entire city can hear their revelry here in the palace dining hall.

Arokh slams his goblet of wine on the table and stands with a great roar. His warriors answer in kind, and he gives another rousing speech about destroying the Mages and the Wraiths.

I do not miss the way he keeps eyeing my A'lyra, and it is difficult to push down my agitation. She is mine. Curling my wing possessively around her side, I pull her closer to me.

Arokh walks to our table and claps a meaty hand on Aren's shoulder. Of all my warriors, Aren is the one they respect most. It seems that tales of his bravery from when he served on the Great Wall reached even their ears.

The Orc King turns his attention to Grayce. "I would ask you a question, Brave One, if you will permit."

She dips her chin.

"You have visions, do you not?"

My head jerks back slightly. *How in the seven hells does he know this?*

"I do," she admits.

"Can you tell me anything of my future?"

"It does not work that way," she replies. "I cannot call upon it at will. It comes to me in dreams and even then, they can be difficult to interpret."

"What of the others?" he asks.

"What others?" I frown.

"The other Sanishon," he replies. "Are their visions like yours? Or are they able to seek answers whenever they ask."

"How do you know about us?" Grayce asks the question that I have held back. "Where did you learn of this?"

"I have studied the prophecies." He cocks his head to the side. "They say the Sanishon will possess great powers. That they will be called upon to make a great sacrifice."

"Those powers are not specified," I counter.

"The tomes are written in the archaic form," he explains. "The word used for powers can also be interpreted as visions."

I sit back in my chair, stunned that an Orc of all beings has discovered this. "And what of the sacrifice?" I ask, because that is the part that concerns me most. "Is there another way to interpret that?"

"The translation states they will be called upon to make a great sacrifice, but when you go back to the original text, it says they will make the *ultimate* sacrifice."

"What does that mean?" Grayce asks.

"Many scholars believe it means that because of their visions, the Sanishon will be aware of what is to come. And still… they will choose to sacrifice themselves for the greater good. Which is why the translation of *ultimate sacrifice* is thought to be the correct one."

Fear unfurls and wraps tight around my spine, and it takes everything within me not to lift Grayce into my arms and carry her back to our room, begging her to remain there under heavy guard until the Order of Mages are defeated entirely.

But that could take many years, and I already know she would refuse. Grayce is brave and determined. She would never be content to hide away, even for her own safety.

Arokh shifts his gaze to me. "Now that we are allies, I would ask a favor."

"What is it?"

"A great darkness is coming. Before peace, there will be war. It was foretold in the prophecy. The Order of Mages and their Wraiths will not be easily defeated. I wish to visit the heart tree in your temple. It is my hope that the spirt of the heart tree will give me guidance for what is to come."

The heart tree is sacred, and I am reluctant to allow an Orc anywhere near it. But when Grayce gently squeezes my hand under the table, I understand what she is trying to convey.

Trust.

I have allowed others, including my friend, Varys, and the High Elf King of Cymaril to receive a reading from the spirit of the heart tree. If this alliance with the Orcs is to have any chance of succeeding, it cannot start off with mistrust.

"Done," I reply. Off to the side, I notice Lord Torien's eyes widen in shock as I continue. "The temple is heavily warded." I gesture to one of my guards. "My guards will take you before you leave."

Arokh dips his chin in a subtle acknowledgment and then returns to his warriors.

Lord Torien walks over to me, his gaze disapproving. "May I have a moment of your time, my king?"

I dart a glance at Aren, and he immediately moves to my

side. "Stay with the queen," I whisper, and he nods. I turn to Grayce. "I will return as soon as I can."

"We will speak in the council chambers," I tell Torien over my shoulder.

He follows silently behind me. I'm certain he will voice a protest at my granting the Orcs access to the heart tree. My father always believed him to be a skilled negotiator, especially when dealing with the humans. He is familiar with the inner workings of the council and the royal court. It is the reason I have kept him as my advisor even though his prejudices against other beings that are not Fae are well-known.

When we reach the Council chambers, I turn to face him. "I'll not change my mind about the Orc," I state firmly, trying to head off an argument. Lord Torien can be quite adamant when he believes in something. "Is that what this is about?"

"You would allow that savage brute to speak with the spirit of the heart tree?" he asks incredulously. "It would be sacrilege, my king."

I expected his protest, but his words are even more dramatic than I'd envisioned. I arch a brow. "You raised no objections when the Dark Elf and the High Elf King sought the tree for guidance."

"That was different," he replies. "They were not Orcs."

"And what about humans?" I ask, deciding to test him. His answer will tell me if he'll continue to serve as advisor or not. If he is prejudiced against my mate, I cannot allow him to remain in his position as advisor to the crown. "The queen, as all monarchs who have come before her, will undergo the sacred heart tree ceremony when she receives her crown."

His face pales. "Surely, you do not mean to take her as your true mate."

Wrong answer. "Why would I not?" I ask, forcing my expression to remain impassive despite my anger.

"Because she is human," he says as if it should be obvious. "You married her to secure a treaty. She will be queen in name only, just as was done with your grandmother's sister when she married the Dark Elf King to create our alliance with the kingdom of Ithylian."

I only saw my grandmother's sister a few times before she passed from this world, but I remember, even as a child, thinking of how lonely it must have been for her to be queen, but never true mate to her Dark Elf King husband. He took another Dark Elf female as his mate and mother of his children.

Torien continues. "I have already sent word to the four corners of the kingdom, inviting eligible females to the winter solstice ball for your consideration. So that we may find you a Fae true mate to rule by your side and give you heirs. I—"

"Enough!" I snap, anger burning in my veins. "How dare you dishonor my mate in such a way. You already knew I intended to make her mine in all ways, and *still*"—I growl—"you persist in trying to dissuade me from making her my true mate."

All the color drains from his face. "My—my king?" His voice quavers. "I—I thought that—"

"When I wed Princess Grayce, I did so with the intention of making her my queen and my true mate in all ways. I told you this when you first brought your concerns to me." I seethe. "And yet you act as though we never spoke of it."

His jaw drops but he quickly snaps it shut, brow furrowed deeply. "Because I did not truly believe you would muddy the great line of Fae royalty with human genes."

Curling my hands into fists, a deep growl rises in my throat as I stalk toward him. "Get out of my sight," I grind out.

"But—but, my king, I—"

"You are relieved of your position as advisor to the crown, Lord Torien." I clench my jaw. "Leave now before I strip you of your title. The only thing staying me from taking that as well is the knowledge that your mate and children would be shamed along with you."

He turns on his heels and rushes out the door and into the hallway, knowing better than to try my already thin patience.

Anger roils deep within, and I drag my claws across the table as I struggle to quiet the rage that burns in my chest.

A muffled sound behind me is Aren's warning of his approach. He is able to move silently, but he often makes noise when he wants to alert me to his presence.

"I had no choice." I curl my hands into fists at my sides. Sighing heavily, I look down at the marks I've left on the table. Waving my hand, I conjure magic to repair it. "He does not respect my mate."

"Not that it is for me to judge you, but I do believe that you did the right thing," Aren offers. "But people will talk. Lord Torien has many friends on the council. And I am certain he is not the only one to harbor such prejudices against the new queen. I'm sure there are some already whispering about how you have yet to give her your mark."

Resolve fills me and I turn back to face him. "Let them whisper," I growl low in my throat. "I will not rush Grayce into fully sealing our bond just to quell a few wagging tongues. But I *will* make certain that everyone knows, without doubt, that any show of disrespect toward my queen will not be tolerated."

"Invite the public to witness her crowning," Aren suggests. "The queen is your A'lyra, and a Sanishon. Even the Orc King knows she is special. Lord Torien may have some support among the nobility, but it is the support of the people that matters more. Win them to her side by publicly announcing what she is."

He continues. "Once the people hear she is your fated one, I believe she would be even more protected."

He has argued this before, and I was not sure about it then, but after what just happened with Lord Torien, I see no way around it.

"It will strengthen the position of your joint rule," he adds. "The people will know you have been blessed by the gods."

Yes, I have been blessed, but I also believe that the will of the gods is hardly ever clear. I sought guidance from the heart tree spirit. She is a messenger from the gods, and yet she told me I must keep the secret of who I was from my mate. How can I promise Grayce that she is my equal while I still carry this lie? How can I protect her from harm when I withhold something that could destroy her trust?

On our bonding night, I wanted to claim her, but part of me was also relieved that she wants to wait. As much as I want to seal our bond, it feels wrong to do so without her knowing the truth.

"Once you decide upon a new advisor, they could help you plan the crowning ceremony to include the public instead of just the nobility. They could—"

"You," I cut him off, and his brow furrows in confusion. "You will be my advisor, Aren."

His head jerks back. "But I am not from one of the noble houses. I—I am a commoner. I know little of politics beyond what I've seen as your personal guard, and—"

"If I am to rely upon the people to help protect my mate, would it not be wise to choose an advisor from among them?" I arch a brow. "A hero from the Great Wall?"

Aren lowers his eyes to the floor. "I am a warrior. Not a hero."

"You are an honest and honorable male," I correct. "You would have sacrificed your entire life on the Wall to protect our people. An advisor's job is to consider the needs of the kingdom when serving the crown. I have no doubt you will do this."

"Are you certain?" he asks.

"I am." I clap a hand on his shoulder. "It is good that you are a warrior." I arch a teasing brow. "For you will find that many of the skills needed to assess a battlefield are the same ones you will need to navigate the royal court."

Aren huffs out a laugh before his expression sobers. "The Dark Elf King's personal guard is also his advisor." He bows low. "I ask to be allowed to do the same."

I dip my chin in agreement. "You will remain my personal guard. But as my advisor, your first duty will be to send a raven to Florin, inviting the queen's brothers to attend her crowning. It will be a public affair witnessed by the people, the nobility, and our new allies."

Aren leaves to do as I've asked, and I head back to my chambers. *Our* chambers, I remind myself. A hint of a smile crests my lips as I think of my mate, waiting for me in the room.

Guilt dampens my mood as I remember the secret that lies between us. The one that could destroy Grayce's trust in me. Tomorrow, I will take her to the heart tree.

The official crowning ceremony has always been for show. A tradition done for the sake of tradition. As far back as history remembers, the mate of the king or queen is automatically accepted as joint ruler upon their bonding ceremony.

But Grayce is human, and I know there will be some who doubt her status as my equal. Just as Lord Torien did. Turning her crowning ceremony into a public event where it will be revealed to all that she is my A'lyra, it will not take much for the people to draw a line straight to the prophecy of the Sanishon from there. It will send a message that she is the queen and not simply a figurehead to satisfy the terms of an alliance.

Taking her to the heart tree, as is the right of every ruler, will not only legitimize her standing among our people, it will hopefully provide clarity to guide our paths. I only pray that the heart tree spirit guides me as well.

I have never questioned the will of the gods, but in this I cannot help it. How can it be better to hide the truth from my mate, instead of revealing it to her?

Closing my eyes briefly, I send a silent prayer to the gods, praying that Grayce will forgive me once she learns the truth.

* * *

WHEN I REACH OUR CHAMBERS, Grayce is already in bed. I gaze at her sleeping form. Her silken, chestnut hair is spread out on the pillow beneath her like a lovely halo. Her long, dark lashes fan across her cheeks.

Careful not to wake her, I undress and change into soft knit pants before carefully slipping into the bed. I love how she instinctively moves toward me. I wrap my arm and wing around her, tugging her the rest of the way. She snuggles into me, and my heart is so full it feels as if it will burst.

Grayce is everything to me. I want so much to tell her the truth, but I also dread it in equal measure. She said she wanted only honesty between us, and I have already lied. And although it was a lie of omission, it is still a deception.

As she lies in my arms, guilt threatens to overwhelm me. She trusts me. Completely. And I am so undeserving of it. I want to seal her to me, but I am not worthy of her love and devotion. Not while I harbor this secret.

CHAPTER 38

GRAYCE

When I awakened this morning, I studied my mate as he slept. I've come to the conclusion that I can no longer deny my feelings. I am madly in love.

And now, I find myself blindfolded and my heart completely ensnared as I stand outside, trying to guess what he has planned for me.

A smile crests my lips as Kyven whispers in my ear. "Have you already guessed at your surprise?"

"I have no idea what it could be." I tip my head up as if that will somehow help me see past the blindfold over my eyes, but it does not. I only know that wherever he is taking me, it requires flight. "Care to offer me a hint?"

The wind whips through my hair as his wings flutter furiously behind him. He curls his arms tighter around my form as we glide through the air. To where, I am uncertain. I only know that my fear of heights has been diminishing every day since we left Florin. Perhaps it's because I know for certain that Kyven would never let me fall.

"It is something you wished for."

I frown, trying to think of what I may have told him I wanted, but nothing comes to mind.

Before I can ask anything else, he presses a quick kiss to the tip of my nose. "That is the only hint you will receive, my beautiful mate. If I say anything else, it might give it away."

"Fine." I huff in mock exasperation. "How much farther?"

"We are nearly there."

True to his word, he touches down gently and then carefully lowers me to my feet. His strong hands remain around my waist a moment before he slips his palm into mine. "Are you ready?"

"Can I take this off?" I gesture to the blindfold.

"Not yet."

A crisp breeze wraps around my form as he guides me, carrying the smell of fresh hay, reminding me of the stables back home.

A loud trill sounds nearby, followed by a strange shriek, and I freeze. A frisson of worry ripples down my spine as it starts again, this time echoing back even louder. I press myself closer to Kyven. "What is that?"

He folds his wing around me and kisses my temple. "You are safe, Grayce," he murmurs. "I promise. Now, stand right here."

Kyven's palm slips from mine and I feel a slight tug on the blindfold as he loosens it. "Keep your eyes closed," he whispers in my ear. I do as he says as the fabric falls away. "All right. Now, you can look."

I open my eyes and stare in shock at the nylluan before me. Behind him is the rookery, with several others nested in the carved-out alcoves.

At least twice the size of a horse, it has the head of an owl with a sharp yellow beak and what appear to be horns, but are actually pointed tufts of black fur that stick up on either side of its head. Dark gray and black fur frame its cerulean eyes. The rest of its body is covered in thick white fur with black spots, like a snow cat with a long black and white spotted tail. Massive feathered white wings with black tips are folded at its sides.

Bright blue eyes regard me with piercing intensity, and it is easy to read the intelligence behind them as we study each other.

"This is Greywind." Kyven gestures to him. "He came from Corduin. His rider was a warrior who died in a scouting mission on the other side of the Great Wall."

Sadness clogs my throat. I know from experience that the bond between a horse and its rider can be very strong. I imagine it must be the same with nylluans.

Kyven rests a hand on Greywind's neck. "We offered him the choice to return to the wilds, but he decided to remain."

Before I can ask, Kyven volunteers. "Nylluan are highly intelligent, like Dire Wolves." He takes my hand and guides it to rest lightly on Greywind's neck. "They understand language."

His fur is thick and silky beneath my fingers, and I smile as he leans into my touch with a low, trilling coo. "Hello, Greywind. I'm Grayce."

"Would you like to ride him?" Kyven asks.

"I—" I swallow hard. I have been better about heights, but I'm not sure how I'd feel about flying on a nylluan.

But as I study Greywind, I realize that this is what Kyven meant when he said that my surprise was something I wished for: the ability to fly on my own when we travel. I am queen of the Fae and this is my life now, and I've decided to embrace it entirely. Squaring my shoulders, I turn back to Kyven. "Yes."

A handsome smile curves his mouth. "I will show you how to saddle him."

Another Fae appears off to the side with a saddle in hand. Kyven takes it from him and hands it to me. It's small and light compared to the ones I'm familiar with for horses, and it has two straps instead of one. The first one goes around his neck, just above his shoulders and the other around his waist to secure it firmly in place. The only problem is that he's so tall, it is difficult for me to reach his back.

"Lo." Kyven uses the Fae word for down, and I observe as Greywind lowers himself enough for me to put the saddle on his back and tighten the straps.

"What about a bridle and reins?" I ask.

He slips a bridle over Greywind's beak, and then turns to me. "Nylluans understand language and verbal commands. Bridles are not normally needed," he explains. "But Greywind knows that you are new to this."

Once more, I'm amazed that the nylluan can understand such a thing, but I do not question it.

Kyven continues. "You may also simply tug lightly at his fur to let him know if you'd like to go left or right. Many Fae also choose to ride without the saddle, but I thought it might be best to use one for your first flight so you can see how it feels."

"Good idea." I offer him a warm smile.

"Are you ready to fly?"

My stomach twists in a knot, but I force myself to remain calm as I climb into the saddle. As soon as I'm settled, Greywind stands. Worry slithers down my spine, but I draw in a deep breath and sit up straight.

"Let's fly," I tell Greywind.

He extends his massive wings and then lifts into the air. My stomach drops as the world falls out beneath us, but I close my eyes and take several deep breaths to calm my racing heart.

When I open them again, I find Kyven flying beside us. He flashes a devastatingly handsome smile that warms my heart and eases my worry, for I know he will catch me if ever I were to fall. I glance down. The rookery and the castle grow smaller as we ascend. The wind whips through my hair as we spiral up toward the clouds.

Greywind dips to the right and slips into a strong current, carrying us even higher. A strange mix of anxiety and exhilaration courses through me as we climb toward the sun. Each beat of Greywind's powerful wings seems to resonate in my very bones, as his powerful downstrokes lift us higher into the sky.

My apprehension disappears as I gaze at the scene beneath me. The world below unfurls like a lush tapestry, the city of the Fae sprawling before us. It is enchantingly beautiful, and my breath catches as Greywind makes a long, slow arc out over the city.

Lightly, I tug on the fur on the left side of his neck, and he turns back toward the castle, weaving between the thick trunks and branches of Ryvenar effortlessly.

Several Fae observe, a few of them even bowing midflight as we pass.

Greywind flies over the castle, toward the mountain behind it. He flaps his wings, and my heart slams in my throat as we ascend up the steep side, our shadows racing beneath us. Breaking through the clouds, he rushes toward the peak. My pulse pounds in my veins when we reach the top as my fear of heights threatens to raise its ugly head once more.

I quickly force it back down when I see the kingdom of Anlora beyond the mountain. My heart is full at the beauty of this wondrous land.

"What do you think?" Kyven asks beside me.

Nervous excitement flows through my veins as the thrill of the flight clashes with the still lingering worry that I cannot completely ignore, despite my best efforts to reassure myself that this is safe. "It's beautiful."

"Grayce." Kyven rushes toward me, his hand on his heart. "I can feel your concern." Reading the small spike of worry through our bond, he quickly sits on the saddle behind me. He wraps one arm solidly around my waist and I lean back against him with a heavy sigh of relief. "Thank you."

"You have done well." He gently nuzzles my temple. "Especially considering how afraid you were the first time we flew from Florin."

A smile crests my lips at the memory. "A definite improvement," I agree.

With Kyven at my back, my fear disappears entirely. I cannot deny that I'm disappointed in myself, however. I sigh heavily. "I thought I had nearly conquered my fear of heights."

"Do not judge yourself so harshly," he replies. "It takes more than a few days to gain mastery over a long-held fear. It—"

He stops abruptly and I twist back to find him staring off into the forest.

"What is it?"

A wide smile spreads across his face. "Turn left. There is something you must see."

I gently tug on the reins and Greywind makes a wide arc to the left, flying to the outer edge of the city.

We are just outside Ryvenar. The forest is thick with trees. Greywind hovers a moment before touching down softly onto the ground and Kyven and I dismount.

He takes my hand we tread softly through the lush forest, my heart aflutter with anticipation. The ground is carpeted with moss and leaves, damp from the recent rainfall, the scent of petrichor filling the air. Sunlight filters through the emerald canopy above, casting dappled patterns upon our path.

In the distance, a silvery glint catches my eye. My breath hitches as we edge closer, the steady rhythm of my heartbeat resounding in my ears.

When we step into the clearing, I am struck by the sight before me. A majestic unicorn stands in the sunlight. Its coat is as pure as freshly fallen snow, glistening in the sun's rays, and its mane is like moonlit silk. The spiral horn on its forehead glows with a gentle iridescence, casting a soft aura of magic around it.

My pulse races, but I remain rooted to the spot, afraid to break the spell of this enchanted moment. Standing at my side, Kyven smiles as he watches my reaction.

"What do you think, my A'lyra? Is it what you imagined?"

Tears prick at the corners of my eyes, and I blink them away, too overwhelmed by emotion to speak.

Kyven's lips curve into a gentle smile as he holds me close.

"Thank you." I lean into his embrace, my heart swelling with gratitude for the man who has given me so much love and tenderness.

* * *

WHEN WE RETURN to the rookery, Kyven slips off the saddle and then helps me down as well. I loosen and remove the straps and slide the saddle off Greywind's back. He flexes his wings, and then stretches forward on his front feet like a giant cat before turning his attention back to me.

My heart melts when he gently bumps his forehead against my arm and coos softly. I run my hand along the soft fur of his jaw and down his neck. "Thank you, Greywind. I hope that I can ride you again someday."

"He is yours," Kyven says. "If you wish."

I turn back to Kyven, shocked. "He's mine?"

Before Kyven can answer, Greywind nudges my arm again as if in agreement, his trilling coo growing louder as I run my fingers through his fur. I stare, gaping at Greywind, remembering how Kyven said nylluans understand languages. "You... will accept another rider?" I ask, a bit cautiously because I don't want to assume.

All doubt leaves my mind as he nuzzles my side again.

I use both hands to pet the thick fur along his neck, and his trilling coo grows ever louder. I lean into the silky fur of his shoulder as I continue to pet him. I love the soft cooing and chirruping sounds he makes as I stroke his fur and the way he keeps bumping his head lightly against my arm in affection.

When I'm finished petting Greywind, Kyven turns to me. "We should go. I have another surprise for you this day."

Although I'm reluctant to leave Greywind, I nod.

The nylluan rubs his head against my shoulder one more time before turning to walk back to the rookery.

"Was it a good surprise?" Kyven asks as he takes my hand.

A beaming smile lights my face in return. "Yes."

"Good." He grins. "Because I have one more."

"What is it?"

He holds his arms out, and I step into them without hesitation. Gathering me to his chest, he lifts into the air and gently spirals back down toward the castle.

"You cannot possibly have a better surprise than the one you already gave me today," I gently tease.

Kyven's laughter fills my ears, rich and warm, as the exhilaration of our descent courses through me. "And if I do, will it earn me a kiss?"

His intense gaze holds mine as he waits for my answer. I bite my lower lip as heat flushes through my veins. "Yes." A smile tugs at my mouth. "Will my surprise require a blindfold again?"

"Not this time. We are already here." As we near the ground, he gestures to a bridge spanning from the castle courtyard to another tree. "This is the Great Library of Anlora."

It's a breathtaking sight, a testament to the grandeur of the Fae. Built within the embrace of an ancient tree, the library is unlike any I've seen before. Its massive, pine-like trunk stretches heavenward, its great branches supporting the library's exquisite architecture. Golden light spills from the countless windows, casting a lovely glow on the garden that surrounds it.

I can't help but gaze in wonder at the intricate carvings that adorn the library's exterior, a stunning depiction of the Fae's rich history and lore. The masterful artistry speaks of the dedication and reverence the Fae hold for knowledge, and I am reminded of the countless hours I have spent in similar hallowed halls back in Florin, my fingers brushing the spines of countless tomes, my mind expanding with each new world revealed to me.

As we touch down gently on the ground, I turn to Kyven, my heart swelling with love. He sets me down and takes my hand, his warmth spreading through me, as we walk to the library.

The massive doors stand before us, carved with intricate scenes of Fae history and mythology. With a wave of his hand, they open smoothly, revealing the sanctuary within.

When we step inside, I am immediately enveloped by the familiar and comforting scent of aged parchment and old leather. A quiet hush blankets the space. The library is a cathedral of knowledge, its vaulted ceilings adorned with murals that depict celestial beings and otherworldly land-scapes. Sunlight spills in from the windows, highlighting the countless shelves lined with books and scrolls that seem to stretch into eternity.

"This library contains ancient scrolls and texts that are found nowhere else in the world," Kyven explains. "Their secrets have been passed down through generations, kept and guarded by our people."

I follow Kyven as he guides me down one of the many aisles, my fingers trailing along the spines of the tomes that stand sentinel on the shelves. We pause before a glass-encased scroll, its parchment yellowed with age. Beside it are rows of shelves with dozens of tall, thick candles. Markings are etched into the wax. "Each line represents an hour." Kyven gestures to them. "Pick one and I will show you what it is for."

I grab the closest one, placing it on a holder while Kyven unlocks the case with a whispered word, and carefully, almost reverently, unrolls the ancient text.

"What is this?" I ask.

"A spelled parchment," he replies. "It was created by one of our scholars over five hundred years ago. It is a spell that allows one to read and understand any language as if it were their own."

I stand in awe as my gaze travels over the library. "I can read anything in here," I whisper in amazement.

"Yes." A faint smile curves his lips. "To activate the spell, light the candle and then speak the words. The enchantment will last as long as the candle is lit."

He takes my hand and holds it over the lock on the glass encasement. Closing his eyes, he whispers words in the ancient Fae tongue. A glowing blue ribbon of light wraps around our joined hands and then fades. "Now you can unlock this anytime you wish," he explains. "All you must do is wave your hand over the case and it will open for you."

Soft footsteps echo behind me, and I turn to find a Fae male with orange wings walking toward us. He is dressed in dark robes and his long silver-white hair is tucked behind his pointed ears.

He bows low as he approaches. His yellow eyes studying me a moment before turning to Kyven. "It is good to see you here, your majesties." His voice is low and soft as if trying to maintain the quiet atmosphere in this sacred space.

"This is Scholar Nolyn." Kyven introduces him. "He is in charge of the library."

I dip my chin in greeting. "It is lovely to meet you, Scholar Nolyn."

"It is an honor to meet you, Queen Grayce," he replies. "I understand you are a scholar yourself."

My brow furrows slightly.

"Word reached us before you arrived about what happened in Corduin. Your in-depth knowledge of Orc language and culture." He gestures to several high shelves of books to the left. "That section of the library contains information on the various cultures of our world. But I am afraid it is severely lacking in anything to do with Orc culture. It is my hope that you might aid us in rectifying this situation." His gaze darts briefly to Kyven. "It seems there is more to their people than a robust enthusiasm for drink and for war."

"There is," I agree. "Perhaps I can write to my brother and ask him to lend a few of the books from Florin's library so that your scholars may make copies. We have many tomes on Orc language and customs."

His eyes light up. "Any new knowledge would be most welcomed here."

Kyven turns to me. "There are a few things I must attend to, but I thought you might like to explore while I am gone."

"Yes." I smile. "I'd love to learn more about this place."

He presses a tender kiss to the back of my hand and then leaves. I notice Talyn leaning against a column a few aisles down, his amber wings folded tightly to his back.

Talyn is good at his job. He never hovers, like some of the Florin guards used to, and whenever I look up, I am always able to find him easily.

"You do not mind spending time in here?" I ask.

"I quite enjoy this place," he replies, his amber eyes traveling over the large room. "It is quiet in here. Peaceful," he adds. "Like a sanctuary from the outside world."

"That's part of the reason I used to love the library in Florin," I agree. "It is a good place for reflection." A faint smile curves my mouth. "I am glad you appreciate it, because I anticipate spending much time here."

He dips his chin. "I look forward to it, my queen."

Scholar Nolyn's pride in the collections housed in the library is easily heard as he gives me the tour. The entire structure is massive, consisting of multiple levels. Fortunately for me, there is a spiraling staircase carved into the inner ring of the tree that allows access to each section. Orbs of gold and white fae lights hover throughout the space, illuminating the book spines and scrolls along the shelves.

I'm still carrying my candle with me, so it's easy to read the spine of each book and the labels on the ends of the shelves. It's amazing that such a spell even exists.

By the time we reach the lower levels, it's nearly midday. Nolyn turns to me with an apologetic look. "Forgive me, my queen, but I must go. Part of the enchantment upon the candle can be used to guide you through the library. If you ask it for something specific—a certain book, or a genre or interest—follow the direction of the flame. It will guide you true." He clears his throat. "I regret cutting our tour short, but I need to see to the calming spells."

"Calming spells?"

"Yes. Many of the books in this library are old and they have seen many things. Depending upon whose hands they passed through, some of them are prone to violence."

My jaw drops. "What?"

"In ancient times, it was popular to enchant the pages," he explains. "To make them come alive, so to speak. It made them more engaging to the masses, it seems." He shrugs. "But that practice fell away after the first few hundred years of use because the books became... agitated, for lack of a better word."

"Agitated?"

"Oh, yes," he replies quickly. "Some of them violent even. The other scholars and I spend an hour each day casting a calming spell over levels five through ten."

"That many?" I ask incredulously.

"Yes." He sighs heavily. "As I said, it was a popular practice during the time of our ancestors, and they produced a great many tomes during those centuries."

"What happens if the calming spells are not used?" I ask, curious to know.

"Destruction... mayhem of all sorts." He shakes his head. "It's why we decided to group those books together. They can fight amongst themselves if the calming spells do not take, instead of damaging any of the other books that lack the magic to mount a defense, you see."

I blink several times, my mind attempting to conjure an image of a rabid book, but coming up short.

And now that he mentions this, I realize that we bypassed those levels entirely, and I cannot help but be curious. "May I see one of the spelled books?"

His brows shoot up to his hairline a moment before he regains his composure. His gaze shifts behind me, and I glance back at Talyn. "I—I suppose it would be all right. You do have your guard after all."

"Are these books dangerous?" I ask.

"Oh, some of them are revolutionaries. They grow extremely agitated when they sense royalty or nobility nearby." He gives me a pointed look. "You see, they still believe they are living in the time of King Danvyr and Queen Catheryl," he says as if that explains everything. "Complete and utter tyrants they were." He shakes his head. "Trying times, my queen... a rather dark page in our people's history. Fortunately, King Kyven's ancestors gained control of the throne and things were soon righted."

He tips his head to the side, considering. "However, there is one book I could safely show you. If you are still interested."

"I am," I reply quickly, eager to see a book literally come to life.

"Follow me," he says, and Talyn and I trail behind him.

CHAPTER 39

GRAYCE

As we walk among the stacks, several of the books rattle on the shelves. If Scholar Nolyn had not explained these enchanted books to me, I would have assumed this place was haunted by a ghost inhabiting the library.

He pulls one of the ancient tomes from the shelf and we follow him to a sitting area near the spiral staircase.

Nolyn sets the book on the table and turns back to me. "This is the story of Queen Ilyra's sacrifice to our kingdom."

My ears perk up at the mention of this Queen as I remember the portrait in the castle. She is Kyven and Emryll's famous ancestor, and owner of the necklace at Corduin.

Nolyn continues. "It is one of the few enchanted books that can still be viewed. In fact, every member of the royal family and each warrior chosen to guard the Great Wall is shown this historical account."

"Why?" I ask.

"So they may understand the sacrifices of those who have come before them."

He turns to me. "If at any time you feel discomforted, let me know and I will close the book," he says, and I nod.

Carefully, Nolyn opens the book. The moment he turns to the first page a burst of light and magic pulse out from the tome, creating a glowing clear bubble around us. My jaw drops as it transforms and suddenly we're standing on a balcony overlooking a battlefield below.

"What happened?" I blink several times. I glance back at Talyn, his eyes wide as he looks around us. "Where are we?"

"In the pages of history," Nolyn replies solemnly. "The great battle at Corduin over a thousand years ago." He glances back at us. "Do not worry. What you see can neither touch nor harm you."

I stand at the edge of the balcony of Corduin fortress. The cold wind brushes against my cheeks as I gaze out over the Great Wall to the ruined and bloodied battlefield below. The setting sun casts a fiery glow on the ancient structure, as if aflame with magic.

I shiver slightly, drawing my velvet cloak tighter around my shoulders, my breath forming a mist in the crisp air. I glance back at Talyn and find him staring at the scene in wonder—a look I'm certain is mirrored on my own face.

A gentle voice breaks the silence, narrating the pages of the book. It is strange—as if I can not only hear the words, but feel them as well. *"The Fae queen who once ruled these lands was a woman of immense power and unyielding devotion to her people."*

A Fae woman, dressed in armor, stands at the front of her warriors, gathered along the Wall. Her white hair is twisted in a braid that hangs down her left shoulder, her verdant wings fluttering and her green eyes blazing and intense as she stands beside her mate and King.

"The Wraiths had come," the book continues its narration. *"A dark storm of malice and destruction, their only purpose to tear through our kingdom and leave naught but ashes and despair in their wake. The queen knew that she alone had the power to stop them, but the price would be great."*

A black cloud gathers on the horizon, moving toward the Fae army. As they draw closer, hundreds of red eyes glow in the darkness as the Wraiths fly toward them. Their skeletal bodies covered in tattered, black shrouds and their talon-like claws fully extended as they gnash their fangs.

The battle unfolds before us—the terror in the eyes of the Fae as they fought against the Wraiths, the desperate cries of the wounded, and the relentless advance of the enemy.

A pain-filled cry rips through the air as the queen watches her beloved mate fall—his life force drained by the savage Wraith before her very eyes.

"The queen looked up from her grief, watching in horror as her warriors fell in droves. With her mate dead, she knew what she must do," the voice continues. *"Grasping the powerful gemstone of her necklace in one hand, she dropped to her knees and slammed her other palm to the ground, drawing energy from her life force and from the very essence of the land itself... the roots of trees and the hearts of mountains lending her their strength."*

I watch in stunned silence as power surges through her, a torrent of energy threatening to consume her from within as she struggles to control it. With a battle cry, she releases the pent-up force in a cataclysmic explosion, obliterating the Wraiths and sacrificing her own life in the process.

"She gave her life to protect her people," the voice speaks solemnly. *"The force of her magic was too great, and it claimed her in that final moment. But her sacrifice was not in vain, for the kingdom was saved, and her legacy has lived on through the ages."*

The sun disappears below the horizon, and the cold night settles in around us. As I look out upon the Great Wall once more, tears sting my eyes as Scholar Nolyn closes the book. The magic of the pages slowly bleeds away, and we are standing in the library once more.

I blink several times as if coming back to myself, and notice Talyn doing the same. Nolyn turns to me. "Now you understand the power of these books," he says soberly. He rests his hand reverently atop the tome. "Fortunately, this one has not turned like the others."

"Why do you think that is?" I ask. "Why does this one not need a calming spell like the rest?"

"Because the one who created the spell for this book took great care when weaving it into the pages." His eyes brighten with tears. "The Queen's daughter—and direct ancestor of our king—wanted to make sure that her mother's sacrifice and bravery would never be forgotten. Some stories are meant to be remembered."

When Nolyn leaves to perform the calming spells, I decide to head back to the castle.

My heart is full of sorrow as I walk across the bridge from the library. Talyn follows behind me. His normally happy mood somewhat dampened as well. I understand now what Nolyn meant when he warned of discomfort.

The Fae queen's story resonated deep within me, a reminder of the power, the responsibility, and the sacrifice that comes with carrying the weight of the crown.

I think of the prophecy of the Great Uniters, wondering if there is any truth to be found in the ancient tomes of the Lythyrian. And if there are, I wonder if it would be better to leave them undiscovered as I remember the Orc King's words about the ultimate sacrifice required of the Sanishon.

When I reach the castle, I make my way to the gardens. The roses along the back wall remind me so much of Florin. Sadness steals through me as I trace my fingers over the delicate petals. I miss my family. A tear slips down my cheek as I move my hand over one of the unopened buds and concentrate, filling it with magic so that it spirals open in a beautiful, vibrant bloom.

Strong arms slip around my waist from behind as Kyven pulls me back into the solid warmth of his chest. "Are you all right?" he whispers. "I sensed your sadness through the bond, and I came at once."

"It's nothing," I lie. "I'm fine."

Kyven curls his wings around me and turns me in his arms to face him. His violet eyes search mine in concern as he cups my chin and gently brushes the tear from my cheek. "You are not fine," he murmurs. "Why are you troubled, my beautiful Grayce?"

"Scholar Nolyn showed me the story of Queen Ilyra," I explain. "He warned that it could be discomforting." I swallow against the lump in my throat. "And he was right. I know it's strange, but it made me feel so sad."

"It is meant to be powerful." He drops his forehead gently to mine. "Her daughter made sure the spell on the book was strong. I suspect she wove her own emotions into the enchantment as well."

A tear slips down my cheek. "It made me think of home and my family." I cup his cheek. "It made me think of you, guarding the Wall for all those years before we met. And it makes me afraid."

His brow creases. "What is it that you fear?"

"Losing the war to the Mages and the Wraiths." Emotions lodge in my throat, but I manage to speak around them. "Everyone I love is in danger because of them. The Orc King believes I'm a Sanishon—one of the Great Uniters of the prophecy. If that's true, then I need to learn as much as I can about my powers and—"

"No." Kyven pulls me to his chest. "I will not risk losing you."

"I thought you wanted me to learn how to wield my magic."

"I do, but only so that you can protect yourself. Not so you can fight in a war."

"If the prophecy is real, then we may not have a choice," I tell him.

He places two claw-tipped fingers up under my chin, tipping my face up to his. His violet eyes are ablaze, his expression a strange mixture of panic and devotion as he studies me intensely. "There is always a choice. I love you. I have already lost too many people I love, and I will not lose another. As long as I draw breath, I will protect you, Grayce."

My heart swells. Although he has shown me many times and in several different ways, this is the first time he has spoken the words aloud. "You love me?"

He tightens his arms and wings around me. "More than anything." He lowers his gaze. "And I know we've not known each other long, and I do not expect you to feel the—"

"I love you too," I say quickly, cutting him off.

His eyes snap up to mine. His gaze travels over my face as though I am the most precious thing in the world to him. "Say it again," he whispers.

I touch his cheek. "I love you, Kyven."

A handsome smile lights his face a moment before he crushes his lips to mine in a searing kiss, stealing the breath from my lungs.

Without warning, he breaks from our kiss and hauls me to his chest, lifting into the air and flying to our balcony. As soon as he lands, he rushes us inside, carrying me to the bed.

Kyven lays me down atop the fur blankets and then quickly crawls over me, capturing my mouth and sweeping his tongue inside to curl around mine.

A low moan escapes my throat as he tugs down the neckline of my dress, freeing my breasts. He cups one soft globe in his palm, rolling the sensitive peak between his thumb and forefinger.

He rips his mouth from mine and closes it over the other breast, laving his tongue across my tender flesh and making me cry out with pleasure.

There are too many clothes between us, and I want to feel his bare skin against my own. I unfasten the ties of his tunic, pushing it back from his shoulders to reveal his muscular chest and abdomen.

I trace my fingers over the hard lines of muscle before fumbling with the fastener of his pants. He groans low in his throat as he helps me remove them.

He slices a line down my dress with his claws, careful not to nick my skin, leaving me bare beneath him.

His violet eyes turn raven-black as they travel over me, his fangs extending into sharpened points. Instead of being afraid, it only drives my desire even more, knowing that I have this effect upon him.

"You are perfect," he murmurs. "My beautiful mate. And you are mine."

"If I am yours," I breathe. "Then you are mine in return."

Pleased by my claiming of him, a deep growl of arousal rumbles in his chest and he crushes his lips to my own.

I wrap my fingers around his length, and he groans. "My stav is sensitive," he rasps. "If you keep doing that, I will not be able to hold back."

"Is that a bad thing?" I tease, breathless as he kisses a heated trail down my neck. I reach up with my other hand and trace over the pointed tip of his left ear, remembering how sensitive he said they were.

He growls low in his throat and quickly moves down my body, leaving a trail of kisses down my abdomen. He smooths a hand up my inner thigh and whispers against my skin. "Open for me."

Breathless with anticipation, I do as he asks. His gaze holds mine, full of hunger as he dips his face between my thighs. I cry out in shock and pleasure as he drags his tongue through my slick folds. He concentrates his attentions on the small pearl of flesh at the apex, driving me mad with desire.

I dig my heels into his shoulders, writhing beneath his skillful ministrations. "Kyven," I breathe. "Please."

He slips two fingers inside my channel, reaching a spot deep within that drives my pleasure even higher while he continues to tease his tongue through my folds. It's too much and not enough all at once.

"Let go," he whispers. "I have you."

A low growl rumbles in his throat and the vibration moves straight through my core, igniting a fire in my veins. My release roars through me, and I cry out his name as I fall over the edge into blissful oblivion.

I tug at his shoulders, pulling his lips back to mine. "I want you," I breathe between kisses. Reaching between us, I grip his stav. I want him to feel as good as I do.

"Grayce," he growls low in warning.

A loud knock on the door startles us both. Kyven drops his head to my neck and groans, seemingly just as irritated as I am at the interruption.

He presses a quick kiss to my lips and then stands from the bed. He tugs the blankets and furs over my naked form to cover me before slipping a pair of pants back on himself and going to the door.

He opens it just enough to peek outside. "What is it?" he practically snarls.

"I would not have interrupted if it were not important." I recognize Aren's voice right away. "But there has been a Wraith attack."

"Where?" Kyven asks.

"Along the edge of the city."

"The Queen's brother, Prince Raiden, was injured and so was his friend, Prince Lukas."

Alarm bursts through me. "Where are they?"

"Our guards brought them to the palace. The healers are tending to them now."

CHAPTER 40

GRAYCE

K yven and I quickly wash up and dress, and then he flies me through the corridors to the healing ward. As soon as we reach them, I rush to the nearest bed. Raiden is laid across it, his eyes closed and his face set in a painful grimace as Healer Draymon moves his hands over him.

Lukas is standing beside the healer, growling. "Will he be all right?"

"Yes," Draymon snaps. "This is not my first patient. I *do* know what I am doing, Wolf-Shifter."

"Lukas, what happened?" I ask.

His head snaps up and he pulls me into a crushing embrace. "Grayce, thank the gods," he breathes. "You are safe."

"Safe?" I pull away from him. "What are you talking about? Why did you think I wasn't safe?"

He opens his mouth to speak, but quickly wrinkles his nose. "Oh, gods, you stink."

"What?" I ask sharply.

"You smell like—" His eyes sweep to Kyven behind me. "Are you all right?"

"Of course I am. Why would you think I was not?"

Raiden grips my arm. With a heavy groan, he sits up in the bed.

"Lie down," Draymon commands. "I am not finished."

Ignoring him, Raiden stands. He hisses in pain before leveling a dark glare at Kyven. "We received word that your new *husband* took you to the Great Wall."

"How on earth did you hear of this?"

"That does not matter," Lukas says darkly. "We decided to come at once to check that you were safe."

Lukas stalks toward Kyven, and jabs an accusing finger at his chest. "We entrusted her to you, and you took her to the most dangerous place in the seven kingdoms. What were you thinking?"

Kyven's eyes darken with rage, his fangs and claws fully extended. "We had no choice," he grinds out.

"We took a detour because—" I start, but Raiden cuts me off.

"That's my sister, Fae King! And if you think I'm going to leave her with you when you take such little care with her safety, you—"

"Enough!" I place myself between them. "This is ridiculous," I chastise, eyeing my brother and Lukas. "You could have just sent a raven like a normal person if you wanted to check on me. You didn't have to come all this way just to—"

"How could I trust a raven?" Raiden asks. "*He*"—he points at Kyven—"could have sent any message he wanted to make us think everything is fine."

"It *is* fine," I counter. "We're happy, and I love him."

Raiden's head jerks back. "You *what?*"

Lukas pulls a small pouch from his tunic and before I can

ask what he's doing, he opens it and flings a puff of glittering blue dust in my face.

Kyven pulls me behind him. A deep rumbling growl fills the air as he bares his fangs at my friend.

Blinking, I sneeze several times. "What in the seven hells was that, Lukas?"

His eyes remain locked on Kyven's as he grits through his teeth. "An enchantment breaker."

"You really think I would cast a spell on my mate to make her love me?"

"I don't know." Lukas cranes his neck to look at me. "Do you still love him?"

Kyven snarls.

"Yes," I reply, completely exasperated. Crossing my arms over my chest, I glare at him. "Do you believe me now?"

He exchanges a look with Raiden, and they both nod. Lukas turns back to me. "Yes."

Draymon places a firm hand on Raiden's shoulder and pushes him back to sit on the edge of the bed. "I need to finish tending your wounds."

"Fine," Raiden grumbles. "Go ahead."

"What happened?" I ask. "Does Edmynd know you're here?"

Raiden and Lukas exchange another glance, guilt easily read in their features.

"Of course not," I huff. "Only the two of you would come up with this crazy plan to throw magic dust in my face to see if I've been enchanted."

"It's not *magic* dust," Lukas points out. "It's *anti*-magic dust."

I roll my eyes. "You know what I mean."

"We're sorry, Grayce." Raiden gives me a guilty look. "We just wanted to make sure you were all right."

My anger instantly dissipates. I cannot stay mad at them when they were only doing this out of concern.

"What happened?" Kyven asks. "My guards said you were attacked by Wraiths."

"There were at least a dozen of them," Lukas explains. "They ambushed us when we reached the border of the city. We killed most of them, but a few got away." His gaze shifts to one of the guards. "Your warriors helped and then brought us here to be treated."

"Take two dozen warriors. Search the woods outside the city," Kyven instructs one of his guards. "Find the Wraiths and kill them."

The guard crosses his arm over his chest. "Yes, my king." He quickly leaves the room.

Kyven turns back to Raiden. "Have there been any more Wraith attacks near Florin?"

"No."

"What of Valren?" Kyven asks Lukas about his kingdom.

"None." Lukas tips up his chin and puffs out his chest. "They know better than to attack wolves."

Kyven purses his lips and then turns his attention back to Raiden. He arches a brow. "I assume you did not receive your invitation by raven then to come for your sister's coronation?"

Raiden shakes his head.

"You did not ask me about my invitation," Lukas crosses his arms over his chest. "Or am I to assume my raven was lost trying to deliver it?"

Kyven narrows his eyes. "I sent you a raven too, Wolf-Shifter."

His response catches Lukas off guard. "Really?"

"Yes," Kyven states firmly. "My mate considers you like a brother to her. Of course we would send you an invitation."

He walks up to Kyven, claps a hand on his shoulder and

grins. "Maybe you're not as bad as I thought you were, Fae King."

"I'm glad you finally recognized this," Kyven replies, a hint of sarcasm lacing his tone.

"Kyven, what happened?" Emryll's voice rings out from the hallway before she rushes into the room.

She stops short when she sees Lukas and Raiden, her eyes widening as they land on my brother.

Raiden's mouth gapes as his gaze locks onto hers.

"Raiden, this is Emryll—Kyven's younger sister." I gesture to her. "Emryll, this is my older brother, Raiden."

He bows low before her. "It is an honor to meet you, Princess Emryll."

She smiles. A blush spreads across her cheeks. "And you as well, Prince Raiden."

Lukas stops short of rolling his eyes, and then elbows Raiden, pulling him out of his lovesick daze.

A hint of a snarl curls Kyven's lips. He's just as protective of Emryll as Raiden is with me. It seems he noticed the way they are looking at each other too.

Her gaze drifts down to Raiden's torn and bloodied shirt. "You are hurt." Concern is easily read in her features. "What happened?"

"I'm fine," Lukas teases, gesturing to his own bloodied shirt. "No need to worry about me."

A hint of a smile tugs at Emryll's mouth. "Of course you are, Wolf-Shifter. I was not concerned because I know your kind heal quickly. But he"—she points at Raiden—"is human, and they do not."

Raiden straightens his back and flexes one very muscular bicep, trying but failing to appear casual as he does it. "I'm all right." He smooths his dark blond hair back from his brow. "I've had worse."

Now, I'm the one trying not to roll my eyes.

"You have?" Emryll asks, her wings fluttering slightly behind her.

"I'm not easy to kill," he teases.

She laughs—a bright sparkling sound of happiness.

Raiden smiles at her as if she hung the moon and the stars. I've never seen him look at anyone that way before, but I do know what it means. My brother is completely and utterly smitten. And from the look on Emryll's face as she stares at my brother, I believe the feeling is mutual.

Emryll turns to Kyven. "I'll ask the servants to prepare chambers for them in the family wing." She looks back at Raiden. "Are you hungry?"

"I am." A mischievous smile curves Lukas's mouth. "If anyone cares, that is."

Raiden elbows his side, and Lukas laughs. "I was only joking."

"Come," Emryll tells them. "I will take you both to your chambers to change and dress, and then we will go to the dining hall for a meal." She looks back at me and Kyven. "You two should go back to your rest and we'll all have breakfast in the morning."

I hug Lukas and Raiden before they leave with Emryll.

Kyven's gaze tracks his sister with a look of concern before they disappear around a corner and down the hallway.

"It's all right. My brother is a good man, Kyven."

"Yes, but will he be careful with her heart?" he asks.

A smile crests my lips. "I think he is the one more in danger of having his broken."

Kyven arches a brow. "Why do you say that?"

"Because everyone knows the Fae are skilled in placing poor, unsuspecting humans under their thrall," I tease. "There are many stories about it, you know."

Kyven laughs and then gathers me to his chest. He drops

his forehead gently to mine, his expression sobering. "I apologize for the way I reacted to them at first. I just—" He clears his throat. "My kind are very possessive of their mates. And while I know that you only consider Lukas like a sibling to you, it is difficult to suppress my instincts because he is an unbonded male and—"

"I understand," I tell him. "It's all right. You two actually seemed to be getting along there toward the end."

"He cares for you," Kyven says. "I cannot fault him for that."

As we make our way back to our rooms, Kyven is unusually quiet. "What is wrong?" I ask.

"The Wraiths along the city's borders... it is concerning that they made it this close to Ryvenar without anyone knowing." He sighs. "We will need to check all the wards and double the number of guards on patrol."

He turns back to Aren, who is walking silently behind us. Aren nods. "Consider it done," he says, before relaying the order to another guard beside him while Talyn takes up his post outside our chamber doors.

When we step inside our room, I turn to Kyven. I know that what I have to say will probably upset him, but it needs to be done.

"I'm going to start studying the prophecy." He opens his mouth to protest, but I quickly add, "If what the Orc says is true, isn't it better to be prepared for what may come?"

"Not if it means you must place yourself in danger. I will not allow you to—"

"I am your equal," I remind him. "You swore this to me before we wed."

"I did." He hangs his head. "Forgive me. I just... cannot stand the thought of any harm coming to you."

"I know." I wrap my arms around his waist, and he curls his wings around us both. "But if there is anything in the prophecy that will help us to defeat the Mages and the Wraith, I think we should learn what it is, Kyven."

Reluctantly, he nods. "We will speak with Nolyn tomorrow. The ancient tomes of the Lythyrian are guarded by several wards. He will need to remove them to give you access. But first, I will take you to the heart tree." He cups my cheek. "It is tradition for a new monarch to seek guidance from the spirit of the tree before their crowning."

"You were crowned not very long ago. What sort of guidance did the heart tree give you then?" I ask, curious to know. "Did it mention anything about us?"

A dozen emotions flicker across his expression before he lowers his gaze. "I cannot speak of it, or else I risk altering my fate."

"It's all right," I reassure him, gently squeezing his hand. "Whatever it was, I understand that you cannot tell me."

He lifts his gaze back to mine. "I need you to remember this moment, Grayce."

Worry tightens my chest at his ominous words. I want so much to ask what he means, but I know that he cannot answer.

When we lie down in bed, Kyven holds me close. And although his wings and his arms are wrapped solidly around me, he has never felt further away.

CHAPTER 41

KYVEN

I listen as Grayce's breaths become soft and even as she drifts off to sleep. She lies so trustingly in my embrace that it threatens to break me. I do not deserve her trust or her love. I am anxious to speak to the heart tree myself tomorrow.

I cannot keep this secret from her any longer. She has asked for honesty between us, and she deserves nothing less than the truth.

Closing my eyes, I send a silent prayer to the gods to guide me. To show me what to do. The spirit of the heart tree told me not to reveal my secret to Grayce, but I cannot continue to lie to her, to hide the truth of what I did.

When I was secretly courting her as Joren, I had plenty of opportunities to tell her that I was not human—to admit to who I was, but I did not. Now, I fear that if she discovers what I did, she will never forgive me for lying to her.

I curl my wings tightly around her form as dread twists

deep in my gut. For better or worse, I cannot keep this secret any longer. The spirit of the heart tree told me that to admit my deception would alter my fate. Worried, I did as she instructed and remained silent. Before now, I have always trusted the will of the gods, but now I am finding it hard to do.

I only pray that Grayce will forgive me when she learns the terrible truth.

* * *

I BLINK my eyes open and find it is still night. Moonlight spills through the window, casting a silver glow across the chamber. Still half asleep, I struggle to focus through the fog of exhaustion as I lift my head.

Alarm bursts through me, and I whip my head around the chamber, searching for any signs of danger. Worry grips my chest in an iron vise, seizing my lungs. It takes me a moment to realize that this emotion is not coming from me. It is flowing across the bond from Grayce.

She is still wrapped up in my arms, but her brow is creased in fear. Her breath comes in shallow gasps, and she begins thrashing against my hold, lost in the throes of a nightmare.

"Grayce, wake up," I murmur, shaking her gently, trying to rouse her from this torment. But she does not wake, her body only growing more rigid, her whimpers more pronounced.

Desperate to help her, I close my eyes and place my fingers on her temple. Our connection flares to life, and my mind pours into hers like liquid pouring into a glass as I dive into her dream, determined to save her from whatever haunts her.

Grayce stands in a dimly lit room, her mother's lifeless body lying across the floor behind her. Her face is streaked with tears, terror and determination etched into her features. Blood trails down her front from the blade lodged just beneath her collar. The assassin towers over her, a dark figure with a mask obscuring his face, a cruel smile playing on his lips.

He lunges toward her, readying to end her life, but Grayce rips the dagger free of her chest with a primal scream and slashes it across his left cheek.

The assassin stumbles back, covering his face with one hand as black blood oozes from the wound.

My gaze is drawn to a sudden flash of movement at his back—the unmistakable glint of a wing.

My heart clenches with realization: her mother's assassin was a Fae.

"Grayce!" I cry out, and she spins toward me. I reach for her hand, our bond pulsing with urgency, ripping her from the nightmare and pulling her back to the waking world.

She awakens with a start, her breaths ragged and her eyes wide with terror. I gather her close, pressing her trembling form against my chest. "You're safe, my A'lyra," I whisper into her hair. "I'm here. I won't let anything happen to you."

She clings to me, her fingers digging into my skin. "His back." Her voice quavers. "Kyven, he had wings. I never noticed them before."

"I saw them too," I whisper.

"He's Fae, Kyven. And he is coming for me." A broken sob escapes her. "I can feel it."

"I will not let him touch you," I vow. "I will protect you."

"How?" she asks. "We do not even know who he is."

"You scarred his face with an iron blade," I tell her. "We will find him, Grayce."

We remain entwined in the moonlit silence, as I send a wave of love and comfort across our bond. I smooth a hand across her back and shoulders, listening as her heartbeat begins to slow and her breaths even out.

"I love you, Grayce, and we will face whatever darkness awaits us together," I whisper. "My vow."

CHAPTER 42

KYVEN

The echoes of Grayce's remembered fear pulses through our bond as we sit across the table from her brother and Lukas. I reach for her hand under the table and squeeze it gently.

She offers me a faint smile, and I press a tender kiss to her temple.

When I turn back to our company, I notice Lukas's eyes practically boring into me. "What?" I snap. "Is it wrong to kiss one's mate?"

"No," he replies. "I'm still getting used to the idea that you're not the villain I thought you were." He leans forward in his seat, arching a teasing brow. "And I'm thinking we might end up being friends. Which is strange, because I never thought that would happen."

Grayce laughs.

I'd heard Wolf-Shifters were rather blunt, but I also find his honesty refreshing. Unlike my kind, his people do not hide behind words.

"Neither did I," I admit.

"Who knows." He flashes a wolfish grin. "You might even grow to like me so much you'll name me godfather to your first child."

I narrow my eyes. "I highly doubt that."

As we continue our breakfast, I notice my sister smiling and laughing with Raiden. It is difficult to suppress a snarl as he smiles at her in return.

I know he is an honorable male, but Emryll is my sister, and it is hard to not be protective of her. She is the last of my family, and I want her only to be happy. I also cannot bear the thought of her moving away. If she were to bond to Raiden, I doubt he would wish to remain here among our people.

When we're finished with our food, Grayce turns to Lukas and Raiden. "I had a dream last night."

"What was it about?" Raiden asks. "Was it a vision?"

"I believe it was both a vision and a memory."

"What do you mean?" Lukas asks.

"I dreamed of my mother's death. And in my nightmare, I noticed something I had not before." Her gaze darts to mine, and I nod before she continues. "He had wings." Raiden's shock is evident on his face as she continues. "Father was right. He was Fae."

A low growl rises in Lukas's throat as he turns a dark glare to me. "Do you know anything about this?"

"Of course not," I vehemently deny.

"What about your father?" Raiden presses. "Would he have ordered it?"

"Do not *dare* disparage my father's name," I grind out. "He was an honorable male, and he would never have ordered the death of Florin's queen."

"Then who would have done this?" Lukas asks. "And why?"

"I do not know, but I will not stop searching until I discover who was behind the assassination and the attempt on Grayce's life." I curl my hands into fists at my side as the memory of him standing over my mate in her nightmare resurfaces. "And I will end him."

"He has been hidden all this time," Raiden says. "How do you intend to find him?"

"I scarred his face," Grayce points out. "Surely, such a mark is not common."

"It is easily hidden though," Lukas says darkly. "Use of a glamour or a shade stone could conceal such an injury."

I flinch inwardly at the mention of a shade stone. It is how I disguised myself to appear human. Although they are rare, it would not be impossible for someone to procure one. I should know. I had to deal with rather unsavory characters, but I was able to obtain one rather easily.

Anything can be had for the right price.

"There is more," Grayce murmurs.

"What is it?" Raiden asks, concerned.

She tells him about the Orcs and their claims about the Wraiths and the shadow assassins. When she brings up the Orc King and the prophecy, Raiden clenches his jaw. "It is a myth." His gaze sweeps to me. "And if you truly care about my sister, you will do everything in your power to quell this superstitious nonsense."

"Why?" Grayce asks.

"Because it is dangerous for you," he snaps. "High Mage Ylari says the Mages believe in this prophecy. And they are doing everything they can to prevent it from coming to pass."

Ylari turned on his own Order to protect the kingdom of Florin. I do not believe he would lie about this.

Raiden continues. "If the Mages truly believe in the prophecy of the Great Uniters, and they think *you* are one of the Sanishon foretold, how long do you think it will be before they send someone to try to kill you?"

"But if I truly am part of the prophecy, that means I can help stop the Mages and the Wraiths," Grayce counters. "I could help keep everyone safe."

"But at what cost, Grayce?" Raiden asks pointedly. "Your life? Because that is what it might come down to."

Raiden turns to me, his brown eyes full of anger. "What about you? Do you believe in any of this?"

While I wish I could deny it, I cannot. "There are too many things that point to it being true for us to ignore the possibility that Grayce, her sister Inara, and her cousin Freyja are the Great Uniters foretold by the ancient tomes of the Lythyrian."

Raiden opens his mouth to protest, but I cut him off.

"Each of them are Outsiders—the first to marry into the Dark Elves, the Dragons, and the Fae. And they all have inherited powers through the bonds with their mates. It cannot simply be coincidence that these events are happening now."

Raiden turns to Grayce. "What powers?"

Grayce reaches for the vase in the center of the table. It is full of flowers, but she touches her finger to one of the unopened buds.

Raiden and Lukas's jaws drop as they watch her use magic to make it unfurl, blossoming into a mature bloom before their eyes.

"We were attacked by Griffins on the way here," I tell them. "Grayce used magic to help save us. It was the first time her powers manifested, and I realized she had inherited them from me. Just as Inara gained hers through her bond with Varys, and Freyja from her bond with Aurdyn."

Emryll reaches across the table and takes Grayce's hand, her eyes full of worry. "We need to train every day to strengthen your powers. Make sure that you are able to defend yourself if you are in trouble."

"No," Raiden says. "You need to stay hidden. You must discourage the rumors of the prophecy at all costs."

Grayce meets his gaze evenly. "I'm going to study the prophecy. See if there is anything I can learn to help in the fight against the Mages and their Wraiths."

"This is madness," Raiden counters. He looks at me. "Surely you can see this as well."

Aren steps forward. "There are many who believe in the prophecy. The queen is a symbol of hope. The people should be told what she is."

Raiden's eyes snap to his, understanding dawning on his features. "The crowning ceremony…" He turns to me. "You mean to announce it to everyone."

I cannot deny the truth. "Yes."

"You would knowingly put my sister in danger?" He narrows his eyes. "All for some belief in some ancient prophecy?"

"This is my decision too," Grayce interjects.

"This is madness," he grinds out, his gaze locked on hers. "Do you want to die? Like your mother?"

Grayce inhales sharply, and Raiden's expression morphs from anger to regret in an instant, realizing he has gone too far. "Grayce, I'm sorry. Please, forgive me. I—"

"I know you love me and that you're afraid for me, Raiden." Her bottom lip quivers slightly as frustration burns in her eyes. "Do you think I'm not worried? That I am not afraid too? You cannot protect me from the world. This is my decision, and if there is any way I can help in the fight against the Mages and Wraiths, I must see it through."

Raiden stands and walks around the table to her. He pulls her into his arms and hugs her fiercely. "I'm sorry. I'm just worried for you, Grayce. I love you, and I cannot bear to think of you being hurt or worse."

"I know."

I'm not entirely surprised when Lukas rounds the table and embraces them both. "We will figure this out." He turns to me. "In the meantime, I believe we should meet with the Orcs as well. See about combining our efforts to discover how the Wraiths are crossing the Wall. Because the more of them on this side, the greater a weapon they are for the Mages."

"I'll send a raven to Edmynd, informing him that we are traveling to the Great Wall to meet with the Orc King." Raiden turns to me. "We should leave as soon as possible."

"The crowning ceremony can be held later today." I exchange a glance with Grayce, and she nods. "But first, I must take Grayce to the heart tree. It is tradition before a monarch takes the crown."

Raiden and Lukas each nod in agreement.

CHAPTER 43

GRAYCE

The sun scatters golden light across the temple grounds, its warmth caressing my skin as I step through the towering archway. The scent of wildflowers and ancient magic fills the air, a heady combination that leaves me feeling both awed and humbled.

When Kyven and I were wed here in our Fae ceremony, we were in a different part of the gardens that surround the temple. I had no idea how sprawling the grounds are here.

As we approach the heart tree, my breath catches in my throat. Its tear-shaped white leaves shimmer in the sunlight, their ethereal beauty almost too much to behold. They fall gracefully, floating on the breeze, but never leaving the tree bare–new leaves sprout instantly, a testament to the ancient Fae magic that created this wonder.

A mix of emotions swirl within me as I stand before the sacred tree. Awe courses through my veins, but so too does a tremor of nervousness. The spirit that resides in each one is believed to be a messenger from the gods.

I have come for guidance, and I cannot help but worry about what I may learn. I have had enough experience with my visions to know that knowledge of the future can be either a curse or a blessing, depending upon what is revealed.

Gathering my courage, I step closer, feeling the magic thrumming in the air around me. The delicate white leaves dance in the wind, some brushing against my skin as if whispering secrets from another world.

"What do I do?" I ask Kyven.

His expression is one I cannot discern, somewhere between concern and sadness. It worries me. "You must place your hand on the tree, and it will connect you with the spirit that resides within."

Nervous, I reach out a tentative hand and rest it on the bark. It is surprisingly cool and smooth beneath my fingertips. Closing my eyes, I take a deep breath to clear my mind, letting my worries and fears fall away, focusing only on the question that has brought me here.

With a whispered plea, I ask the spirit of the tree for guidance, for wisdom to navigate the challenges that lie ahead.

A sense of calm washes over me. Whatever the spirit of the heart tree may tell me, I will face it with the strength and courage that has brought me this far.

The moment my fingers graze the heart tree, the world around me shifts. The temple vanishes, replaced by an expansive field bathed in an ethereal, golden light. I'm standing amid a swaying field of grass, the air suffused with a sense of otherworldly serenity.

A glowing figure approaches me, her movements fluid and graceful. "I am the spirit of the heart tree," she says, her voice a melody that resonates in the very soul of my being.

Her face is obscured in the light emanating from her form, but her eyes are a vivid shade of amber.

I'm desperate for guidance, seeking clarity and hope.

The spirit gazes at me with ancient, knowing eyes before she speaks. "You are one of the Sanishon of the prophecy of the Great Uniters. But you already knew this in your heart."

I nod.

"You will be betrayed by someone you hold dear." Her words are heavy with sorrow and my breath. "But trust your heart to guide you through your pain and remember the promises you made."

My heart constricts with fear. "What does that mean? Who will betray me?"

The spirit does not answer my questions. Instead, she speaks solemnly. "If you knew the truth, your future would have been altered, and the world would have fallen into darkness. Only a heart forged in the fires of adversity can be strong enough to withstand what is to come."

Her words send a shiver down my spine. Before I can voice any further questions, she gestures, and the vision shifts. The Great Wall crumbles before me, and Wraiths surge through the breach, their dark forms spilling in the kingdom of Anlora like a giant wave of darkness sweeping over the land.

Desperation claws at my throat. "How can I prevent this?"

"This future has already been written," she replies ominously. "It will be up to you to decide what to do and what to sacrifice."

As the weight of her words sinks in, the vision fades, the golden light receding until I find myself once more standing beside the heart tree. Disoriented and reeling from the revelations, I stagger back, my vision swimming.

Strong arms encircle me, steadying me as I struggle to regain my equilibrium. I look up to see Kyven's concerned face. His presence anchors me, reminding me that whatever trials and betrayals lie ahead, we will face them together. And with the heart tree's guidance echoing in my soul, I am determined to find the strength to protect him and our world, no matter the cost.

CHAPTER 44

KYVEN

As I hold Grayce close, her warmth pressed against my chest, my thoughts drift back to my own encounter with the heart tree. The memory of the spirit's words still echo in my mind, a haunting melody that both soothes and torments me.

In that golden, otherworldly realm, the spirit appeared to me, her luminous form radiating ancient wisdom.

"I know your heart is torn," she said, her voice resonating with empathy. "Keeping the secret of who you are from your mate fills you with guilt."

I fell to my knees before her, my soul raw with anguish. "Please," I begged, "tell me why I cannot reveal the truth. Why would the gods want me to lie to my mate?"

The spirit looked upon me with a mix of sorrow and determination. "If Grayce had known, she would never have bound herself to you, and the prophecy would have been broken. The fate of the world rests upon the strength of her heart and her love for you."

"I don't understand," I told her.

"Love is the only thing more powerful than the darkness that is coming. Without it, the world will fall away."

I stared at her, my heart aching with the weight of this revelation. "I want to tell Grayce the truth now," I said, desperate for an end to this torment. "Each moment I keep this from her is torture. I have lied to her... betrayed her trust. I have hurt she whom I love above all else. Tell me why I cannot speak the truth. I need to understand."

"Grayce must discover the truth on her own," she said, her voice resolute. "That is the only way for her heart to remain strong and steadfast. To face what is to come."

"What is the sacrifice she will be called to make?" I asked. "Tell me so I can protect her."

"The sacrifice is hers. Not your own," she said. "You cannot alter her fate."

Now, as I stand with Grayce in my arms, I struggle with the burden of this secret, terrified of what it means and what it has to do with our future. I do not understand how the fate of the world rests upon the love we share. I only know that it is dangerous to defy the will of the gods. But how can I continue to keep the truth from Grayce, knowing the pain it will cause?

As I study my mate, the ominous warning of the heart tree spirit echoes in my mind. I may not be able to alter Grayce's fate, but I resolve to do everything in my power to protect her, no matter the cost.

CHAPTER 45

GRAYCE

Seated before the vanity, I watch as Emryll deftly weaves my hair into an intricate design fit for my crowning ceremony. Her fingers move with practiced ease, creating a masterpiece that mirrors the elegance of the Fae. The room is filled with soft murmurs and the delicate rustle of silk as two of the seamstresses lay out my dress, a comforting backdrop to our conversation.

"Grayce," Emryll asks hesitantly, her eyes meeting mine in the mirror, "why did Raiden refer to your mother as if she were not also his own?"

"Raiden was born of our father's mistress. My mother was rather cold to him when we were growing up. She resented having to raise the child born of her husband's affair because Raiden's mother died in childbirth."

Pausing for a moment, I continue. "But my siblings and I love Raiden dearly. It has never mattered to us that we do not share the same mother."

Sadness reflects in her gaze. "Do others look down upon him for this? For the circumstances of his birth?"

"Some do, but not all."

"Does he... have anyone back in Florin?" she asks. "A betrothed?"

A faint smile curves my lips because I know why she asks this. "No, he does not."

Her eyes brighten, her wings fluttering behind her.

"My brother is an honorable man. He has a good heart, and he is not afraid to speak the truth. It's why Edmynd relies on him so heavily as his advisor."

"We are so different: Fae and humans," Emryll muses. "But it seems to work well for you and my brother. There are so many misconceptions our kind have about each other." She shakes her head. "Raiden and Lukas were telling me all the myths they've heard about the Fae."

"Like what?" I ask, curious to know what they spoke of.

"About our males luring unsuspecting human maidens into the forests to seduce them." She laughs. "And that we are unable to tell falsehoods, but we can bend the truth to serve us instead."

I frown. "I thought Fae could not lie as well. Is... this not true?"

"We are like any of the other races." She arches a teasing brow. "But I suspect my ancestors may have spread this myth in the hopes that it would make others trust us more."

My heart stutters and stops. Everything Kyven has said I have accepted as truth because I believed this myth about his people.

"Are you all right?" Emryll frowns. "What is wrong?"

The heart tree's words echo in my mind. "Emryll, have you ever spoken to the spirit of the heart tree?"

Her eyes light up with a mix of reverence and wonder. "Yes, I have."

"Did the guidance it gave truly help you?"

"I believe so." Emryll smiles, her gaze thoughtful. "The priestesses say that what it tells you may be hard to interpret because the spirit of the tree only tells you what you need to hear to set you on the right path."

My heart clenches with worry, recalling the cryptic words the heart tree's spirit shared with me. I can't help but remember Kyven's expression of sadness when we were there. My voice trembles as I confess my deepest fear. "The spirit said that someone dear to me will betray me, Emryll."

Her fingers pause in my hair. "Who do you think she was speaking of?"

My thoughts turn to Kyven, but I cannot voice this aloud for fear that my heart will shatter. I love him, and I cannot bear the thought that he could be my betrayer. "I—I do not know."

Taking a deep and steadying breath, I force myself to push down my worry. Whatever happens, I will face the future, unafraid.

When we walk into the Grand Hall of the castle, it is a breathtaking sight. A gorgeous display of the craftsmanship and artistry of the Fae. Towering walls adorned with intricate carvings stretch toward the high, vaulted ceiling, their surfaces gilded with gold and silver. Graceful archways frame the hall, each one crafted from polished wood and adorned with delicate filigree, leading to opulent rooms beyond.

Large, floor-to-ceiling windows flood the hall with natural light, their panes crafted from enchanted glass with delicate, swirling patterns that capture the essence of the elements, a tribute to the Fae's deep connection with nature.

A majestic chandelier, crafted from shimmering crystal, hangs from the center of the ceiling, bathing the hall in a golden glow. The chandelier's myriad of crystal prisms catch the light, reflecting a mesmerizing dance of rainbows upon the smooth wood floor.

I'm nervous as I look out upon the crowd gathered to witness my ceremony. A sea of Fae nobility adorned in garments that gleam with the colors of gemstones and precious metals. Their faces reflect a mix of curiosity, anticipation, and a subtle undercurrent of skepticism as they watch me, a human queen, ascend to a position of power among them.

Whispers rustle through the assembly like the soft sigh of a breeze, but I cannot make out the words. My heart races in my chest, pounding like the beating of a thousand wings as I take slow, measured steps up the aisle towards Kyven.

He waits for me at the altar. His eyes are warm and steady, a beacon of reassurance that guides me forward.

My nerves buzz beneath my skin, but I do my best to maintain an air of composure. I draw upon my inner strength to steady my trembling hands and quell the storm of emotions brewing within me.

Despite the crowd's scrutiny and my own anxiety, I am determined to stand tall, to face the challenges and uncertainties of my position with courage. For Kyven, for our people, and for the future we will build together.

A hush falls over the crowd as Kyven stands before me, the ceremonial crown in his hands. The common people stand behind the line of nobility, their eyes wide with anticipation as they bear witness to this historic moment.

My brother, Raiden, and my best friend, Lukas, stand off to the side, steadfast in their support.

As Kyven places the crown upon my head, his eyes meet mine, and my heart squeezes in my chest. He takes my hand, and we both face the crowd.

"I present to you Queen Grayce of Anlora, Princess of Florin. My fated one," he says solemnly. "My A'lyra."

A hush falls over the audience at this revelation, the weight of their collective realization settling upon us all.

"Sanishon," someone says in the crowd.

"One of the Great Uniters," another chimes in.

"She is the Sanishon Queen foretold," someone else speaks aloud as several voices overlap, almost all of them repeating variations of the same thing.

As the ceremony ends, the crowd erupts in cheers, their voices rising like a symphony of hope and joy. Kyven takes my hand and guides me down the aisle. Many of them stare at me in awe and wonder.

Yet, I notice that some of the nobility, including Lord Torien, have only expressions of skepticism and anger. Their disdain for humans is evident in their stony expressions, a stark contrast to the jubilance that surrounds us.

Tangled emotions swirl within me: Fear as I wonder if we did the right thing announcing who I am. Sadness that Raiden and Lukas will be leaving now that the ceremony is done. Worry that Kyven may be my betrayer.

I gaze up at him. The thought is insidious and painful, and I decide that it cannot be him. Not Kyven. After everything we have been through, I refuse to believe it.

Pushing down my dark thoughts, I squeeze his hand. The warmth of his touch is a balm to my troubled soul, reminding me that we stand together, united against whatever may come.

CHAPTER 46

KYVEN

It has been a week since Grayce's crowning ceremony, and I cannot help but marvel at the way she has taken to her new role with grace and determination. We have not yet sealed our bond, and although part of me yearns to do so, I am hesitant to press her. My guilt over the truth she does not yet know gnaws at me, making our bond a bittersweet thing.

"Is something wrong?" Aren asks beside me. "You seem rather quiet today."

We have spent the past several hours reinforcing the wards around the city, ensuring our people are protected against any Wraith that might threaten our safety. He is right. I have barely spoken.

"I am worried," I admit.

"About what?"

"Losing her."

"We will protect her, Kyven." He rests a hand on my shoulder. "Talyn and I will make sure she is safe. I swear it."

"It's not just that. There is… something else." I lower my gaze. "Something I have not told you."

"What is it?"

"I have lied to her about something, and I fear that when she discovers the truth, I will lose her."

Concern crinkles his brow. "What is it that you have withheld? What have you—"

"If I tell you, you must give me your unbreakable promise that you will speak of this to no one."

"You do not have to bind my tongue with magic." He purses his lips. "I am loyal to you. I would never repeat anything you have told me."

"I ask you to swear it for your own good," I tell him. "Because I will not have you carry the same guilt that I do in my heart."

His eyes widen slightly. "Fine. I swear it."

I extend my hand, and he clasps it in his, sealing his promise with magic.

"When I left Corduin, before Father and Lyrian's deaths, I went to Florin."

"Why?"

"My father told me he planned to offer my hand to Princess Inara in exchange for a treaty. I was curious to learn more about her. So, I used a shade stone and disguised my appearance. I took on the glamour of a human."

"You could have been executed as a spy if they'd caught you. You should have taken me with you. I would have—"

"I saw Grayce then," I interrupt him. "I knew immediately what she was to me. And I—" I swallow hard. "I courted her in my human disguise as a man named Joren."

"You *what*?" he asks, his voice rising.

"I—I wanted to tell her who I was. And I was going to, but then I received word about Father and Lyrian and I had to return home before I could." I clench my jaw. "I hurt her,

Aren. She thinks Joren rejected her. I broke her heart, and she does not even know it was me."

"You have to tell her. If she finds out before you do, she will—"

"I want to, but I cannot," I say grimly. "The spirit of the heart tree says that she must find out the truth on her own or else it risks altering our future."

"Then you have no choice, Kyven." He meets my gaze evenly. "Our histories are littered with stories of those who have gone against the will of the gods, and I would not see you suffer their wrath."

Although I know he is right, guilt gnaws at my heart. "She trusts me, Aren. I do not deserve her trust or her love."

"Spend every day earning it. Worship her and show her how much you care. So that if the day comes that she learns the truth, she will remember and she will understand why you made the choices that you did."

* * *

As THE SUN begins to set, I make my way to the library in search of Grayce.

I find her there, nestled among the towering shelves of ancient tomes, fast asleep with her head resting on an open book. My heart swells with love as I study her face, serene and lovely in the fading light. A strand of her hair has escaped her loose braid, and I carefully tuck it behind her ear, my fingers lingering on her soft skin.

Grayce is the most precious thing in the world to me, and I would do anything to protect her. The thought is a fierce, burning resolve that courses through my veins, a promise I silently swear to her as she sleeps, oblivious to my presence.

As I watch her, the weight of my secrets and the love I bear for her war within me. But for now, I simply cherish the quiet moment we share, the warmth of our bond thrumming lightly between us.

Gently, I brush my fingers across Grayce's cheek, rousing her from her slumber. Her eyes flutter open, her expression drowsy and endearing. A hint of a smile curls her lips. "What are you doing here, my love?"

"I came to spend time with you." I offer her my hand. "Come."

A radiant grin lights her face, curiosity sparkling in her eyes. "Where are we going?"

My heart nearly breaks as she trustingly slips her palm into mine, allowing me to pull her up from her seat. "You will have to come with me to see," I tease gently.

With our hands intertwined, she follows me out of the library. As we step into the gardens outside, the scent of blooming flowers and the gentle rustle of leaves greet us.

Grayce gasps in delight when she spots Greywind, waiting patiently among the lush greenery. The majestic nylluan bows his head in deference to his chosen rider, his eyes gleaming with intelligence.

With a laugh of pure joy, Grayce climbs onto his back, her fear of heights momentarily forgotten in the face of her excitement.

"Are you coming?" She smiles over her shoulder at me, and I nod.

Spreading his wings, they take to the sky, soaring high above the city.

I follow close behind, my own wings carrying me effort-lessly through the air.

My heart swells with happiness as I watch Grayce conquering her fears, her laughter ringing out like a sweet melody as she and Greywind weave through the clouds.

Her face is alight with exhilaration and wonder, the wind

tousling her hair as they climb higher and higher, spiraling up on a swift current.

As we fly side by side, the city sprawling beneath us, I cannot help but stare at my mate in wonder. I am blessed beyond measure that the gods chose to cross my path with hers.

Aren is right. I will show her each day how much she is cherished and treasured. She is my A'lyra and I will do whatever it takes to be worthy of her love.

CHAPTER 47

GRAYCE

I awaken to soft shades of buttery yellow filtering in through the window as the warmth of the morning sun caresses my skin. I reach out for Kyven, but my hand meets only the cool, empty expanse of the bed. With a frown, I notice a folded piece of parchment resting on his pillow.

A grin crests my lips as I unfold the note to read Kyven's message. My smile fades and a chill runs down my spine as I study his writing. The elegant script is etched in my memory, as familiar to me as my own, for I have seen it many times.

This is Joren's handwriting. I am certain of it.

My heart races, and my hand trembles as I hold the note. It cannot be the same, and yet, I would recognize that handwriting anywhere. Joren and I exchanged numerous letters.

Dread twists deep within and tears gather in the corner of my eyes, but I force them back down, refusing to believe the worst. I know the Fae can use glamours to change their appearance, but at the time I met Joren, the Mages were still allies with Florin.

JESSICA GRAYSON

They had spells and wards upon our kingdom, preventing the Fae and Otherworldly beings from using magic in our lands.

I force myself to read Kyven's note, trying to focus on the message instead of his writing. He says he has gone to check the wards around the city and will return for our midday meal together.

A sob bubbles up in my throat, but I swallow it back, clutching the letter to my chest as sadness threatens to overwhelm me.

"No." I squeeze my eyes shut. "Kyven would not lie to me. I know it. He promised."

Drawing in a deep breath, I rise from the bed and walk over to the desk. My heart hammers as I check each drawer, searching for a sample of his handwriting to compare it. Surely there has been some mistake. Kyven could not have written this.

Maybe he had an assistant do it. Or Aren. Frantically, I try to think of any reason why the handwriting cannot be his.

When I pull out the bottom drawer, a sharp click slices the air and I glance down to discover a hidden compartment in the base, the top lifting along the edge. Tracing my fingers up under the panel, I carefully push it open.

My jaw drops. Inside is the embroidered handkerchief I once gave Joren. My entire body trembles as I pick it up. Something solid and heavy is wrapped in the material. When I pull back the corner, a small black polished stone falls onto the desk.

A purple glow lights the center, swirling across the strange rock. Carefully, I pick up the stone and a pulse of energy moves through me. Gasping, I lift my gaze to the mirror and my heart stutters and stops.

Instead of my own appearance, a Fae woman with silver-white hair stares back at me. My lips part as I draw in a shaking breath, and she does the same. I jerk back, the stone falling from my hand and clattering onto the desk.

With shaking hands, I feel inside the back of the drawer, catching on a stack of parchment. I pull them out and my eyes widen as I stare down at the stack. Written across the top is my own handwriting and Joren's name.

Scrambling to unfold the first one, my eyes fly over the page as I read the words aloud. I wrote this. It was the last thing I sent him. There is no mistaking that these are my letters.

Tears prick at the corners of my eyes, my world falling down around me as my mind processes the terrible truth.

The man I cared for, the man I believed had rejected me, and the man I now call my husband are one and the same. A broken sob escapes my throat as my heart shatters beneath the weight of Kyven's betrayal.

Panic and fear build in my chest, and it takes me a moment to realize these emotions are not mine. They are his.

He can sense my distress. He is worried, and he is nearly here.

The bedroom door crashes open, and Kyven rushes inside. "Grayce!" he calls out, frantic. "What is wrong?"

I lift a tear-filled gaze to him as the letters tumble from my hands to the floor.

CHAPTER 48

KYVEN

Grayce's pain is so intense, it takes my breath away. Her tear-filled eyes meet mine as the letters I had hidden from her fall from her trembling hands to the floor. My gaze follows the trail of evidence to the shade stone and handkerchief on the desk.

Devastation twists deep within as the realization crashes over me: she has discovered the truth. She knows I lied to her.

"Grayce, please, let me explain," I beg, my voice strained with desperation.

I reach for her, but she recoils as if struck.

"No," she chokes out, her voice cracking with emotion. "Do not touch me." Her words are a devastating blow. "I need you to go."

My chest tightens with anguish, the fear that she will leave me now gnawing at my very soul. "Please, Grayce, forgive me," I plead, the weight of my own guilt threatening to crush my heart. "Grayce, I—"

Her gaze holds mine, full of hurt and anger. "Leave." Her voice trembles. "Now."

Everything inside me wants to drop to my knees and beg her forgiveness. To gather her in my arms and not let her go until she understands why I lied. But as her devastating hurt and anger pulse across our bond, I cannot speak. The knowledge that I have hurt her is more than I can bear.

Agony builds in my chest as I take a step toward her, but she quickly steps back.

"Do not." Her voice is low and angry. "I want you to leave, Kyven." Tears stream down her cheeks. "Please. Just go."

With a broken heart, I step out onto the balcony and spread my wings. Devastated, I lift into the sky, soaring above the castle.

As I ascend toward the clouds, my emotions threaten to tear me apart. An anguished cry rips from my throat as I curse the gods for forcing me to keep this secret. For hurting my mate, my A'lyra, my queen, my heart, my very soul.

As I fly through the endless sky, a maelstrom of emotions swirls deep within. I have lost her. She will never forgive me. Our love and trust have been shattered by my lies.

"My King!" Aren's voice calls out, and I spin to face him. "What is—"

"She knows." The words spill from my mouth like bitter poison. "I hurt her, Aren. I broke her heart." I swallow against the lump in my throat. "She will never forgive me."

"You do not know that for certain."

"I can feel it here." I slam my palm to my chest, directly over my heart. "I can feel her pain and her agony through our bond, Aren." I shake my head. "What I did was unforgivable."

"Go back to her," he urges. "Explain to her why you lied. She will understand, Kyven. She has to."

"She told me to leave," I say defeatedly. "She does not want me near her."

"She's hurt. She lashed out. People do that when they're in pain. But it does not mean she never wants to see you again."

"What if she leaves me? How will I live without her?"

"You are fated. The gods set this path," he states firmly. "There must be a reason. There has to be. They would not bind you to her only to have you separated."

"We are not fully bound," I remind him. "We have not yet sealed our bond." I draw in a shaking breath. "She will leave me now. And I do not blame her."

"If you love her, you must fight for her, Kyven. Do not let her go. Not without explaining yourself. She doesn't understand why you lied, but she will when you tell her the truth." He rests a hand on my shoulder. "Even though she is hurt and angry, she still loves you. She will listen. I know she will."

I wish I could believe his words as truth, but I cannot. Even now, her agony flows across our bond; the weight of her sadness threatens to tear my soul in two.

"Return to the castle," I tell him. "Make sure she is well-guarded." I sigh heavily. "When you get there, please ask Talyn if she has eaten. And if she has not, have something prepared."

"It will be done." He gives me a pitying look. "I hate seeing you like this. I hate knowing she is in pain as well. You are both... important to me." He sighs heavily. "Think on what I have said."

"I will."

Aren thinks I should go back to her... try to explain myself. I want to. More than anything. But she asked me to leave. She does not want me near her. And yet, every instinct inside me demands that I return to her, gather her in my arms and do whatever it takes to earn her love and her trust again.

But I do not know if love and trust can be mended once broken. The thought that they cannot, terrifies me more than anything because I can't bear the thought of being without her. She is everything to me.

"Kyven?" Emryll's voice rings out. "What is wrong?"

Emotions clog my throat and I cannot speak.

She flies up beside me and rests a hand on my shoulder. "Kyven, please tell me." She presses her hand to her heart. "I can feel how sad you are. What has happened?"

"It's Grayce," I barely manage.

Worry pales her features, but I quickly add. "She is safe, Emryll."

"Then, what is it?"

I fly to a nearby branch and she alights beside me. "Please, Kyven. I want to help."

I drop my head into my hands as sadness threatens to overwhelm me. "I lied to her, Emryll. I promised that I would tell her the truth, but I lied."

"About what?" Her eyes flash with concern. "What did you lie about?"

She listens as I explain how I met Grayce, courting her in the disguise of a human. When I am finished, she rests her hand atop mine. "I'm sorry you have carried this all on your own ever since Father and Lyrian passed," she murmurs. "I knew you were sad, and I know how hard it has been for you to wear the crown. But I never asked you what was wrong. I merely assumed you were grieving, like I was."

"I was grieving. I miss them," I murmur. "And I missed her too." I rest my hand over my heart. "Leaving her... lying to her... it tore my soul in two. The guilt of not telling her the truth has haunted me every day."

"Now that she knows, you can explain yourself," Emryll says. "You can tell Grayce that the heart tree forbade you to speak of it, at the risk of altering the future."

"Yes, but... do you not see?" I swallow hard. "I could have

297

told her at any time before I had to leave her. I could have revealed who I was from the start."

"Yes, but that was not your path," she murmurs. "And you cannot change the past. Grayce loves you, Kyven. I am sure of it. I have felt this from her, and I believe she still does. She will forgive you, my dear brother. But you must tell her the truth. All of it. Once she knows everything, it will be the beginning of mending her broken heart. And yours."

Determination fills my chest. Emryll and Aren are right. If I love Grayce, I must do whatever it takes to earn her forgiveness. I cannot risk her leaving without knowing my heart and understanding why I made the choices I did.

"Thank you." I embrace Emryll warmly. "I will go speak with her."

Lifting off, I make a wide arc out over the city to return to the castle. Resolve burns deep within. Grayce is mine and I will do whatever it takes to earn her forgiveness.

CHAPTER 49

GRAYCE

The weight of my heart feels like a stone, dragging me into a murky abyss. Sadness churns deep within as I walk through the palace gardens, overwhelmed by the knowledge that the man I once loved and lost was, in truth, the man I now love and married.

It's a bitter, painful irony that threatens to tear me apart. Kyven, my husband, my mate, is Joren—the man who stole my heart only to abandon me, seemingly without care. And he never told me the truth.

I thought I knew Kyven. I thought I could trust him. But now, as the reality of his deception sinks in, I feel as though I'm drowning.

I close my eyes, taking a deep breath as the scent of roses wafts through the air, reminding me of when Kyven first brought me here. Every flower, every tree, and every stone seems to hold a memory of time spent together in this space. I recall how he taught me to use my newfound powers to make the flowers bloom. The gorgeous blossoms now only serve to remind me of how much I miss him.

I think of the first time he smiled at me. It was so genuine and warm, my heart fluttered in my chest. A heavy sigh leaves my lips as I wander further into the garden. I can almost hear the echoes of our laughter and our easy conversations.

I think of the day we confessed our love. He gathered me in his arms and flew me to the balcony, kissing me as the world faded away until there was just him and me.

Tears prick at the corners of my eyes as I trace my fingers over a rose bloom. I thought my heart was strong but right now, it feels as fragile as the petals beneath my fingers.

"Your Majesty," a deep voice calls softly, and I turn to see Aren approaching. He bows his head in respect, his blue eyes filled with concern. "You look troubled."

Despite the terrible ache in my chest, a wry smile tugs at my lips. I can only guess how terrible I must look, with tears streaming down my cheeks and my face red from crying. "You have a talent for understatement, Aren."

He gives me a sad look. "May I speak freely, my Queen?"

I nod, curious about what he might have to say.

"I spoke with Kyven. I know what you've learned. And I understand why you feel hurt and betrayed. But, my Queen, I've seen how much he loves you, and I know how much you love him."

I want to protest, to claim that my love is now tainted with doubt, but I know Aren speaks the truth. My love for Kyven still burns, even as my heart aches with betrayal.

"Before you make any decisions," Aren continues, his voice gentle, "I encourage you to speak with him. Ask him about the truth, and listen to what he has to say."

A spark of determination ignites within me as I listen to Aren's words. He is right; I owe it to myself and to Kyven to confront him and learn the whole truth. As painful as it may be, I need to know why he kept this secret from me.

"Thank you, Aren," I murmur, grateful for his support and advice. "I will speak with Kyven."

Aren bows, his eyes filled with relief. "I believe that is wise, my Queen."

As he takes his leave, my resolve strengthens. I will face Kyven and demand the truth, no matter how much it may hurt. Perhaps, there is a chance we can find a way to heal and return to the happiness we once knew. I make my way to the palace, determined to face the man who has both broken and mended my heart.

CHAPTER 50

KYVEN

When I reach the balcony, my nostrils flare as I scent the nylluan. A fluttering of wings catches my eye and I turn to find Talyn approaching.

As if sensing my question, he gestures to the bedroom. "Aren told me the queen was upset. So, I sent for her nylluan."

I look around him, peering into the bedroom. Greywind is lying on a nest of blankets at the foot of the bed. Turning back to Talyn, I arch a brow. "Did you do that?"

"Yes." He tips his head up with pride. "When I was a child, my grandfather was injured on the Great Wall. He had a nylluan, and when I would stay with my grandparents, she would sleep in my room every night. She was a great source of comfort to me after the death of my parents."

I look in again and my heart squeezes in my chest as Grayce sits down next to him and leans back into his side. Greywind drapes his wing over her, nuzzling her shoulder and cooing as she pets him.

Turning back to Talyn, I smile. "Thank you. You have done well."

A beaming grin lights his face. "Thank you, Kyven."

Quietly, so as not to startle her, I step back into our chambers.

Grayce turns toward me. Her eyes are swollen and red from crying. The hurt in her expression is like a dagger to my heart.

If I'm not mistaken, Greywind narrows his eyes at me, covering Grayce even more with his wing.

"May I speak with you?"

She sniffs and then gives me a reluctant nod while Greywind practically glares at me from behind her.

His reaction is understandable. He is her nylluan and they are very attuned to the moods of their riders. And right now, he has correctly deduced that I am the source of her tears and sadness.

Lowering myself to the floor, I sit across from her.

As I try to find the words to begin, she does instead. "It's my fault."

My head jerks back. Of all the things I thought she might say, this was not one of them. "Why do you say this?"

"I thought you could not lie." Her voice quavers. "I heard my entire life that Fae could not lie and instead of asking you about it, I simply took it as truth. So, when we spoke that night, in the gardens at Florin, I did not ask you the most important question."

"What question was that?"

"Can I trust you?"

Her words pierce my heart. Unable to look into her eyes, I drop my gaze to the floor. "My father wanted to betroth me to Inara. To forge an alliance through marriage by marrying a second born son to a second born daughter." I clench my jaw. "Willful as I was, I obtained a shade stone, even though they are the type of trickster magic we are taught not to use. I wanted to see Inara. To learn what sort of female my father wanted to bind me to."

"You never told me your father wanted you to marry my sister, and Edmynd never mentioned anything about it either."

"My father never officially reached out to your brother about this." A pained smile crests my lips. "Because when I made my way to the palace, I saw you instead. You were standing on the balcony of the castle, gazing out at the gardens, and I knew." I swallow thickly. "It was as if a bolt of lightning had struck my chest because I knew immediately what you were to me."

"Why did you lie?"

"Our people had been enemies for so long, I was afraid that if I told you the truth of who I was, you would reject me."

"So, instead you rejected me." A tear slips down her cheek. "You broke my heart, you know. I had never cared for anyone before then. Not… in that way."

She bites her bottom lip to stop it from quivering. "You told me that you needed to speak with me. To tell me something. You asked me to meet you." She sniffs. "I waited until dawn, but you never came."

"I was going to tell you that night, Grayce. I swear it." I meet her gaze evenly. "I could not bear keeping my identity secret any longer. I was going to reveal who I was… I planned to ask you to run away with me if our families did not agree to allow us to be together."

"What?" She blinks at me in astonishment.

"Can you imagine?" I shake my head. "I was naïve and foolish. Even if you'd agreed, I doubt we would have gotten very far before we were discovered."

A short huff of laughter leaves her lips. "If we had left,

Lukas would have tracked us down. He would have probably killed you, thinking that you'd stolen me away against my will, and sparked a war."

"I believe you are right." Despite my sadness, a smile curls my lips. "He would have done just that."

"Why did you leave?" she asks.

"I received word that my father and brother were dying. I —" My voice breaks. "I did not want to leave you, but I had no choice."

"I'm so sorry, Kyven." Her expression turns sad. "I should have realized the timing... now that I know..."

"If I had told you, would you have accepted me?" I ask the question that has plagued me ever since I left her to return to Anlora.

"I... do not know," she replies. "In truth, I probably would have believed you meant to use me to spy on my family."

Sadness reflects behind her eyes. "What I don't understand, is why did you not tell me? When I asked you that night in the garden, before our wedding, why not tell me then?"

"If I could, I would have," I offer. "I wanted to tell you so many times, but I—"

"The heart tree," she murmurs. "That was what you could not share. But why?"

"The spirit of the heart tree said it would have altered our fate... broken the prophecy."

She lowers her gaze. "The gods are cruel, are they not?"

"I agree. I did not want to hurt you, Grayce."

"I know that. And yet you did and I—" Her voice catches. "I need time to forgive you."

Unable to hold back any longer, I ask the question that burns in the back of my throat. "Do you think you can love me again?"

Her eyes lift to mine, tears gathering at the edges. "I never stopped."

Hope flares brightly in my chest.

"I understand now what my mother must have felt for my father." She sniffs. "She loved him, but he had hurt her and… she did not know how to let him back into her heart."

Despair floods my veins like ice.

She leans forward and takes my hand. "But I would like to try."

I turn my palm up to hers and squeeze gently. "So would I."

CHAPTER 51

GRAYCE

I t has been a week since I found out the truth. Kyven and I still share his chambers, but he sleeps on the couch, insisting that I have the bed. Greywind has taken full advantage of the situation by sleeping in our bedroom every night.

Apparently, it is improper to have a nylluan in the house, but I like having Greywind close. He is a comfort to me right now.

Nylluan are exceptionally intelligent, and I'm certain he knows he is supposed to sleep in the rookery, but he is also smart enough to know that Kyven and I are in no mood to press the issue.

This morning, I caught Kyven eyeing him with pursed lips as he lay on his back, completely stretched out at the foot of the bed in a makeshift nest of furs and blankets with his head on a fluffy pillow, like a giant cat with wings.

After this, I doubt Greywind will ever wish to return to

the rookery. Not when he can sleep in the castle in a comfy nest of blankets and warm furs.

"Again," Emryll calls out, interrupting my thoughts.

Drawing in a deep breath, I force myself to concentrate as I focus my powers on the target ahead. An arc of green light shoots out from my hands, straight to the ground. Thick vines explode from the surface, wrapping tight around the scarecrow dummy and caging it in.

"Good!" Emryll yells. "Your powers are getting stronger."

I smile at her praise and then laugh when I turn to find Greywind on his back and Emryll giving him belly scratches before she gives him another treat.

"If you keep feeding him like that, he will grow too wide to fit through the balcony door," Kyven's voice calls out from the side as he lands nearby. He turns to me, and my heart melts as he flashes a handsome smile.

Despite what happened between us, I still love him. I'm just taking things slowly, trying to protect my heart. But when he grins at me like that, it makes me want to rush into his arms as if everything were back to the way that it was before.

He walks over to Emryll and Greywind, and the unashamedly, attention-seeking nylluan gives him an affectionate head bump, begging for pets.

Kyven scratches up under Greywind's chin and he begins his low trilling coo that he makes when he's happy.

Emryll looks between the two of us. "I forgot that I have to be somewhere."

A faint smile twitches my lips because I know what she is trying to do.

"Perhaps Kyven can stay and help with your practice?"

Kyven's gaze sweeps to me, with a somewhat nervous look. "I can stay... if you'd like."

My heart practically jumps at the idea, but my mind

counsels caution. I consider him a moment before my heart wins the argument. "I would."

He sets up several targets and then we begin. Kyven offers himself as a moving target, instructing me to catch him as I did the Griffins. A few weeks ago, I would have been worried about accidentally hurting him, but now I have much better control of my powers.

Magic gathers in my palms and the tips of my fingers before shooting toward him in a wide arc of green light. A burst of vines erupts from the ground, tangling around his legs and his feet, but he manages to counter them with his own power, challenging me to think of new ways to catch him off balance.

After a few hours, I feel completely drained. I'm so tired, I'm exhausted. This always happens when I have a long practice session. Emryll thinks it's because I'm human and my powers are new. She says I'll build up my strength the more I use them. But right now, I'm so tired I can barely walk.

"I think I'm done for the day," I tell Kyven. I start back toward Greywind, so he can fly me back to the balcony of our room, but I stumble.

Strong arms wrap around my middle, stopping me before I can fall as Kyven pulls me back into his chest. For a moment, I bask in the solid warmth of him against me before I remember that things are different between us now, and I start to pull away.

"I can carry you, if you will allow me," he says, stopping me abruptly.

I glance over my shoulder. "All right."

A smile curves his gorgeous mouth as he hoists me to his chest. Greywind follows as we fly back to the castle. Gently, Kyven sets me down at the small table on the balcony. He goes inside and comes out a moment later with a tray of lavender tea and chocolate biscuits.

Now that he has told me everything about when he pretended to be Joren, I have also learned how he studied me, learning my likes and my dislikes and committing them to memory.

Perhaps, before I knew him, I would think it strange, but he is Fae, and according to Emryll it is not uncommon for a male to become completely and utterly obsessed with his mate.

"I have a surprise for you." He grins. "I think it's one you will love."

"What is it?"

He hands me a book. The title is in Faerinesh. *"Her Fae Admirer*, I murmur, reading the cover.

"It is a good one. It reminds me of *The Queen's Knight*."

My eyes snap to his. "You read *The Queen's Knight*?"

As the question leaves my mouth, I realize how ridiculous it is. Of course he read it. He followed me for weeks, learning everything he could about me, before I even knew who he was.

He nods. "You used to fall asleep with it still in your hands."

His statement catches me off guard. "You watched me when I slept?"

"Many times."

I study him, unsure how to respond.

"You asked me for honesty in the gardens the night before our wedding, and I withheld... so many things. I regret this, and I am sorry, Grayce."

"Is this your way of trying to make amends?"

"Nothing can excuse what I did, and I cannot change the past." His gaze holds mine evenly. "The only thing I can do, is offer you the truth that I should have given you from the very start."

His words settle in my chest like a heavy stone. He's right.

The past cannot be altered. It is the future that will shape things. Now I must decide whether to allow him back into my heart or fortify the barrier I have placed around it.

His eyes search mine as I pass the book back to him. "Read it to me."

A handsome grin lights his face as he flips it open and begins.

When I'm finished with my tea and chocolate biscuits, we move to the sofa. As I struggle to keep my eyes open, I find myself leaning close to him. After a moment, he cautiously wraps his arm around my shoulders, curling his wing around me like a giant cocoon while he reads to me in his rich, warm voice in front of the fireplace and the glowing l'sair crystals.

A soft cooing sound fills the air. Greywind is lying at our feet, his long tail curled around his body as he rests his head on his front paws.

After a few more pages, I succumb to the call of sleep and fall away into the void.

CHAPTER 52

KYVEN

When I wake, it's dark outside. I'm still on the sofa and Greywind is at my feet, but Grayce is not beside me. I look around the room and realize she is not in our chambers.

Sensing I'm awake, Greywind lifts his head. Gently I pat his neck and then tip up my nose, scenting the air to search for Grayce's scent, trying to determine where she is.

I follow it out onto the balcony. Movement in the gardens below catches my eye, and I flap my wings and fly toward her, landing behind her as she walks along the back wall of rosebushes.

"I could not sleep," she murmurs. "So I thought I would walk in the garden." She studies the thick vines and their vibrant blooms with a contemplative look. "You made this for me, didn't you?"

"I missed you when I returned to Anlora." I trace my fingers over one of the roses. "It made me feel close to you when we were apart. I was desperate to return to you, but…

my father and brother had just died and there was so much I had to do. I—"

"I understand," she whispers. "It was the same for Edmynd after the death of our father. The crown is a heavy burden to carry, especially when you were not expecting it so soon."

"Or ever," I add. "It should have been Lyrian who assumed the throne. If my father had had his way, my brother would have been your husband."

She turns back to me. "What would you have done?"

"I already told you my plans." A smile curves my mouth. "I would have convinced you to run away with me if our families did not endorse our bonding."

"And what would *we* have done?" She laughs. "Lived in the woods?"

"I planned to ask Varys to take us in. I would have asked him to give me a position as a healer so you could live in the palace... in conditions that were similar to what you would have left behind to be with me."

Amusement sparks behind her eyes. "You truly thought this through, didn't you?"

"I did. It was all I thought about... before I had to return here unexpectedly."

Cautiously, I cup her cheek. I'm pleased when she does not pull away. My gaze drops to her full, pink lips and I long more than anything to taste them again.

She stretches up on her toes until her face is nearly even with my own. Her luminous gaze holds mine as she slowly leans in, and I meet her halfway, brushing my lips to hers in a tender kiss.

When we pull back, I gently rest my forehead against hers. "Would you like me to fly you back to our chambers? Or would you prefer to climb the trellis as you did back in Florin?"

A hint of a smile tugs at her mouth. "You saw that too?"

"The first time I observed you do this, I thought you were running away."

"What would you have done if I had?" She crosses her arms over her chest. "If I had decided to leave my life at the palace and run off in search of adventure."

"I probably would have followed you."

She arches a teasing brow. "Probably?"

A sly grin curls my lips. "Definitely."

A soft huff of laughter escapes her. "Are all Fae males so obsessive?"

"Only when it comes to their mates."

She studies me a moment more before turning her gaze back to our balcony. "Let's go back to our chambers."

I love that she still refers to them as ours and that she allows me to share her room. I want to sleep in her bed, but I will not press her. It will take time, but I have hope that we can rebuild what we once had.

By the time we return to our chambers, the sun is already beginning to rise.

A soft knock on the door is Aren. "You asked me to wake you early to inspect the perimeter."

I turn back to Grayce. "Would you like to have midday meal together later?"

She smiles. "I would like that."

When I leave with Aren, he waits to speak until we are far enough away that he knows she cannot hear. "Things are going well?"

"As good as can be expected, I believe."

"Good." He rests a hand on my shoulder. "I am glad to see you are mending things." He arches a brow. "I have some disturbing news, however."

Worry arrests my heart. "What is it?"

"Your sister has begun receiving correspondence from Prince Raiden. Another raven came for her this morning."

I rake my hand through my hair. "Do you think it is serious?"

As if my very thoughts have summoned her, Emryll comes fluttering down the hallway. She hums, smiling to herself as she reads what I'm assuming is the message she received from Grayce's brother.

"Good morning," she says, practically beaming. "Isn't it a lovely day?"

I purse my lips. "I suppose it is."

Grayce's brother is an honorable male, and I suppose if Emryll were to be attracted to a human he would be a good choice. But I hate the idea of her leaving Anlora if things become serious between them. I would miss her terribly. For the first time, I realize how sad Grayce's brothers must feel to be apart from their own sisters.

I turn to Aren. "Perhaps we should invite King Edmynd and Prince Raiden to the spring festival."

Aren's head whips to me. "You wish to encourage your sister's relationship with Prince Raiden?"

I shrug. "It's not as if I can stop her. It is her choice who she wishes to pursue. Besides, my mate would probably appreciate a visit from her brothers. We could invite Inara and Varys too."

"What about the Dragon King and his mate—the Queen's cousin?"

I purse my lips. "As long as he vows not to make any more threats to burn down our kingdom, we can invite him as well."

CHAPTER 53

GRAYCE

As I enter the Fae library, the hallowed silence wrapping around me like a cloak, the scent of ancient parchment and leather filling my nostrils. A sea of books stretches out before me, shelves upon shelves of knowledge collected over millennia. The whispers of a thousand stories call out to me, but I am here for one purpose—the ancient tomes of the Lythyrian.

I walk to the scrolled parchment that Kyven showed me. The one that will allow me to read and understand any language. I pick one of candles from the shelf beside it and light the wick as I recite the spell to understand the words of an ancient race that wrote such cryptic words.

The prophecies of the Lythyrians have been the subject of much debate and study. No one knows what happened to this race of seers. They disappeared without a trace, leaving behind their sacred texts and ruined cities—the only proof that existed.

Fae Scholar Nolyn, greets me with a respectful bow, his

orange wings folded tightly at his back. His gaze drifts to the candle in my hand. "Your Majesty, how may I assist you today?"

"I wish to study the ancient tomes of the Lythyrian."

His eyes widen slightly, but he nods. "Of course, my Queen. But first, I must use the spell to understand their writing, as you have."

I wait patiently as he lights a candle and recites the enchantment. When he is finished he turns his attention back to me. "This way, my Queen."

He leads me through a labyrinth of bookshelves until we reach a wall adorned with strangely carved symbols. Nolyn murmurs a spell, and the wall shimmers, revealing a hidden passage.

This is obviously a secluded section of the library, hidden away to guard their most important texts. I marvel at the rare and sacred books that surround us. Nolyn approaches a shelf and retrieves a set of ancient, weathered tomes, their pages yellow and fragile with age.

He guides me to a table, carefully setting the tomes on the surface. He takes great care as he carefully opens the pages. "Here." He points to one of the chapters. "This is the prophecy you seek." He looks at me. "I am familiar with the tomes. Is there something, in particular, that you wish to study?"

"Is there anything that could help in our fight against the Mages and their Wraiths?" I gesture to the page. "It says the Sanishon will have to make a sacrifice, but beyond that it is rather vague."

"There is something curious I have read." Nolyn scrolls through the prophecy and then gestures to a passage. "Here, Your Majesty, the translation mentions something. Loosely translated it is... an enhancement to the powers of the Sanishon. Interpreted another way, it could be read as an *amplifier.*"

"An amplifier?" I study the passage, my heart pounding with excitement and trepidation. "What does that mean?"

"They are objects that can enhance one's power."

My thoughts turn to the pixie dust I still carry with me, wondering if something like that could be considered an enhancement. "Would pixie dust count?"

"The magic of pixie dust is unpredictable," He dismisses it. "The dust is a potion, but in powdered form."

"The Lythyrians took an interest in amplifiers. There is much written in their ancients scrolls about them." Nolyn's eyes narrow in thought. "One of these texts speaks of powerful magic. Magic only found in the Great Divide. They tried to harness this power by attaching it to objects to enhance their natural energy, creating some of the first amplifiers."

"The World Between Worlds," I murmur, remembering my conversation with Emryll. "Queen Ilyra's mate came from that place."

Surprise flits briefly across Nolyn's face. "You are familiar with our history."

"I first heard of Queen Ilyra when we were in Corduin."

"Ah." He nods. "You saw her necklace in the fortress library, did you not?"

"I did."

"It's a very powerful gemstone." His brow furrows deeply. "It could be considered an amplifier. It was forged by the magic only found in the Great Divide. It is what allowed her to tap into not only the energy of the elements, but also her own life force."

My thoughts return to the memory of the book about her. I remember how she gripped the gemstone as she drew power from the earth to obliterate the Wraiths.

"The gemstone enhanced her powers," I murmur more to myself than to him.

"Yes," he muses. "It did. But at great cost. It is the reason she was killed."

"Why?"

"She used the power of the gemstone to draw upon herself to power her spell, draining her life force."

"The gemstone is powerful because it came from the Great Divide," I point out. "What if that is one of the amplifiers spoken of in the prophecy?"

"I have considered this," he says. "But if so, it is too dangerous to do any good. Anyone who used it would end up like the Queen."

"The ultimate sacrifice of the Sanishon," I murmur, repeating the words of the prophecy.

His eyes snap to mine.

"What if there was a way to harness that energy safely? What if that is the key to defeating the Mages and the Wraiths?"

He gives me a cautious look. "What you are considering is dangerous."

"If we look further into these amplifiers spoken of in the prophecy, we might find something helpful." I turn to him. "If I am truly part of the prophecy of the Great Uniters, I am fated to make a sacrifice. And I'd prefer to have as much knowledge as possible before I'm faced with an impossible choice." I meet his gaze evenly. "Will you help me?"

A deep frown mars his brow as he considers. He looks down at the ancient text before he finally nods. "I will."

Determination and resolve fill me as I continue to delve into the ancient tomes. The weight of the prophecy rests on my shoulders, but with the knowledge contained within these sacred texts, perhaps there is hope.

After a few hours, Nolyn leaves to cast the calming spells

over the enchanted books. While he's gone I lose myself in the cryptic words, searching for answers to the prophecy.

The door creaks open, interrupting my concentration. I lift my head and I'm surprised to see Lord Torien, his dark eyes narrowing as they meet mine.

Torien dislikes me for being human and not Fae. Kyven dismissed him as his personal advisor because of his prejudice against humans. His disdain is as palpable as the air in the room, and worry knots in my stomach as I wonder why he is here.

"What are you doing here, Lord Torien?" I ask, trying to keep my voice steady.

"I came to find you." A sinister smirk twists his lips. "I understand you enjoy spending time in the library." His gaze drops to the tomes. "I am surprised you are studying the prophecy. I would have thought you would rather pretend it does not exist."

"Why?"

"Because if it is true, those ancient texts foretell your doom, Queen Grayce," he says darkly. "And that of your sister and your cousin, as well."

His words send a chill down my spine, and my thoughts turn to the pixie dust in my tunic pocket. Kyven said I would be drawn to it if it was needed. Dread fills me as the pull to reach for it becomes stronger.

"Did you know that some of the Mages have the gift of foresight?"

"I suspected as much." Unease moves through me, but I force it back down. I will not show any fear to his man despite the goosebumps that pebble my flesh as he regards me like a predator that has cornered its prey.

Cautiously, I stand and take a few steps toward the door. "As enlightening as this conversation has been, I have things that I must—"

"Your mother was not the one the assassins came for," he says, and my heart slams in my throat as he positions himself between me and the door. "The target was you and your sister."

I inhale sharply. "How do you know this?"

Torien advances slowly, his sinister gaze locked on mine. "The Mages foresaw your powers, but your High Mage Ylari swore you and your sister had no magic. Even so, there were some who did not believe him." He narrows his eyes. "Did you know this section of the library is spelled to prevent the use of anything stronger than a glamour? It is to prevent any accidental damage to the ancient books."

I look at the door, praying Talyn or Nolyn will enter.

"Nobody's coming, Your Majesty," Torien says, his voice laced with venom. "I used an invisible glamour to enter. You're alone here."

The chilling certainty in his words sends fear coursing through me. My heart slams in my throat. Alarm bells ring out through the city, their clamor slicing through the air.

"What is that?" I demand.

Torien's sinister grin widens. "A distraction to keep your mate from coming to your aid."

A glint of metal flashes in his hand and my eyes widen when I realize he has a dagger.

Desperation fuels me as I reach for the pixie dust in my pocket. I don't know what it will do, but I'm praying that it saves me.

Ripping open the pouch, the golden dust slips through my fingers, and I feel an irresistible force tug at my very being. The word goes dark and I'm pulled into a void.

When I blink my eyes open, I'm back in my chambers in the castle. I only have a moment to realize it was a teleportation spell as the sounds of alarms clang throughout the castle.

"Wraiths are attacking the city!" a voice cries out from somewhere in the castle. "They've slipped past the protective wards!"

Greywind is on the balcony, his fur bristled as he gazes up at the sky. I rush toward him and rest a hand on his neck, drawing his attention to me. "We have to help fight," I tell him.

He lowers himself to the ground and I quickly climb onto his back. Spreading his wings wide, we take to the air.

CHAPTER 54

KYVEN

Alarms ring out throughout the city.

"What's going on?" I turn to Aren. "What is happening?"

"My king!" One of the guards shouts. "There has been an attack along the outskirts of the city. Wraiths. Dozens of them."

My wings beat furiously as me and the guards we race to the edge of the city. I turn to Aren, flying beside me. "We must check the wards and recharge them. We cannot risk a breach."

When we reach the edge of the city, several guards have already fortified the wards. The Wraith are fleeing into the forest, and I give the order to hunt them down.

Aren and I start after them, when one of the guards yells out. "Look!" He points in the distance to the Wraith. "They are disappearing!"

Stunned, we watch as several of them wink out, leaving

behind only a handful. "Most of them were illusions," Aren mutters. "But how? Why?"

I turn my gaze back to the castle. "They were a distraction." Panic constricts my chest. "We have to get back to the queen!"

Flying as fast as I can through the city, I reach out across the bond, trying to sense Grayce. To see if I can warn her through our connection.

As if reading my mind, Aren asks. "Can you feel anything through the bond? Is she in any distress?"

"No, she—"

Unbridled fear rips through me like a sharpened blade. Power sparks like lightning between my fingers as rage builds deep within. Whoever is behind this will pay with their blood. I vow to all the gods that I will end them for daring to attack my queen.

Alarms blare through the city and panicked cries fill the air as dozens of dark figures hover between the trees, their glowing red eyes striking terror in the hearts of the people below.

In the distance, a winged figure takes flight from the castle. My heart stutters and stops when I recognize the flash of Greywind's wings. Grayce is on his back, sending out spiraling arcs of green magic, attacking the Wraiths as they charge.

Grayce's fear and anger pulse through our bond, echoing my own emotions as we fight our way through the city. My wings beating furiously as I rush toward her.

Greywind releases a battle shriek, gripping a nearby Wraith in his claws and shredding it mid-air as Grayce rides astride him.

As I draw closer, I call out to her. Her eyes meet mine, burning with determination. Her face is a picture of fierce resolve as she uses wields her magic, directing it at our enemies.

Green sparks of magic spiral out from her fingers, hitting the trees and the soil, sending vines shooting up toward the Wraith, the lethal tendrils wrapping tight around their forms and ripping them from the sky to slam them to the ground.

The Wraiths cry out in agony as the vines trap them, twisting until they are crushed.

I can't help but feel a swell of pride as my mate fights with the skill of a battle-trained warrior. My guards rally around their queen and our people watch as she defends Ryvenar, protecting them from the devastating scourge of the Wraith. She is magnificent, and I am completely in awe of her strength and resilience.

When the battle is over, and the last Wraith is killed, Grayce and Greywind land in the palace courtyard. I start toward her, and panic stops my heart as she slips free of the saddle and falls toward the ground.

Talyn catches her at the last second. "What happened?" I pull her from his arms. "Was she injured?"

"No, they did not touch her."

"Fetch a healer!" I cry out, running my hands over her form, checking for any wounds I may have missed, but I find none.

Before I was king, I trained as a healer but never had the chance to finish my apprenticeship. I've never felt as lost as I do now, staring down at my mate, unable to help her.

Healer Draymon flies toward me as I cradle Grayce to my chest, her face pale and her body limp.

He lands beside us. "Lay her on the ground," he instructs.

I do as he says, and he raises his hands, hovering them above her form as he assesses her for injury.

Panic rises within me like a tidal wave, threatening to pull me under. "What is wrong with her?"

My heart aches with worry and fear as I stroke her hair, whispering words of comfort, praying to the gods that she will be all right.

"I do not understand it," Draymon says. "Her life force energy is waning."

My mind flashes to Varys and Inara. She inherited his power, but she draws the energy from herself instead of from the earth around her as the Elves and Fae do. The same must be true for Grayce.

Before I can share this with Draymon, he turns to me. "It is her own life force that she uses to conjure her magic. It makes it more powerful, but it can be deadly if she uses too much."

I cannot bear the thought of losing her: my world, my love, my everything. She is the light in my darkness, and without her, I am lost. "Will she live?" I ask frantically. "Tell me!"

"Yes," he replies.

"Why will she not wake?"

"Her life force was almost completely drained to power her magic. She came close to death." He gives me a grave look. "She is alive, but she will need much rest to recover."

"Can I take her back to our chambers?"

He nods. "I will come check on her in a few hours."

"You will stay in the room." I meet his gaze evenly as I give the command. "I want you close in case she needs anything."

He bows his head. "Of course, my King."

CHAPTER 55

GRAYCE

My eyes flutter open, and the first thing I see is Kyven, standing beside me with a relieved smile on his face. My head is fuzzy, and I struggle to remember what happened before I lost consciousness.

"Grayce," Kyven breathes. "You're awake. I was so worried about you." He takes my hand in his, squeezing it gently. "Thank the gods."

"What happened?" I ask, my voice weak. "I remember we stopped the Wraith, but then... I was so tired, and I remember feeling strange before I passed out."

"My queen." Talyn steps forward. "How did you leave the library? I saw you enter the room with the ancient texts, but when the alarms rang out you were already gone."

"Lord Torien," I murmur. Images flit through my mind and I inhale sharply as the memory returns. Fear constricts my chest. "Where is he?"

"I do not know." Kyven glances back at Aren and Talyn. "Why are you—"

"He found me in the library, Kyven. He used an invisibility glamour. He would have killed me but I used the pixie dust." My gaze shifts to Talyn. "It transported me back to the castle." I struggle to sit up. "Lord Torien is the one behind the Wraith attack on the city."

Kyven's eyes flash with anger as he turns to Aren. "Find him," he growls. "Now."

Aren barks orders at three of the guards and they quickly leave the room to gather more for the search.

"Torien also mentioned my mother's death." Dark memories rush forward, but I force them back down. "I think he knows who killed her."

"What did he say?" Aren asks.

"He said that she was not the target. That Inara and I were. He said that it was because of the prophecy. That the Mages suspected Inara and I had powers."

"Why is Lord Torien working with the Mages?" Aren asks the same question that burns in my mind. "He always claimed to hate them."

"Maybe they promised him something," Aren adds. "Power... position... wealth. He is a small male and any one of these things would appeal to him."

"As soon as he is found, bring him to me," Kyven grinds out. "I will tear his mind apart if I must. But I *will* have answers." He turns back to me. "Do not worry. I will not allow him to get anywhere near you."

Talyn steps forward. "I will not fail you again, my queen."

"You didn't fail me, Talyn," I reassure him.

Kyven looks at him. "The Queen is right. You couldn't have known."

Talyn dips his chin in acknowledgment, but guilt flashes behind his eyes. It will probably be a long while before he forgives himself, even though it was not his fault.

Healer Draymon moves to my side, his expression serious. "My Queen, you need to lie down. You nearly died."

"I don't understand." I blink up at him. "I remember feeling weak before I collapsed, but I wasn't injured. So why did I faint?"

"You did not just faint," he stresses. "When our kind use magic, we draw from the earth and nature around us to create it, but you draw from your own life force. And you used so much it almost killed you."

"Just like Inara and Freyja," I murmur, and Kyven nods.

Both my sister and my cousin nearly died using their magic for the same reason.

"Why does this happen to humans?" Kyven asks. "Why can they not draw from nature as we do?"

Draymon shakes his head. "I do not know, my king. I only know that because they draw from themselves, the magic they do create is more powerful."

"Scholar Nolyn says that's how Queen Ilyra died," I offer. "She used her necklace as an amplifier to draw power not only from the earth but also from herself."

"I'm not sure about the Elves and the Dragons, but it is possible for our kind to tap into our own life force to create magic if there is no other source available," he explains. "But because of the risk, it is only done in the direst of circumstances."

Draymon gives me a stern look. "You must take great care how much magic you use, my queen. Your fight with the Wraiths left you very near death."

"You're awake," Emryll's sing-song voice calls out as she walks into the room. "Thank the gods." She playfully nudges Kyven's side. "It's a good thing you are awake, because I doubt poor Healer Draymon has had any rest since you fell unconscious."

My eyes snap to Draymon only now noticing the dark circles under his eyes.

She continues. "Kyven was constantly insisting that he check you."

"Is this true?" I ask Kyven, and he gives me a reluctant nod. I purse my lips and then turn my attention to Draymon. "I apologize, Healer Draymon. If you would like to leave to get some rest, I—"

"It was no hardship to tend you," Draymon says. "You saved my young daughter from the Wraiths when we were under attack. I can never repay you for this." He brings his hand to his heart and bows his head. "Thank you, my queen."

Draymon leaves and Emryll hugs me tight. "I'm so glad you are all right, my sister," she whispers in my ear. "I am off to the temple to give thanks to the gods for answering my prayers." She flashes a quick grin at me before leaving.

I try to push myself up to sitting, but I'm still weak. Kyven places a hand at my back and helps me the rest of the way. He studies me, worry etched in his features. "You could have died, Grayce. Promise me you'll be more careful."

"I had no choice, Kyven. I had to help defend the city."

"Not if it means risking your life."

"That is what leadership is about." I meet his gaze evenly. "How can I ask others to do that which I will not?"

He clenches his jaw, and I know he means to argue, but I'm tired.

"I'm exhausted. I do not want to argue with you, Kyven. Please."

"You were so pale and still in my arms when you fell." He drops his forehead gently to mine, closing his eyes. A tear escapes his lashes and rolls gently down his cheek. "I cannot bear the thought of losing you."

"I'm here." I cup his cheek as he studies me with a look of such intense love and devotion it takes my breath away. "And

I do not plan on dying anytime soon," I tease, trying to lift his sadness. "I promise."

"Good." He huffs out a laugh and then pulls me close, curling his wings around me. "I will hold you to it."

His violet eyes stare deep into mine as he touches my face. "You are everything to me," he whispers. "And I—"

A low cooing sound fills the room and we turn to find Greywind walking in from the balcony. He comes to the side of the bed. When I reach out to pet him, he leans into my palm and begins his trilling coo that means he is happy.

"He has stood guard on the balcony ever since you fell unconscious." Kyven smiles as he rubs a hand along his jaw. "He is very attached to you."

"And I'm attached to him." I grin at the nylluan.

Kyven pulls a book from the side table and holds it out to me. "Would you like me to read to you?" He arches a brow. "We were just about to reach the part where the Fae knight declares his undying love for the princess."

I nod. "That's my favorite part."

"Mine too," he agrees.

He sits in the bed, his back propped against the headboard and I rest my head on his shoulder as he reads. Greywind lies on a pile of furs at the foot of the bed, his front paws folded in front of him as he listens too.

As the time wears on, my eyelids grow heavy with exhaustion. Despite my attempts to remain awake, the smooth and rich sound of Kyven's voice eventually lulls me back into sleep. As I'm drifting away, I feel him shift on the bed as if to get up, but I open my eyes and grab his hand. "Wait."

He turns to me, his gaze full of concern.

Feeling bold, I pull him toward me. "Stay with me. Here in the bed."

"Are you certain you wish me to stay?"

"Yes, but just to sleep."

A smile spreads across his face. "All right."

He settles back down in the bed, beneath the blankets and loops his left arm and wing around my form.

With a deep sigh of contentment, I nestle into his side. His familiar masculine scent floods my nostrils as I close my eyes and fall away into sleep.

CHAPTER 56

KYVEN

"Another raven came from Corduin." Aren hands me a small, scrolled parchment as I sit at the desk in my chamber. "They report that Wraith sightings have increased along the Great Wall."

Clenching my jaw, I read the message. "The Orcs have reported more Wraiths in the forests as well," I add. Frustration simmers deep within as I crumple the message in my hand. "Now that we know Lord Torien was behind the attack on the city, I'm sure he is somehow involved in them crossing the Great Wall."

"Yes, but where could he be hiding?" Aren asks. "Who would take him in now that he is a traitor to the crown?"

That is the question that has plagued my waking hours and my sleep. It has been nearly a week since the Wraith attack on the city, and I am no closer to finding any answers. "I do not know, but we must find out."

I gaze out the window as the sun dips below the horizon,

and my thoughts are consumed by my mate and the safety of our people. "Is the queen still in the palace library?"

"Yes," Aren replies. "Talyn says she has been studying the prophecy ever since the attack, trying to find a way to defeat the Wraiths and the Mages. He also reports that she has become obsessed with the story of Queen Ilyra, trying to understand how she used her necklace to destroy the Wraiths when they breached the Great Wall."

My heart stutters in my chest, but I force my expression to remain impassive. I am concerned about Grayce's fascination with Queen Ilyra. The warrior queen gave her life when she destroyed the Wraiths and as much as I wish to defeat them, I do not want Grayce in anywhere near danger.

"Talyn says he overheard her speaking with Scholar Nolyn. They are researching amplifiers. She hopes they may be used to strengthen her powers."

"Amplifiers?" Worry tightens my chest. Ilyra's enchanted necklace strengthened her magic, but it is also the reason for her death. "What did he tell her?"

"They are pouring over ancient texts to study the origins of Queen Ilyra's necklace, trying to uncover its secrets."

I curl my hands into fists at my sides. Curse Nolyn and his loose tongue. Fortunately, the necklace is in the fortress of Corduin. If it were here, I'm sure my mate would insist upon experimenting with it to see if it could strengthen her powers so she could aid in the fight against the Wraiths.

"Talyn says they are also researching information on the powerful magic of the Great Divide—the World Between Worlds."

"Amplifiers are dangerous. So is the Great Divide," I grind out. "Did Nolyn bother to tell her that?"

"Yes." Aren rests a reassuring hand on my shoulder. "I specifically asked Talyn about this, and he said Nolyn warned her."

"Still... the queen is stubborn," I muse, more to myself than to him. "I doubt that has entirely dissuaded her."

"In that, you are the same." A hint of a smile tugs at Aren's lips. "The queen is like you: when you become obsessed with something, you have a hard time letting it go."

I narrow my eyes for I know he is speaking of my mate. He knows how I watch Grayce, how I observe every detail about her. I cannot help it. I'm completely and utterly fascinated with everything she does.

* * *

IT IS GETTING LATE, and I stand from my desk, finished for the day with my royal duties. "I think I'll take a walk in the gardens," I tell him. "I will see you in the morning."

He dips his chin in a subtle nod and leaves the room.

Deep in thought, I stroll along one of the narrow pathways in the palace gardens, seeking solace in the fading light. The cool evening air brushes against my skin as I walk among the flowers, listening to the gentle rustle of leaves in the breeze.

I want more than anything to go to Grayce, but I am trying to give her space. She has still not forgiven me for lying to her about being Joren. We kissed once in the garden, but that was before the attack on the city. Every night after that, we have shared the same bed, and I hold her, but we have done nothing but sleep.

As much as I want to seal her to me, I will not push her into something she is not ready for. I am fortunate that she even allows me to be near her, especially after how deeply she was hurt by my lies.

She still loves me, but things are not the same. She is cautious now, and I cannot blame her. I just wish things could be as they were. I long more than anything to kiss her, to hold her in my arms and—

"Kyven?" Her soft voice rips me from my thoughts, and I turn to find her walking toward me. "What are you doing out here?"

"I came to think."

"Me too," she replies, moving to my side. "What's on your mind?"

I gaze at the rose-covered wall, gathering my thoughts. Before I can answer, she takes my hand, squeezing it gently. "I'll go first."

A smile tugs at my lips as her words make me recall the night we spoke in the palace gardens in Florin, before we were wed.

"Things have been a bit strained between my husband and me these past few weeks. And he has been trying very hard to bridge the gap that has grown between us."

Swallowing hard, I lower my gaze. "Strange you should say this, for things have been understandably strained with my own mate as well. It is entirely my fault. And I have been trying desperately to earn her forgiveness even though I do not deserve it."

"Why do you believe you are undeserving?"

"Because she is my mate. The one I swore to love, to honor, to protect, to cherish until the end of my days, and... I hurt her." I swallow hard. "But that is not the worst part."

Her eyes snap up to mine. "What do you mean?"

"I could have defied the will of the gods. I could have told her the truth before she discovered it, but I did not. And it wasn't because I was worried about breaking the prophecy or about the world being plunged into darkness. It was because I was worried I would lose her."

Her gaze holds mine as I continue. "The truth is... *she* is all that matters to me. And in trying so hard not to lose her, I have driven her away instead. I am a selfish male, and I do not deserve her."

"What if she loves you so much she has already forgiven you?"

As her luminous gaze holds mine, a spark of hope ignites in my chest. Boldly, I step closer.

She stretches up on her toes until her face is nearly even with my own.

I cup her cheek, pleased when she does not pull away from my touch. Cautiously, I curl my arm around her waist, staring deep into her eyes. "When we are apart, you are all I can think of," I murmur. "You haunt my both my waking hours and my dreams. I never knew anything could feel this way... this intense need to be near you. To know you. To see you and to be seen."

Worried that I am dreaming, I remain still, afraid I will awaken at any moment as she brushes her lips to mine.

"I see you, my love," she whispers. "And I forgive you, Kyven."

I crush my mouth to hers, lifting her into my arms as I spin us both around. Setting her back on the ground, I fold my wings around her, holding her close as I drop my forehead to hers. "You truly forgive me?" I ask, because I need to be sure.

She cups my cheek. "Yes."

I capture her mouth with my own in a passionate kiss. Threading my fingers through her silken chestnut hair, I stroke my tongue against hers, relishing the taste of her kiss and the feel of her body against me.

I have done nothing to deserve her love and forgiveness, but I will do everything I can to keep it.

My nostrils flare as I breathe deeply of her delicate scent. It is enticingly sweet. She is at the peak of her fertile cycle.

Something dark and primal awakens deep within, demanding that I claim my mate.

I feared she would never want me again. And I have waited so long to bind her to me. Gods help me, I do not want to wait any longer.

A soft moan escapes her as I cup her breast through the fabric of her dress.

Movement in the distance catches my attention, and I growl low in my throat. Although I know it is only Talyn, trying to discreetly give us space, fierce possessiveness burns in my veins.

"Hold on to me," I whisper as I hoist her to my chest and take off, flying toward the balcony. As soon as we step inside, I am glad to see we are alone. Even Greywind is gone. I kick the door closed behind us and then capture her mouth again in a searing kiss.

She moans, threading her fingers through my hair, as our mouths mesh repeatedly.

Desire burns in my veins as I carry her to the bed. I'm so lost in our kiss, my knees bump the edge and I fall forward, twisting at the last second so that she lands on top of me as we tumble onto the mattress.

Her gaze holds mine a moment, her hair forming a curtain around us as her hazel eyes stare deep into mine. "I love you." I reach up and touch her face, watching in wonder as a pink flush blooms in the wake of my fingers. "More than anything."

A beautiful smile curves her lips. "I love you too, Kyven."

I rise up just enough to capture her mouth with my own as I hold her against me, her thighs straddling my hips.

Without breaking our kiss, I sit up on the edge of the bed, curling my wings around her. I groan as she rolls her hips against mine, the delicious friction is the most exquisite torture.

The scent of her need fills the air and the desire to claim her is almost more than I can bear. Palming the left globe of her breast through her dress, I kiss a line down her neck and trace my tongue across the pulsing artery.

My fangs extend with want to pierce the delicate flesh beneath, but I force myself to pull back. "We should stop," I whisper against her skin.

"Why?" she asks, breathless.

"I am on the edge of my control," I rasp. "I do not want to rush you into—"

"I want you, Kyven," she whispers.

I still. Need pulses deep within, and I am desperate to claim her, but I need to be sure this is what she wants. I touch her face. "Are you certain you want me?"

She nods. "Yes."

Happiness floods my veins as I crush my lips again to hers in a searing kiss. She reaches between us, undoing the fastening of my tunic and pushing it back from my shoulders.

Extending my claws, I slice away the fabric of her dress, reveling in the feel of her petal-soft skin as I cup the creamy mound of her breast, rolling the hardened peak between my thumb and forefinger.

She arches into my touch, and I lean down, closing my mouth over the tight bud, laving my tongue across her sensitive flesh as she threads her fingers through my hair and writhes against me.

When she rolls her hips against mine, I groan as the damp heat of her center seeps through the silken fabric of my pants, directly over my already hardened stav. Her scent is intoxicating, and I am desperate to be inside her.

Her delicate fingers fumble with the fastening of my pants before I help her, freeing my stav from the confines of my clothing.

A deep growl leaves my throat as she wraps her hand around my length and swipes her thumb across the already weeping tip before she positions me at her entrance.

Cupping her jaw, I stare deep into her eyes as I begin to push up into her. The tight clasp of her body around my stav as I advance is so intense, it takes every bit of my control to go slowly when all I want to do is flip her onto her back, bury myself deep inside her, and fill her with my essence.

CHAPTER 57

GRAYCE

Kyven's eyes are raven black, his fangs fully extended as his gaze holds mine, full of possession. I gasp at the slight twinge of pain as she pushes through my barrier, but it's quickly replaced by pleasure.

Tight heat blooms in my core as he slowly sheathes himself deep in my channel, each gentle roll of his hips advancing him further until he is fully seated.

"Are you all right?" he whispers, going still.

"I just need a moment to adjust," I breathe as my body begins to relax around his. I shift slightly and he groans as he sinks impossibly deeper inside me, the base of his knot pushing into my channel.

His gaze holds mine as I begin to move against him; he raises his hips to meet my own, creating the most delicious friction as the ridges of his stav touch some place deep within that makes my head fall back and my toes curl with pleasure.

He grips my hair and gently guides my lips back to his, stroking his tongue against mine as he moves deep inside me. I inhale sharply as his knot expands, locking us together. The completely fullness and the gentle tug only adding to the desire building within.

He reaches between us and I cry out as he teases his thumb over the sensitive pearl of flesh between my thighs. Everything tightens and my entire body goes tense a moment before I clamp down hard around his stav, crying out his name as my release sweeps through me like fire in my veins.

His stav begins to pulse in my channel. "Mine!" he roars as intense heat erupts deep within, flooding my core as he fills me with his seed.

His release triggers another orgasm within me, this one even stronger than the last. I'm not even fully recovered when he flips me onto my back. Our bodies are still joined by his knot and I wrap my arms around his back, holding tightly to him as he pumps into me.

His wings are fully extended as he stares down at me. I reach up to touch his face. With his black eyes and sharp fangs, he is both fierce and beautiful. And all mine. Just as I am his.

Wrapping his arms tightly around me, he leans in and traces his tongue along the artery of my neck as each thrust becomes longer, deeper, and more forceful. "So tight," he rasps in my ear. "You are perfect, Grayce."

Sensation threatens to overwhelm me as I hold onto him, my arms and legs wrapped around his body as my release builds deep inside. Pleasure coils tight in my core as the small muscles of my channel quiver and flex around his invading length.

I gasp at the sharp sting of his fangs as he marks me, but the pain is quickly forgotten as my body clamps down around his stav and intense heat floods my core as he fills me again with his seed.

He laves his tongue over his mark, sealing the two small punctures. When he pulls back, he drops his forehead gently to my own. "You are mine," he whispers and gives me a tender kiss.

I touch his face, as our bodies remain locked together. I never knew anything could feel like this. "And you are mine," I speak tenderly in reply. "Always."

* * *

AFTER WE'VE MADE love three times, Kyven lays us on our sides, facing each other. Gently, he tucks a tendril of hair behind my ear and then presses a sweet kiss to my lips. "I can have the healer bring you tea. If you wish to take precautions."

"Precautions?"

"To prevent conception."

"We do not even know if it is possible for us to have children," I reply. "And if we can, it would be a blessing, don't you think?"

His eyes darken again, twin pools of black in his ethereally handsome face. His fangs extend into sharpened points as he carefully moves over me, rolling me beneath him.

I trace my hand across his chest and down his abdomen, but he quickly snatches my wrist, pulling it away. "Don't," he says sharply. "I need a moment."

When I frown in confusion, he adds, "The thought of you swollen with my child…" He splays his palm across my lower abdomen. "I am struggling with the primal part of me that wants to take you again and again until my seed takes root deep in your womb, but I know you need rest."

A faint smiles curves my lips. "Who said I'm tired?"

He captures my mouth in a claiming kiss, and I moan as he begins to push inside me again, his stav touching some secret place deep within that makes my toes curl with pleasure.

I'm glad I'm not exhausted, because I doubt we'll be getting any sleep this night.

CHAPTER 58

KYVEN

Morning light spills in through the window. I focus on my mate. Her long lashes cast shadows against her high cheekbones, the faintest hint of a smile playing upon her lips as she dreams. She is more beautiful than anything I have ever seen, and she is completely and utterly mine.

Her eyelids flutter open and she gives me a sleepy smile. "You're watching me again," she teases gently.

"I cannot help it," I whisper. "Part of me is still worried this is a dream and that I'll awaken at any moment."

She cups the back of my neck and pulls my mouth to hers, kissing me long and deep. I glance down at her body, wincing when I notice the slight bruising in the shape of my hands on her hips. "Are you all right?" Guilt tightens my chest. "Forgive me, I—"

Her gaze follows mine to the bruising, and she takes my hand. "It's all right. I'm fine."

"I must take greater care with you," I whisper.

"I'm not going to break, Kyven," she gently admonishes.

Carefully, I gather her in my arms and stand from the bed, walking us to the cleansing room. I set her down in the bathing pool and a soft sigh of contentment leaves her lips as she settles beneath the warm water.

"Join me." She tugs at my hand.

I do as she commands and sit behind her, my legs bracketing hers. She leans back, resting her head against my chest and shoulder as she takes my arms and wraps them around her waist.

I fold my wings around her and gently nuzzle her head.

"This is lovely," she whispers. "I don't want to leave."

"Leave?" I ask. "Where would we go?"

She twists back to face me. "I had a dream a few nights ago. A vision," she corrects. "We had to go to Corduin—to the Great Wall."

"Why? What happened in your dream?"

"It was strange," she murmurs. "I was watching the story of Queen Ilyra and the Wraiths were rushing toward the crumbled part of the Wall." Her eyes meet mine as she cups my cheek. "You and I stood side by side and we defeated them, Kyven. We pushed back the Wraiths, sealing the breach to prevent them from crossing into our kingdom."

"There is no breach," I tell her. "If there were, I would have received word. "

"Not yet," she says ominously. "But there will be."

Fear coils tight in my chest. I cannot bear the thought of anything happening to her. "How did we do it?" I ask. "How did we push back the Wraiths?"

"I do not know." She rests her head back on my shoulder. "I only know that we did."

"Why do you not seem worried by this vision?" I ask. "It means we will be in danger."

"Yes, but we will defeat it together," she counters. "It is a good vision. It means we will win."

I wish I was as confident as her, but I cannot still the worry in my heart. I must speak with Aren—have him send a raven to Corduin, informing them of Grayce's vision so they can be prepared.

My thoughts turn to my conversation with Aren about Grayce asking about Queen Ilyra's necklace. "Aren said you were researching magical amplifiers with Scholar Nolyn."

"I am. If we can learn how to harness something like that, it might allow us—Inara, Freyja, and me—to draw the energy needed to power our magic, from nature, like your people do, instead of drawing from ourselves."

"That is not how it works," I reply grimly. "Queen Ilyra used it to draw the energy of her own life force, amplifying the powers she drew on from nature. That is why she was destroyed along with the Wraiths. If you were to use an amplifier, it could kill you because it would take even more of your own life force than you already utilize."

"What if it doesn't?" she counters. "Nolyn believes that it could have the opposite effect when used by a human."

I clench my jaw. Nolyn and I need to have a serious talk soon. I tighten my arms possessively around Grayce. "Nolyn can test that theory out on his own human mate, if he ever gets one," I say, trying to add a teasing note to my voice when I am anything but amused that he is planting these ideas in my A'lyra's head. "I do not want to risk you getting hurt, Grayce."

Gripping her waist, I turn her to face me, her thighs straddling my hips. "Promise me you will stop pursuing the idea of using an amplifier."

She lowers her gaze. "I cannot."

Why must my mate be so stubborn? "Why not?"

"What if amplifiers are the answer, Kyven? What if they

can help us defeat the Wraith and the Mages once and for all?" She sighs. "In the prophecy of the Great Uniters, it says the Sanishon will have powers beyond any seen before. And just as the Orc King suggested, there are many ways to interpret the translations. For instance: the words "great powers" can also be translated as "amplifiers.""

Worry snakes down my spine. "If you are wrong, it could cost you your life, Grayce." I touch her face. "Please, do not pursue this. You could be hurt. I don't want to lose you."

"You will not lose me, Kyven," she whispers.

"How do you know?"

She places her hand over mine on her cheek, leaning into my touch. "I dreamed last night of our daughter."

My heart stutters and stops. "You... what?"

"I saw our future." A lovely smile curves her mouth. "It was beautiful."

I press my palm to her lower abdomen, searching for any sign of a life spark in her womb, but detect nothing. Then again, if she were Fae, it would be too early to tell. "You are certain it was a vision?"

She nods. Relief fills me as I hug her to my chest. My A'lyra will be safe, and we will have a child. Fierce possessiveness flows through my veins

"I want you," she whispers, pressing her lips to mine as she rocks her hips against me.

"You are not hurting?"

"Not anymore."

She reaches between us, gripping my stav and notching me at her entrance. A low growl of pleasure vibrates in my chest as she carefully lowers herself onto me, and I lose myself in my mate.

* * *

AFTER WE MAKE LOVE AGAIN, I carry her back to the bed. It is well past breakfast, and I am sure she must be hungry, but I decide to let her sleep just a bit longer.

As I study her, a nagging thought keeps circling in my head. The prophecy speaks of a great sacrifice—the ultimate sacrifice, if the Orc's translation is correct. And yet, Grayce saw our future.

If her vision of the Wall crumbling comes to pass, I will insist that she remain here. I will not risk her. While the Wraiths and the Mages remain a threat, I must not let down my guard. Just because she saw a future does not mean we will not have to fight for it.

CHAPTER 59

GRAYCE

I've had three blissful days and nights making love to my husband. We have hardly left our bedroom. But our days of indulging in each other cannot last forever. We have to figure out how to defeat the Wraiths. More importantly, we must determine how they are crossing the Great Wall.

Lord Torien is still missing and we do not know who else he may be working with.

Not wanting to be caught unprepared, I've started training again with Emryll. This time, however, I'm pacing myself so as not to use too much of my power. Facing my target, I raise my hands and try to focus. I'm trying to control how much energy I use with each casting, but it is not an easy thing to learn.

Now that I must be more controlled in my use of magic, it does not always come to me when I call it forth.

Emryll told me to form an image in my mind of what I

want my magic to do while also controlling how much energy I harness. Closing my eyes, I picture vines springing up from the ground, wrapping around my target. When I open them again, nothing is happening.

Disappointment fills me and I turn to Emryll. "It's not working."

"Try again," she encourages.

Turning my gaze back to the wooden post, I hold out my hands. Gritting my teeth, I concentrate on trying to reach deep within for the magic inside, struggling to bring it to the surface with as little use of my life force as possible.

Sweat beads across my brow as my focus remains locked on my pretend enemy. My hands tremble as I try to conjure my power.

Emryll comes up beside me and gently touches my shoulder. "It's all right," she whispers. "It will come eventually."

"I don't understand. Why is this so difficult?"

She gives me an understanding look. "Magic is not an easy thing to master, and you have only recently inherited your powers."

I nod and then raise my arms again, but she calls out. "You should rest, Grayce. Give yourself some time to relax before you try again tomorrow."

I'm impatient. I want to learn how to control my powers now, but I know Emryll is right. I nod, and we start back for the castle. Although I'm disappointed that I cannot access my magic like I want, I'm determined not to give up.

Something shimmers in the trees, catching my eyes. I stare into the darkness, searching for the source, but I can see nothing.

"What is wrong?" Emryll asks, moving to my side.

"I thought I saw something," I murmur. "It was like a flash of light."

She turns her gaze in the direction of the trees, her entire body still as she scans the woods.

Only now do I realize the forest is completely silent. The ambient sounds of birds and insects are absent; even the wind has grown deathly still. My breath begins to fog with each exhalation as the air around us grows cold.

Mist billows from the woods and onto the training fields, rapidly covering the ground and rushing toward us.

"Get behind me!" Emryll calls out.

Raising her arms, she creates an invisible barrier. The fog slams into the shield. The dark tendrils of smoke covering her magic completely, blocking the light of the sun.

Glowing red eyes pierce through the inky blackness as a dark-cloaked figure moves toward us. Fear trips my heart at the skeletal face beneath its hood. Its gray lips pull back to reveal two rows of gleaming, dagger-sharp fangs. "A Wraith," I barely manage to speak through my panic.

Emryll's entire body trembles as she struggles to maintain the shield around us. Fine fissures spread across the surface, threatening to crack the protective barrier as the fog continues its assault.

I raise my hand, desperately trying to call upon my own magic, but it is no use.

"When I tell you to run, you must run," Emryll grits through her teeth. "Get to the castle and—"

A sharp crack rings out as the barrier collapses. Dark tendrils rush inside, completely enveloping Emryll before wrapping around my form like icy fingers. Sharp pain stabs at my body, and I open my mouth to scream, but nothing comes out.

The Wraith's blood red eyes fix upon mine and it extends one skeletal hand to my neck, gripping me in an iron vise. I thrash against the dark tendrils of magic that hold me immobile, but it's no use.

My pulse pounds in my ears and all rational thought is stripped away as terror wraps tight around my spine. *"Kyven!"* I call out with my mind, praying he will hear me.

A maelstrom of emotions—fear, panic, and unbridled rage—consumes me. And somewhere within comes the understanding that it is his. *"Grayce!"*

Heat builds in my chest, flowing through my veins. Power erupts from my palms in a brilliant display of green light. Vines burst from the ground, their thick, long tendrils curling around the Wraith and tightening before jerking him away from me and slamming him to the ground.

Another Wraith races toward me, flying through the trees with inhuman speed.

I raise my hands and send an arc of power rushing to him. It explodes on the ground before him, and vines burst from the ground, churning rock and soil as they grow and expand to capture their prey.

The Wraith releases an ear-piercing shriek before the vines tighten, cutting him off abruptly and trapping him against the earth in a living cage.

The fog recedes, and Emryll pushes to her feet beside me.

Movement in the trees catches my eyes, and a bolt of bright red light races toward us. Desperate to stop it, I raise my hands. Heat surges through my veins and magic erupts from my palms, striking the ground. A wall of vines shoots up from the soil, forming a barrier to shield us.

Time slows as the dark magic slams against the protective barrier, scorching the vines and threatening to burn through it to ash.

Magic hovers between Emryll's palms a moment before she sends it out in the direction of our attacker. My eyes widen at the sight of the dark robed figure with pale gray skin and pitch-black eyes. A Mage.

His sharp, white fangs are bared in a feral snarl as he sends another bolt of dark magic racing toward us.

Gritting my teeth, power burns through me, scorching my veins and exploding from my palms as I concentrate my energy on the earth. The ground quakes beneath us as soil and rock ripple beneath the surface and roots expand and lengthen, heading straight for the Mage.

He cries out in shock as they explode from the ground in a burst of rock and earth, wrapping around him and forcing him to the ground.

Writhing in their grasp, his dark magic pulses through the roots, traveling back to me. A pained cry rips from my throat as it blasts into my veins. Blinding pain crashes over me like a giant wave, but I refuse to let go.

The ground trembles beneath us from the force of my magic. Sweat beads across my brow and I brace myself, struggling to maintain my power. A sharp crack splits the earth, crumbling in on itself as the line races toward him.

His anger ripples through me, the dark magic whispering through my veins and promising a painful end if I fail. If he breaks free, we're both dead.

An arc of green light races toward the Mage, slamming into him and freeing my magic before rendering him unconscious.

I jerk my head toward the source and Kyven's eyes lock with mine. A dozen of his warriors stand behind him.

"Grayce!" He rushes toward me.

Breathing heavily, I lower my trembling arms. My heart pounds in my chest as raw pain and exhaustion wash over and through me, and I stumble forward, dropping to my knees before falling to the ground.

Kyven's strong arms wrap around me, lifting me to his chest. His warm hand cups my cheek and my eyelids flutter open. A strange mixture of pain and devotion mar his features as his eyes search mine. "Grayce, you must stay awake." He lifts his head, shouting at someone. "Get the healer! Now!"

CHAPTER 60

KYVEN

R aw panic rips through me as I stare down at my beloved. Blood trails from the corners of her eyes. She struggles to remain conscious.

"Kyven," she barely manages as tears track down her cheeks. "The Mage and the Wraiths... are they—"

"You are safe," I reassure her.

The Wraith are dead, their bodies crushed in a cage of vines. Out of the corner of my eye, I observe as Aren drags the Mage back to the castle to take him to the dungeon.

Gently, I wipe the blood from her face. "I need you to stay awake, Grayce. Can you do that?"

Weakly, she nods.

Over my shoulder, I hear Emryll directing the healer to us. Healer Draymon comes up beside me. His eyes widen briefly as he takes in the scene around us. The displaced earth and the open fissure in the ground. "Lay her down," he commands.

"We should take her inside," I argue.

He moves his hand through the air, just above her body as he assesses her. His expression turns grim. "There isn't time."

I lay her on the ground, and he closes his eyes as he concentrates on his healing powers. A soft white glow envelops her entire body as he works.

My heart stutters and stops as she closes her eyes. "Grayce!"

"She is only resting. She will live," Healer Draymon says solemnly. "I put her in a sleeping state so her body may recover faster. She used too much of her power."

"The Mage and the Wraith attacked without warning," Emryll's voice sounds over my shoulder. I turn back and her eyes are fixed on the dead Wraith with a faraway look. "We would be dead now if not for her."

I clench my jaw and lift Grayce into my arms. "I want you to remain at her bedside until she awakens," I command Healer Draymon as I start back toward the castle.

He and my sister follow closely behind me as I push through the doors and into the hallway. Several guards look on with shocked expressions as I pass them on the way to my chambers.

Gently, I lay her down in the bed. I doubt Grayce would appreciate waking only to find herself covered in dirt and blood. I rest my hand upon hers and close my eyes as I cast a cleansing spell. When I'm finished, I turn back to Draymon and Emryll. "I will return as soon as I can. If she awakens while I am gone, send someone to find me. I want to be notified immediately."

Draymon dips his chin.

"Where are you going?" Emryll asks.

A low growl rises in my chest. "To the dungeon to question the Mage."

* * *

WHEN I REACH THE DUNGEON, I find Aren standing before the Mage, his eyes burning with anger. "How did you get past our wards?" he asks, his voice low and deadly. "Why did you attack the queen?"

I move to his side, and he gives me a subtle nod of acknowledgment. The Mage is bound with chains to the bars of his cell, unable to move save for lifting his head and glaring at me in defiance. "Your wards are not as strong as you think," he replies darkly. "As for the queen"—his eyes lift to mine, narrowing—"I believe you already know the answer."

I do not believe for one moment that he was able to pass through our wards without help. It had to have been Torien's doing that they were able to slip past our wards. The magic that is used to create them is strong enough to repel even the Mages.

"You think to give me cryptic replies." I seethe. "But I assure you." I snarl. "I *will* find out the truth."

His brow furrows in confusion a moment before I press two fingers to his temple. Closing my eyes, I brace myself, shielding my own mind and my thoughts as I dive into his.

Panic grips me in an iron vise, but I realize this fear. It does not belong to me.

"Stop!" he cries out in my mind, but my powers surge forward, tearing through his memories as I seek the truth.

He throws up a brick wall, trying to seal away his innermost thoughts, but I smash through it. Another rises to replace it, but it crumbles beneath my power. Frustrated, I grit my teeth and push harder.

Blood pours from his nose, eyes, and mouth as I focus all my intent upon tearing through his defenses, searching for anything of Torien's location and any plans they may have for the Great Wall.

Aren inhales sharply beside me as the Mage begins to

thrash, struggling against my powers.

She is fated to the Fae King—a Sanishon from the prophecy. Wisps of thought and memory collide as a cloaked figure stands before him, pointing at a scroll. I focus my concentration, trying to break down his defenses entirely.

"She is one of the Great Uniters, and she must be killed." His voice trembles. "She cannot be allowed to live."

"Where is Torien? Why are the Wraiths gathering along the wall? Tell me!" I demand. "Now!"

"Never!" he roars. A surge of energy rushes forward. A wall of dark magic slams into me a moment before another wall rises between our minds, sealing me out. I push at his shield and the image of Lord Torien flashes in his thoughts.

Before I can search more, he falls still, his head and shoulders slumping forward as he goes unconscious.

Unwilling to give up, I mean to search his still mind, but find only a darkened void. His thoughts and memories completely hidden from me by his dark and terrible magic.

Breathing heavily with exhaustion, I turn to Aren. "I saw Lord Torien in his mind. He must be working with them. Find him," I command. "And place extra wards on this cell, and post guards at the dungeon's entrance. I'll not take any chances on him escaping."

Aren dips his chin and goes to work on the wards. I would do them myself, but I'm exhausted. The mental strain of trying to read the Mage's thoughts has weakened me.

When Aren is finished, he walks over to me. "I don't why Lord Torien would turn against his own people to ally with the Mages and Wraiths?"

"I do not know." I curl my hands into fists at my sides at the memory of Grayce's terror as she reached for me through the bond. I turn to Aren. "Double patrols along our borders and the guards along the city's perimeter. Until we discover the truth and find Lord Torien, my mate will not be safe."

CHAPTER 61

GRAYCE

The sound of people talking breaks through the hazy fog of sleep as awareness slowly trickles back into my mind.

"Double the patrols along our borders and the guards around the castle," Kyven commands. "You are my best warriors, and I want you to guard my mate... shadow her every movement when we are apart."

"Yes, my king."

I open my eyes to see Aren and Talyn bowing to Kyven.

"Did you send the raven to King Varys and King Aurdyn?" Kyven asks.

"They have already been sent," Aren replies.

I sit up in the bed, leaning forward on my knees as the world spins a bit before settling.

Kyven rushes to my side. "How are you feeling?" His violet eyes search mine in concern before he snaps at someone behind him. "Fetch Healer Draymon. Now."

"I'm fine." My voice comes out a rasp. "What happened?"

"You don't remember?" Emryll asks, moving to my side. "You saved us from the Wraith and the Mage."

Images flit through my mind as the memory of our attack rushes to the forefront of my thoughts.

The doors open and Healer Draymon enters, his expression grave as he looks at me. "How do you feel?" he asks, his hands hovering over my form as he assesses me with his magic. "Any pain? Weakness?"

"A little," I reply honestly. "But nothing debilitating."

"Can you stand?"

Slowly, I slide my legs off the edge of the bed and then stand up. My knees give out, and I start to fall forward, but Kyven's arms wrap around me, catching me before I hit the ground.

Gently, Kyven sets me back on the bed.

"Why am I so weak?" I lift my hand, unable to stop it from trembling.

Kyven takes it between his and presses a tender kiss to my palm. His gaze flicks to Draymon before returning to me. "You used too much of your life force again."

"Yes," Draymon agrees.

Kyven squeezes my hand. "You must be careful when using your magic. If you use too much, it will kill you, Grayce."

"Before the attack, I had already been training and I was exhausted." I glance down at my hands. "So I'm not even sure how I did it," I reply honestly. "It just… happened when we were attacked."

Healer Draymon nods. "That is how most fledglings first learn to use their powers. It is instinct to defend yourself when you feel threatened."

Worry tightens my chest. "If I cannot even control my magic to protect myself, what if I accidentally hurt someone? I wasn't worried about this before, but if I can't even help how much I use... what if it gets away from me?"

Kyven cups my cheek. "It won't, Grayce."

"How can you be certain?"

Before he can answer, Emryll interrupts. "If you had no control, your power would have sought any target, indiscriminately. Instead"—she smiles warmly—"you saved us both from the Wraith and the Mage. Your magic did not harm me. It *protected* me."

"What happened to the Mage?" I ask. "The last thing I remember was—"

"He is in the dungeon," Kyven replies. "For questioning."

"What did he say?"

Kyven turns to Emryll and Draymon, motioning subtly for them to leave the room. Once they are gone, he turns to me, his expression grim.

"The Order of Mages knows that you are my fated one. They believe you are one of the Great Uniters of the ancient tome of the Lythyrians—one of the Sanishon foretold in the prophecy."

"Because you are my A'lyra, it has made you their target."

"What about Lord Torien? Has he been found?"

"Our warriors are still searching for him."

Aren walks in, handing him a scrolled parchment. He bows low. "We've received word from Corduin. There are more Wraiths gathering along the Wall."

"My vision," I whisper, and Kyven's head snaps to mine. "It's coming to pass. We need to send a raven to my brothers and Lukas. They need to be warned. If the wall were to collapse, it would not be long before the Wraiths reached their kingdoms."

"I will send a raven immediately," Aren says. He turns back to Kyven. "And I suggest that we return to the Wall to assess the threat firsthand as well."

"Agreed," Kyven says.

"I'm coming with you."

"No," Kyven states firmly. "You will remain here."

"I will not," I counter. "You agreed that we would be equals and I refuse to stay behind."

"Grayce, please." He takes my hand. "You must listen to me."

"I'm not completely helpless," I remind him. "I am able to wield magic and—"

"I'm not saying you are helpless, Grayce. I just do not want to risk you."

"We've had this argument many times, Kyven, and I feel the same about you. That's why I'm going with you to the Wall."

He opens his mouth as if to protest, but quickly snaps it shut again. Pulling me into his arms, he sighs heavily. "I would argue with you, but I cannot. You are right. You are my queen and my equal, and it is not for me to tell you what you can or cannot do."

I'm glad he understands this, because I did not wish to argue. "We should leave first thing in the morning," I tell him.

His entire body goes tense before he reluctantly agrees. "We will leave at first light."

CHAPTER 62

KYVEN

It is midday and we are a little more than halfway to the Great Wall. Although I am worried about what we will find when we reach it, I push down my concerns as I concentrate on scanning the forest for any trouble.

Aren, Talyn, and a dozen of our guards fly in formation around us, alert and watchful as they constantly search the trees for threats.

The air whips around us as we soar through the emerald canopy of the forest. The ancient trees with thick, tower-like trunks stretch towards the heavens. Their foliage is so vast that it seems as if the sun has been swallowed by their embrace. I spread my wings wide, feeling the powerful muscles beneath stretch and strain.

Beside me, Grayce rides astride Greywind, his powerful wings carrying them both effortlessly through the sky. Her dark hair billows out behind her, a stark contrast to his black and white feathers and fur. Fierce determination burns in her eyes–the same eyes that captured my heart the moment they met mine.

As we weave through the labyrinth of branches, I'm surprised by how far Grayce has come. She was terrified of heights when we first flew together, but now, she appears completely at ease upon her mount.

Although I know it was her wish to not have to rely upon me for traveling, I cannot deny that I miss the feel of her in my arms.

Up ahead, Aren signals for us to land. It has been many hours of travel and we still have many more ahead.

"What are we doing?" Grayce asks.

"We're going to stop for a bit to rest and to eat. Then we will continue our journey."

Greywind lands on a nearby branch and Grayce remains astride him while I unroll a tarp and secure it to the trees. When I'm finished, I motion for her to join me.

She swallows hard and carefully slides off Greywind's back. With one hand holding onto the saddle, she stands frozen on the branch. It is as wide as three people, but it is easy to see that she is reluctant to walk across it.

I move to her side. "Are you all right?"

"My legs feel a bit weak from sitting for so long," she explains. "I do not trust myself to balance on the branch just yet."

"Will you allow me?" I ask.

She nods, and I carefully lift her into my arms and walk her over to the tarp. A grin tugs at my mouth. "Do you remember the first time we flew through the forest? After our human ceremony?"

She arches a brow. "I imagine it must be an easier flight for you this time, without having to carry a burden."

"On the contrary." I grin. "It made the journey much more enjoyable."

She laughs as a blush steals across her cheeks. "You enjoyed carrying me even when we were new to each other?"

"I was new to you," I remind her gently. "But you… I had dreamed of having you in my arms for months before then."

Gently, I lower us both onto the tarp. She settles in front of me, my legs bracketing hers with one arm wrapped solidly around her waist. Grayce leans back against me, resting her head on my collarbone as I carefully unpack our lunch.

"What do you think happened to Lord Torien?" she asks. "Do you think he fled Anlora?"

"Possibly. But he is a resourceful male. I doubt he would have aided the Mages and the Wraiths without some sort of plan for if things went wrong."

"Like what?"

"I am not sure, and that is what worries me," I admit the fear in my heart. "He was willing to put all of Anlora—all of his own people—in danger, just to get to you. But why? What would *he* have to gain from breaking the prophecy?" I shake my head. "The only ones that would benefit are the Mages and the Wraiths."

"Maybe they promised him power."

"If they did, I doubt they would keep their end of the bargain."

"I agree."

"He knows who killed my mother, Kyven. We have to find him, because I want answers."

Sadness and pain seep through our bond as she speaks of her mother's death. I press a tender kiss to her shoulder. "I tear his mind apart if he refuses to speak."

"Kyven?" she twists back to me, alarmed. "Could that not harm you? Tearing through someone's mind like that?"

"No." I watch her expression carefully, waiting to see the fear in her eyes that I saw even in my own parents when they discovered what I could do. "That is why those with my ability are so feared."

Relief flits across her face instead. She settles back against me, snuggling into my chest. "Just promise me you'll be careful, anyway."

My heart swells at her easy acceptance of me. "I will."

"Why do I sense you are surprised by my reaction?" she asks.

"Most would be afraid of what I can do."

"Not me." She shakes her head. "I know what it is to have an ability that others shun. I had to hide my visions almost my entire life. I will never judge you for what you can do, Kyven."

She turns and reaches her arm to cup the back of my neck and guides my lips to hers in a tender kiss. "I love every part of who you are," she whispers. "Always."

* * *

WHEN WE REACH CORDUIN FORTRESS, I'm not surprised by the warm welcome we receive. This place was my home, and these warriors were my friends and my family for five years. Bonds forged on the Wall are never forgotten.

When Grayce dismounts from Greywind, one of the warriors moves to take him to the rookery, but I stop him. "I'd prefer that he stay close to us in case the queen needs him."

His brow furrows slightly in confusion, but he dips his chin. "Of course, my king."

Grayce turns to the male. "Could you lead him to our rooms? And I'll need extra bedding for him to sleep on the floor."

"Yes, my queen."

Before he leaves, she affectionately pats Greywind's neck. "We'll be in later."

Commander Caldyr bows low. "It is good that you have returned."

"What has happened?" I ask. "Tell me the bad news first."

He guides me to the balcony facing the Wall. As we step outside, a cold wind blusters up from the ground, its icy fingers wrapping around us and sending a chill straight through my bones. My jaw drops as I gaze down at the Wall and the mass of Wraiths gathered on the other side.

"What are they doing?" Aren murmurs beside me, his face pale and his eyes wide.

"They are waiting for the Wall to come down," Grayce says ominously. "Just like in my vision."

CHAPTER 63

GRAYCE

The throne room has been turned into a command center, complete with a large round table and several chairs. Commander Caldyr, Aren, Talyn, myself, and Kyven all sit in the circle, discussing our next move.

Kyven has sent several scouts over the Wall to see if they can determine why the Wraiths have begun to gather here. A few have already returned without answers, and now we await the others as well, hoping to learn something new. Something that will help us win the war against these dark creatures.

"There are no Mages among them," Aren says. "At least, none that have been sighted."

"What about further along the Wall?" I ask.

He shakes his head. "We sent word to Florin's outpost, but no response yet."

"Not until now," a gruff voice calls out from the doorway,

and a smile spreads across my face when I recognize who it belongs to.

"Raiden!" I jump up from my chair and rush toward my brother's open arms.

He gathers me in a bear hug and spins me around in a wide circle. "Did you miss me?" he teases.

"So much." I laugh even as tears gather in my eyes as he sets me back on my feet. "I know I saw you recently, but I miss seeing you every day."

"I miss you too," he says.

He lifts his head as Kyven approaches and gives him a lopsided grin as he claps his shoulder. "I guess I'm glad to see you too."

Kyven narrows his eyes, but it's easy to see the hint of a smile that tugs at his lips. "It is good that you are here. Is your brother—"

"I'm here too," Edmynd's voice sounds from behind me.

I turn and he embraces me warmly as well. He whispers in my ear. "Raiden told me you are happy. Is this true?"

"Brilliantly happy, my dear brother." I smile brightly. "My husband is a good man."

Something akin to relief flashes across his features and he turns to Kyven and embraces him like a brother.

Caldyr, Aren, and Talyn observe in stunned silence. I suppose it is strange to see a human king embrace a Fae one, especially after so many years of trouble between our two kingdoms.

"I didn't think you would be able to come yourself," Kyven tells him.

"You're both lucky he came at all. I had a hard time pulling him away from a certain Dark Elf Princess," Raiden teases, and Edmynd scowls.

"Dark Elf Princess?" I ask. "Varys's sister?"

Raiden nods.

"Princess Nyrala came to visit Florin in the interest of furthering the cooperative peace between our two kingdoms," Edmynd explains.

"That may be why she arrived in the first place, but things seemed to be going in another direction when I saw them walking through the garden of the pal—"

Edmynd elbows Raiden, cutting him off, and I laugh.

"He"—I gesture to Raiden—"should not be teasing you, Edmynd. You should have seen how he fell all over himself around Kyven's sister, Emryll."

Edmynd's jaw drops and he turns to Raiden. "Is that so?"

Kyven clenches his jaw. "It is."

"Nothing happened between us," Raiden says quickly. "I swear. We simply talked and—"

"Nothing has happened *yet*, you mean." Narrowing his eyes, Kyven crosses his arms. "My sister is young and—"

"Oh, Kyven." I grin, looping my arm through his. "Emryll is not a child."

He gives me a look as if he cannot believe I am not taking his side in this. I lean in and whisper. "I'm sorry, my love, but I, for one, believe they would make a lovely couple."

He sighs heavily. "I suppose if she had to pick a human male, your brother is a decent choice," he says in a voice so low I'm sure no one else can hear him.

Smiling, I press a quick kiss to his cheek and then turn my attention back to Edmynd. "What of Varys? Does he have any reservations about you and his sister?"

Edmynd's cheeks flush dark red. "Well, I—" He clears his throat. "Things did not... I mean, we never had a chance to explore—"

"They are still awkward around each other," Raiden finishes for him, rolling his eyes. "But it's easy to see they're both in lo—"

"If you could give us a report on what your warriors have

seen along the Wall," Edmynd cuts him off. "I've received rather disturbing reports from my own warriors as well."

"Come see for yourself," Kyven says, leading him and Raiden out onto the balcony.

Their jaws drop as they stare out at the Wall and the hundreds of Wraiths gather just on the other side. "What in the seven hells are they waiting there for?" Edmynd asks. "My warriors sent ravens from our Outpost stating they noticed the Wraiths migrating this way. And now, we know where they were going. But why are they here?"

"I had a vision about this," I speak up and they both snap their heads toward me. "In my dreams, I saw the Wall crumble and the Wraiths came pouring through like a devastating flood."

Raiden and Edmynd exchange a worried glance. "How do we stop it? Did you see anything in your dream that might help us?"

"I believe I know what to do," I tell them, explaining about the amplifier that belonged to Queen Ilyra.

When I'm finished, Raiden frowns. "Is it safe to use such a thing?"

"I believe so."

"It is not safe," Kyven interjects. "It killed Queen Ilyra."

Edmynd turns to me, concerned. "If it killed a Fae, who is naturally born with magic, why on earth would you believe it is safe for you to use?"

I cross my arms over my chest. "When have my visions ever been wrong?"

Raiden looks at Kyven. "Please, tell me this amplifier is lost to history."

"It's here," I tell him. "In the Fortress."

"Locked away safely?" Raiden presses, and Kyven nods.

"Good," Edmynd says. He gives me a pointed look. "It is not worth the risk. Besides, I have brought an entire regiment with us. Between Florin's forces and those of Anlora, we should be well-equipped to deal with any problems should the Wraiths try to somehow bring down a section of the Wall."

"That's just it," I tell him. "They should not be able to. And yet, I saw it in my dreams."

"And what of the Orcs?" Edmynd asks. "Where are they?"

Aren steps forward. "We've received reports they are tracking and eliminating Wraiths, deep in the Wyldwood, which have already escaped over the Wall."

"How are they able to do this?" Edmynd asks. "It does not make sense."

Kyven clenches his jaw. "I believe they have had help from someone inside my kingdom."

"Who?" Raiden asks, his brown eyes flashing with anger. "Who amongst you would turn on his own kind?"

"Lord Torien," I reply. "We believe he helped them cross the barrier into the city, when we were attacked."

"Why attack the capital?"

"I was their target," I reluctantly admit.

"What?" Raiden snaps. His eyes sweep to Kyven and then back to me. "How close did they get to you?"

"Close enough," Kyven says through gritted teeth.

Raiden looks at me. "You need more guards. A handful are not enough." He gestures to Aren and Talyn. "You need—"

"Do not insult them," I interrupt. "They are two of our best warriors."

Raiden runs a hand roughly through his short, dark blond hair. "Forgive me," he addresses Aren and Talyn. "I am simply protective of my sister."

"As are we," Talyn replies solemnly.

"She is our queen," Aren adds. "Bondmate of our king and

Sanishon of the prophecy. We would give our lives to protect hers."

"Let us hope it does not come to such measures." Edmynd rakes a hand through his short, blond hair before lifting his green eyes back to me, worry easily read in his features.

"There is more," I tell him.

"What is it?"

"The assassin who killed Mother." I swallow against the lump in my throat at the painful memory. "I believe Father was right. He was Fae."

"Raiden told me of your dream," Edmynd says. "Could you tell anything else about the assassin?"

I shake my head. "But I believe Lord Torien was involved somehow. He said Mother was not the target. Inara and I were."

"What if it was Lord Torien?" Edmynd asks.

"And now he is trying to finish what he did not all those years ago, by trying to kill you now," Raiden adds.

"I scarred the man's face. Torien does not carry a scar."

Edmynd's gaze flicks to Kyven. "Whoever it was could be hiding behind a glamour."

"This is true," Kyven replies. "If Lord Torien was behind your mother's death, we will find out."

"Have you had any word from Lukas yet?" Edmynd asks, changing the subject.

I love that my brothers do not ask Kyven if he knew anything about Mother's death. They already know my husband well enough to understand that Kyven would never have taken part in such a thing. And if he knew something, he would have already told us.

I shake my head.

"His father is in poor health and has passed the crown to him. He was forgoing his ceremony to march here with his warriors to meet us."

TAKEN BY THE FAE KING

"He is King of Valren now?" Kyven asks.

"Yes."

Kyven's brow furrows deeply. "But my kingdom has no formal alliance with his. Why would he come to our aid?"

"Because he is a Wolf-Shifter." Raiden arches a brow as he gestures to me. "You essentially married his sister, so that makes you family to him."

Commander Caldyr steps forward and bows low. "I am Caldyr, Commander of this Fortress. If I may interrupt, I have a suggestion."

"What is it?" Edmynd asks.

"I suggest we combine our forces," he says. "Rotate watch along the Wall."

Edmynd nods. He turns back to one of his men, gesturing to him. "This is Commander Larken."

The Commander dips his chin to Caldyr. His black hair falling forward over his heavyset brows as his sharp blue eyes study the Fae commander. "Commander Caldyr," he says by way of greeting.

"You two will work together to come up with a rotation to put extra men along the Wall," Edmynd commands.

The two commanders leave the room and Kyven looks at my brothers. "We have guest quarters, but you will have to share a room."

"That's fine," Edmynd says.

"As long as I get the bed," Raiden teases. "You can have the floor."

Edmynd purses his lips, and I laugh.

* * *

WHEN WE RETURN to our room for the evening, Greywind is already asleep on the balcony. Kyven and I settle into our bed and he curls his arms and wings solidly around me, and I snuggle into his warmth.

"Promise me if things go badly, you will take Greywind and get to safety. You must—"

I press a finger to his lips. "Do not ask me to leave you, because I won't. Do not tell me to run, because it is not in my nature to abandon the people I love."

"But, Grayce, I—"

I silence him with a kiss.

My hands trace over the hard muscles of his chest, feeling the pounding of his heart beneath my palm.

"You are trying to distract me," he whispers against my lips.

"Is it working?" I smile.

He rolls me beneath him. His dark eyes search mine, full of desire and hunger. "Yes."

CHAPTER 64

KYVEN

Carefully, I slice a line down Grayce's sleep gown, leaving her bare beneath me. I cup her breast and she arches into my touch, moaning out my name as I roll the already stiff peak beneath my thumb.

Her entire body is so soft and giving. I lower my head and close my mouth over the soft globe, groaning as she threads her fingers through my hair to guide me to the other side.

She gasps as I lave my tongue across the sensitive bead of flesh and smooth a hand down her body to her center. Gently, I tease my fingers through her folds and find her body already slick with arousal.

My nostrils flare as her delicate scent grows stronger. "I can scent your need," I growl. My every instinct demanding that I take her now.

She pushes on my shoulders, and I willingly go onto my back, curious to see what she will do.

She seals her mouth over mine in a searing kiss before

traveling down my body. When she reaches my stav, the air explodes from my lungs as she traces her tongue over the tip.

I grip her arms and pull her back up my body.

"Did I do something wrong?" she asks, her eyes searching mine. "Did I hurt you?"

"Too sensitive," I barely manage.

I flip her onto her back and settle myself between her thighs. Her gaze holds mine as I notch myself at her entrance. "Forgive me. I can wait no longer."

She opens herself even more to me and then cups my neck to bring my lips back down to hers. "I want you," she whispers into my mouth.

Gritting my teeth, I struggle to hold back my release as I sink deep into her warm wet heat. The tight clasp of her body around my stav is the most exquisite sensation. "So tight," I rasp.

I seal my mouth over hers as I begin to stroke deep inside her. My knot expands, locking us together. My eyes roll up in the back of my head as the small muscles of her channel quiver and flex around my length.

I'm not prepared when she clamps down on my knot. It's too much and the pressure is too great as she cries out my name. My stav pulses strongly and I cry out "mine" as I erupt deep in her core, flooding her with my seed.

Panting heavily, her entire body goes limp as she bathes in the afterglow of our shared release, but I'm not finished yet.

With my knot still swollen within her, I wrap my arms around her back and pull her up as I sit back in my heels. This new angle makes me groan as she tightens around me, moaning my name. "Kyven," she breathes as she wraps her arms around my neck and her legs around my hips.

I fold my wings over her, holding her in place as I thrust

up into her body. Pleasure builds deep and I worry that I will be unable to hold back. But I want her to climax before me.

Reaching between us, I brush my thumb over the small pearl of flesh between her thighs and she cries out, her body clamping down hard around mine as she reaches her peak.

I fall over the edge with her, roaring her name as I flood her womb again with my seed, and then follow her into blissful oblivion.

* * *

WHEN I WAKE, Grayce is still asleep in my arms. I thread my fingers through her long, chestnut hair and then press a tender kiss to her soft, pink lips.

Her eyelids flutter open, and she gives me a sleepy smile. "Good morning," she whispers.

"It is not yet morning." I grin. "We have a few hours still."

She snuggles into me. "Then, go back to sleep," she teases lightly.

"I'd rather watch you." I gently skim the tip of my nose alongside hers, and whisper. "You are perfect, Grayce."

A sharp knock on the door startles us both. "What is it?" I growl, unable to hide my irritation.

"The number of Wraiths have doubled along the Wall." Aren's voice comes through the door. "I thought you might wish to be alerted."

"I'll be right there."

I give Grayce a quick kiss and drop my forehead to hers. "Stay here. I will return shortly."

I half expect her to protest. Instead, she whispers, "Be careful."

"I will."

I quickly dress and then slip out into the hallway. I turn to

Talyn, standing guard at the door. "Remain here with the queen."

He bows low. "Of course, my king."

Aren and I make our way down the hallway to the balcony outside the throne room. Grayce's brothers arrive a moment later, each of them staring wide-eyed at the scene below.

I gaze down at the swirling mass of darkness along the Great Wall. The normally dormant magic embedded in the wall begins to glow brightly as the Wraiths gather against it.

"What is happening?" Raiden asks, pointing to the light blue glow along the rock. "Why does it look like that?"

"The magic that fortifies the wall is being tested," I say grimly. "With so many Wraiths in one spot, it is forming a weakness."

A dozen Fae warriors concentrate their powers, strengthening the wards until the blue glow fades once more into the stone.

"How long will that hold?" Edmynd asks.

"I am uncertain."

"Aren't they attracted to magic?" Raiden asks.

"Yes. Why?"

"Because the more your people send to that spot to strengthen it, doesn't it make it more attractive to them?"

He's right, but there is no other way to fortify the wall. "We have no choice. If we leave it, that section will give way."

"It will collapse eventually though, will it not?" Raiden presses.

"Not necessarily," I reply. "As long as we keep strengthening the wards…" My voice trails off as I consider. "I suppose it's a possibility, but it is remote…"

"Do you have a backup plan in case the wall fails?" Edmynd asks. "Aside from our forces?"

Clenching my jaw, I study the Wall. If a sacrifice must be

made again, it will be made by me. Not by my queen. I turn to Caldyr. "Where is the amplifier?"

He hesitates a beat before answering. "Still in the library."

"Bring me the necklace."

"My king, are you sure?" he asks, his eyes full of concern because he knows what I mean to do.

"Yes."

"Someone has to be controlling them," Edmynd says darkly. "Where are the Mages?" He casts his gaze along the Wall, as if searching for a Mage somewhere among my warriors. "Do you personally know all of these men?"

"Most," I reply. I turn my attention to Caldyr. He too begins scanning the males below. "But not all of them."

"You truly believe a Mage could be hidden here?" Aren asks.

"If not a Mage, then who?" Edmynd counters. "One of yours? One of mine? Who wants to bring down the Wall, and why?"

"The Orcs claim the Wraiths are evolving," I tell him. "Suggesting they may not need to be controlled by the Mages."

"But why are they gathering here?" Edmynd ask. "Your people have magic. Mine do not. Would it not make sense to have attacked Florin's Outpost instead?"

"We still have High Mage Ylari," Raiden replies. "He broke from the Order because of his loyalty to our family." He narrows his eyes as he scans the Wall. "If this is the work of Mage magic, would your people recognize it like he would?"

My heart stutters and stops. Raiden is right. "We would not," I reply soberly.

Commander Caldyr returns with the necklace and hands it to me. Grayce's brothers both snap their attention toward it. It seems even they can feel its raw and terrible power.

Raiden looks at me. "The last time a Mage was in your

midst, my sister was attacked. Your Lord Torien was the one who enabled them to cross your wards." He clenches his jaw. "What if he is here helping them?"

Aren turns to us both. "Last we heard, he fled the capital, but to where, we do not know."

"If he is helping the Mages, then he would be here," Raiden presses. "Would he not?"

"Grayce's vision," I murmur, dread unfurling deep within. "If Lord Torien is here, then"—I gesture to the Wall—"this is a—"

"Distraction," Edmynd finishes my sentence.

Without hesitation, I lift off from the balcony and fly back inside, my wings fluttering furiously behind me as I race toward our chambers, back to Grayce.

CHAPTER 65

GRAYCE

A soon as Kyven leaves, I move to the cleansing room. I bathe and dress quickly and then open the door into the hallway. Talyn turns to me. "My queen?"

"Take me to Kyven," I tell him. "I want to see what is happening along the Wall."

Instead of hesitating like I thought, he dips his chin, and we start down the hallway.

As we make our way to the throne room, I'm surprised by how eerily empty the fortress feels. Most of our warriors are concentrating their efforts on guarding the Wall against the Wraiths.

Movement off to the side catches my eye, and I turn toward it, but a hand clamps over my mouth, jerking me back.

Talyn spins, his eyes wide.

"Do. Not. Move," a voice hisses in my ear. "One wrong move and the queen is dead."

Dread twists deep in my gut as I recognize the voice.

Lord Torien.

"Release the queen at once," Talyn snarls. "Or I'll—"

"Take me to the king," Torien snaps. "Now."

I shake my head, but Torien clamps down even harder. "I thought I told you not to move," he says darkly. "I'm going to remove my hand from your mouth, and if you scream, people will die. Do you understand?"

I nod.

"Good."

His hand lifts away from my mouth, and he grips my arm firmly. "Let's go."

His fingers dig into my flesh as he practically drags me down the hallway to the throne room.

Talyn spins to attack, but Torien sends an arc of magic flying toward him, hitting him square in the chest.

"No!" I watch in horror as my guard crumples to the ground. "You—"

"Silence!" he snaps, pulling me down the hallway.

When we reach the throne room, the two guards at the door charge toward him, but he stops them short with a knife at my throat. "Attack me, and I'll—"

The door bursts open, and Kyven stops abruptly in his tracks at the sight of me in Torien's grasp.

The cold steel of the knife presses against my throat, just hard enough to remind me of my fragile mortality. Torien stands behind me, his breath hot on the nape of my neck. The room is silent as Kyven watches, anger burning in his eyes.

"Let her go, Torien," Kyven commands, his voice low and dangerous, "or I'll end you."

Raiden and Edmynd step forward, their fists clenched. "You're a dead man," Raiden growls.

Torien remains unflinching, his deadly intent unwavering. "The amplifier necklace," he demands, his voice cold and emotionless. "Give it to me."

The clear, sparkling pendant gemstone on a silver chain glows a soft light blue as magic swirls within the stone.

Kyven hesitates, but knowing that my life hangs in the balance, he reluctantly hands it to Torien.

As the necklace is transferred from my husband to my captor, I glance back at Torien. A wave of magic moves across his face, and my jaw drops as his glamour falls away, revealing a long, jagged scar running down the right side of his face.

A jolt of recognition runs through me. This is the Fae who attacked and murdered my mother years ago and nearly killed me as well.

"You," I whisper, my voice trembling. My brothers stare in shock, understanding dawning in their eyes.

"You remember, don't you?" Torien taunts, his eyes locked on mine.

Edmynd's face contorts with rage. "You killed our mother, you monster!"

"And I will kill your sister too if you take one step closer," he threatens, pressing the blade into my skin.

A bead of warm liquid rolls down my neck as the sharp dagger nicks my throat.

"Let her go," Kyven growls. "Now!"

"No."

"You have the necklace," Kyven says. "Now, let her go."

"I still need her," he says darkly. "The Mages need her and so do the Wraiths."

"For what?" Edmynd snaps.

"She is a Sanishon," he grinds out. "I cannot have her interfering when we bring down the Wall."

"You have no idea what you're doing, Torien." I seethe. "If

you use that necklace to bring down the wall, you'll unleash the Wraiths on your own kingdom."

He tightens his arm around my waist. "I know."

Without warning, he leaps off the fortress balcony, taking me with him. I bite back a scream as we plummet toward the ground. At the last moment, he snaps open his wings, and we soar toward the Great Wall that has held back the Wraith for centuries.

The power of the amplifier necklace glows brightly as we approach the wall. I stare down in horror at the dark mass of Wraiths below. "Don't do this, Torien!"

"It's too late," he says as we spiral to the ground. He lands beside the Wall and dread coils tightly within as I think of what lies on the opposite side.

"What did the Mages promise you?" I ask, trying to make him stop. "Why are you doing this?"

"They promised me the crown of Anlora. I will rule by their side once the war is done."

"No, you won't," I counter. "They'll make you their slave. Just like everyone else."

"If I was their slave, would they have given me the ability to control their Wraiths?" he gestures to the Wall. A sinister grin twists his mouth. "They shared their power with me. I am not their slave, I am their ally."

"The Order of Mages only make alliances to benefit their cause, Torien. Once you have done what they asked, do you really think they'll give you what they promised?"

"There is no stopping them," he snarls. "What I do, I do for my people... to save them."

"You are not saving Anlora." I give him an incredulous look. "You are helping destroy it."

"You would destroy it!" He seethes. "The Order showed this to me. That's why I volunteered to end you!"

"They showed you what you needed to see to win you to

their side," I grind out. "They recognized a spineless male who wanted power and was close enough to the crown of Anlora to bring it down," I grit through my teeth. "They used you, Lord Torien, and you let them."

Ignoring me, he raises the necklace in one hand and begins speaking in the ancient tongue of his people. The blue light of the gemstone swirls brightly as it begins to work, Cracks spread like spiderwebs across the stone barrier.

I have to act quickly.

"Torien," I plead, "you don't understand what you're doing. The Wraiths will destroy everything if you bring down this wall."

He laughs, a cruel and bitter sound. "Not everything, Your Majesty," he says mockingly. "Only my enemies."

Panic twists deep within, my mind racing for a way to stop him. For the sake of my people, my family, and the memory of my mother, I cannot allow him to succeed.

A piercing cry fills the air, and I look up to find Greywind heading straight for Torien, his massive wings beating furiously. His claws are fully extended as he barrels toward my attacker, slamming into him and knocking the necklace from his grasp.

A bolt of magic spirals toward Torien, hitting him square in the chest as Kyven flies toward us, taking advantage of the chaos, and sending another arc of magic toward my attacker.

I sprint toward the falling necklace, my heart pounding in my ears. It's within my grasp, but so is the crumbling wall. The magic holding back the Wraiths is on the verge of collapse. I lunge, fingers outstretched, and snatch the necklace from the ground just as the first stones begin to fall.

Torien casts a barrier spell, holding Kyven at bay as he turns his wrath toward me. "Give me the necklace!"

"No!"

I rush toward him. He only has a moment to be shocked

as I grip the dagger from his belt and plunge it deep into his heart. I watch in cold satisfaction as the light leaves his eyes and he drops to the ground in a pool of dark blood.

"Grayce!" Kyven rushes toward me as a section of the wall cracks and crumbles inward. He gathers me in his arms and beats his wings furiously as we take off, flying back toward the balcony and to safety as the Wraiths begin pouring through.

"No! I have to stop this!"

He sets me on the balcony, and Greywind lands beside us.

"Where are my—"

I look down and find my brothers are already at the head of Florin's army, swords swinging as they battle the Wraiths.

"Stay here!" Kyven calls over his shoulder as he dives into the fray, joining his warriors in the fight.

Dozens of Fae concentrate their magic on the Wall, trying to repair it, but it's no use.

A loud horn sounds in the distance, and I glance back to see an army of Wolf-Shifters in wolven form racing toward the crumbling barrier. It's Lukas and his brethren that have come to our aid.

An army of Orcs follows closely behind them, axes and swords swinging wide as they clear a path to the Wall.

I turn my gaze to the Wall as Kyven's warriors try to repair it, but it's a losing battle. Too many Wraiths are pouring through. The image of Queen Ilyra using her magic surfaces in my mind, and I know what I must do.

Without hesitation, I jump onto Greywind's back and we dive toward the Wall.

Clinging to the amplifier, I close my eyes and pour every ounce of my will into mending the fractured magic. Power surges through me, filling me with a strength I've never known. The crumbling wall slows as fractures begin knitting themselves back together.

Energy flows through me, burning like fire in my veins as I focus all my power on repairing the Wall and pushing back the Wraiths. I grit my teeth as my entire body trembles with exertion, but I cannot give up.

Strong arms wrap around my waist. "Grayce, you must stop!" Kyven shouts from behind me. "Please!"

He pulls me from Greywind's back, and a sharp cry escapes his lips as a surge of power moves through me, hitting us both. Unable to remain aloft, we spiral toward the ground, only the sharp snap of his wings as they extend, breaking our fall.

"Grayce!" Kyven yells, and I open my eyes as he extends his hand, casting a barrier spell around us, keeping the Wraith back.

Their blood red eyes watch us with hunger as they press against the barrier, trying to break through.

I focus all my strength, conjuring every bit of magic I can muster. The ground grumbles and quakes beneath our feet and vines explode from the ground in a spray of earth and rock, rising and thickening like castle towers reaching for the sun, twisting around each other and forming a barrier, plugging the gap in the Great Wall.

My entire body shakes as I struggle to remain conscious. The threat of oblivion trying to pull me under.

Kyven grips my hand and a surge of power flows through my veins. My eyes open, and I blink at him in wonder as I realize he is funneling the earth's energy from him to me, fueling my magic and expanding it even further.

As if reading my mind, Kyven's eyes snap to the vine barrier and back to me. "We can do this!"

Together, we focus our energy on the Wall and creating a barrier to seal the collapsed section. As the vines grow and fill in the gap, Kyven's warriors and the Orcs use their combined powers to rebuild the stone Wall, reinforcing the wards as they rebuild the barrier.

Closing my eyes, I give myself over to the power, feeding mine and the borrowed energy from Kyven into the spell. My entire body is shaking, and I'm not sure how much more I can take. "Kyven," I call out. "I don't know if I can hold this any longer."

"Let go!" he yells. "Let go now, Grayce. Please."

I lower my hands, and the necklace falls from my grasp as I stumble forward.

Kyven's arms wrap tight around my waist, and he pulls me to his chest. "Grayce, you did it," he whispers. "You saved us."

Everything hurts, and I bite back a wince as I shift slightly. My entire body feels raw and drained. I reach a trembling hand and cup his cheek. "We did it, Kyven." A tear slips down my cheek. "I love you."

"Grayce!"

"I'm all right," I barely manage.

"You used too much of your life force." His eyes search mine, full of panic and devotion. "You must stay awake."

"I'm not going to die," I brush my thumb across his cheek. "I saw our future, my love. We will have a daughter, remember?"

He nods even as tears gather in the corner of his eyes. Fear and panic flowing from him, through our bond.

"I just need to rest for a bit," I whisper.

My head falls back, and I tumble away into the dark and beckoning void.

CHAPTER 66

GRAYCE

As my mind slowly awakens, I'm aware of Kyven's warm, masculine scent all around me. I snuggle into his warmth and his arms and wings tighten around my form. "Are you awake?" he whispers, gently nuzzling my temple.

"Kyven," I whisper, my voice strained. A faint smile curves my mouth. "I told you I would not die."

He cups my chin, tipping my face up to his. We're lying in our bed back at the castle. "I was so afraid." His voice is thick with emotion. "I thought I would lose you." He drops his forehead gently to mine. "Never scare me like that again."

I touch his cheek. "I'll try not to. Where are my brothers? Talyn?" I ask. "Is everyone all right?"

"Yes." He presses his lips to mine in a tender kiss. "Your brothers are waiting outside the door."

"They are?" I grin.

He nods. "Are you up for visitors?"

"For family?" I smile. "Always."

Kyven goes to the door and as soon as he opens it, Raiden pushes past him, followed by Lukas and Edmynd.

"Thank the gods you're all right," Raiden says. He leans in and hugs me tight.

I sit up as Edmynd hugs me next. Lukas stands behind him, and I inhale sharply when I notice the long, jagged scar on his left cheek.

"What happened?" Even as I ask this, it is easy to see they are the work of sharp claws.

"The Wraiths," he says with a sad smile. "They got a few swipes in before I ended them."

"I'm so sorry, Lukas," I whisper.

Lukas has told me before how many female Wolf-Shifters pass over males with scars, thinking them weaker than others.

"It's all right." He sighs, but I know the truth. It will make his life that much harder to find a mate. And if anyone deserves happiness, it's my best friend. "Just concentrate on getting your strength back."

"Yeah," Raiden says. "You gave us all a good scare."

"Especially me," Edmynd chimes in. "When I saw you fall, I thought you had—" His voice catches and he hugs me again. "I love you, my darling sister."

"I'm fine," I insist. "Truly."

"I don't understand how you did it," Lukas says.

"The amplifier allowed me to channel more power through Kyven. It was not all mine." I look at my husband. "It was our combined powers."

"Yes, but still… you used so much of your own life energy, Grayce," Kyven says.

"It worked though, Kyven. Do you not see?"

His brow furrows deeply. "See what?"

"The amplifier… that's how we win this war."

He frowns, but I continue. "Each of us should have one."

"Us?" Raiden asks.

"Yes. Inara, Freyja, and me."

"It's dangerous," Kyven says.

"But necessary," I counter. "Without it, I wouldn't have been strong enough to plug the barrier on my own. You know that."

He clenches his jaw and gives me a reluctant nod.

I turn to Kyven. "We have to tell the others, and we need more amplifiers."

"Where do we even begin to find them?" Raiden asks.

"I do not know," I admit. "But I know someone who might." I turn to Kyven. "We need to speak with Scholar Nolyn. If anyone knows, it's him."

Sighing heavily, Kyven dips his chin in a subtle nod.

EPILOGUE

GRAYCE

I sit in the dimly lit corner of the palace library, a leather-bound tome splayed open in my hands. The worn pages whisper of amplifier gemstones and the elusive Great Divide—the World Between Worlds—where they can be found.

My heart tightens with worry as I think of Lukas. He volunteered to travel to that mysterious place to locate more gemstones for us, trusting no one else for the task.

According to Nolyn, Wolf-Shifters can pass more easily in the Great Divide, hiding amongst the many monsters that are rumored to lurk there. I hope he was wrong, but all his research suggests there are things in that plane of existence that are the stuff of nightmares.

A soft creak behind me is the only warning I get before Kyven's arms encircle my waist, pulling me back against his warm chest. His lips find the curve of my neck, pressing featherlight kisses along my skin, and my concerns momentarily dissolve.

"You're worried about Lukas," he murmurs, his breath tickling my ear.

I nod, my fingers tracing the words on the page. "He's been gone so long, and the Great Divide is so dangerous."

Kyven's grip tightens around me, reassuring and strong. "Lukas is strong, too. He'll return. I have every confidence in him."

I can't help but tease Kyven, the corners of my mouth lifting into a playful smile. "I thought you didn't like Lukas."

Kyven chuckles, the vibrations moving through me. "I'll admit, he's growing on me. He's proven his loyalty and determination."

His hands move to my hips, guiding me as he lifts me onto the edge of a nearby table, the heavy book forgotten. I wrap my legs around his waist, pulling him closer as his lips find mine in a tender kiss. Our lips mesh repeatedly in a delicate dance, a balance between passionate love and burning desire.

Kyven's fingers tangle in my hair as he deepens the kiss, his other hand pressed against my back, holding me close.

"What if someone sees us," I whisper between kisses. "What if—"

He snaps his fingers, and a clear barrier surrounds us so that no one can see or hear us anymore. I moan as Kyven cups my breast through my tunic dress. "Need you," he murmurs into my mouth. "Your scent is intoxicating. I want to taste you on my tongue."

Carefully, he guides me back onto the table and lifts the hem of my skirt. He pushes it up to my waist, and his eyes hold mine, full of fire and intense possession as he guides first one leg and then the other over his shoulders.

I'm breathless with anticipation as he slices away the small scrap of fabric between my thighs. He presses a series of heated kisses up the length of my inner thigh, and I moan out his name. He is so close to where I want him to be.

Without warning, he goes still.

He lifts his head to me, his brow furrowed deeply.

"What is it?" I ask.

He rests his head against my lower abdomen and closes his eyes. When he opens them again, he splays his palm over my lower abdomen. "You are carrying our fledgling," he whispers.

My heart stutters and stops. "You're sure?"

He stands and cups my cheek, his eyes searching mine. "I am certain."

A smile crests my lips and tears sting my eyes, but I blink them back. "We're going to have a family," I breathe out. "A daughter."

He pulls me into his arms, pressing a series of tender kisses all over my face before capturing my lips in a claiming kiss. "My beautiful, wonderful, perfect, mate," he whispers against my lips. "We're going to have a family."

I place my palm over my lower abdomen, and he rests his hand atop mine. Joy surges across the bond as we bask in the shared wonder of the life we've created.

In the sanctuary of the library, surrounded by the echoes of stories long past, Kyven presses his lips to mine again in a tender kiss. "Everything is too perfect, and it worries me a moment. Tell me this is real and not just a dream or a vision."

"This is real." He cups my cheek, staring deep into my eyes. "I am yours and you are mine. Always."

ALSO BY JESSICA GRAYSON

Next book in series : ***Stolen by the Wolf King***

Sign up for my mailing list via my website and get a welcome gift of
a Bonus Epilogue (ebook) for this book:

http://Jessicagraysonauthor.com/

If you enjoyed this book please leave a review on Amazon and/or
Goodreads.

Jessica Grayson

Of Fate and Kings Series

Bound to the Dark Elf King

Claimed by the Dragon King

Taken by the Fae King *(this book)*

Stolen by the Wolf King

Captured by the Orc King

Check out some of my other books while you're here.

Do you like Fairy Tale Retellings?

Fairy Tale Retellings (Once Upon a Fairy Tale Romance Series)

Taken by the Dragon: A Beauty and the Beast Retelling

Captivated by the Fae: A Cinderella Retelling

Rescued By The Merman: A Little Mermaid Retelling

Bound To The Elf Prince: A Snow White Retelling

Claimed By The Bear King: A Snow Queen Retelling

Protected By The Wolf Prince: A Red Riding Hood Retelling

Claimed: Dragon Shifter Romance

Bound: Vampire Alien Romance

Rescued: Fae Alien Romance

Stolen: Werewolf Romance

Taken: Vampire Alien Romance

Fated: Dragon Shifter Romance

Protected: Dragon Shifter Romance

Want Dragon Shifters? You can dive into their world with this completed Duology.

Mosauran Series (Dragon Shifter Alien Romance)

The Edge of it All

Shape of the Wind

V'loryn Series (Vampire Alien Romance)

Lost in the Deep End

Beneath a Different Sky

Under a Silver Moon

V'loryn Holiday Series (A Marek and Elizabeth Holiday novella takes place prior to their bonding)

The Thing We Choose

V'loryn Fated Ones (Vampire Alien Romance)

Where the Light Begins (Vanek's Story)

For information about upcoming releases Like me on

Facebook at Jessica Grayson
http://facebook.com/JessicaGraysonBooks.

OR

sign up for upcoming release alerts at my website:

Jessicagraysonauthor.com